Siren Reborn

Other Books by Lexi Blake

ROMANTIC SUSPENSE

Masters And Mercenaries

The Dom Who Loved Me
The Men With The Golden Cuffs
A Dom is Forever
On Her Master's Secret Service
Sanctum: A Masters and Mercenaries Novella
Love and Let Die
Unconditional: A Masters and Mercenaries Novella
Dungeon Royale
Dungeon Games: A Masters and Mercenaries Novella
A View to a Thrill
Cherished: A Masters and Mercenaries Novella
You Only Love Twice
Luscious: Masters and Mercenaries~Topped
Adored: A Masters and Mercenaries Novella
Master No
Just One Taste: Masters and Mercenaries~Topped 2
From Sanctum with Love
Devoted: A Masters and Mercenaries Novella
Dominance Never Dies
Submission is Not Enough
Master Bits and Mercenary Bites~The Secret Recipes of Topped
Perfectly Paired: Masters and Mercenaries~Topped 3
For His Eyes Only
Arranged: A Masters and Mercenaries Novella
Love Another Day
At Your Service: Masters and Mercenaries~Topped 4
Master Bits and Mercenary Bites~Girls Night
Nobody Does It Better
Close Cover
Protected: A Masters and Mercenaries Novella
Enchanted: A Masters and Mercenaries Novella
Charmed: A Masters and Mercenaries Novella, Coming June 23, 2020

Masters and Mercenaries: The Forgotten

Lost Hearts (Memento Mori)
Lost and Found

Lost in You
Long Lost
No Love Lost, Coming September 29, 2020

Butterfly Bayou
Butterfly Bayou, Coming May 5, 2020
Bayou Baby, Coming August 25, 2020

Lawless
Ruthless
Satisfaction
Revenge

Courting Justice
Order of Protection
Evidence of Desire

Masters Of Ménage (by Shayla Black and Lexi Blake)
Their Virgin Captive
Their Virgin's Secret
Their Virgin Concubine
Their Virgin Princess
Their Virgin Hostage
Their Virgin Secretary
Their Virgin Mistress

The Perfect Gentlemen (by Shayla Black and Lexi Blake)
Scandal Never Sleeps
Seduction in Session
Big Easy Temptation
Smoke and Sin
At the Pleasure of the President

URBAN FANTASY
Thieves
Steal the Light
Steal the Day
Steal the Moon
Steal the Sun
Steal the Night

Ripper
Addict
Sleeper
Outcast
Stealing Summer, Coming soon

LEXI BLAKE WRITING AS SOPHIE OAK

Texas Sirens

Small Town Siren
Siren in the City
Siren Enslaved
Siren Beloved
Siren in Waiting
Siren in Bloom
Siren Unleashed
Siren Reborn

Nights in Bliss, Colorado

Three to Ride
Two to Love
One to Keep
Lost in Bliss
Found in Bliss
Pure Bliss
Chasing Bliss
Once Upon a Time in Bliss
Back in Bliss
Sirens in Bliss

A Faery Story

Bound
Beast
Beauty

Standalone

Away From Me
Snowed In

Siren Reborn

Texas Sirens, Book 8

Lexi Blake
writing as
Sophie Oak

Siren Reborn
Texas Sirens Book 8

Published by DLZ Entertainment LLC

Edited by Chloe Vale
ISBN: 978-1-942297-96-3

Sign up for Lexi Blake's newsletter
and be entered to win a $25 gift certificate
to the bookseller of your choice.

Join us for news, fun, and exclusive content
including free short stories.

There's a new contest every month!

Go to www.LexiBlake.net to subscribe.

Dedication

I'm not sure why this one didn't have a dedication back when it was first released, but it offers me a chance to thank everyone who made my years as Sophie Oak wonderful. I learned so much writing these books and being able to bring some of my Lexi voice to them has been a joy. I've had a few people who were there in the beginning and who have stuck with me through it all. Thanks to Kim Guidroz and Richard Blake, my first readers. To Shayla Black and Kris Cook who held my hands through those early years. To all those early fans who lifted me up – Tina, Tara, Ashley, Cherie, and all the Righteous Perverts. I know I've forgotten some and please know I am grateful, so grateful for these years I spent with you. Here's to many, many more.

Prologue

Willow Fork, Texas
Four Years Before

"She needs to be in a hospital." Kitten's father frowned down at Finn, using that fire-and-brimstone voice that packed his church every Sunday. "I've found a doctor who can help her."

Kitten sat in the same chair that had been allocated to her at the dining room table. It was her chair and had been for as long as they had lived in this perfectly kept house that seemed more like a museum than a home.

Don't run, Katherine. It's not ladylike.

Don't talk too loud. It's unseemly.

Don't touch anything. You're too clumsy.

"She's been through something traumatic, Uncle Martin. She's not insane." Her cousin Finn had his fists clenched at his sides.

Traumatic was such a simple word for what had happened to her. She'd been kidnapped and held against her will for… She knew it was more than days or weeks. Months, for certain.

She'd been taken by a madman. One day she'd been Katherine Taylor, a junior at a small religious college, and the next she'd been Kitten, a toy, a plaything, useless for anything but bringing her tormentor pleasure.

She wasn't sure who she was at all now.

"I took her computer away because of the things she was pulling up on the Internet. You wouldn't believe it." Her father's eyes narrowed. Cousin Finn was the black sheep of the family. "Or maybe you would."

Her father had caught her visiting BDSM websites. She'd been introduced to something violent, something terrible. And yet, she'd seen the way real, not-criminal Doms acted toward the subs. There had been such beauty in it. She needed to understand. She needed to figure it out.

She couldn't go back to being Katherine Taylor. Katherine Taylor was always quiet and did exactly what was expected of her, and all she got for it was a father who now thought she was damaged goods and a mother who had told her it was all her fault and now she was a whore and no man would want her.

"She's confused," Finn said. "I can help her. Look, I'll pay to bring down Janine or Leo. They're both excellent therapists. Janine is working with the other two women and they're making progress. You should have left her with me."

Her father's face turned a nasty purple color. "My daughter is not staying in some godless heathen club."

She'd gotten to stay at The Club for one glorious night, though she hadn't been allowed in the dungeon. She'd met Julian, Finn's Dom and partner. And Leo, the therapist.

Not all Doms were like Hawk. Hawk was the aberration. He hadn't been a Dom at all. He'd been a killer and a rapist.

"She can't sit in her room every day," Finn argued. "She needs to get out and be with people."

"That's why I'm sending her to Glenville."

"You have got to be kidding me." Finn was the one turning red now. "That is a bunch of bullshit. Those men aren't therapists. They're practically cultists."

She'd heard of Glenville. It was where some of her friends from school had been sent after they'd been caught in bed together. Two girls.

"They specialize in restoring a person to proper behavior," her father explained.

"They scare kids into saying they're not gay. Katherine isn't gay," Finn argued. "Though I think what they do should be criminal."

Her father's hands were suddenly fists, raised against some imaginary foe. He was always like this. Always fighting some invisible evil. "They're working up a program for her, to remove this sexuality she's suddenly discovered. I will bring her back to the righteous if it's the last thing I do."

"I've heard rumors that they use electroshock," Finn said, his voice shaking. "If you think I'm allowing you to torture her all over again, you're insane. I'll block you. I'll shove so many legal documents up your ass you won't be able to see straight."

Her father would do it. He would send her somewhere nasty and tell himself it was all right to abuse her because she was wrong. Might made right in her father's world. The same way it had in Hawk's world. Now that she thought about it, she'd lived in the same world for her whole life. Her life with her parents had been restrictive and there had certainly been brutal punishment when she stepped outside the lines.

Was there another world out there?

She wished Nat was here. For so long it had only been Kitten and Daisy in the cage. Gretchen, she reminded herself. Not Daisy. It had been Gretchen, and Kitten had known they would die in the cage.

And then Nat had been taken. Nat's imprisonment had been Kitten's salvation. Nat was a bright light. Nat was different. Nat was worth fighting with and for.

Nat had killed Hawk and Kitten had helped her.

She missed Nat.

She'd walked away from Nat because her father had called her Katherine Taylor, and Katherine Taylor always obeyed. She'd walked back to this house that held not an ounce of love and she'd taken her assigned seat at the table because that was what Katherine Taylor did.

She wasn't Katherine Taylor anymore.

"Kitten wants to go with Finn."

Finn didn't seem to hear her. He was too busy arguing with her father. "They're a bunch of quacks. She's not crazy. She doesn't need to be restored to your idea of proper behavior."

Her father leaned over. "Your parents might be fine with you going to hell, but I won't let you drag my daughter with you."

It was time to let her wishes be known. "Kitten wants to go with Finn."

"I don't care what you think about me," Finn shot back. "Just know I'm not leaving here without her. I won't let you ruin her life."

Her father got right in Finn's face. "I'm calling the police. You're not going to threaten me in my own home."

They weren't going to listen to her so she stopped trying. She stood up, took a look around the home where she'd grown up. Shouldn't she feel more? She was leaving and she would very likely never return. Her father wouldn't allow her back in. She glanced at her mother, who hadn't left her place in the kitchen during the fight. Her mother would do what her father said. If her father said she was dead to them, then her mother would bury her in her mind.

She didn't want a single thing from this house. It was just another cage. It had taken being in an actual cage to understand that simple truth.

She walked out, past the parlor that she'd never been allowed to play in. Past the hallway where her father kept their family portrait. She glanced at that girl. Katherine was so grim, so resigned to the life she'd been given.

But she wasn't Katherine anymore. For now, she was Kitten. She walked out into the sunlight, turning her face, letting it settle into her skin.

What would it be like to feel that sun everywhere on her body?

"Katherine?" Finn hurried down the steps, coming to stand beside her. "Katherine, what are you doing?"

"It's Kitten, Finn. Kitten's name is Kitten."

He shook his head. "Sweetie, you have to let that go."

The name Hawk had given her? "Why?"

"Because he named you that. It's a symbol."

"Kitten's parents named this one Katherine. That was a symbol. Kitten chooses to be Kitten for now. This one doesn't know what is coming later, but this one is Kitten for a while. And Kitten is going home with Finn. Kitten is an adult and can choose. Kitten chooses

Finn."

And Nat. Nat would help her figure out the whole BDSM thing. Nat would help her figure out the whole Kitten thing, too.

"All right, sweetie." Finn took her hand. He'd always been her favorite cousin. "Hey, I'll take care of you. Don't be afraid of Julian. I know he seems like Hawk…"

Kitten allowed her eyes to roll. "Master Julian is nothing like Kitten's old Master. No. Kitten will give that up. Hawk was not a Master at all. Hawk was a criminal. Kitten is not afraid of Master Julian."

Finn sighed. "See. I told them all you weren't crazy. Come on. If we get out of here now, we can be in Dallas before dinner."

Kitten followed Finn and for the first time in her memory was excited about the future.

* * * *

Bliss, CO
Two Years Before

Cole Roberts slammed his SUV into park. The snow was falling all around him, usually a peaceful thing, but now it felt like a betrayal. The world was far too quiet, too perfect. It should be falling apart. There should be some fucking noise.

She had to be alive. She couldn't be dead. He was panicking. He was a worst-case scenario kind of guy, but usually everything was fine and he found he'd worried for nothing.

It would be that way this time. It had to be.

He'd worked hard with her. He'd put so fucking much of himself on the line. Sure, it hadn't been easy, but he'd made it work. She couldn't be dead. She had signed a contract that made him responsible for her. He'd left her with Mason. Mason would never fail him.

Mason. A single vision of Mason with his pitch-black hair and gray eyes assailed him. Mason would always be eighteen years old in Cole's mind. It didn't matter that he was almost thirty now, with fine lines around those eyes because he smiled so fucking much. He was forever young and shining up at him as they figured out the world together.

He couldn't even think about the fact that Mason might have been in that car with her, and that made his gut churn with guilt. He was supposed to care for them equally. That was the pact, and in a second he knew he would trade Emily for Mason because he loved Mason. Because Emily had been a desperate attempt at completing them. An attempt that might have cost her life.

The snow crunched beneath his boots. He tried not to think about the pass. He tried not to think about the lights of his car illuminating the railing that had been wrenched free of its mooring. That could have happened days ago. He'd been stuck at the lodge for a week. It was probably a truck. It wasn't her car. It didn't mean she was dead.

"Cole?" Nathan Wright stood outside the double doors that led to the station house. Nate was the sheriff of Bliss County. He stood there in his khakis, looking younger than any sheriff had a right to be.

Cole stopped. Nate's face was grim, so fucking grim, and it suddenly struck him. He'd been called to the sheriff's office.

Not the hospital.

His heart dropped.

"Emily?"

A single shake of Nate's head told him everything he needed to know.

"Mason?" Oh, god, he couldn't lose Mason, too. His stomach turned. He couldn't imagine a world without Mason in it. Mason, with that perfect smile that lit up his whole world. Mason, who told him Emily wasn't the one, but he'd gone along with it anyway. He'd signed the contract, too. He'd promised to be involved in their ménage even though he'd doubted that the outcome could be a good thing. Mason had followed him, the way he had for the last ten years.

Mason was the cornerstone of his world.

Nineteen. He'd been nineteen when he'd lost his virginity to Mason. And his heart. But he was a Dom deep down and Mason was such a switch that he didn't completely fulfill Cole's needs. He couldn't bottom for Mason. They required a third, a true sub and a woman. They both needed a female. It was perverse, he knew it, but he couldn't live without both. He'd been searching for her for years, and Emily had been the closest he found.

And now she was dead.

"Mason is all right. He wasn't in the car with her. He actually came down after her." Nate pointed toward the back of the station house. His face remained grim as he looked back. "Though I'll be honest, I'm surprised he could drive."

"They weren't together?" The only reason he'd been okay with her going to a party without him was the fact that Mason would watch over her. Why hadn't he been with her?

"Mason was in a vehicle he apparently borrowed. It's not registered in his name."

"They took Emily's car," Cole explained.

"I found him at the accident site where he damn near killed himself getting too close to the edge." Nate stepped down two steps, his jaw tightening with each word. "Ms. Yarborough was with a friend. From what I can tell, Ms. Yarborough was driving and she lost control of her vehicle on the pass. I have to think from the damage done to the railing and skid marks that she hit the guardrail at a high speed. The friend didn't survive the crash either. I've got her mom coming in. Sometimes I hate this job."

Emily didn't have friends. She was kind of a bitch who didn't like many people but who needed a specific type of dominance to survive and thrive.

He didn't love her but in that moment he felt the loss. He'd had one job in the whole fucking world that mattered and that was protecting his subs.

Nate's words were starting to penetrate his brain. He'd been surprised Mason could drive. Why had he been surprised? "Why are you surprised Mason could drive?"

Mason was supposed to be looking after her. He couldn't look after her if he was drunk. They had rules, damn it. Rules. Rule number one had been she didn't drink more than one glass of wine at a party when Cole wasn't around to supervise. Mason was topping her. He didn't get to drink at all.

"You'll see," Nate said with a sigh. "I haven't arrested him yet."

The doors to the station house opened and Mason staggered out. "I need Cole."

His voice was slurred, his walk not on balance. His gray eyes sought out Cole's own.

A kernel of anger lit inside him as he realized what had happened. Mason wasn't altogether there. That was obvious. He'd had a few and that was against the rules. Blatantly. He'd trusted Mason. Ten years together and Mason still hadn't fucking grown up, and now their sub was dead.

"You can't even walk straight." A deep disgust settled inside him. He loved Mason but he'd put up with this shit for a long time. He'd always been the adult and Mason got to play the gorgeous man-child. Everything had been handed to Mason. Movie-idol good looks, charm to last for days, a brilliant mind. The only thing he'd lacked was money and connections, and Cole had given him both. He was the reason Mason had a high-powered job. He was the reason Mason had money. And he'd only asked one thing in return—a tiny bit of discipline.

"I don't know what happened. I can't remember." Mason slurred every word.

Cole knew exactly what had happened. He'd seen it all before. Mason had told himself one drink wouldn't matter. And then two. He'd spent the night charming every man and woman in sight and he'd forgotten his job. Cole had seen it a million times. He'd cleaned up after Mason time and time again.

Nate was frowning, staring at Mason like he was trying to figure something out. "He didn't register on the breathalyzer. I'm going to have to take some blood."

The hits kept coming. Had there been drugs at the party? Had Mason taken drugs? Had he allowed Emily to take them?

"Cole?" Mason held on to the railing as though it was a lifeline.

He ignored Mason. Mason had broken the rules they'd agreed on. It didn't matter whether he was drunk on alcohol or he'd gone insane and tried cocaine or whatever. This wasn't some faux pas Cole had to fix. This was a dead body and he couldn't even look at

Mason now. He turned to Nate. "Where do I claim her body?"

He owed it to her. She didn't have family. She only had her Masters. She only had him and Mason, and Mason had failed her.

Fuck. He'd failed her. He should have known Mason wasn't strong enough. He should have known Mason was decadent and followed only the rules of pleasure. Tears blurred his eyes, guilt welling inside him. He should never have allowed her to go to the party. He should never have allowed Mason to watch over her.

He thought they'd turned a corner, that Mason had become reliable, the kind of man he not only could love, but who he could depend on.

Mason stopped on the bottom step, his arms outstretched as though he desperately required comfort. "Please. Master."

God help him. Cole hadn't truly loved Emily. All his life he'd only loved Mason, but Mason was a butterfly flitting around and now it had cost him something precious—his honor as a Dom.

Cole took a step back.

"She's at the hospital in Del Norte," Nate replied. "They're going to release her to whatever funeral home you choose."

He had to choose a funeral home. God, he'd failed. He'd failed by not being able to love her. He'd failed by allowing Mason to watch over her. He'd failed on so many levels. He had one job—to keep her safe—and he'd failed.

He stepped back as Mason moved toward him. One thing. He'd asked one thing of Mason and Mason had chosen to disobey when it counted the most.

Mason stopped, that gorgeous face going blank as he seemed to understand there was no comfort waiting for him. "I didn't drink. Master, this isn't what you think. I don't understand what happened. Please."

How many times had he heard that before? It wasn't what he thought. He hadn't meant to get in trouble. It wasn't truly his fault. Nothing was ever Mason's fault.

Cole looked to Nate, who suddenly seemed interested in his boots. It was all Cole needed to know. He turned away.

There was nothing for him here. He had to go to Del Norte. He had one last task to perform for his submissive.

His heart ached. He loved Mason. Mason was his touchstone, but he couldn't trust him.

He couldn't trust anyone anymore.

Chapter One

Dallas, TX
Present Day

Though his elegant office was kept at a perfectly cool temperature, Cole had started to sweat. It was stupid, but he was nervous.

"So to what do I owe this pleasure, Julian?" Cole asked as he offered a chair to his old friend.

And tried to settle the worry gnawing at his gut because he had a suspicion why Julian Lodge had decided to show up in the middle of the afternoon on a Thursday. If the meeting was about business, he would have called or sent an e-mail. So this visit must be personal and if it was personal, then there was only one way in which Cole intersected with Lodge's family.

"I'm here about Kitten." Lodge let the statement drop, a rock he'd dumped in between them. There was a politely blank look on Julian's face that told Cole he was serious.

But then when wasn't Julian serious? He was practically the grim reaper and Cole was suddenly worried Julian had come to end something important to him.

And that pissed him the hell off.

Still, he held on to his temper. It wasn't the time to play the possessive caveman. Not with the man who could very likely take away the possession he wanted to keep. Kitten's primary loyalty was probably still to the people she considered family. He had to view Julian as a potential father-in-law, though Cole doubted he would appreciate the comparison. "We had a nice time at dinner the other night."

It was best to put on a brave front. He was in charge of Kitten Taylor and he didn't want that to change. Not when he was almost certain he was falling in love with the woman.

The trouble was, he couldn't seem to reach her. She'd been living in his home for almost a month and he wasn't any closer to real intimacy with her. He'd taken everything slow. Even after they'd signed a contract, he'd done his version of courting her. He'd allowed her to stay in Julian's home for a while. He'd called and spent time talking to her. He'd walked the dungeons with her. He'd escorted her to a wedding. He'd thought things would move more quickly once he'd actually moved her in.

He needed more time.

"Leo feels she's losing hard-earned ground," Julian stated flatly. His thousand-dollar shoes tapped against the floor as he enumerated his points. "She slipped into third-person speech twice the night you brought her over to the penthouse. She's obviously lost weight. And you haven't brought her to The Club on a regular basis. I don't know that I like that."

"Do you want to complain about the collar I bought her?" He seemed to be complaining about everything else. Why not bitch about Kitten's collar, too? It was Cartier and stunning. If Julian complained about it, he might punch him in the face.

And as Julian was the closest thing his submissive had to a father, that would go over so well for him.

The possessiveness he felt was something new and he rather liked it. It had been so long since he'd wanted someone to belong to him.

"No," Julian replied, his expression never changing once. "Her collar is perfectly satisfactory."

Her collar had cost him twenty grand. He'd meant it as a promise of the future, one he hoped to have with her. "You have to give me time, Julian. What happened to Kitten can't be erased in a month."

Now the club owner's mouth tightened, his eyes narrowing slightly. "It's been years."

Sympathy crept up on Cole. In the end, Julian was simply watching out for a woman he viewed as family. And he understood. As a Dom, Julian wanted to be able to do something. To command the problem to go away. Life wasn't as simple as it was in the dungeon. "And it will likely never truly go away. She was kidnapped, raped, and molded into something she wasn't before. She has to figure out who she is now, and that's a difficult process."

Julian finally sighed and sat back in his chair, his left ankle resting on his right knee. "I hoped she would be better when I found her a proper Dom."

At least Julian still considered him "proper." "We're working on her problems, but you know I move cautiously."

Patience was required to forge a good relationship.

Except sometimes a wildfire took over. Sometimes passion couldn't be contained. Like Mason. Images rushed through his brain. Their hands tearing at each other's clothes. Mouths fusing into one. Arms and legs tangled.

But he had to be patient with Kitten. It wouldn't hurt to remind himself that wildfires tended to burn a man. He was done with the wildfire portion of his life. Now he would plan out his future and that included using everything he knew to help Kitten find herself again.

"I understand, Cole. It's one of the reasons I selected you," Julian said finally. "I believed you could truly be patient with her. You have a reputation for working with difficult subs. I still find myself worried about her now that she isn't under my roof. She's important to Finn, you see."

Liar. She was important to Julian, though he would never admit it. Julian liked to play the stoic, cold bastard, but Cole had watched him over the last few years. He'd watched Julian Lodge go from heartless Dom to family man.

Damn, but he wanted that for himself. He'd known he might be able to have it if he could help Kitten. If he could show her that she could find herself through discipline and careful work. She would never be the same person she was before. She would be someone new, but she would be able to choose for herself.

He wanted to make sure that when she chose, she truly chose him. That was the delicate balance he was walking.

"I care for her. I honestly do. She's a sweet woman and I want this to work. And I think we can expect her to slip more than once. I know she's been under a Dom's authority before, but I'm her first real Dom. I'm the first one she's lived with and truly submitted to. She slips back into the habits that bastard taught her. It's only to be expected. She didn't know anything before him. And in some circles, referring to herself in the third person would be perfectly acceptable. You have full-time Masters and slaves at The Club."

Julian was right back to being the hawk, his eyes sharpening. "Is that what you're looking for? To own her?"

Frustration welled, a wave that threatened to swallow him. "You knew what I was looking for when I inquired about her. I prefer a Master-slave relationship. I prefer a firmer power exchange than most of the couples and trios at your club. And that's what she needs as well. We simply have to find our footing. I can't do that if you continually threaten to take her away from me."

This wasn't Julian's first visit. Julian had inspected Cole's home, tested his private dungeon equipment for sturdiness, run multiple, invasive personal checks through his in-house private investigators. Setting Chase Dawson on a man proved that Julian Lodge was a complete sadist. He'd had to submit to interviews by not one but two psychologists. He'd expected to deal with Leo Meyer, The Club's resident psychologist. He hadn't expected to be treated to an afternoon with Eve McKay, a lovely woman who used to profile serial killers for the FBI.

Cole truly worried for the first young man who was stupid enough to try to date Julian Lodge's daughter.

Cole had suffered through it all because from the moment he'd heard her story, he'd wanted to help her. And the minute he'd actually seen her… Fuck, his dick got hard thinking about her. She was the first human being to move him since Mason left, and he meant to do right by her.

"Is she happy?" Julian asked, his face softening slightly.

He had to be honest. “I don’t know.”

She was with him one moment and somewhere in her head the next. Kitten was elusive. She was fragile and he had to be careful not to harm her when he caught her. He didn’t truly want her in a cage. He wanted her to find her freedom through submission.

“Perhaps you would consider bringing her to The Club more often.”

Cole nodded, relaxing a bit. The tension had gone out of the room. “Yes. I will if you think it might help. I wanted her to settle in with me. We’ve been playing privately on a regular basis. Nothing heavy, just some impact play to get her used to me.”

“I appreciate your patient approach. I truly do, but you should know that she’s performed some hard-core scenes with her handlers. She’s a bit of a pain slut. She needs it.”

“And she’ll get it, but not until I discern what is for her pleasure and what she’s forcing her Doms to give her in order to punish herself.” He couldn’t move on until he was sure.

“And how about affection? You didn’t even hold her hand at dinner the other night.”

Because in the last two years he’d forgotten what real intimacy felt like. Since Mason had betrayed him, he’d become cold. Perhaps he’d been born that way, but at least with Mason around, he’d had someone to remind him to show his affection. Mason always prodded him for kisses and rarely allowed him to leave a room without a hug. Mason had been the one to teach him how to curl up on a couch and that dinner tasted better when someone else fed it to him.

Kitten couldn’t ask for the affection she needed. He struggled to remember to show his emotions in a physical way.

He was starting to feel inadequate.

“I thought I should give her time,” he reiterated.

Julian took over. “To get used to you. Yes, you’ve said that. Are you giving her time? Or yourself?”

“Maybe a bit of both,” he admitted. “I don’t want to screw this up. She’s been through a lot. She doesn’t need a ham-handed Master making things uncomfortable for her. She needs to settle in. We signed a six-month contract. There’s no rush. I’m not going to force her into bed with me."

"No one is worried about that." Julian stared at him for a moment. "I am worried that you won't see the signs that she genuinely wants to sleep with you."

"With me? Or with any Dom?" It was a definite worry in the back of his mind. He didn't want to be a stand-in for some other Dom. She'd had several and she talked about her former Masters often. Including Logan Green. He definitely didn't want to be the stand-in for a kid he'd watched grow up. Sometimes he wondered if he was too old for her, but then he would catch glimpses of the sadness that lay under her surface and he knew that no matter what her chronological age was, she'd seen enough that she wasn't truly young, not the way other twenty-five-year-olds were.

"She only tried to sleep with one Dom," Julian said, his face so serious that Cole knew he was struggling with what he had to say. "I don't like to gossip, but this is important. She wasn't in love with the men who watched over her."

"But she wanted one of them." He hated the fact that jealousy was burning through his gut.

"Not really. She wanted something familiar. She went to Chase one night and begged him to hurt her." Julian shook his head as though releasing some terrible memory. "Chase declined. Finn had to calm her down. I worried for her sanity that night. I worried she would never be able to tell the difference between love and abuse. You have to understand that she didn't receive love and affection from her parents. They were cold. Hawk was a monster, but she found some physical affection from him. And she became close to her fellow hostages. I believe she thought if she allowed Chase to hurt her, he would pay her back with affection. She's come a long way since that night."

Chase Dawson had a dark side, but he wouldn't hurt a woman. God, Cole could only imagine how Chase had felt about being the man Kitten picked to hurt her. Cole was trying everything he could to make sure she didn't make that mistake with him. "We need more time. I've been working a lot lately, but in a week I should be free and I plan on spending plenty of time with her."

"And if she disappoints you?"

What the hell was that about? "I don't expect she will."

"But if she does?" Julian prodded.

"Then I suppose I would try to work it out. If I couldn't, I would find a way to ease her out of my life."

A single brow rose over Julian's eyes. "That's good to know since you didn't do that with Mason."

Fuck. Even the mention of his name caused an ache. "What happened between Mason and me is my business."

"No, it's my business if it's the way you treat your submissives. Kitten is my family. She's my responsibility and she will remain that way until such time as I trust the man who cares for her. I do not trust you yet, Cole. Not with her. She's had a hard life. Even before her unfortunate kidnapping, her life was marked with intolerance and harshness. Her father has a limited view of what love means. Of what love is. There was no affection for her. No kindness. If you can't give that to her, I need to take her back." Julian's face tightened, the closest Cole had ever seen to the man becoming emotional. "I have to do right by her. I hope you understand."

He did. Julian was one of a few men that Cole understood. His life was defined in a particular way. He needed to make things right for the people he cared about. He needed to be important, and that included placing boundaries and guarding them. Kitten was firmly within Julian's fence line—the one between him and the outside world. That made her important to him. Cole needed him to understand that she was in his fence, too.

"I'll take care of her. What happened between me and Mason was different. He let me down. We had a sub we shared and she died on his watch. She died because he couldn't control himself. Can't you understand that? I loved him, but I did what I had to do."

Julian sighed and stood. "I truly do understand, but not in the way you think. I understand that you did what you thought you had to. I merely question the fact that you think what you had with him was love. I believe if it was love, you couldn't have broken him the way you did. And you should watch out for it. I also happen to know that breaking a man that way can come back to haunt you. If you choose to break with a person, it's almost better to eradicate them. I should know. I had a relationship very much like the one you had with Mason. The man let me down and I cut him out of my life. My Mason almost killed Danielle."

Cole had heard the story. Julian had caught his male submissive with drugs in his club and had dismissed the man. He'd come after Julian, nearly killing both him and his now wife, Dani, in the process. "I don't discuss Mason with anyone. That part of my life is over."

Though lately Mason had been more and more on his mind. He didn't quite understand what Julian meant by "breaking" Mason, but he was unwilling to ask for clarification.

"That's a shame. I watched you with him. I rather thought it was love. You proved something different. Know that if you treat Kitten with such indifference, you will deal with me. I will not be as simple to handle as Mason."

Julian stood and walked out the door, his message plain.

What the hell had Julian meant? He'd loved Mason with everything he'd had. How was he supposed to forgive him for what he'd done? Mason had broken with everything that they had agreed on.

Julian was married to Danielle and Finn. Wouldn't he break with them if they harmed each other?

Or would he simply try to figure out what had gone wrong?

Cole took a long breath. Julian didn't understand. Mason had caused the death of their sub. His sub. Mason had put pleasure before the woman Cole had pledged to protect.

He was in the right. Surely.

He stared at the door Julian had shut behind him, memories of Mason playing through his head.

* * * *

Kitten Taylor let the sun warm her skin as she lay out by the pool. She took a deep breath. The air was humid, sultry. Not that sultry would help her in any way. There was nothing hot about her world except the temperature.

"Do you need anything?"

She kept her eyes closed because the last thing she wanted to see was Ms. Hamilton frowning down at her. Ms. Hamilton's face was in a perpetual frown that not even Botox could solve, though Kitten had thought several times about injecting the woman in her sleep.

"No, thank you." The Dallas sun heated her up. She was wearing a modest two-piece that Julian had purchased for her the prior summer. It made her resemble a Hollywood star from the sixties, but she had to admit, it fit her look.

The housekeeper sighed as though horribly put out and Kitten heard her functional heels begin to tap impatiently against the cool-crete of the pool area. She couldn't stand Ms. Hamilton. Her eyes were always judgmental, and she didn't even try to disguise her hatred of Kitten.

Of me. Sometimes it was hard to remember to refer to herself in the first person. It was a sure sign that her life had taken a wrong turn that she had to remember narrative terms outside of her English class.

"Really," she said quietly. "I'm fine, thank you."

"The schedule Cole left says it's time for your snack."

She opened her eyes and sighed. Ms. Hamilton had a tray in her hand. She was sure it included something incredibly healthy. Apparently Cole wanted her thin as hell. It was working. The food he fed her during the day had caused her to lose five pounds during the month she'd been his submissive. The only time she ate well was at night when she ate with him. If he didn't come home for dinner, she was given a salad and nothing else.

She was starting to think this had all been a horrible idea.

She was also starting to think she didn't need this anymore. She'd longed for her own Master. Cole Roberts was everything she'd dreamed of, but he didn't seem to want her the way she wanted him. He wasn't cold. He could be quite warm when he wanted to be. He just didn't seem to want her.

She was starting to understand she needed a little indulgence in her life. She wasn't the piece of trash Hawk made her believe she was. She was something more. She was the same girl who'd earned straight A's in high school and was voted Most Likely to Succeed. Unfortunately, she should have been voted Most Likely to Get

Kidnapped and Forced into Slavery, but she was out of that now. "I'm not hungry."

"Your hunger doesn't matter. Cole said it's time for you to eat. You will eat or break your contract."

That contract was starting to chafe. Mightily. "Just leave it."

There was a clatter as Ms. Hamilton placed the tray on the table near her. "Well, I'll make sure Cole knows how you feel."

She was sure Ms. Hamilton would. She was sure the housekeeper wrote up reports on her daily. Cole would soon ship her right back to Julian Lodge, and Kitten wasn't sure how many chances she had left. Julian had taken care of her because Finn Taylor was her first cousin. Finn was Julian's male submissive. Julian loved both Finn and his female sub, Dani. He loved them so much he took in their stray relatives who had been traumatized.

Years of living under Julian Lodge's roof had taught her a couple of things. First, it taught her that she was fucked up. Like totally, maybe irrevocably. Second, even if she could never find that girl she'd been, she could find a new her. She could find a Katherine Taylor who could live and love and have a happy life. Julian had taught her that. Masters Chase and Ben had taught her that. Her friend Nat had taught her that.

She was more than a victim. She was Kitten. She was an I.

I am worthy.

It was her new mantra. That and *I hate kale salad.*

She turned away from the "snack" she'd been brought. Kale wasn't a snack. Popcorn was a snack. Chocolate was a snack. Undressed kale salad was a punishment and she hadn't earned one.

She'd been damn near perfect, not that it had gotten her anything. Sure, he'd spanked her a couple of times and he'd gotten her off, but no sex for Kitten yet.

Damn it. No sex for me.

Maybe her Master didn't find her attractive. He'd bought her clothes and cuddled her while they watched television, but every night he sent her to her room and he went to his.

It made a girl think. And not good things.

Her phone rang, a trilling sound that reminded her of bunnies and flowers and daisies. She glanced down and grimaced. Cole.

He was the most gorgeous man she'd ever met and she was thinking about ducking his call.

She sighed and flipped the switch to answer. "Hello."

"Hello? Is that what I get?" His dark voice did things to her feminine parts.

"Hello, Sir." When he was with her, when she could see him, she had hope. When he was away, there seemed to be so many walls around him.

"Hello, pet." If only she truly was his pet. "Tell me what you're doing."

She smiled. That made her feel wanted—the hitch in his voice that let her know he actually was interested in the answer. "I'm lying by the pool."

A deep chuckle came over the line. God, the man had the sexiest voice. "Tell me you're not wearing a thing."

She wasn't supposed to lie to her Master. "I'm in my swimsuit."

He sighed. "Tell me you're wearing sunscreen."

He was deeply interested in sunscreen. And vitamins. And her diet. "Yes, Sir."

"I'm so glad to hear it, pet. I don't want my lovely sub to be sunburned." That sexy voice might mean something if he'd ever touched her with pure affection.

"Did you need something, Sir?"

There was a pause and then he sounded slightly disgruntled. "Not really. I wanted to call you. If I've interrupted something, I certainly apologize."

This was what they seemed to be best at. Getting themselves into uncomfortable situations. It wasn't like her relationships with Masters Chase and Ben and Master Logan. Well, except for the fact that Master Cole didn't want to have sex with her either. "No, Sir. I was worried I had forgotten something."

His voice softened. "You never forget anything, sweetheart. You're very good at remembering. I'm looking forward to our session this evening."

Her body tightened. The only time she felt connected to her gorgeous Master was when they spent time in the dungeon. In the month she'd been living in his home, she had spent six glorious evenings getting familiar with his excellent flogging and spanking techniques. While he was working her over, she was relaxed and happy, but being sent to her own bed was getting old. She hated to sleep alone. She rarely slept more than an hour or two when she was all by herself.

"I am as well."

"We'll begin an hour after dinner. I thought we would start adding in some protocol. I'd like you to be naked tonight for dinner."

That was promising. She quite liked being naked. Her exhibitionist side was one of the things she'd discovered about herself. "Yes, Sir. If it would please you."

"Would it please you?"

"Yes, Sir. It would very much please me."

He chuckled. "I rather thought it would. You prefer your own skin."

She'd fought hard to be comfortable with her body. Sometimes she could still hear Hawk shouting at her that she was too thin or too fat. She was never perfect. Never attractive. "It is nice to feel the air on my skin."

"You don't have to wear a suit to swim." There was a small pause. "I was surprised to find you owned one."

"Oh, Master Julian was worried about The Club becoming a nudist resort. He said if I did it then Master Chase would want to as well, and he didn't want to look at that."

Now her Master laughed long and hard. She enjoyed the deep sound of his amusement. When he laughed like that, she felt like she was giving him something he needed. "All right, then, pet. I'm going into an important meeting. I won't be available for the rest of the afternoon. If you need anything, ask Ms. Hamilton. I'll see you at dinner."

The phone disconnected and she was left with that odd feeling she'd come to associate with Cole. It was somewhere in between hope and desire and a bleak acceptance that nothing worked out.

She wanted Cole. He was big and strong but had such kind eyes. They were a stark blue that warmed up the minute he looked at her. She'd thought at first that it was desire in those eyes, but now she wondered if what Cole felt for her was something closer to pity.

She'd been an object of pity for long enough. Still, she wasn't sure she was ready to walk away. Walking away meant disappointing the few people who loved her. Finn. Nat. Her friend Haven. They would all think she'd gone backward.

She sighed, allowing the sun to warm her skin. Maybe she should slip out of her suit and feel the air against her flesh.

She was going to have to make a decision soon. She was twenty-five years old. She had to figure out who Kitten Taylor was. She knew who Katherine Taylor had been. She'd been a college student studying education and dating a boy her mother approved of who she'd barely kissed but talked about marrying.

Her father didn't talk to Kitten Taylor. Her mother turned her back on Kitten.

On her. Her parents had turned their backs on her. Because they didn't understand this version of their daughter. Because in so many ways they believed she'd done something to justify her kidnapping. Her rape. Her torture.

Tears pierced her eyes, but they were actually a lovely feeling. They came on their own now. She didn't need a spanking to cry. She could do that all on her own. She could find a well of sorrow and it was pure. How sad was it that she was grateful to be able to cry?

Or how beautiful? Katherine Taylor had taken her emotions for granted. Kitten did not. Kitten found a profound beauty in the small things.

Like sitting near a pool on a sunny day. She sat up, her nose wrinkling at the sight of the salad Ms. Hamilton had left. Snack? Barf. She would wait for dinner. For now she would sit by the pool and hope that tonight brought something new. Maybe a long kiss from her Master.

A nice long fuck would be better though.

She was on the edge of her lounge chair when the phone rang. Not the cell at her side, but the one inside the house. She could hear it ringing in the distance. One. Two and then three rings.

Kitten wondered why Ms. Hamilton wasn't answering. Four rings. And then nothing.

She looked at the back of Cole's ridiculously large house. Her

Master was wealthy. There were five bedrooms in the house plus a lovely pool house. Ms. Hamilton lived in a small one-bedroom guesthouse on the grounds. Kitten squinted and as she'd feared, Ms. Hamilton was walking toward her home, her gait sure and stately.

The phone began to ring again.

Kitten sighed. She wasn't supposed to answer the phone, but someone obviously needed to talk. She crossed the patio and slipped into the house, the conditioned air cool on her skin. She shivered as she answered. "Hello?"

"Is Cole Roberts there, please?" a crisp, feminine voice asked.

"I'm sorry. He's at work. May I take a message?" She'd been Leo's administrative assistant for over a year. She'd learned a few things. Sometimes she missed working.

"I'm a patient advocate at Parkland Hospital. There's a patient here named Mason Scott. Mr. Roberts is his emergency contact. I need to get in touch with Mr. Roberts or a woman named Emily Yarborough."

She'd heard the name Mason Scott before. Julian and Leo had talked about a Mason and being worried about him. And they'd talked about the fact that Mason had been close to Cole.

She knew she shouldn't, but she couldn't help herself. "This is Emily."

She was definitely going to get in trouble for that.

There was a sigh over the line. "Thank god. Mr. Scott has been in an accident. He's got a concussion and a sprained ankle. He's in and out of consciousness. It would be helpful if one of you would come down here and stay with him until we can release him. Are you his sister?"

Kitten wasn't dumb. She knew that her Master had been involved with Mason Scott. She knew her Master had loved him. She was interested in meeting Mason Scott. "Yes. I'll be down there as soon as I can. What is his prognosis?"

Her Master no longer talked to this man, but that didn't mean a thing. He was important—the way her college boyfriend had been important. Michael Rhodes had been her everything and then she'd been nothing because she wasn't pure and perfect. Kitten needed to see Mason. She needed to understand why Mason was no longer special to Cole Roberts.

"It's good. He'll be fine if he gets proper care."

Like she had needed proper care. Nat had saved her, and Finn and Nat and Julian and everyone at The Club had made sure she was all right. "I'll make sure. Can you give me a list of what's required? I can be very precise if I know what to do."

She would take care of him. Like she'd been taken care of. She could make sure Mason Scott survived. Her heart swelled at the thought. She could be important to someone.

There was a long sigh over the line. "Yes, miss. I can make sure you know what to do. Thank you. He seems like a nice man. I wanted to ensure that he gets what he needs. He seems to think no one will care what happened to him."

Tears welled in her eyes. She knew that feeling. She'd been alone for so long. Even when she'd met Nat, she'd wondered if she was expendable. She didn't know this man, but her heart ached for him. "I'll take care of him."

Mason Scott. He didn't know it yet, but he needed her.

Chapter Two

Mason stared at himself in the mirror. Sure, he looked a little tired, but otherwise he couldn't tell he'd been in a terrible accident. How the hell could he have a concussion? "There's not even any bruising."

The nurse sighed. "You can't see the egg on the back of your head, Mr. Scott. Put down the mirror and slide your fingers over it."

He stared at himself, feeling that odd sense of disconnect he'd felt every day for the last two years. Like he didn't quite recognize the man in the mirror. One day he'd known exactly who he was and then the next he'd been a complete stranger.

A stranger who might have finally hit rock bottom.

He ran his hand over the back of his head, wincing slightly. Yep, there it was. Proof that he couldn't even fucking drive right. And he had no idea how he was going to pay this damn bill. He'd lost his health insurance years ago when Cole had decided he wasn't worth knowing anymore. Not only was he not worth knowing, he was worth utterly destroying.

God, that still ached. He could remember the moment when his boss had fired him and told him he wouldn't work for any of the big firms again. When Cole Roberts was done with a person, he was finished. There were no apologies, no discussions. Cole hadn't listened to him in any way. The doors to the house they'd shared had been locked and there had been a note explaining that Mason's belongings would be delivered to his new address.

Years he'd loved Cole, supported him, propped the fucker up, and that was what he got.

And now he worked for shit money and was sliding into thirty-five without anything or anyone to call his own. And he didn't even have a fucking car since he'd apparently wrapped it around a truck.

"How's your pain level?" the nurse asked, her clipboard in hand.

Tell her it's horrible. Get some good fucking drugs and go out the right way. No one gives a shit. His parents had dropped him because he was gay. They didn't care that he wasn't gay. He was bi. The fact that he liked men had been enough. All his friends had dropped him, too. It hadn't mattered because he'd had Cole. And now he was utterly alone and had been for years. *Take the drugs. Like you take the alcohol. Take a couple of hydrocodone with a bottle of vodka and none of this will be meaningful. You can go where you've always been going. You can finally have some peace.*

"I'm fine, thank you." His head was pounding and his ankle hurt worse, but he didn't trust himself to take only what he needed. That piece of him that had always wanted to self-destruct was so much louder now. One day it might drown out all the other voices, but not today. He could hang on today.

The nurse frowned down at him as though assessing his stubbornness. He was pretty sure she'd come to the right conclusion when her eyes went all sympathetic. "All right. If that's what you want. How about some ibuprofen? It will help with the swelling."

He nodded. He could handle a little less swelling, especially since it was only his head. God knew his ego hadn't swollen in forever. Rather like his cock. His cock had become a useless thing, never twitching or demanding anymore. Somewhere along the way it had realized what it needed was gone forever.

"I've got the paperwork almost ready for you." The nurse stood by the doorway.

Wow. He was going to get thrown out pretty damn quick. When he'd first walked through the door, she'd explained that he couldn't be released without someone to watch him and wake him every hour or so. Now they were willing to dump him on the street. So much for patient care. And he'd learned not to fight it. He hoped he had the money for a cab. "All right. I'll get cleaned up and out of your hair."

There had been a time when he would have charmed his way into the woman's home. He didn't see a ring on her finger. She was of an in between age where he would have to decide if he would play the charming potential lover or the son she'd never had. He would likely have gone the son route, playing on her sympathy. Oh, he would have found a way to help her, to pay her back, but he would have taken every comfort she offered as well.

Now he simply gave in to the fact that he would have a few days to vacate his rattrap apartment because living there was contingent on him having a job, and he needed a car to get to work.

Would he end up in a shelter? He had absolutely no idea where he would be in two days. Maybe he'd been wrong to turn down those drugs.

He knew where Cole was. Cole was still in his big, gorgeous house. Cole still had everything.

The nurse stopped at the door, her body half in the stark white room. "I'll get this done so you can head out when your sister gets here. She sounds lovely, by the way. So polite."

The door closed behind her.

Sister? He didn't have any siblings. Hell, he didn't have any friends. Certainly no one polite.

A horrible thought struck him and he stood up. His head started to pound and the world did a 180, but he was determined to get to his wallet. He found it on the table, opened it, and was utterly horrified to discover that the small card he'd placed in the back pocket was still there, weathered and wrinkled from being folded.

In case of emergency, call Cole Roberts or Emily Yarborough.

It gave his old Master's cell phone number as his emergency contact. And one other. It was the house phone in Dallas where someone nearly always answered. Cole had insisted Emily be made aware as well, as though Mason pretending to be close to her would bring them together.

Use the house phone, love. I sometimes turn off my cell, but I want someone to answer if there's an emergency. You're very important to me. You're the most important person in the world, Mason.

Fuck. The hospital had called Cole. But the nurse said a female had answered. Ms. Hamilton was the one who answered the house phone. Ms. Hamilton, with her pinched face and the never-ending gloom cloud that seemed to follow her. Some people were like that—vampires sucking away all the joy. But Ms. Hamilton wasn't polite either.

"Oh, my. You have a lovely backside. It's completely obvious to me that you work out often."

Mason nearly jumped out of his skin at the sound of that sweet, feminine voice. He turned, his head more than a little woozy. He swayed on his feet as he caught sight of a gorgeous woman in a black-and-white polka dot sundress that could have come straight out of a Doris Day film.

She gasped and was suddenly beside him, reaching out to balance him so he didn't fall. It gave him the most spectacular view of her pert breasts. They weren't big, but they were lovingly rounded. And the skin displayed around them was sun-kissed and smooth. He would bet she was soft all over.

"This one is so sorry. I mean, I am so sorry. I didn't mean for my ogling to cause you distress. I like to tell people when I find them pleasing. There aren't enough compliments in the world." She bit at her plump lower lip as sea green eyes widened in regret.

And his dick decided to wake up for what felt like the first time in forever. Fucking hallelujah. Despite the ache in his head, it felt damn good to be hard.

And then he remembered he was in a paper-thin robe that opened at the back. She'd seen his backside in full-screen vision.

But the sweet thing seemed to have liked the view. Maybe the day wasn't looking so nasty. He needed a place to go. She was walking around a hospital alone. No ring on her finger. Yeah, he could see this working out nicely. "Not distress, gorgeous girl. I was just surprised. I'm glad you liked ogling me. Sometimes a man works his hardest and no one notices."

It was the first time he'd felt the need to turn on the charm in forever. He wasn't sure why the gorgeous thing had walked into his room, but he intended to walk out with her. He wasn't sitting around waiting for Ms. Hamilton to show up because Cole wanted to humiliate him again. No way. No how.

Maybe it was time to start living again. If Ms. Hamilton had a cloud of gloom following her around, then Little Miss Luscious was a ray of sunshine.

She smiled, the sweetest expression he'd ever seen. It did things that went way past his dick. "I can't imagine that any female with eyes wouldn't appreciate the sight of your muscular backside. You've done a spectacular job with it, Sir."

There went his cock again. It was twitching now, an eager puppy who had found a playmate. Maybe his head didn't hurt so much. He could probably perform with a concussion.

Sir. Had she meant sir or Sir? Or was she merely being polite? The nurse had said the woman who was coming to pick him up was polite. Exactly like Cole liked his subs. *This one.* She'd corrected herself. His eyes found her neck and sure enough she was wearing a delicate filigreed collar around her slender throat.

Fuck all, Cole's sub had come for him.

His heart took a long plunge. "You belong to Master Cole."

Her high-wattage smile dimmed slightly and he could see the faintest hint of pain there. All was not well with the sub and her Master. He was brilliant at finding tells and Gorgeous Girl had a multitude of them. God, Cole would die over her. She was so soft and innocent. "I am the Master's submissive."

Not his slave. In his truly intimate relationships, Cole would call her his slave. Oh, he didn't necessarily mean anything by it. Cole treated his slaves like queens, meeting their every want and need, but he found the word slave to be intimate. It meant the woman belonged to him in every way.

But this woman was merely a submissive. So they weren't far into their relationship yet. Cole liked to take things slow. He liked to spend months training a submissive before he would even fuck her. It could drive the sub crazy.

Something nasty took root in Mason's gut.

Cole had taken so fucking much from him. What if he could get a little of his own back? Why should Cole get the pretty girl? Now that he looked at her through different eyes, he could see that Cole was dressing her, molding her. She wasn't Cole's usual type, which meant he was engaged emotionally in some way.

Wouldn't it hurt if Mason had her first?

He sighed and took a step back. He had to play this perfectly. It had been a long time since he'd bothered with games, but suddenly he really wanted to win. And that meant manipulating the sub. He gave her a weary smile. "Well, sweetheart, you should know that I won't be welcome in your Master's home. He no longer speaks to me. I don't want to get you in trouble."

She stared at him as though trying desperately to figure out what to do. He attempted to look as pathetic as possible, sitting on the edge of his bed. "Can I at least give you a ride somewhere?" she asked. "I have a car outside. I'm quite a good driver. The Master made me prove to him that I could be safe."

He was surprised Cole let her drive at all after what happened to Emily. "I would have thought he would get you a driver."

She shook her head. "I wouldn't sign the contract until he allowed me to drive. I'm not a child. I need my independence. I'm allowed to go wherever I like during the day as long as I let someone know where I've gone. I left the Master a nice note."

Oh, god, she was a brat. Fuck, yeah, that did it for him, too. Revenge was going to be sweet indeed. "It's all right. I'll take a cab."

Now her brow furrowed, giving her the sweetest line between her eyebrows. It would be her stubborn look. "You have a concussion. Who will take care of you?"

She wanted to be needed. He would bet Cole wasn't giving her that yet. He knew how the Master worked. He would prefer that his submissive lie around waiting for him to return, but it was plain that this one needed something more. Mason could give it to her. It was why they had always worked well together in the first place. Mason gave the sub affection and Cole handled the discipline.

"I'll be fine. I've been alone for a long time, honey. Don't you worry about me." He turned his head. It chose that exact moment to pound and swell and send him off balance. He put both hands on the bed and gritted his teeth to survive the wave.

She was right beside him, her hands on his forehead. She grabbed the cool rag the nurse had left and gently put it against him. "I looked some things up on the Internet before I left. You'll feel better if I can keep your body cool. I set the thermostat in the pool house to sixty-eight degrees. It should help with any nausea."

If she wanted to keep him cool, she should keep her hands off him because damn his dick was hot. "I don't think Cole will let me in."

Her sunny smile was back. "Oh, I will handle the Master. I've found it is largely better to ask forgiveness than permission. It's easier to get what I want that way. And don't worry about making the Master angry. He is easily handled with tears and apologies. Most of the time he doesn't even spank me."

The last bit was said with a sad regret. God, Cole was fucking up with this sub. How many had he gone through since Emily? Had he turned tentative since Emily? It made sense. Cole would be apprehensive. Mason could use that to his advantage. Once he was in the pool house, Cole could toss him out.

But if he gave in to his sub's wishes, Mason would be in. And then he could start to work on the sub Cole so obviously was treating with kid gloves.

He would make his way into her bed. He would have her spread-eagled, penetrated, and fucked, and he would make damn sure Cole caught them.

He sent her a grateful look. "Are you sure? I don't have anywhere else to go. I'm alone."

She softened even further and a light took up in her eyes. "I can take care of you. Let me handle everything."

He sat back as she stood and started organizing his sad possessions. "I didn't even ask your name."

Her shoulders straightened and her chin came up. Carmel-brown hair flowed almost down to her waist. God, she was beautiful. He could almost see her wearing all that hair and nothing else. "I'm Kitten. Kitten Taylor. It's nice to meet you, Mr. Mason."

"Just Mason, darling." It was so nice to meet her. Oh, yes. She scurried around, arranging things for their departure, and Mason relaxed for the first time in a long time.

He would have his revenge and then maybe it was time to move on. Maybe it was time to finally figure out who he could be without Cole Roberts looming over his life. A little revenge would close the circle and he would leave Texas. He would make his way north and find a new life.

And maybe he would take Kitten, if she proved to be as sweet as she looked. He would give up his switch needs. They'd done nothing but get him in trouble. He would be in control. He would be the Dom this time.

Yes, he would take care of her. And he would ruin Cole.

Chapter Three

Cole looked up from the notes he was making as his assistant walked into the room with a mug of coffee in her hand.

"Don't mind me," Lea Schneider said with a tight smile. "It's almost three and I know how you drag at this time of the day."

She was a slightly plump woman with a plain face. Cole thought she might be pretty if she ever smiled, but she had a two-by-four shoved so far up her ass it would never come out. He'd been shocked at how young she was when she'd first hired on. He'd thought she was squarely in middle age, but she'd been in her twenties. Something about the way she dressed and the frown she had most of the time aged her.

He'd hired her over eight years ago and he thought about firing her from time to time. Not because she wasn't competent. She was always on time, never complained about working late. She was chained to her job. No, she was almost the perfect assistant. It bugged him.

In the end, he simply didn't want to take the time to find another one.

He accepted the coffee that was brewed to his specifications. As with everything she did, it was perfect. It even had about an inch of space at the top because she knew he sometimes didn't look at what he was doing and spilled.

How utterly different she was from Kitten Taylor. Kitten forgot things because her head was in the clouds. She tried to hide it, but there was a bratty mouth on her.

She completely fascinated him. He got hard just thinking about her.

He had to take it slow or he would screw everything up with her. She couldn't know that he was already a bit in love with her. She'd been through so much. She needed the firm hand of a loving Master. He couldn't screw up with her the way he had with Mason. Julian was wrong about how he'd truly felt about Mason. Love was where he'd gone wrong in that relationship. He'd been far too soft, and it had cost them all.

A vision of Mason floated across his brain. It happened more and more now. Especially since Kitten had moved in. He'd thought about how sweet they would be together. Mason needed a playmate, a woman he could dance with and watch silly TV shows with. Cole had little time for such things, but he enjoyed knowing that his subs were happy and together. Kitten liked games. He could join them for quiet nights at the lodge where they would share wine and board games and end up in an intimate pile together.

Except Mason was gone from him. Where was he living now? God, he hadn't been able to stop thinking about Mason since Julian's visit this morning. Had he found a new Dom? Was he happy with his new lover, or did he occasionally think of Cole?

"Did the meeting go well?" Lea shuffled around the room, cleaning up things here and there. The boardroom was always messy after a long meeting where they fought about acquisitions and mergers. He was tired. He wanted to close everything up and head home where Kitten was probably still in her swimsuit. He could order her out of it, order her to take down his pants and suck his cock until his eyes rolled to the back of his head and he forgot about everything but the way she was drinking him down. Then he would take her to bed and lick her pussy until he knew her taste better than any other. He would make her come and then cuddle with her and fuck her all over again. They could shut out the world and there wouldn't be anyone except the two of them for a few hours.

God, he was a bastard. She'd been brutalized and he wanted to order her to suck him when he hadn't even given her a month to get used to being around him. She wasn't eating. He'd left strict instructions that she was to get anything she wanted when he wasn't around. She was to be offered everything he had, and Ms. Hamilton had announced that she turned down every given opportunity to eat. She would ask for a salad and then refuse to eat it. She barely ate any of the soup she would order. What he wouldn't do to get her to eat a burger or some ice cream.

Her abuser had used food, or the withholding of it, as a punishment. The only time she ate was at night, when he watched over her. Then she ate with gusto, clearing her plate every time. She was trying to please him.

She was afraid of him.

Until she started to show signs that she trusted him, until he earned it, he had to keep the relationship platonic.

"Cole?"

He was drifting. He never drifted, damn it. What had she asked? Oh, yes. The meeting. "It was fine. We fought about the property in Colorado, but what's different about that? Bob is bugging me again about developing it. I have to hold a hard line until I can get the funds to buy it from the company."

The trouble was the property had tripled in value since he bought it years before. The board was getting anxious about selling it or developing it, and neither of those outcomes was acceptable to Cole.

She frowned again, her face pinching. She didn't like Colorado. She'd made that plain to him time and again. Or rather she didn't like the town they stayed in when he was in Colorado. She didn't fit in there. "Bliss? Why are you wasting money there? No one wants to go to that weird town."

Ah, yes. Now he remembered why he wanted to fire her from time to time. He let his eyes go stony cold. "My grandfather loved that weird town."

And so did he. He felt comfortable at the Elk Creek Lodge. It was the beautiful ski resort his grandfather had left him. That lodge was his real legacy, his prize. He couldn't wait until the season began. He would take Kitten with him. He would buy her a pink parka with faux fur around the hood because she would cry if she thought he'd killed some bunny to keep her warm. He would teach her to ski and sled, and they could play in the snow. She was so much sweeter than Emily had been. Kitten looked at the world with wonder. Like Mason had.

Fuck, when would he stop missing Mason? Years had done nothing to fill the hole in his heart.

Lea shook her head. "I'm sorry. I've always thought it was a risky investment. I know the lodge does well, but the people of that town always give you hell when you try to help them out. They're very unreasonable."

He smiled, thinking about the last time he'd had to face the Bliss citizens and tell them his plans. He wanted to build some outlet malls on the property he owned outside of Bliss. Yeah, that hadn't gone over well. He'd been protested vigorously. Nell and Henry Flanders had chanted outside the lodge. He'd gotten numerous letters asking him why he hated the earth and thought cheap and damaged goods were a reason to ruin the beauty of the planet. Nate Wright had started ticketing him regularly. Max Harper had been more obnoxious than usual, though Cole was damn near certain the man had regular hormonal cycles. Callie Hollister-Wright had cried and begged him not to ruin the valley. But it was all over when Stella refused him breakfast and Zane Hollister had delivered lukewarm beer to his table and told him if he wanted something cold he should put in a tavern at the Outlet Hellhole.

The people of Bliss had spoken. If he couldn't get hot pancakes and cold beer, life wouldn't be worth living.

"I'm not going to ruin the earth this time. I've given up on those plans. The board is wrong about them. It's why I finally had to strong-arm them down. I'm going to turn it into a nature refuge where people can pay to hike and enjoy bunnies and shit. Let's see Nell Flanders protest me now." He would never admit it, but he actually wanted to fit in there. And he definitely wanted to be able to get a cold one at Trio.

Kitten would like Bliss if she gave it a chance. She'd been there for a wedding, but she hadn't seen the snow yet. Would they still be together when the winter came and he moved to the lodge? Or would she have moved on to a kinder Master?

"Will we make money off that?" Lea asked.

There was no real "we" there. She didn't have stock in the damn company. "There are some things that are worth more than money. This is about our company image. That land is going to be a good tax shelter."

It had been a shitty day where everyone questioned his judgment. He'd made a horrible mistake by not buying that property with his own cash. When it had come up for sale a few years back, he'd gotten it in his head to develop that land, to help the town he loved. Yeah, he'd been out of his head at the time. Now he couldn't imagine what he'd been thinking. It was better as it was. He couldn't imagine building on that gorgeous land.

The trouble was, he had some stockholders who wanted to do exactly that. It had been a hell of a fight.

"Speaking of Colorado," Lea began with a long-suffering sigh. "That woman called again. She's very rude."

Gemma Wells was a pain in his ass. She ran the sheriff's department for the county, but no one had told her she needed to be polite about it. "Tell her that if Nate Wright wants me to donate to the police fund, he should have a damn bake sale. I paid three hundred dollars in tickets the last time I was in town. He can kiss my ass. And while you're at it, tell him he should get a better fundraiser. Gemma's crappy. She bitches at me until I give in. I'm not dealing with her anymore."

Lea nodded. "I'll deflect everyone for you. You know I try to give you the peace you need. I'll be in the outer office should you require anything further."

He shook his head. "Nah. Knock off early. I think I'm going to get out of here before the board decides to call another flipping meeting. Sometimes I wish my father had kept the company private."

Stockholders were also a pain in his ass. He couldn't wait. Three months and he could head to Colorado and leave everything in his second-in-command's hands. He would have three months of freedom. He could be an innkeeper like his grandfather for a few months. All he would have to worry about was whether or not his

EMT caught a venereal disease.

He loved the lodge. He loved the staff. Sure Tyler Davis was a dipshit lothario, but Cole found him amusing.

Lea shook her head. "I stay with the boss. I'll be here with you, Cole."

The door shut behind her. God, he wasn't looking forward to telling her he was leaving her behind this winter season. He'd decided it the first time he'd had a meeting at the house and Lea hadn't been able to hide her disdain. Kitten was completely adorable. She was a bundle of sweetness, but Lea had taken an instant dislike to her. He wouldn't put Kitten through that in close quarters the way they would be in Colorado. He wanted her happy and relaxed. He wanted her comfortable in Bliss so they could spend time there.

But he didn't have to deal with that today. Lea could do her work from Dallas and Kitten would travel with her Master.

She was the one. He was almost sure of it. He felt something for her he hadn't felt for anyone with the exception of Mason. He just had to control it better than he had with Mason. He had to always stay in control.

His phone vibrated. He'd turned it back on not five minutes before and he was already getting calls. Yes, he was counting down the days to Colorado where half the time he couldn't get a signal. Ms. Hamilton. He slid his finger across the screen to answer. "Yes?"

"She took the Benz, sir."

He had to think about firing Ms. Hamilton, too. He could only think though. He couldn't actually do it. How could he convince her to retire? God, when had he become surrounded by grim reapers? He hadn't noticed it until recently. Ms. Hamilton had been his father's housekeeper. He had the feeling she didn't approve of his lifestyle, but he couldn't care less. He hadn't thought about it at all until she'd started giving him daily rundowns of all the ways Kitten was a disappointment. Ms. Hamilton had loved Emily. Emily had been perfect in her eyes.

Of course, he worried she was going a little blind.

"Did she tell you where she was going?" He struggled to find his patience. Kitten wasn't a prisoner. At first he'd worried because

Julian had told him she had a habit of getting lost, but he'd discovered quite quickly that Kitten liked to pretend to be dumber than she was. He was putting up with it—for now—but he saw through her act. She rarely didn't know exactly what she was doing. She could be a manipulative brat.

And that got his dick hard. It gave him hope that they could get somewhere.

If he could get past the fact that a piece of his soul would always be missing.

Lately he'd been wondering if he shouldn't at least find out what was happening with Mason. Maybe he'd gotten his life together. Maybe they could talk. Maybe Mason would apologize and they could at least be friendly again.

"She said she was going to run a few errands."

He frowned. He would have to be clearer. She wasn't a prisoner, but he also didn't like the vagueness of "running errands." "I'll call her. She'll be fine. I'm sure she ran out for a snack or something."

"I would be surprised. The girl refuses to eat. When you're gone, she simply becomes difficult."

"I'll talk to her." When he got her to Colorado, he would keep her with him all day. He would feed her himself, not in a commanding way, but indulgently. Slowly, he would draw her out of her shell. He would show her the good side of D/s.

"All right then. Also, there were two calls on the answering machine I thought you might need to deal with. First some brusque woman named Gemma Wells called and requested that you contact her. She seemed rude."

"I'll call her." Gemma could be a bulldog when she wanted to be. Most of the time she wanted to be. He would have to be firm with her. "What was the other message?"

She huffed. "It was the hospital. You don't need to do anything about it. I called them and told them we would have nothing to do with it."

He sat up a bit straighter. "With what? Who's in the hospital?"

"Apparently Mason Scott hasn't managed to drink himself to death yet. He was involved in an accident and he has you listed as his next of kin. The nerve of the man. I can only hope he hasn't killed someone else with his recklessness. Why they didn't prosecute him before I have no idea. The laziness of the police is atrocious."

"What hospital?" His whole body had gone tense. Mason was in the hospital? God, he wasn't supposed to give a shit, but Mason was in the hospital. Mason was hurt.

"Does it matter?"

"What fucking hospital?" He bit off every word. He'd been fooling himself. He'd pretended the world was all rosy and shit, but the thought of Mason dying still had the power to make his heart seize. He might never be able to forgive him, but he couldn't leave him alone to die in a hospital.

"Parkland," she replied. "They also asked if you would be responsible for the bill."

"What? For his deductible?"

"Apparently he doesn't have any insurance. I would only expect it from someone like him. Freeloader."

How could Mason not have insurance? Mason worked for one of the biggest law firms in Dallas. Mason was a high-powered attorney.

God, had he lost his job because Cole hadn't been there to rein in his self-destructive tendencies? Guilt rolled in his gut. Had he made a mistake? He didn't know. He was only certain of one thing. He needed to see Mason. "Tell Kitten I'll be late for dinner."

He hung up the phone, pushing away his unfinished paperwork. He had to get to the hospital.

When Lea called out to him, he ignored her. There were some things in life that were more important than work.

* * * *

Kitten looked down at Mason Scott as he settled into the bed in the pool house. She'd decided to keep him out here for a while because it was easier than dealing with Ms. Hamilton. She wondered if she could keep him a secret, like a treat she kept just for herself. It was selfish, but it had been a long time since she had something for herself, something that had nothing to do with getting better or labeled as therapeutic.

"You're so kind," he murmured as his eyes drifted closed.

God, he was a beautiful man. He could be a male model with his to-die-for face and his lean body. Though he was a tad on the thin side, unlike her very muscular Master. She wondered if he was simply vain or if he didn't get enough to eat. She intended to fix that though it meant either going up against Ms. Hamilton or sneaking around her.

What was she doing? She couldn't hide the man. She'd been impulsive, but she wasn't sure what else she could have done.

He was alone and he needed someone, and she hadn't been able to help herself. She'd claimed him and was driving him back to the Master's estate before she'd taken a second thought.

"You're worried." Mason's eyes were open again, the gray orbs narrowed as he studied her.

"A bit." She hadn't disobeyed the Master before. Not like this.

"I could leave. I could be gone before Cole knows I was even here. You don't have to do anything more than call me a cab. Well, and loan me the money to pay for the cab."

Somehow that would seem even worse than allowing her act to be discovered. "No. If he makes other arrangements, I'll decide what to do."

"You're not his usual, you know."

"What do you mean?"

"His usual sub," Mason explained. "You're calm, collected. You already have quite a bit of discipline about you. You've been in D/s relationships before. Cole typically likes to do his own training, and he prefers newbies."

"Well," she said with an air of sorrow, "I'm sure I'm very different for Master Cole. I've been wondering lately if he didn't contract with me as a favor to my cousin's Master. I've been living under my cousin's roof for a couple of years. They recently had a child. I think it was time for me to move on, but nothing had worked out."

She often wondered if Julian had thrown his hands up when it came to her. After her therapist had cleared her for a permanent relationship, Julian Lodge, the owner of The Club, had interviewed several Doms, but they always seemed to have something Finn didn't like about them. One had flunked Leo's psych evaluation. One had gotten so far in the process that he'd performed a scene with Kitten to prove to Julian, Finn, and Leo that they could work well together. He'd used a whip on her and opened up her skin. Though Kitten had thought it was an accident, Julian had run the poor man off.

And then little Chloe had been born and she'd been out the door within five months. Cole hadn't been forced to go through all the hoops because he was a longtime member of The Club.

Mason frowned. "I know Cole. He wouldn't take you on out of pity. He might have helped to find you someone, but he wouldn't take you on himself. I was only saying that you're a bit different from the last sub I saw him with."

"The one who died?" The Master never talked about her but Ms. Hamilton did. She constantly compared Kitten to Cole's former submissive. It was no great surprise that Kitten found herself coming up short.

"Yeah. I don't know how many he's been through since then, probably a couple, but you're much more innocent than Emily was."

"I'm the first." That's what Finn had explained to her. At the time she'd thought she could help him. Now she'd decided that he was either still in mourning for his lost love or he had taken her in for Julian's sake.

"The first?" Mason sat up as though the thought had disturbed him. "Cole's had a sub with him since he was eighteen years old. I thought he would take a month off and then find some new subs. Most of the time he had two."

Because he'd had Mason with him since he was very young. She'd been told to expect to have to share Cole with a male submissive at some point in time. Like her cousin, Cole was bisexual. But as far as she knew he'd been alone for a while. "Master Julian told me Master Cole hasn't had a permanent submissive since Emily's accident. He believes Master Cole hasn't even dabbled. He's been to The Club and he's scened with unattached submissives, but he hasn't taken one home."

"No. I can't believe that. Cole has the sex drive of a teenaged boy. He has to have it at least twice a day."

Well, he didn't seem to have a sex drive at all when it came to her. She shrugged. "Perhaps he's changed since he only has me now and our relationship is strictly D/s."

His hand came out, covering hers, making her skin tingle. It reminded her how long it had been since someone touched her. Nat hugged her when they got together, but she was busy with her husbands now. She had a small group of friends at The Club who were affectionate. Haven, Tara, and Marcy were always hugging her or reaching for her hand, but the males of The Club didn't touch her unless they were giving her discipline. Cole was the same way. Mason was the first man in forever to simply reach out and brush his hand over hers.

Thank god he was gay. She would be in so much trouble if he wasn't because she was totally turned on simply being in the same room with the man.

"Cole takes his time with a new sub. It's why he usually kept two. He was always looking for the perfect female submissive. Like I said before, I didn't mean you weren't gorgeous because, honey, let me tell you, you are." He brought her hand to his lips and kissed her with a gallant sigh. "You're a vision in that dress. What I meant was Cole liked to deal with the fucked-up ones, and you're obviously not that. Emily was incredibly self-destructive. She was wild and required a Master-slave relationship to curb her more dangerous tendencies. Some people thought she should be in therapy, not D/s. I was one of them."

She pulled her hand away because he had a deep misimpression of her. She would like to continue their talk, but it seemed her past always caught up with her so quickly. And it explained a lot. At least she understood why Cole had agreed to take her in. She wished it didn't hurt so badly. Once in her life she would like someone to care for her because they found her worthy and not out of pity. "Well, I'm afraid many people believe the same thing of me. Is there anything else I can do for you? You don't need to take your medications for another three hours. I'll come back and make sure you can easily be awakened."

"Hey." Mason's eyes had softened, his hand gripping hers now. "I didn't mean to insult you. God knows I can't claim any semblance of normalcy or sanity myself. I was trying to compliment you. You seem so calm and self-possessed. I find you quite lovely, and it's not merely your looks. You have a glow about you that I find some submissives have. You enjoy serving and being worshipped for it. There's something about being in the room with you that puts me at ease."

Now she laughed and relaxed a bit. Perhaps he wouldn't turn her away because she was damaged. "I don't know that any of my friends would think I could put someone at ease. I'm actually behaving quite properly. I can be a bit of a handful on the dungeon floor."

She was comfortable in her fet wear, walking the dungeon with a Dom as her guide. But she'd never walked a dungeon with her Dom. She understood who she was when she was in her PVC. She understood obeying a Dom's orders. She still wasn't sure how to ask for what she wanted, but she'd decided that particular problem went back further than her kidnapping. Her sad inability to assert her own will had begun when she'd been born to her suffocating parents.

But she didn't need to think about them now. She had bigger problems. She had to figure out how to tell her Master she'd brought home a stray.

Mason's hand played along her skin, his thumb rubbing across the back of her hand. "All I know is you're an angel to me. I don't know what I would have done without you. I have an apartment, but it's kind of run down. And not exactly clean. I have a roommate, but I'm pretty sure he isn't the nurse type."

"Should I call someone for you? Your family?" He didn't seem like a man who would be alone in the world.

He withdrew slightly, his high-voltage smile dimming. "No, dear. My parents would tell you that I deserve whatever I get. They didn't appreciate my 'lifestyle choices,' as they would say."

"They didn't approve of you being gay?"

He shrugged, his eyes sliding away from hers. "Among other things. The fact that I was in a relationship with a man was certainly enough to get them to kick me out of the house."

She knew how that felt. "How old were you?"

"The first time I was kicked out of my home? I was seventeen. Luckily enough my boyfriend at the time had a marvelous set of parents. They actually took me in and sent me to college. They were good people."

Like Julian and Finn and Dani had taken her in. Julian had offered to pay for her to finish college, but she wasn't sure what to study anymore. The idea of being a parochial school teacher like her parents had planned seemed farfetched now. "That must have been nice. You lost one home and found another."

"In a way." His hand found its way back to hers, as though he couldn't stop himself from touching her. "And then I lost it all again, but I don't want to talk about that right now. I want to talk about you. I want to know about you. You said almost nothing about yourself the whole time we were coming back here."

Because talking about her past was difficult. "I'm boring. I would rather talk about Sir." He had her flustered. "I mean you."

He was being polite with her, but she couldn't see him as a sub full-time. It made her wonder about his relationship with the Master. She'd been told that Mason and Emily had been Master Cole's subs, but they hadn't gotten along well and it had caused trouble. Kitten had believed it was because they were each jealous of the other. A threesome like that worked best when everyone was involved. Julian made love to both Finn and Dani and Dani and Finn made love. She knew some threesomes worked when the men shared a female but not each other, but she rather thought it would be difficult for one Master to have two slaves who didn't care for one another.

But what if Mason's problem was that he didn't acknowledge his Dominant side?

A grin caught on Mason's face, lighting him up. When he smiled, the sun seemed brighter. "Caught that, did you, darling? Smart girl. I'm a switch, but lately I've decided I prefer my Dominant side. It gets me in less trouble. I'm well trained."

She felt so much more comfortable with a Dom. She knew how to behave. "I'm sure Sir is excellent."

His smile turned slightly sad. "Sir is out of practice. Sir lost his club membership when he lost everything else. He really will be mad, you know."

Master Cole. She hoped not, but then it wouldn't be the first time she'd upset someone. She was getting better and better at handling the fallout. She was only human. "We'll see."

What would she do if Master Cole turned this man out? How would she handle it? He needed so very much, and he was a former submissive. She knew something had happened between the two and suspected it had to do with Emily's death, but it would tell her a lot if Cole tossed him on the street. It would tell her much about the man she now called her Dom.

Out in the hallway, a door slammed open.

"Kitten? Honey, are you in here?" Cole's voice rang through the small pool house.

Her gut knotted. She turned to the door. This was it. "I'll be right out."

She gave Mason her most positive smile, praying all the while she wasn't about to get them both tossed out on their asses. She wasn't entirely sure where she would go except that her newfound pride wouldn't allow her to go back to The Club.

Her hands were actually shaking. What would Cole do? There seemed to be a deep calm in Cole Roberts, but she wondered what would happen when that calm was shaken away and she was left to deal with the man underneath.

God. She'd been through enough therapy to know why she'd done this. She was waiting for Cole to turn into Hawk. Hawk, the man who had kidnapped her from a campus party she knew she shouldn't have been at. Hawk, the man who had beaten and raped her. Hawk, the man who had shown her how small she was.

"Are you all right?" Mason asked.

But she barely heard him. She was waiting for the pain, for the humiliation. Tears pricked at her eyes as she watched Cole walk through the door, but it wasn't Cole she saw. Hawk was back and she wondered if she would survive.

Chapter Four

"Kitten?" Cole walked through the pool house doors. It was the only part of the house that hadn't been redone since his parents passed away, his mother to cancer almost ten years before and his father to a heart attack shortly after that. He didn't like to walk into the pool house. He could still see them in here, still remember that it was wrong that they weren't still with him. It was also the place where Mason had stayed after his own parents had kicked him out.

He could still see Mason's face, tears in his eyes as they'd led him in here and his dad had told him he was welcome to stay. His father had known damn well that they were close to being involved, and his dad had said that whoever Cole loved, well, he would love that person, too.

Damn, but he missed his dad.

"Are you all right?"

There was no way to mistake that voice. Mason had a melodic voice that had the power to bring men and women to their knees. In a courtroom, he commanded attention. Out of the courtroom, that voice turned into a siren call, all seduction and sweetness. He'd made a study of Mason over their long years together, and he heard the fine edge of worry in the question he asked.

Mason was here. In his house. And there was only one person who would have brought him here.

Kitten. Her errand had been to fetch Mason, and Cole wasn't sure how he felt about that.

He stepped into the room and felt caught between a deep rage and sweet relief that he knew where Mason was. Mason was alone in his pool house with his sub, and it was obvious that she'd helped him. Mason didn't have a shirt on. He was thinner than before, as though he hadn't been eating well, but he still worked out. He was leaner, rawer, more defined.

Damn it. He'd been sure that he would never want a man again. Mason had been the only man he'd ever been attracted to. He'd blown through women in college and his early twenties, but there had only been Mason, and it was deep and true and done.

So why did his whole body tense at the idea of being in the same room with Mason? He was over that part of his life. He could have some normalcy. He'd simply needed to find the right female submissive and then he wouldn't need Mason.

Why did it feel so right that he was standing in the same room with them both? "Mason, would you like to explain what you're doing here?"

His eyes slid over Mason, taking in every inch of the man he once loved. He was down to his boxers. He was familiar and yet foreign now, as though the years they had spent apart had changed him in ways he couldn't understand.

"Kitten, sweetheart, what's wrong? Cole, she shut down." Mason was standing behind Kitten. His hands were out, but he didn't touch her.

Cole felt a growl start in the back of his throat. "Sweetheart? Are you serious? You've known her for all of an hour and she's your sweetheart?"

Mason was a terrible flirt. He'd never used charm on men before, but he would lavish a woman with affection. And they would fall right into bed with him. For the longest time, falling into bed with Mason meant falling into bed with Cole, too.

The thought of Kitten fucking Mason made him crazy. When had he gotten so possessive?

"Chuck the attitude, Cole. Look at her."

That got his back up. "You come into my house and tell me

what to do?"

Mason's body stiffened, his eyes narrowing, and for a moment, Cole wondered if he was about to throw a punch. "Are you her Dom or not? I'm fucking asking you to be her Dom. Or have you forgotten how to do that? I understand that you toss everyone to the side when you're done with them, but I didn't realize you had started ignoring a sub when she still lives with you."

He might have had something to say about Mason's comments, but he was finally looking at Kitten.

Her eyes were open but there was a vacant look to them that he didn't like. "Kitten, sweetheart. Could you tell me what's wrong?"

Her lips curled up slightly, but it seemed like a practiced thing, like an automatic response to stimulus. Her eyes slid submissively to the floor, her shoulders hunching slightly, as though she was trying to make herself smaller. To become less of a target.

She'd gone somewhere deep inside herself.

"Kitten, it's Cole and I need you to come back to me. I need you to come down from wherever it is you are."

She seemed to only hear one word. Down. The minute the word left his mouth, she dropped to her knees, her hands coming up to work on the fastening of his waistband.

Shit. He backed away. "Kitten, no."

Her hands began to shake.

"Hey, sweetheart." Mason got to his knees behind her, his voice soft as silk. That charm that Mason used to work was being poured onto Kitten. "I'm not sure what's going on, but I don't think the Master is interested in a hummer right now." He reached up and touched her hair, drawing her back against his chest with more delicacy than Cole could have managed. "Why don't you come out of Crazyville and we can all sit down and talk. Cole and I promise to be on our best behavior from here on out. We're not going to yell anymore. We'll be polite, and there won't be any reason for you to be scared."

Kitten blinked a couple of times, Mason's affection doing what Cole's commands could not. "I…I am sorry. I got lost for a moment."

Mason hugged her tight, rubbing their cheeks together with an ease that Cole envied. "It's okay. You want to talk about where you went? Was it nice there?"

Mason didn't know her history.

Kitten seemed to sink into Mason's body, reveling in the contact. "No, Sir. It is not a good place, and I haven't been there in so long I thought it was gone forever." Her eyes came up, finding Cole's and she stiffened again, pushing her way out of Mason's arms. She got to her feet and the polite girl who had come into his home weeks before was back.

Cole missed the sensual thing who'd cuddled up to Mason.

Maybe he was handling her wrong. Maybe he wasn't the right Dom for Kitten.

Maybe he should grow some balls.

He stepped forward and put his arms around her. He remembered how to do this. Sort of. It had been a couple of years and he'd always been a little standoffish about pure affection, though he didn't know why. His parents had been loving. He had this core part of himself that felt untouchable.

Except when he was with Mason.

It was awkward at first, Kitten stiff in his arms. And then Mason came in behind her, placing her between their bodies.

Kitten sighed, and her head came down on Cole's shoulder. "I'm sorry, Sir. I know you're not him."

But he reminded her of Hawk. He hated that. "I shouldn't have yelled."

He felt her chuckle. "Sir, I think I likely deserved a bit of yelling. I realized that I was pushing you to see if you would hit me and then I didn't want to know."

"Hit her?" Mason asked. "Why would Cole hit you?"

"I wouldn't. Kitten, pet, I would never strike you in anger. I would never hit you. Mutually agreed upon spankings are different. I'm not the monster who kidnapped and caged you. I've been trying so hard to give you time to get used to me, but I've been screwing it up." Watching how quickly she'd accepted Mason's affection had made him understand that she didn't need his distance. She needed to be close, to have gentle hands on her body even while she received the rough play and discipline she craved.

He wasn't sure how to do that.

Kitten's head came up, shaking in the negative. "No. Sir is very good at handling Kitten. Me. Sir has been good to me."

Kitten liked to praise everyone. This time when he hugged her, he pulled her close, allowing himself for the first time to revel in her softness. "Sir is going to be better."

He held her close for a long moment, breathing in her scent. She smelled like peaches and cream. His hand sank into her hair and he squeezed her tight. She didn't complain, simply relaxed against him in a way she never had before.

After a long moment, he broke his hold. "Pet, why don't you go and change for dinner? I think we're having a nice roast. Is that all right?"

She nodded, but her smile was tight. "Of course."

He'd noticed she didn't love red meat. Perhaps it was time to soften a bit. Normally he followed a rigid schedule and never would change plans. Julian's discussion with him had him thinking about the fact that he should bend to Kitten's needs as well. "Actually, I think I'm in the mood for Chinese. Why don't you go and order some takeout?"

Her eyes lit up. "I would love to. I know a great place. What would Sir like?"

He had no idea. He didn't eat a lot of Chinese, but he was bending today. He knew Kitten loved it and tonight she would have anything she liked. "Surprise me. Order your favorites and I'll try them."

"And Mason?" Her eyes were wide with anticipation.

He sighed. She was going to force the situation, and he couldn't work up the will to disappoint her. He'd already watched her sink into the past. And it did appear Mason could use a good meal. "Yes, of course. Order for three, please."

He was such an idiot because the way she smiled up at him made him feel about twelve feet tall. God, she could manipulate him. He was supposed to be harder than this.

"Thank you, Sir." She scampered off happily.

Mason shook his head. And then winced. "Wow, she changes moods quickly."

Cole stared at him, taking in all the changes that the last few years had brought. He looked different, harder, older. Cole had the sudden need to peel away all those new layers to see the Mason he remembered, a frantic, almost panicked need. He didn't know this person. This person was leaner than his Mason, colder. What had happened to him in the last two years? "What are you doing here, Mason?"

Mason's hands went to his hips, his body on display. He'd always been lean but now he seemed to be all predatory angles. Every muscle was toned, but there was a hunger to them. If Mason was his sub, he would feed him, force him to rest, to put on some weight so he didn't look like he would eat anyone who strayed onto his path. "The hospital fucked up. They called your house and Kitten answered. She came down and got me."

"And you went with her?"

"I needed a ride."

"You couldn't have had her take you back to your place?" He was being perverse. He wasn't exactly sure what he would do if Mason tried to leave. It was obvious he needed help and Cole couldn't stand the thought of not understanding what had happened to his former love to bring out this side of the man.

A nasty smirk went across Mason's face. "I'm afraid your submissive insisted on bringing me home with her."

God, despite the fact that he was too thin, had a mean look to his eyes, and was obviously here for more than a ride, Cole's cock was rock hard. This man did it for him. "She's got a soft heart."

"She's got a soft everything." Mason's eyes trailed toward the door.

Yeah, Mason would be totally into her. Which was precisely why it was a horrible idea to keep him here. And yet he was curious. He couldn't take his eyes off Mason, couldn't stop wondering what had happened to him. Now that he was standing in the same room with the man, he was struggling to send him away again. "She's been through a lot. You should try being kind to her."

"I have no interest in being anything but kind to that woman," Mason shot back. He faltered for the first time, taking a moment before speaking. "She's very sweet. And she's obviously had some sort of trauma. What did you mean when you talked about the man who kidnapped her?"

How much should he tell Mason? Nothing. He should tell him absolutely nothing. He should turn and walk out and not come back in here again. All of his ghosts were in residence here. And yet it would be so good to talk to someone about her. Mason had been his sounding board, his second, often better brain.

"Do you remember the story a couple of years back about the man selling women in Central Texas? He kept them in his guesthouse. Trained them in order to sell them." He remembered sitting in their living room watching the news reports and wondering about those girls.

Mason suddenly looked more like Mason than he had the entire time. His face softened and he shook his head. "Yeah. Are you telling me Kitten was one of those girls? That she was kidnapped?"

What he didn't say, what sat there without explanation, was that Kitten hadn't merely been kidnapped. She'd been tortured, raped, abused. He suspected something else. He suspected that she'd been a virgin when she'd been taken, that her only real experience with sex had been rape. "Yes."

"Shit," Mason breathed. "We were sitting in the main house when that story broke. I remember hoping my firm got to sue someone for those women."

"Yes. You and me and Emily." He was wistful at the thought, though the vision that ran through his head didn't include Emily. It was Kitten who was sitting in between him and Mason as they lounged on the big couch watching TV.

God, he was lonely. Having Kitten around and now Mason clarified how singular his existence had become.

"Yes, I remember." Mason's tone turned hard again. "I remember that your girl laughed and said that the women who had been taken probably deserved it. What exactly did Emily say? Oh, yes. She said they should probably be grateful since it was likely the only way the bitches could get laid."

"Keep your voice down." The last thing he needed was for Kitten to hear shit like that. "And you know I spanked her for that."

"Yes, because a spanking can change the nature of a human

being. You never saw it." Mason shook his head. "You're still in denial. You still think she was some perfect flower who was damaged by daddy or some shit."

"You never understood her." He simply hadn't had enough time with Emily. She was rough and could seem cruel, but surely she would have softened with plenty of affection and discipline.

"You know what? It doesn't fucking matter." Mason held up a hand and sent him that look that let Cole know he no longer gave a shit. "You want to believe what you want to believe. Fine. So Kitten had a flashback? She thought you were the guy who kidnapped her?"

It was easier to talk about Kitten. Mason had been good with her. Unlike the way he'd been with Emily, but then time actually had lent Cole some wisdom about her. She had been wild. She'd been cruel. Had she been cruel to Mason? He hadn't asked because Mason had never given him a reason. Cole had thought Mason had been jealous since his charm hadn't seemed to work on Emily. What if it had been something more? "I have to think so. She's been in therapy for the last several years. This is the first time she's attempted to take a permanent Master. I worry I could be a bit rigid for her, but Julian says she's had trouble with the more lenient Doms."

Mason seemed to think about that. "I'm sure it's a delicate balancing act. She seemed to respond to physical affection. She won't get much of that from you."

"I can be affectionate when I choose to be." God knew he'd been that way with Mason, for all the good it had done him. He'd spent hours kissing Mason, their tongues tangling, limbs merging until they couldn't take another second and he had to have him.

"You also work all the time. You're leaving her here alone with that gloomy housekeeper of yours. Maybe that's why she ran the moment she had something to do. She wanted to get out of this house and away from Mrs. Doom."

He wanted to kick Mason out of the fucking house, but unfortunately, he might be right. Kitten wasn't getting what she needed from his housekeeper. "You know I promised Ms. Hamilton a job until she was ready to retire. I promised my father I would take care of her."

"Yeah, and you always keep your promises." There was no way to ignore the bitterness in his tone.

"I try to. Sometimes it's not possible because the person the promises were made to turns out to be unworthy of them." He needed ice in his veins, but Mason was pushing his every button. It was something he'd always been able to do. No one could push his buttons like Mason.

Mason stood, his chest puffed out, invading Cole's space. "Let's talk about unworthy, Cole. Let's talk about who kept up their promises and who tossed the other one out like a fucking piece of trash. Let's talk about your version of being a good Master."

He was going to wrap his hand around the nape of Mason's neck and squeeze. He would lift him up, just so he could keep him off balance as he dragged the fucking brat into the dungeon and taught him what his version of being a good Master had become. He would tear Mason's ass up.

And then he would probably shove his dick up Mason's asshole, and that couldn't happen.

He forced himself to take a breath, to give up the raging need to dominate this man. If he started down that path, he wasn't sure he could recover. "I think we should both calm down. What happened between us is in the past. Maybe we should leave it there."

"Sure. Let's leave it." Mason's shoulders were tense, his eyes tight. Pain. Mason was still in pain.

"What happened?"

Mason sat down on the edge of the bed, holding his head as though he was trying to keep the damn thing on his body. "Today or the last two years?"

All of it. He wanted to know everything. He forced himself to stop. "Today. I don't think we gain anything by rehashing the past."

"Of course, you wouldn't give a shit about the last couple of years. You just want to know why I'm bugging you." Mason's eyes slid toward the door.

"You're evading my question." His Dom voice was coming out. It was a habit with Mason.

Hard eyes came up to look at him and Mason stood again,

though Cole could tell what it cost him. His hands shook, and he struggled to gain balance. "I can evade anything I like. You're not my fucking Master anymore so don't order me around like you are."

He hated it when a sub spouted filth at him. "You're in my house. You're under my roof and you will treat me with a modicum of respect."

Mason took a long breath and seemed to calm down. "I apologize. I've forgotten my manners over the last several years."

"I'm surprised your Dom hasn't kept you in line." He was fishing. Damn he wished he hadn't said that.

"I don't have a Dom. I haven't been to a club in years." He sat back down on the bed, all the aggression seemingly gone.

"I'm surprised. You always needed play more than others." Mason had required it. He'd enjoyed dominating the women they shared, but he had a deep need for submission. Cole had been completely certain that Mason would find a new Dom and quickly. It was why he'd avoided going to The Club on the nights Mason preferred.

Stark gray eyes looked up and there was no way to miss the lines around them. The years showed on Mason's face. "We don't always get what we need."

"What happened?" Now that Mason wasn't yelling at him, Cole found himself softening.

"I was on 35. I was trying to get to work. Some asshole changed lanes and sideswiped me. I don't remember a lot from there. I think my car rolled a couple of times. I woke up when the fireman was getting me out. I was upside down."

Cole's stomach turned. Mason could have died and he would never have known. "I thought the Benz wasn't supposed to roll."

It was why he'd bought it for Mason. Kitten was in a safe vehicle as well.

"I sold the Benz a long time ago."

"May I ask why? Did you want a newer vehicle?" Mason had always liked flashy cars. He could definitely see him turning in the staid Benz Cole had purchased for him in order to get a snazzy sports car that would likely kill him.

"I sold it because I needed the money."

Fuck. "Are you on drugs, Mason?"

His eyes came up, a steely will in them. "I have never taken a single goddamn drug in my life. I refused the fucking pain meds the hospital offered me today. I sold the car because I needed the money for rent."

It didn't make a lick of sense. "You make plenty of money."

"I did before I lost my job. Don't pretend you don't know about it. When you pulled your business from the firm, they fired me."

Cole felt like someone had kicked him in the gut. He'd changed law firms because he couldn't stand the thought of sitting across the table from Mason. "I didn't know."

A bitter huff came from Mason's throat. "Sure. You didn't think that they would fire me when their biggest client left because of me. You were the only client I took care of. You were my entire roster."

God, he hadn't thought of it like that. He'd thought Mason would find a hundred new clients and move on without him. Fuck, he hadn't thought at all. After Emily died, he'd been caught up in his own guilt, in his own failures. "I'm sorry. I should have handled it differently. Please know that I didn't mean to get you fired. Where are you working now?"

"Benedict and Wright."

He searched his memory. "I haven't heard of them."

Mason shrugged. "It's not so surprising. You probably don't need a criminal lawyer often. Look, all of this is moot. I'll get out of your hair. I can see you have a whole thing going on here. I didn't want to let the lady down. She seemed so intent on helping."

Mason was the first thing Kitten had been excited about since moving in. God, he shouldn't even be thinking about doing this. He couldn't have Mason stay. It would be a huge mistake. But it appeared he owed Mason a debt he hadn't thought he needed to pay. "I think you should let Kitten watch after you."

Gray eyes found his. "I don't know that's such a good idea."

"Do you have someplace better to go? Someone who'll look out for you?" He'd imagined Mason likely had a whole group of men and women who would pamper and baby him, but it looked like he'd been wrong. No one who was well taken care of could possibly look so rough.

"No. I'm alone." He said it simply, but his eyes slid away, finding the window and staring out at the grounds.

Alone. Cole had been alone since that moment he'd made the decision to break with Mason. He might have Kitten in his home, but she wasn't in his bed yet. She hadn't truly accepted him as her Master so he still felt his solitude.

He'd never been more in tune with another human being than Mason Scott. It was right there, the urge to reach out and touch him, the instinct to take care of him.

All of his life he'd seen the world in black and white, but what if there were a million different shades? Why had he been harder on Mason than he'd been on any of his other subs?

Because he loved Mason. Because the others might have been transitory, but he'd always thought Mason would be with him forever.

Julian had told him it couldn't have been love if Cole had been able to break with him.

To break him.

God, had he broken Mason?

"Sir?" Kitten's voice cut through the silence that sat between him and Mason. She stood in the doorway looking vulnerable and young, and he wondered how much she'd heard.

He schooled his expression, attempting to give her a reassuring look. "Yes, sweetheart?"

"The police are here. I think they've come for Mason."

Cole strode out of the room, his mind a whirling mess.

Chapter Five

Kitten found herself smiling as she entered the living room. When Ms. Hamilton had told her the police were here to talk to Mason, she'd gotten scared. Police tended to mean someone was in serious trouble, and perhaps Mason was, but this was a friendly face. "Darin!"

Darin Craig was married to her friend Tara. He was also a Dom at The Club. A tall, well-built man, Darin gave her a grin before opening his arms to her. He was athletic, with dark hair and warm brown eyes. "How's our Kitty Cat?"

After the pressure of the day, it was good to see someone she knew. She walked into his hug, wrapping her arms around his neck and accepting the needed affection. The thing she missed most about The Club were the hugs and touches and handholding with friends. "I am well, Master Darin."

"Darin." Cole's voice sounded positively arctic as he walked into the room.

"Wow, I thought she was your sub, Cole. I didn't know she belonged to Detective Craig." Mason's voice wasn't exactly warm, either. "Have the rules of The Club changed, then? Is Julian allowing Doms to manhandle someone else's sub?"

Darin slowly released her, an apologetic expression on his face. He took a step back, holding his hands up as though in surrender.

"Sorry about that. Kitty Cat is just a friend."

"Kitten or Katherine is preferred," Cole said between gritted teeth.

"Her name is a term of affection. You don't need to come up with your own." Mason stood beside Cole, both men frowning Darin's way.

She'd done something wrong again. "Master Darin is only a friend. He's my friend's husband. There's nothing going on between us."

Cole stopped glaring at Darin and seemed at a loss for what to say. "Sweetheart, I wasn't trying to say something about you."

Mason's expression softened. "What the Master is trying to say is he knows how sweet you are. He became jealous when he saw you in another man's arms. You're gorgeous, honey. You have to expect that men will get possessive."

He was a charmer. She knew exactly what he was doing and still couldn't help the smile that crossed her face.

"Mason is right. I was jealous. You rarely hug me with such enthusiasm," Cole said.

Master Cole wanted hugs? He seemed so distant that she held herself apart, but what if he simply wasn't sure how to ask for what he needed? Doms were merely men. Kitten gave him her most brilliant smile and basically tackled him. If her Master needed affection, she would be the one to give it to him.

Cole's big arms wound around her, and she felt him sigh as he lifted her up. He was so big. Her feet didn't touch the floor, but she loved how secure she felt with him when he touched her. It was only when they were apart that she worried. Cole rubbed their cheeks together. "I am sorry I scared you before, love. I don't ever want you to be afraid of me."

"No, Sir. I won't be afraid." She was still smiling as he lowered her down. She turned to Mason. He was a man who needed hugs, too, but she worried that her Master wouldn't like it.

Cole chuckled. "Go on, then. I'll simply have to deal with the fact that you're an affectionate thing. Hug away."

She gave Mason a gentler hug, well aware he was still not feeling well. When she was done, she placed herself between them, enjoying how the two big men surrounded her. "Master Darin, were you attempting to begin an inappropriate affair with me? Because I have to warn you, I promised Tara I wouldn't sleep with you when she wasn't around."

Tara and Darin were always joking about their crazy sex life. They loved it when their friends joined in. Not for the sex, but for the laughter.

Darin let loose a laugh. "I will remember that in the future, Kitty Ca, uhm, Kitten." He sobered. "I didn't come here to see you. I came to talk to Mason. You left the hospital before I got there. I was surprised to find out you were at Cole's."

Darin knew Mason. That was interesting. Darin and Tara had been playing at The Club for the entirety of their marriage. Ten years. They had likely been friendly with Cole when Mason had been his submissive.

Tara was getting a phone call later because she was utterly fascinated with the men and why they had broken up.

And maybe, just maybe, she could tell Kitten how she could get them back together.

She hadn't missed how the two men had looked at each other. Yes, there had been suspicion and anger in their gazes, but there had been such a spark, and Master Cole was already softening up and it had everything to do with Mason. Mason had walked in the door and suddenly the house seemed warmer, more filled with emotion.

Mason, with his stormy gray eyes and pitch-black hair. Mason, who called her "gorgeous girl" and made her feel comfortable.

She so loved having a scheme. It made the days go by faster.

Mason nodded. "All right. Where should we go? Uhm, we could go back to the pool house so we don't bother anyone."

"Sit down, Mason," Cole commanded. He indicated the couch and softened his order slightly. "Please. I think we're all in this now, don't you?"

The last thing she wanted was to get the two of them in another fight. She was under no illusions that they had spent their time in a pleasant conversation.

It was obvious that there were still strong feelings between Master Cole and Mason.

"If something's happened, I'd like to know," Cole said.

Mason stood there, his eyes down as though waiting for the next blow.

She knew exactly how that felt. She'd spent years of her life simply waiting for something bad to happen. She took a place on the couch, reaching her hands out toward them both. "Please come and join me."

Cole smiled ruefully as he let her pull him down. "I have to admit, I like this side of you. I like you asking for what you want."

She'd been wary of doing that. Master Cole didn't laugh the way her other keepers had. He didn't joke or play. She'd decided it was best to simply do as he asked.

God, she was worried about him turning into Hawk, but the way he settled in beside her made her think she should give him more of a chance. "I would like Mason to sit beside me as well."

Cole gestured him over. "Don't even try to resist, Mason. Have a seat. Let's find out why the Dallas Police Department sent a detective to investigate an accident."

Mason frowned and lowered himself down. "That's a good question. Darin, what's going on? What's this about?"

Darin took a seat on the opposite couch and leaned in. "I'm here because my lieutenant knows I have connections to Mason. Lieutenant Brighton wanted me to come out and talk to you."

"Is he in trouble?" Cole asked.

There was a tightening that went through Mason's body. "I haven't done anything for the police to be upset about. Unless they've started arresting people for being late on their rent. Cole here probably thinks I was drunk in the middle of the day and decided to kill a couple of people for fun."

"I didn't fucking say that," Cole shot back.

"If you don't stop fighting, I will be forced to cry because the two of you are making me sad." They were kind of making her mad, but she'd noticed many men responded more quickly to the threat of tears than anything else. Besides, it was true. She often cried when she was mad.

"Kitten." Cole's voice had gone all dark and commanding. It meant he was getting irritated with her. It also made her shiver, and not with fear. He had the most delicious dark chocolate voice.

Perhaps it was time to try out some of the tricks her friends had taught her. She turned her eyes to Cole, attempting to make them large and soft. "I am sorry, Sir. I thought I should warn you. Next time, I'll just cry."

Mason laughed and then immediately put a hand to his head. "Damn, Cole. She's going to be trouble."

Cole's lips curled up. "Yes, she is. We'll keep the fighting to a minimum. Now, Darin, why don't you tell us what brought you here?"

Darin leaned forward. "Mason isn't in trouble. He wasn't at fault in the accident."

"Damn straight, I wasn't." Mason sat back, a frown on his face.

"What exactly happened?" Cole asked.

Mason touched his head as though the memory actually hurt him. "I was driving down the freeway. Some jerk cut me off. I swerved to avoid him and the next thing I remember is the firefighter trying to get me out and I was upside down."

Darin pulled a tablet out of his briefcase and his fingers worked the device. He turned it around. "These are some pictures the officer at the scene took."

She felt Cole stiffen beside her as he looked at the photo slide show playing on Darin's tablet. Her stomach turned. The damage to the small vehicle Mason had been driving was massive. It was shocking he was sitting beside her with nothing more than a concussion.

The car was upside down, its wheels in the air like a turtle trapped on its back. It appeared that the top of the car had partially caved in. Mason had been in that car. He'd been driving one moment and the next he'd nearly died.

"Holy shit." Cole leaned forward. "How did you survive?"

"He had his seat belt on," Darin commented. "If he hadn't, he almost certainly would be dead. He was hit on his right side as he went over one of the steepest embankments in the city. Normally the car in front causes a sideswipe like this because the driver's sight line has been impaired. You see, there's a blind spot…"

Mason nodded. "Yeah, I think every kid who ever went to

driver's ed knows about that, but I wasn't switching lanes. I actually needed the exit ahead of me, the one for 75. It's a left exit so I wasn't even thinking about moving to the right."

"The witness said as much. There was a truck driver behind you. He was the one who called the ambulance. Several people stopped to help. He saw the car that hit you move into your lane. Unless the driver was blind, there's no way they could have missed seeing your car. Several of the witnesses described the driver of the car in question as aggressive," Darin explained. "The driver didn't even try to stop."

"The driver could have been texting," Cole pointed out.

Darin frowned. "I don't like it and neither does my superior. Something doesn't feel right. The witness only got the plate number, but it was a fake. The vehicle that hit you was an SUV, but the plate is registered to a minivan. We found the van along with the mom and three kids who drive around in it all day."

"That tells us next to nothing," Mason said. "Fake plates are easy enough to buy off certain sites. Especially if you know where to look. Fuck."

Mason went pale, as if he'd figured something out.

Kitten looked at him, taking in the hard lines of his face. "A criminal hit your car?"

"What kind of cases have you been taking on, Mason?" Cole asked soberly.

She didn't like the sound of that. "You think one of his clients is angry with him?"

"Oh, sweetheart, I have any number of people who could be angry with me. In the last couple of years, I've been defending some, well, some unsavory clients," Mason admitted. "I'm actually surprised that Darin's here. I kind of thought you wouldn't give a crap if someone wants to kill me."

Darin's eyes hardened slightly, looking more like the Dom she knew him to be. "Lawyers like you are a necessary evil. Everyone deserves a defense. Our justice system doesn't work without it. I won't let my distaste for your clientele stop me from doing my job. But this is as far as I can go. This isn't my department and the cops working the case think it was an accident and the driver fled because they had something to hide. They're going to poke around and move on. I disagree with them. Something about this gets my back up. Call it instinct, but I've been on the job for ten years. My instincts are pretty damn good. I thought I would let you know so if you want to put the Dawson brothers on it, you can. Or you can call my lieutenant's friends. McKay-Taggart would be good at running this down. The Dawsons will call them in anyway."

The snort that came from Mason could only be described as snarky. "Yes, I'll get right on hiring a set of private detectives or a security firm who make more on a single case than I make in a year."

Cole stood up, reaching his hand out. "Thank you, Darin. If you hear anything else, we would love to know about it. We'll get someone looking in on it as soon as possible."

Darin stood as well, shaking Cole's hand, his eyes moving warily to Mason. "All right. But be careful. If he was gunning for you, he might take another shot."

She didn't like the way it felt either. There was something about Mason that called to her. She understood him. She might not know his whole story, but she certainly understood what it meant to feel alone in the world. He could put on a good front, but that was what he seemed to be—alone.

She trusted her instincts and she certainly trusted Darin's. And it wasn't like the Dawson brothers didn't owe her. She'd been instrumental in their wife accepting them. Ben was the weak link. She needed to get Ben on her side because while he was the weak link, he was also not anywhere near the investigator his brother was. Chase was Sherlock Holmes but with several undiagnosed personality disorders.

Ooooh, Leo and Wolf owed her as well. Wolf was a former Navy SEAL who worked security for Julian. She'd saved their wife by forcing her to swallow a GPS locator that was attached to Kitten's collar. It had been hidden in a pretty charm that they hadn't even given back. Surely that was worth some investigating time.

And she had friends at McKay-Taggart. They handled Julian's company security and were employed by Cole as well. Ian Taggart was shockingly easy to manipulate. All she had to do was talk incessantly, all the while reminding him how traumatized she was, and the man gave over. If she did it while he was trying to watch a sporting event, he worked even faster.

"Has she zoned out again?" Mason was asking.

"I don't think so. I think she's plotting. I always thought she was spacey, but there's a glimmer in her eyes. It kind of scares me." Cole was watching her intently.

She smiled. It was silly but she liked how they were looking at her. There was a trepidation in Master Cole's eyes and a sort of breathless anticipation in Master Mason's, as though he would enjoy any chaos she wrought. It sparked her inner brat and made her want to play. "I'm thinking. I want to call Master Ben."

Cole snorted. "Brat. You think he's the weak link."

Well, at least they thought along the same lines. "He is. Master Chase is difficult. I believe Master Chase often has his mansies, and he's terribly irrational during his time."

Mason coughed and covered his mouth.

Cole's eyebrows rose. "What is she saying?"

Mason coughed again, obviously trying to regain his composure. "I believe she's talking about male menses. I think she's accusing that big bastard of having his monthly."

Cole stopped, his face shutting down for a second. Oh, she'd been right to hide that bratty part of herself. She shouldn't have said something bad about a Master. Certainly not her former Master. She should have been respectful. Polite. It was how to get on in the world.

And then a booming laugh seemed to reverberate through the room. Master Cole threw his head back and laughed and laughed. His face went the tiniest bit red as he let go. It was quite a lovely thing to see.

Master Mason was laughing, too, though he grimaced and held his head. "Don't do that again, sweetheart. At least not until I'm healed."

Cole leaned over and the sweetest kiss brushed her forehead. Precious. It made her feel beloved. "You are right about Chase Dawson. That is a man with manstruel issues. But he's also the one we need to hire to look into this. He can work with our security firm.

I'm pretty sure Taggart has mansies, too, but the bastard knows what he's doing."

Mason stopped. "I can't afford any of this."

"You're not paying for him." Cole slung an arm around her shoulder. "I am. And you're not leaving here until a doctor okays it. So relax. Do we have dinner coming, baby?"

He'd never called her baby before. He'd never called her anything but Kitten or pet. She fought back tears because being someone's baby was meaningful. It meant she belonged. Like being someone's sweetheart. Mason called her that.

She knew it was dumb. She knew it was too soon. And it didn't matter. So many things had been bad that she kept clinging to the good things. Even when they let her down, she simply looked for the next one. She might die someday still hoping for something good to happen, but she would hope.

It was funny when she thought about it. Her parents had taken her to church after church. Some good. Those were the ones they ran the fastest from. Some bad. But she figured that wasn't God's fault. When she'd been kidnapped, that hadn't been God's fault either. God had sent her Nat and Finn and maybe, just maybe, God had sent her Cole and Mason, too. All those years and all that pain and she still believed. She still had faith.

Cole reached out, his hand on her cheek. "Sweetheart, you're crying. Are you all right?"

He didn't understand that sometimes it was so good to cry. She could do it now without a spanking, without pain. She could let herself feel and she owed Julian and Finn and Leo and Ben and Chase and Logan for that great gift. She gave Cole a smile. "I'm fine, Mast…Sir. I'm actually quite happy."

His eyes softened. "I want you to know that makes me happy, baby. I will do a lot to keep it that way."

She felt Mason's hand on her shoulder. Surrounded by Masters. Yes, that was a nice place to be.

Chapter Six

Mason couldn't quite shake the feeling of déjà vu as he sat down in the dining room an hour later. There were three place settings, and the food from the Chinese place had naturally been removed from the takeout boxes and placed in good china serving bowls. Heaven forbid they eat like animals.

That had been Ms. Hamilton's doing. She'd brought the dishes with her nose in the air as though the food stank to high heaven when it smelled like pure pleasure to him.

"I had a perfectly good roast," she muttered under her breath. "I suppose this is your doing."

Ms. Hamilton had never liked him. She hadn't liked him as a kid, and the years hadn't changed her opinion.

"I believe you will find it's Mr. Chow's doing," he said with a smirk because he'd never once been able to simply deflect. When someone nudged him, he nudged back. He couldn't stand a bully. "You should take up all your complaints with him."

She turned to him, her rheumy eyes narrowed. "You have no right walking back into this house. You should be in jail."

Ah, there it was. The lovely dulcet tones of guilt. "And you should be in an asylum because you're a crazy old bitch."

"Mason!"

The sound of Cole's voice sent a shiver down Mason's spine,

and not a spooky one. Nope. That shiver went straight to his dick because it was the tone Cole used right before he dealt out the punishment.

"I'm sorry, Mas…" Habit was a bitch. "She started it."

Cole shook his head, but there was no way to miss the uptick of his lips before he turned all Dommy and cold again. "Very mature, Mason. Ms. Hamilton, that will be all for the evening."

"He can't stay here. He has to leave." Ms. Hamilton pointed a bony finger Mason's way.

Cole turned those cold eyes on his housekeeper. "Ms. Hamilton, I was not aware that the ownership of this house had transferred to you."

She seemed to shrink a bit as though she understood she'd pushed the Master too far. Her steel gray head shook. "I didn't mean it that way. I only meant that there is no possible way you could want him here. You loved Emily. You couldn't want him here."

A shadow passed across Cole's face, the past playing out again in guilt Cole obviously still felt. "I said that will be all, Ms. Hamilton."

She strode from the room, muttering under her breath.

"I'm sorry about that. You know how she felt about Emily," Cole said, shaking it off.

"Yes." He watched her go. "I certainly do."

Being back in this place was doing odd things to his emotions. He'd kind of thought he'd left emotions back in the dust a long time ago. He'd gone through all those stages of grief. At first he hadn't been able to believe that Cole was gone. He'd called daily and begged for forgiveness. He hadn't even understood why he'd needed forgiveness, but he'd been so lost that he was willing to offer Cole anything so they could talk.

Then they had talked and Mason had moved right to rage. That had been the good part. He'd enjoyed that. He was a little ashamed of the bargaining he'd done. One phone call in the middle of the night when he was drunk off his ass, he'd begged Cole to take him back. Of course, he'd had to leave that rambling mess on his voice mail. He'd woken up the next morning and there had been no call back. A year's worth of depression had led to finally accepting that this was his life now.

Or maybe he hadn't moved on because he felt like he was right back to rage as Cole took his place at the head of the table.

Smug bastard. He still had everything. He had the money, the company, the girl. He'd moved on as though Mason had never mattered.

There was an oppressive silence that filled the elegant dining room. Kitten wasn't here yet to mediate, to bring her unique sunshine into their gloom.

"Is your head feeling any better?" Cole asked solicitously.

Oh, they were going to be polite now, were they? He could do polite. He would very politely steal Cole's woman right out from under him. "It aches a bit, but I'm fine. I always land on my feet."

Cole's jaw tightened. "So where are you living now? I'm surprised you didn't stay in that apartment I found for you."

Of course. Cole had hired a real estate agent to find Mason an apartment when he kicked him out. "Shockingly enough, I couldn't afford it."

"Because you lost your job." Cole seemed to be trying to wrap his big brain around that one. "Why didn't you find a new one?"

"Are you serious? If there was one thing I always admired about you, it was that you owned up to the things you did." There had been a time when he admired everything about his Master. From his strong good looks to his solid morals, Cole Roberts had been everything to him. Like most things in his life, Cole had turned out to be an illusion. He'd learned a few valuable truths about life. People put up with him for a while. They liked to fuck him, to use him, to show him off, but in the end he always proved unworthy of lifetime affection.

"What exactly is it you think I've done?" So calm. Cole was calm, as though this was merely an academic discussion.

"You blackballed me. I interviewed with every firm in the city and three in Houston." He remembered sitting in the beautiful apartment that overlooked downtown and realizing the trap he'd been caught in. He'd packed up and walked out that day. It was better to start living the way he would be forced to than to try to hold on. He'd found a one bedroom on the outskirts of the city and a year later, he couldn't even afford that.

"I certainly did not. Mason, I never even received a call about a reference. I would have been unbiased had I been asked. I would merely have talked about your proficiencies as a lawyer."

"You weren't taking my calls. I didn't put you down as a reference."

Cole sighed a bit and drew his napkin across his lap. "Then you should have used Julian. Come to think of it, why didn't you call Finn? His firm would surely have hired you."

"Your friends, Cole. Yours. I doubt they would give me the time of day. Julian tried to call me, but I wasn't about to sit and listen to him kick me out of The Club." He'd called back and left a nasty message with Julian's secretary explaining that he wouldn't be returning. Sometimes it was better to torch a bridge before it burned him.

Pride. He had to maintain some small piece of his pride. It had become necessary for his survival.

It was why he was sitting here, looking at Cole and telling himself that it was all for revenge. He didn't feel at home again. He didn't enjoy looking at Cole. He was simply going to have his revenge on the man and then they could be done.

It didn't matter that every inch of this house held some memory for him, from the front door where he would kiss Cole good-bye every morning because the bastard always went in before the sun rose, to the pool house where they'd first made love in the bed he was supposed to sleep in tonight.

No. Instead he held on to that moment in Colorado when he'd reached out, begging his love to help him, and he'd been turned away.

Revenge was all that mattered now.

"They were your friends, too," Cole replied. "It was why I never explained myself to them. I didn't want to poison your relationships. It didn't seem fair."

Mason wasn't going to buy that one. "But it was all right to tell every firm in town that if they hired me, you wouldn't work with them?"

"Mason, I never did that. I would never have done that. I have spent the last two years certain that you were working away at your office and living in the apartment the realtor found." He cleared his throat, his eyes sliding away. "Or that you had found another Dom and were living under his roof."

"You mean sugar daddy, don't you?" He couldn't stop himself. He needed to be calm and cool. He needed to flirt with the fucker, to pretend that all was forgiven between them, but he couldn't seem to stop needling him.

The fire was back in Cole's eyes and the ice in his tone. The Dom had stepped back in the room. "No. That is not what I meant."

"But that's what you were. That's what you like to be."

"Mason, if you don't..." Cole's eyes went wide, his stare going to someplace behind Mason's head.

Mason turned and realized why Cole had stopped in his tracks. Holy fuck. Kitten was standing in the doorway and she wasn't wearing a stitch of clothing apart from the collar around her neck. In the low light from the overhead chandelier, her skin was glowing and luminous. She was slender but womanly. No way that gorgeous girl got mistaken for a guy. Her hair flowed over her shoulders, reaching her breasts. Firm and tipped with perky pink nipples, they peeked through her glossy tresses like treasures waiting to be found and devoured.

Her stomach was gently curved, and those hips flowed into graceful legs.

His mouth watered at the sight of her perfectly groomed pussy. It probably tasted as sweet as she looked. It had been forever, for fucking ever, since he'd licked and sucked and loved a pussy. He liked sucking Cole's cock, but damn he loved to dive into a sweet pussy.

His head started to hurt again, likely because all his blood seemed to have rushed straight to his cock.

"Kitten?" Cole's face had flushed, his eyes wide.

Kitten grinned, the smile lighting up the room. She was one of those women who glowed, her sweet nature shining through. Mason loved those women, tended to worship the ground they walked on. Would she still glow when she realized he'd used her to get back at her Master?

He shoved the thought away. When they were done here, he would take care of her in a way Cole couldn't. He would never shove her away for some perceived weakness. No. He would be her kind and loving Master. He would be better for her than Cole.

"Good evening, Sir." She stepped inside, her feet moving across the carpet like her namesake—a sultry cat gracing the room with her presence.

"Is there a reason you're naked?" Cole asked, his voice going icy.

Oh, that was a massive mistake. She was obviously happy. Cole was allowing his jealousy to override his good sense, as he always had.

And that was excellent for Mason.

Kitten stopped, and her body seemed to shrink, to be less than it had before. "I'm sorry, Sir. You had told me to be naked for dinner. I will find my clothes. Please go ahead and begin. I won't take long."

Yes, let the Master fuck up because it would be so easy for him to slide in. When Cole had completely screwed up and made her feel like shit, she would come to Mason's hand. Cole never explained himself.

As she was walking back out, Mason saw the distress on Cole's face and knew why. He wasn't sure how to fix the situation. He'd learned long ago that Cole had spent so much time in his youth with his nose in a book that he'd never picked up on the lessons his parents had to teach him about communicating. They'd indulged their only son, accepting him as he was. Once, Cole's father had sat with Mason and told him how happy he was to have Mason in Cole's life because Mason seemed to smooth the way for him.

It had been the first time he'd been accepted lovingly for who he was, the first time he'd felt like he belonged.

He told himself it was strictly in honor of Colin Roberts that he opened his mouth. "Cole is jealous, sweetheart. You look amazing and he's completely forgotten that he asked you to do this. He never would have asked if he'd known he would have company tonight. He wants to keep your nakedness all to himself, but I personally think you're too beautiful to have only one man's eyes on you."

Kitten stopped, and he could see her tentative smile.

"He's right," Cole said quickly. He stood and strode over to where Kitten was. "I forgot I told you to be naked tonight. I forgot. My fault, Kitten. Forgive me."

He stood in front of her, towering over her. He had to give it to Cole. He was a stunning man. Alpha as the day was long. Cole's broad shoulders could block out the sun. They could make a sub feel like Cole was ten feet tall, a bulwark against all the bad things of the world. Cole reached out to touch Kitten and she walked right into his arms.

He was a stupid bastard. He should have kept his mouth shut.

And then Kitten would be crying somewhere, thinking she'd offended them when all she'd done was sparked her Master's jealousy.

No matter what, Kitten should be protected. He would have his revenge, but he would protect her, too. He hadn't lost that much of himself. He could still find some kindness.

He could damn straight still find lust. His cock was practically thumping against his sweats. She was stunning.

Fuck, so was Cole. Damn it. He wasn't going there. He wasn't going to think about what it would mean to stand beside Kitten as her supportive fellow sub. Because he couldn't go there. He would never sink to his knees beside her and reach for her hand as they waited for their Master. He wouldn't play and kiss and gossip with her while they rolled in bed at their Master's command.

He would be the Master and then he couldn't be hurt again.

"Do you want me to put on clothes?" Kitten asked, her eyes on Cole. She wasn't looking Mason's way now. She only had eyes for her Master.

Cole chuckled. "No. I think I prefer you like this, and if that means Mason sees you as well, then I'm all right with that. Come and sit with us. You promised to tell me what's good. I have no idea. You know I'm a meat-and-potatoes kind of guy."

Cole handled it well after his initial stall. He hadn't changed at all. It was the same Cole from years before. He struggled to express himself, had trouble with apologizing even when it was his fault. He tended to look a bit like a deer in the headlights until Mason stepped in and gave him a chance to turn it around.

Cole kissed the top of her head and Mason would have bet his miserable life that it was one of the first times Cole had done that with Kitten. He'd likely been holding himself back. Given Kitten's history, Cole would attempt to be patient and wait until the time when he was sure that Kitten was capable of making her own decisions without her prior history coming into play. He would try to almost reset her to a place where she could make decisions without thinking about the trauma.

That wasn't possible. The trauma had reshaped Kitten, turned her into something different than before. Mason had always known that no one was without damage. The scars he bore made him who he was. Not that he liked who he was much these days.

Kitten took her place across from him, sitting down in her chair with a complete unselfconsciousness he rarely saw in women. She almost seemed more comfortable without her clothes, as if she preferred the lack of walls and barricades.

He had the sudden urge to get rid of his own clothes. Sitting with the Master and his playmate, feeling content that he belonged, that was all he'd ever wanted since that first moment that he and Cole had visited a club and realized what their places were. Mason liked having that place. He craved being the switch because it was the best of both worlds. He got to top a gorgeous woman and be served by the Dom of his dreams.

Except the woman Cole had chosen had been an outrageous harpy, and Cole himself had turned into a nightmare.

"Mason? Are you feeling all right?" Cole's deep voice cut through his thoughts and brought him back to the present.

He looked up, catching Cole's eyes. "It's a headache. That's all."

"Should we call in a doctor? Perhaps the doctors at the emergency room were wrong and your injury is worse than we thought." Kitten leaned forward, concern on her pretty face.

No one had given a damn about him in years. He soaked it up like a sponge because he was stupid and never, ever learned. The first person to reach out to him had him panting after her. He needed to be colder, but he couldn't work up the will. Not tonight. "I'm fine, sweetheart. Just a bit woozy. I haven't eaten since breakfast."

She was back on her feet, walking around the table. "You should start with the soup. It'll be easier on your stomach." She began to reach for the covered crock. "I have wonton and egg drop."

No one had served him, either. Not in years. Not anyone who wasn't looking for a twenty-percent tip. "Wonton, please."

There was no way to miss the jealous look in Cole's eyes as Kitten fawned on him.

Yes, his day hadn't turned out so badly after all.

* * * *

Cole entered his private dungeon with his head spinning. The day hadn't exactly gone as planned, and he didn't like the feeling of not being in control.

Mason was under his roof. He was asleep in the pool house. Cole had followed Kitten, who insisted on making sure Mason took his medications and tucking him in before they had their session. She'd fussed and fawned all over him and the years had peeled back and he'd seen his mother there doing the same thing. She'd stood over Mason that first night.

Don't worry about a thing, sweetie. You have a home here. Our Cole loves you so we love you, too. And stop calling me Helen. I prefer Mom. You sleep tight, and in the morning we will all sit down as a family and figure out what we're going to do.

His mother had turned off the light and taken Cole's hand as she walked back to the main house. He remembered every word she'd said that night.

Imagine that woman calling herself a mother. A mother doesn't toss her child out because he's not exactly what she wanted him to be. You know I'll love you no matter what, don't you, Cole?

Would his mother be proud of the person he'd become? She would accept him. He had no doubt about that, but would she wonder where she'd gone wrong that he'd become so rigid and controlling? His life had become so bland and predictable that eating

Chinese food was a feat of daring for him.

He was the Dom, but he had to wonder if Kitten wasn't the brave one.

He held the door open for her. "Find your position."

He was relieved to close the door and shut out the rest of the world. This was his dungeon. He was in control here. He had the power.

Kitten immediately sank down, her knees gracefully finding the wood of the floor. Her legs spread wide in a conscious show of her beauty. Palms up. Back straight but with no real tension to it. Her head was at the perfect angle.

Her slave pose was flawless. She needed not an ounce of his teaching when it came to this.

"Which of your Doms taught you how to greet him with such perfection?" He was curious. He would bet it was one of the Dawson brothers. Chase, most likely. He was known to have very particular tastes.

"It was Hawk. He made me practice until I got it perfect."

Cole's stomach turned. He didn't want to think about what that psychopath had done to ensure she was sheer perfection. "I'm sorry I brought it up."

Kitten's head lifted, and there was a frown on her face. "Does where it came from change the beauty of a thing? Should I not take pride in how I greet my Dom because it came from something ugly?"

A minefield, but then half the time he felt like he was walking in one with her. He needed to be honest and forthright. "I think you're beautiful, but I worry that every time I ask you to find your position, you'll think about how you obtained the knowledge."

She bit her bottom lip, a thing he'd come to associate with her thinking. "That time is a part of me. Maybe it's an ugly part, but it's always here. Should I not accept it? Should I fight to forget?"

"You should fight so you don't have to think about it every day, so you can get back to the girl you were. That way you can get on with your life. With the life we could have here."

She was quiet for a moment and he rather hoped they were ready to move on, but these sessions were about her and if she chose to spend them talking, then he would listen. Finally her eyes came up and she caught his. "Sir, I'm twenty-five. Is any twenty-five-year-old truly the same person she was at eighteen? At twenty? Even if I hadn't been taken, I would have changed. I can't pretend like my life was put on pause and go back to that moment. Besides, I didn't particularly like the person I was before."

This was exactly what he worried about. This was why he'd held back. "So you like the person your captor turned you into?"

"No, but I do like the woman who survived." There was a sheen of tears in her eyes but there was something prideful about them. These weren't tears of sadness. They were the emotions of a woman who was standing up for herself even as she was on her knees.

He didn't understand her, but he admired her. He wanted her. He couldn't have her yet, not until he found that understanding he needed to move on, but he could certainly give her what she needed. "I like that woman, too, pet. Now let's get on to tonight's session."

A flogging. It would relax them both. That was what they both needed, a good long session to ease all the tension. He would find his top space. She could spend her time in subspace. It would all be fine, and they would begin again in the morning. He turned and studied the wall of impact toys. Each had been lovingly handcrafted.

Deerskin to start? He preferred to ease into it. Deerskin was gentle but she liked a big bite of pain.

"What happened between you and Mason, Sir?"

"Have you forgotten protocol?" The question came out a bit harsher than he'd intended, but then her words had been completely unexpected. Kitten was perfect. When she got to the dungeon, she only spoke when spoken to and followed every rule. She wasn't the type of sub who misbehaved to get punished. She expected the punishment as a reward for good behavior, not the other way around.

Her eyes slid to the floor and she was silent again. Though she didn't move a muscle, some of the ease of their company had left. There was a tension between them now that he hated, a definite distance.

"I don't talk to my submissives, Kitten. Not in that way." He hadn't covered this in their contract and it hadn't come up. "I will listen to anything you want to say, but I'm not the type of man who needs to talk things out. What happened between Mason and myself is ancient history and it will remain that way. All you need to know is that he and I had a falling out and it will not affect you. We will mind our manners around you. Is that understood?"

"Yes, Sir." Her voice held none of the warmth from before. It was soft, submissive, but the personality had leeched away.

They were back to Dom and sub, and for a moment, they had seemed like something close to friends.

Did he want to be friends with her? He hadn't been what he would call friends with his other submissives. There hadn't been many. Only three. Anna was happily married with a couple of kids and living in Oregon now. She'd been the first, but she'd known what she wanted and it hadn't been a permanent ménage. Susan had been a wild thing. She and Mason had gotten into so much trouble together, but she left, too. And Emily. He'd certainly not been friends with Emily. He'd been an odd combination of father figure, Dom, and therapist. He'd certainly had to be her disciplinarian.

What did he want to be to Kitten? Merely her Dom? Did he want to put her in a space slotted for relaxation and a sense of accomplishment?

What did she truly need from him?

He looked up and realized minutes had passed. How many he wasn't sure, but Kitten hadn't moved. Discipline. She was the definition of the word.

And he rather missed the brat who tried to manipulate him, the one who grinned in a wickedly sensual way, the imp who'd brushed her breasts against his arms as she'd served him dinner.

"Come here." If he was going to do this, he could at least kill two birds with one stone. "I'll talk while I warm you up. Would you like that? I warn you, it's not a happy story."

The smile on her face as she got to her feet was worth any discomfort talking about his relationship with Mason would bring.

"Yes, Sir. I would like that very much." She practically ran to the spanking bench, her breasts bouncing sweetly.

"Hey," he said in a moment of complete impulse. "You should kiss your Dom before he services you."

He'd gotten her off a couple of times, but he'd never kissed her, and now that seemed like such a stupid thing to have put off. Perhaps he was being too cautious. They both needed some affection.

She bounced back up. One of the things he adored about her was her boundless enthusiasm. The minute she walked into a room, it felt like the lights came on for the first time. The energy went up or down based on her mood. And that grin she had when she was truly happy did weird things to his heart.

The way looking at Mason used to move him.

"Is this a new protocol?" Kitten asked with wide, innocent eyes as she went on her tiptoes.

He loved protocol because it taught him how to behave. It gave him a structure to his life he needed because he didn't always understand the social niceties. It taught him how to act. Like his father had taught him to always look a person in the eyes when he talked to them, even though it hadn't been his instinct. Like Mason had taught him that hugging and kissing could be nice, and then he'd shown him an entirely different world. "Yes. The new protocol is that your Dom gets a kiss before and after a session."

She put her hands on the side of his face and the sweetest look came over her. She seemed to study him for a moment, her eyes taking him in to the point that he almost felt uncomfortable.

"Do you not want to kiss me?" He wasn't sure how he would handle that.

"No, Sir. It's the first kiss. Our first kiss. I want to remember it."

It felt like a fist closed around his heart, squeezing tight. "Kitten, I'm going to ask you a question and I need a real and true answer from you."

"Yes, Sir."

"Have you ever willingly kissed a man?"

Her hands found his hair and she ran her fingers through slowly, as though she was attempting to memorize the feel. "No. I had a sheltered childhood and then I was taken. When I got to The Club, I had Doms, but none of them wanted to kiss me. The rest was not my choice so this is my first kiss, and I want to make it count."

Now he knew why he'd hesitated, why he'd waited. He was afraid. He was afraid he would screw it up for her. Afraid that what that monster hadn't managed to ruin with his violence, he would do with his coldness. He didn't want to be cold with her, but he wasn't certain how to loosen the reins.

You've never kissed a man before. Have you kissed a girl, Cole?

"Mason was my first kiss."

"Really?" Every time he offered her some piece of his soul, she lit up like fire being stoked to life.

He nodded. "I was single-minded in my studies in high school. Very competitive. A little shy. Hell, I was a lot shy, Kitten. I was overweight and I wore these thick glasses because I couldn't stand the thought of contacts. I met Mason at my father's country club. His father was the groundskeeper. I kissed him in the woods behind the ninth hole."

"You kissed him?"

He nodded. "He insisted. He said he'd kissed a bunch of girls and a couple of guys by then, and that I should be allowed to discover what I liked. So why don't you kiss me?"

There were tears in her eyes as she went on her tiptoes. They still terrified him but now he was beginning to see her willingness to show her emotions as a type of strength.

She touched his face, her eyes carefully taking him in as though studying him. Her fingertips brushed along the planes of his cheeks, over his nose, tracing the lines of his jaw.

He was always in control except for those brief moments when he'd tangled with Mason and they wrestled like wildcats trying to prove their strength. He'd never once had this singular instant of discovery, never had a woman stare at him like he was a treasure she'd found, and in that one moment, he realized why a sub was a sub.

There was a beauty in trusting someone to not harm him, in giving over and allowing another to have their way. It wasn't something he could do often, but as he allowed Kitten to explore, he realized that he hadn't given her everything she needed. She needed to be worshipped, to feel like a thing of beauty.

She rubbed her cheek against his and his cock hardened painfully. Her body was so close. He could feel her heat, smell the shampoo in her hair.

Mason had understood what she needed immediately because it was what he needed, too.

Could he ever trust Mason again? Could he willingly stand still and let Mason rip his heart out again?

Still. It was odd to be so still because he was always in motion. Even sitting quietly, his mind always raced at a million miles an hour, but now he was forced to stop and pay attention to her. Kitten was more animated than he'd ever seen her. Her green eyes were lit up, glowing with some deep desire, some glorious discovery.

She was discovering him, and if he took this as seriously as he should, he suddenly knew he could discover her, too.

"I don't think I've ever wanted a kiss as much as I want this one." He owed her honesty. He wanted her to know how crazy she was making him, how she was tearing down his walls and he felt like a kid again.

She bit her bottom lip. "Then I should make it a good one."

She leaned over and Cole wondered if he hadn't started something glorious.

* * * *

Kitten loved the way his skin felt under her fingertips. It was odd how touching another person with such singular intent made her feel so alive. Her sexuality had been explored in snatches of time spent in bondage. When her former Masters would bring her pleasure, she'd been tied up or bound down. Even in that consensual act, sex had been something that was done to her.

This was more. This required action from her. This was something she had to do. Discovery. Exploration. Kindness.

Tears filled her eyes and her hands shook slightly because kindness always got to her. Through all of her pain and heartbreak, she'd managed to not cry, but simple acts of kindness brought out her every emotion.

Cole was being kind, but she rather thought it was more than that. He wanted her kiss. No one had ever simply wanted her kiss.

Oh, she hoped she was good at it.

He remained still though she could feel how tense his muscles were. Growing up she'd been very isolated. She'd gone to an all-girls school and her father had told her she couldn't be friends with boys. If this had happened to her as a teen, she would have worried he was angry, but she could read the signs now. Her Master was aroused but in control. As she moved closer and allowed her body to brush against his, she could feel the hard line of his erection.

She knew she should fear it, but years of therapy and work had done their job and now she wanted so badly to know what it felt like to make love, to have a man who cared about her inside, to be truly intimate with another human being.

Or two. A vision of Mason crept across her brain like a spider waiting to strike.

She couldn't go there. She couldn't even think like that because Mason wouldn't want her that way. Cole certainly didn't seem ready to welcome Mason home with open arms.

Still, the thought of Mason moving behind her as she kissed Cole was right there, so vivid inside her head. She would be between them, but not the whole focus because they would love each other, too. The three of them would be a family.

Except she knew it didn't work that way and the smart girl dealt with it. She only got one first kiss and she needed to think about that.

But not for long because he was right here. Yes, she often got distracted by shiny objects, but Cole was far more than shiny. He was hard and wanting.

She finally let her lips brush against his. Warm. So much softer than she imagined. Like a flower. Somehow she'd expected him to be hard everywhere, but he wasn't. There were pieces of him that were soft, vulnerable. He was offering those to her, and she couldn't turn it away.

Heat sprinted through her system, sparking through her from her lips to her toes. The sensation sizzled along her spine, a clear answer to the question she asked every day. What do you want? What moved her? What made her want to dance?

Cole. Her Master offered her his body, his mouth, his trust.

She was going to take it, to truly enjoy it because that was how she honored what he was offering her.

Kitten played at his mouth for a moment, allowing her lips to move softly over his. She let her nose touch his and that seemed intimate, too. There was an endearing awkwardness that came with the act, but the minute she felt him chuckle, she let go of her self-consciousness. He wouldn't be angry with her if she wasn't good. He wouldn't hurt her if she did it wrong.

"Give me your tongue, pet. I want to know how you taste." His words seemed to rumble along her flesh.

She wanted to know how he tasted, too, so she let her tongue run along his lower lip. He groaned, a delicious sound, and then his mouth opened slightly and she felt the touch of his tongue to hers.

Pure fire seemed to race through her and she realized that all those flares of arousal she'd felt before were nothing to this. This was desperate, wanting.

His hands found her hair, fingers sinking in, and then he was in control. His tongue surged into her mouth, rubbing and playing along hers. He moved against her. Their bodies nestled tight, fitting together with a perfection they hadn't found before. The Master had cuddled her after scenes, but there had always been an odd disconnect as though they weren't truly comfortable, as though Cole were only playing out something he thought he owed her. But this was pure. This was passionate.

As his tongue danced with hers, she felt her body come to life. Her nipples were hard against his chest, her pelvis rubbing that hard cock like she could ride him through his leathers. Her hands explored. She hadn't touched him before because the Master had rigid rules about how he played. He took control and until this night, she hadn't even thought to ask if she could touch him. That was a mistake because he was a thing of beauty. Every muscle was sculpted to perfection, every line of his body a pleasure to feel and mold under her hands. As she kissed him, her tongue every bit as engaged as his, she realized that this was why they called it making love. It was active and required the both of them.

She felt his groan along her spine as he deepened the kiss. His hands ran down her body. He'd caressed her before but as with everything Cole did, there had always been determined control about his touch. It seemed as if he planned out every stroke, every move, but not now. His hands moved restlessly over her body like she was a store full of treats and he couldn't decide which one to fully sample first. He skimmed her breasts, running down to her belly where the pad of his fingers touched her clitoris.

She gasped as he touched her more firmly.

"You're already wet," he moaned against her mouth.

So wet. And so hot. She couldn't think about much beyond the fact that he was playing with her pussy. It had been a single kiss, but it went out of control and she loved it. She obeyed the distant Dom, but she was crazy about the desperate lover. A lover. Her lover.

"Please, Sir." She wanted to call him Master, wanted for him to belong to her, but she couldn't. She didn't have permission.

His hand slid against her pussy. He was right. She was desperately wet, wetter than she'd ever been. Her pussy had gotten slick and she felt a pulsing need that seemed to come from her core, blanketing her in a pleasant haze of lust. She could barely breathe as one finger slid inside her body.

Even his finger was big. Cole was so huge. He made her feel delicate beside him. He pressed up against her pussy and Kitten could feel him moving, searching, exploring. She had to hold on to his broad shoulders to stay upright.

"Give it to me." His tongue came out, licking along her lips before he sucked her bottom lip into his mouth and began kissing her again.

She wasn't sure what he meant until she felt his thumb on her clitoris. He pressed down as his finger seemed to curl inside her, finding that magic place. She cried out, but his mouth covered hers as though he was capturing and drinking down her pleasure. He kept up the rubbing, but it softened as her orgasm pulsed and played along every nerve ending.

Her body felt drained, pleasantly so. A dreamy happiness filled her. This was better than play. This felt real, true.

"Well, perhaps we won't add that last part into our protocol." Cole pulled his hand out and steadied her on her feet. "We might never get to our sessions."

Some of her haziness faded. How could he sound so calm when her mind seemed fuzzy and off balance? "Sir?"

His smile was a tight thing. "We'll start on the bench. I'm going to go clean up. Place yourself there and wait for me. We'll start with a flogger."

Kitten stood there, her whole body languid, but her mind was suddenly tense. "Flogger?"

Cole stopped, turning and frowning her way. "I'm sorry I lost control. I meant to allow you to kiss me and I took that from you."

"I liked it. I liked all of it." Why was he talking about control now? What they'd just done hadn't required control. It required passion, and for a moment, she'd had his passion and his focus and energy, and it hadn't been a cool exchange of D/s power. It had been powerful without a contract or mutually agreed on boundaries. She'd trusted him and it felt like he trusted her, too. "Please, can't I give back to you?"

He nodded, but she couldn't help but feel some grim cloud had descended on him. She could still see his erection against his pants. She wanted nothing more than to drop to her knees and take him in her mouth. Or better yet, she could lie back on the bench and he could have her, take her with him, share the pleasure of their bodies together.

"Yes, you can by lying on the bench. I need a moment."

"But I could ease you."

His jaw tightened, and for a moment she thought he was going to get angry with her. He took a deep breath, closing his eyes. When they opened again, he was back to being the Dom. In control. Slightly cold. "I don't want to be eased, Kitten. I want to be obeyed. I've given in to everything you've asked for today. I've been more than indulgent, so you will lie on the bench or say your safe word and we'll both go to bed and you can meet me in the morning to discuss your role here."

Her whole body flushed with embarrassment, shame. She moved quickly, lowering herself face down on the bench, attempting to hold in her tears.

He was gone for what seemed like the longest time. She lay

there, trying to find that place in her brain, her subspace, but that bit of nirvana eluded her. When she heard his boots thud against the floor in an even rhythm, she knew he'd found his control once more and she wouldn't touch him again this evening.

"I didn't mean to be harsh."

But he had been. "I'm fine, Sir."

Damn, but she was good. Her voice was even, calm. Sometimes she thought she should leave Dallas and become an actress because she'd gotten so good at pretending. She pretended she was calm, pretended she didn't need things, pretended that not asking for what she needed was a sign of selflessness and not cowardice.

"But I wasn't for a moment. I wasn't fine." He sounded sad, a bit heartsick, and it occurred to her to sit up and talk to him. "I need my control, pet. I need it for me and I need it for you. I hope you can understand."

She didn't. Not really. She had no idea why he needed control, but he didn't talk to his subs. Not that way, so she would likely never know. It seemed easiest to simply let it go. "Of course."

There was a moment when she almost thought he was going to continue talking. He reached out and touched her back. "I don't like feeling as though I've failed you. I'm not sure what else to do to tell you the truth. I think it's a bad idea to follow my instincts. I could hurt you. I need to be in control so neither of us gets hurt. That's the nature of our contract. Do you still want the contract? I don't want to hold you to something you no longer want."

She wasn't sure what she wanted anymore. She'd thought she wanted a pure D/s relationship. What Cole had offered her seemed perfect. He was in control so she didn't have to be. But now…now she wondered if there wasn't something more. If she wasn't something more…

They had months left on the contract she'd signed. She had months to figure out what she wanted, and she thought that he might not open this particular door again. He was safe. He would go out of his way, deny his own obvious needs in order to avoid hurting her. He would keep her body safe. Her heart was another story.

"I don't want to leave, Sir."

She heard his long sigh.

"I'm glad because I think we can make this work if I try harder. I want to give you what you need. We'll start with a count of fifty. Where are you, pet?"

She said what she always said. "Green, Sir."

Green meant go. Yellow meant she was nervous. Red stopped the scene so they could talk. Kitten was never red. She was never, ever red. She'd learned to say yellow at times because it made her Doms less nervous.

She would throw him a yellow at some time in the session.

The first thud hit her back and she sighed. The deerskin flogger was a warm-up device. It was like a long massage. Cole worked quietly, moving it over the large muscle groups. He was careful to avoid her spine, her kidneys. She looked at him in the mirror on the far side of the dungeon. She almost never watched him. She preferred to close her eyes and let her brain float, but now she watched the man who was working on her.

There was an odd tenderness in his eyes as his hand worked the flogger.

Kitten knew she wasn't good at asking for what she needed, but what if Master Cole had the same issues? What if he was being honest and truly worried he would hurt her?

She thought about Mason alone in his room. What if Cole had been burned before and he was afraid of that fire?

Kitten let her eyes drift closed. She wasn't afraid of the fire now that she'd felt it. She wanted it again. She simply had to show her Master that she wasn't going to burn out of control. And perhaps show him that sometimes fires that had burned themselves out could be stoked back to life.

Mason was the key. If she could get them to talk, really talk, perhaps they would see that whatever happened between them wasn't so insurmountable a wall. She'd seen how they looked at each other.

The gentle thud of the flogger was doing its trick and she relaxed, her mind already plotting because she wasn't the type of girl who ever gave up.

Chapter Seven

Mason woke feeling more rested than he had in years. He opened his eyes and realized why. He wasn't in that fleabag apartment of his with the neighbors screaming at each other or the sound of gunfire booming through the air. It was quiet here.

Because here was home and home felt so good. Warm and safe and comfortable.

Mason forced himself to sit up because he didn't get to be warm and safe and comfortable anymore. He might be in the house he'd lived in once, but it belonged to Cole and it was no longer Mason's home.

"Huh?"

He turned and saw an unusual sight. Kitten had been sitting at the edge of his bed and he'd obviously woken her up. She was in a chair she must have pulled from the desk. He couldn't imagine she'd been comfortable, but she seemed to have fallen asleep leaning over with her head across her arms. The minx was wearing pink pajamas, her hair tousled to a sexy mess and her eyes sleepy. And he got his morning friend for the first time in what felt like forever. Damn, but it was good to know his dick still worked. "Good morning, gorgeous girl. Did you have fun watching me sleep?"

The sweetest blush pinkened her cheeks. "I wanted to be close in case you needed me in the night."

"That's what the intercom is for." He couldn't help but sit up straighter as he gestured to the tasteful box on the wall that worked the house-wide intercom system. She'd snuck in after her session with Cole. She'd gotten off his bench, gotten dressed, and made her way not to Cole's bed, but to Mason's.

Yeah, he had a real shot with her. She was desperate to be needed. The good news was, Mason was pretty desperate himself.

Kitten frowned. "I forgot about the intercom. The doctor told me to wake you every few hours, but I fell asleep. You could have died because I was asleep."

He chuckled. "Not at all. I only had to stay awake for twelve hours, sweetheart. I was perfectly fine to go to bed. You're cold and that can't have been a comfortable position. Come here and warm up. I'm afraid I turned the air conditioner down because I like to sleep in the cold and I haven't been able to in forever."

She hesitated for a moment, her eyes going to the door.

"It's not locked," he said quietly. "Cole can walk in at any moment, but then we wouldn't be doing anything naughty now, would we?"

A new plan had started to form in his head the night before. It was better than his old plan. His old plan had lacked a certain passion. His new plan had plenty of it, and a nice side dish of karma to go with it.

He was going to get back in Cole's good graces. He could do it. He just needed a bit of his old charm. It was obvious that Cole had softened up the tiniest bit. It was also plain that Cole was lonely, and he wasn't quite sure how to reach his precious new sub.

But Mason knew exactly how to handle her. And Cole. He would spend a few weeks getting back in Cole's bed, enjoy his time as a switch again. If Cole was on his side, he would have access to any number of helpful items including Cole's computer and contacts. He would find a new job in a new city and then Cole could be as alone as he wanted to be.

Bye-bye.

Yes, that was a much better plan and it meant much quicker access to Kitten and her gorgeous body. He didn't even think about the fact that it also meant access to Cole. No. That was merely something he would have to get through.

"He didn't forbid me from being near you, and I'm sure he wouldn't want me cold." She slid under the covers, sighing as she settled in. Her eyes were sleepy as she gave him a grin. "That's so much better. Why do you prefer to sleep in arctic-like temperatures?"

He rolled to his side so he could look her in the eyes. There was something intimate about being in the same bed with her even though they weren't touching. He had to be careful or she would find out he was interested in way more than a quick cuddle. "My body temperature runs high. Some people, and they shall remain forever nameless, used to call me a living furnace."

"Was it Cole?" Kitten whispered the question like they were kids and didn't want their parents to know they were staying up late sharing secrets.

"How can he be nameless if I name him?" He liked looking at her. Sunlight played across her skin, and he wished she was naked. He could explore her, see how quickly he could get her to purr for him. "Anyway, my nameless boyfriend would turn the air conditioner way down and he had this place in Colorado, so when we would go there and it was cold, he sometimes wouldn't turn the heater on and we would cuddle all night. He took me camping a couple of times. He said he didn't need a campfire to sleep by if he had me in his tent."

"You've been to Bliss?"

"Yes. I spent months and months of every year in Bliss since I was seventeen." He'd thought he would hate it the first time Cole dragged him up there. He was a city boy, and then he'd gotten a view of those mountains. He'd smelled the clean air and he'd sat. For the first time in his life, he'd just sat and been content because there was something about that place that settled him.

He missed Bliss. It had been the best of both worlds. Part of the year in the city with the energy and competition, and then he got to let go, to relax in Bliss. There had been no reason to compete there. People had to work together to survive, so they thought nothing at all about helping a neighbor.

He'd had a good life with Cole.

"I went to a wedding there." She reached out and smoothed back his hair. God, it felt right to be with her—like they'd been waking up together all their lives. "I liked it. It was weird. I went to a party in a bar and I swear I heard a Russian guy talking about there being a body in the freezer. I'm sure he was joking though."

Mason chuckled. "Well, the last time I was there the only bar was at the lodge and some biker place that Cole wouldn't let me check out. Apparently it's filled with criminals." He winced. "At the time, I thought it sounded interesting. Now I actually work with criminals and I absolutely have zero interest in having a drink with them."

Her eyes widened slightly. "Criminals?"

"My new job is somewhat less than respectable, one would say."

"More than one, Mason." The sound of Cole's voice nearly made Mason jump. "Most people would say your new clients are shady, to say the least."

Both he and Kitten turned and there was Cole, standing in the doorway wearing nothing but a pair of sweatpants. His muscular chest was on full display and Mason had to work to avoid drooling. He was still the sexiest man he'd ever seen. The last few years had refined and honed him, turning him from merely hotter than hell to deadly gorgeous.

It was another joke the universe played on him. Mason looked older and the years had blessed Cole with more beauty.

Mason schooled his expression. His first instinct was to spit bile and vitriol Cole's way, but that hadn't worked. Charm. He still had some of that. Charm had won Cole over when they were kids, and Cole was still that same insecure rich boy on the inside. "I'm sorry. Kitten was kind enough to check on me. She was worried about my poor brain being fried." He held his hands up. "I asked her to join me so she wouldn't be a Popsicle. No touching."

Cole seemed to think for a moment and then he came to a decision. "I don't want to be a Popsicle either. Scoot over."

Kitten's eyes widened as Cole moved quickly, lifting the covers and starting to climb in. She moved over, lying on her back in between them.

So that was how Cole was going to play it. He thought this was a competition, but Mason intended to turn it into something else. Cole seemed to have gone for a long time without a sub when he was used to having two. Hell, he was used to having Mason around to smooth over the rough spots of his life. He needed to remind Cole of how easy he'd made his life. How good it could be.

Cole rolled to his side, his elbow up, head resting in his palm. "Did you sleep all right, pet?"

Kitten was obviously tired, but Cole never picked up on those clues. He was an incredibly smart man, but all of his intelligence tended to be in books and business. He'd relied on Mason for social skills. Mason wondered how he was doing at the office these days.

"I slept fine, Sir," Kitten replied.

This was where he could start making inroads. He could be what he always was—the conduit between Cole and the outer world, or in this case between Cole and his sub. "She was sleeping in a chair in here."

Cole frowned down at her. "What was the purpose of that?"

Kitten seemed to shrink a bit. "I was worried about him. The doctor told me…"

She seemed to falter and Mason took over. He put a hand on her shoulder, stroking gently. It wasn't an intimate touch. It was friendly. Kind. "The doctor told her to wake me up every couple of hours. She didn't remember that she only had to do it the first twelve. She was trying to be nice."

Their eyes met over her body and Cole deliberately placed a possessive hand on her stomach. "She's a nice woman. She tries to take care of the people around her. It's up to me to make sure they don't take advantage of her."

Cole had never been a stupid man. Mason nodded and backed off. "Of course. You know best, Sir."

Cole's eyes flared.

Mason shrugged. "I can remember my manners."

Cole seemed to think about that for a moment. "All right. I suppose if you're polite, I can do the same. How are you feeling this morning?"

Kitten cuddled back against Cole. The minute he showed her

any affection, Kitten lapped it up like a flower that hadn't been watered in years. "Is your head hurting? I could get your pills for you."

He shook his head. "I'm surprisingly clearheaded this morning." He was a bit suspicious though. Something about her manner had him on alert. He was a lawyer so he was used to reading signs, though he'd been doing it for far longer than his career. He'd also had an alcoholic father who liked to smack his son when he was feeling down. Mason had learned at a young age to read people's emotional states. Kitten wasn't completely comfortable. "Are you sure that the only reason you came in here was to check on me?"

It was the way she'd looked at the intercom. She hadn't forgotten about it. She wasn't being entirely truthful.

"Kitten?" Cole stared down at her.

"I…had a bad dream and I didn't want to be alone," she said haltingly.

"You had a bad dream?" Cole asked.

Typical Cole. He wasn't a bad man. His brain simply didn't work that way. Unless Kitten told him something was wrong, he assumed everything was fine. Mason knew better. "You have a lot of bad dreams, don't you, sweetheart?"

Given what she'd been through, it was a good bet.

She shrugged. "I'm not used to sleeping alone. It's been an adjustment."

Cole sat up. Again, typically Cole thought because he'd given her a princess-like bedroom that she would sleep well in it. "I didn't realize you were used to sleeping with someone."

She managed a watery smile. "People took turns. My friend Haven stayed with me at the end of my time at The Club. Before that Finn would stay with me or one of the subs. I will get used to it. I need some time."

This was where he came in. "Or your Master needs to up his timetable a bit. Don't worry. Now that Cole knows what the problem is, he'll make sure to fix it."

"Of course I will. And I'll also thank Haven. She works for me, you know. She's a very kind lady." Cole looked down at her. "Sweetheart, why don't you stay here for a few minutes and Mason and I will go and make you some coffee?"

"I can do it," she said, attempting to get up.

Cole caught her. "No, let me. We're going to The Club this weekend. There will be plenty of time for you to serve me there. Allow me to make your morning better."

She sighed and sank back down. "I wouldn't mind a nap. As long as I know someone's close by, I should be able to sleep."

So Cole wanted to talk to him. He certainly wasn't fooled that Cole needed help making coffee. That was ridiculous. Ms. Hamilton would have left a pot. Mason rolled out of bed and was happy to find he hadn't lied about his head. He felt surprisingly clear. Weak. There was a bit of that, and his stomach was already grumbling, but it would have to wait.

Cole got out of bed and gently tucked Kitten in. Mason liked the way she reached for the pillow he'd used and laid her head there. She was out in seconds.

With a grim face, Cole turned and walked out of the room. Mason wrapped himself up in the robe Kitten had laid out for him and followed. It was too big, but it wouldn't do at this point to tell Cole to wait and find his old clothes. Obedience did something for Cole. He remembered how to play this game.

This was it. Cole would ask him to leave or Mason would start to wiggle his way in. It was easy to see that Cole was floundering when it came to Kitten, and that had to be killing him. He wouldn't necessarily understand that Kitten wasn't the same as the other subs he'd taken in. She needed more than discipline. She wasn't some pampered rich girl with daddy issues.

They were quiet as they walked across the lawn and Cole held open the door and allowed him to go through. Another good sign. Cole was treating him like a sub.

How long had it been since anyone held a fucking door open for him?

"Take a seat, Mason. We obviously need to talk, and if I don't feed you soon I'm pretty sure you're going to eat the staff." He stalked over to the fridge and pulled out eggs and cheese.

Mason took a seat in the breakfast nook, the smell of coffee already wafting through the space. "When did you learn to cook?"

He pulled an omelet pan off the rack above the island. He had the gas on and was cracking eggs into a bowl with a natural ease. "I hired a new chef at the lodge last year. He showed me a few tricks. And I always could make eggs. Usually over a campfire, but this isn't so different. I already had everything prepped. I typically only cook breakfast for Kitten on Saturdays, but Ms. Hamilton had a doctor's appointment this morning so I thought I would step in."

"Shouldn't you already be at the office? The sun is up. I thought the world would fall apart if you didn't beat the sun to work."

"I thought we should talk. I can take a single day off. You know I work hard when we're in Dallas so I can take time off to enjoy Colorado. Don't paint me as something I'm not." He poured the eggs in and turned. Cole stared at him, that particular stare he got when he was desperate to figure a person out. "Why are you here?"

"I thought we went over this yesterday." He could feel his sullenness. He had to stop it.

"I understand why Kitten retrieved you. I'm sure it would surprise you to discover I went to the hospital myself when I found out."

Yes, it was definitely intriguing. "Why would you do that?"

Cole used a spatula to stir the eggs and added some mushrooms and peppers. He hadn't lied. He seemed to have prepped for a nice breakfast for two. "Because I would want to know if something bad happened. I don't want you dead."

"You could have fooled me."

Cole stepped over and filled a mug with coffee. He placed it on the table in front of Mason. "Can we speak civilly?"

Something about the dark nature of his voice pulled at Mason. "Of course."

Cole was back at the stove turning the omelet. "I'll ask again and hope you give me an honest answer. Why are you here?"

He let himself do what felt natural around Cole. He didn't hide. He didn't lie. "I'm here because I didn't have any place else to go. I don't have a car now. I probably don't have a job. I have some money saved up. I can handle my rent for a month or so."

"What about the hospital bills?"

Mason sighed. "I'll take care of them."

"How?" Cole could be a bit like a dog with a bone.

"I'll probably look into bankruptcy," Mason admitted. No lies there. He was tapped. Done. He'd lived hand to mouth for the last two years, always knowing that if anything went wrong he would be fucked and hard. Something had gone wrong. He had a month or two before his roommate would kick him out.

"And if I offered you a job?"

Mason stilled, his hand on the coffee mug. He hadn't expected it so quickly. He certainly hadn't expected anything like a job offer. The most he'd hoped for was to be invited to stay in the pool house for a bit. "I doubt you need a lawyer."

Cole's shoulders were a straight line over his back, a sure sign that he wasn't comfortable. The Master was tense and the instinct was right there inside him to go up to Cole and rub those shoulders until he relaxed. He'd done it for years, and he knew exactly how to touch him to get that tension to go away.

It was a habit, an old habit, so he stayed in his chair, watching Cole.

Cole put a perfectly cooked omelet in front of him and he couldn't help the way his stomach rumbled. Hungry. He was so fucking hungry and it was for more than food.

"I don't need a lawyer, but I do need something from you. Are you willing to listen?"

He had an idea about what Cole was going to ask him, and every cell in his body came alive at the thought. He picked up his fork. The omelet looked superb. It wasn't the only thing in the room that looked damn fine. "Yes. Of course I'll listen, Sir."

He took his first bite and realized his day was looking up.

* * * *

Cole was fairly certain he was making a massive mistake, but he couldn't help himself. It might be a mistake, but it felt like the right thing to do. In a single day Mason had greatly enhanced his relationship with Kitten. He hadn't missed his cues this morning. It had been Mason who had subtly urged him to touch Kitten. He'd been fairly hands off up to this point, but Mason seemed to understand what he didn't—that Kitten needed physical affection. He'd been too worried about taking advantage of her, but Mason had simply moved in.

"I want you to help with Kitten." There, he'd said it. He didn't have to commit to anything beyond a few weeks. Just enough time to understand what she needed to feel comfortable with him and enough time for him to figure out what was really going on with Mason. Despite everything that had happened, he couldn't shove Mason away.

Mason swallowed a forkful of eggs and his eyes closed in pure pleasure before he looked up. "You want to know why you're struggling? I like Kitten. I'll tell you where you're going wrong with her. You certainly don't have to hire me to get me to talk."

"Then let's call it a temporary gig. I'll admit that I don't like the thought of you being alone after your accident. You can stay here for a few weeks. Kitten's comfortable with you. I'm afraid she's been lonely. She's not like the others, or maybe I made a mistake by taking her in without another sub."

"Like a puppy who needs a friend."

"Damn it, I didn't mean that."

Mason held a hand up. "I'm sorry. I've gotten quite bitter over the years. You're making a mistake by treating her like the other subs you've worked with. They had some problems, but their problems came from themselves and not external events."

Mason had always been too hard on them. "They deserved help."

"I'm not saying they didn't. I'm strictly saying that Kitten's problems don't stem from an inner flaw. Anna had body issues."

Anna had more than body issues. She'd hated her body. She hadn't been able to see how lovely she was until he and Mason had shown her. "She's happy now."

"Yes. Once she was comfortable with herself she moved on. And Susan did as well. I doubt Emily would have moved on. She had a different agenda."

He didn't want to get into the Emily fight. There was something that felt good and right about sitting here and talking to Mason. He didn't want an argument to ruin it. "And Kitten? You always were good at summing people up. You were an excellent judge of character most of the time. What's your take on her?"

Mason was thoughtful for a moment. "She could fall in love with you. She isn't using you for anything beyond having a need to find a place to belong. She's invested in the lifestyle. Perhaps too invested."

This was exactly what he needed, a real conversation about all the things he didn't understand. "What's that supposed to mean? I thought it was important that she be invested in the lifestyle since I signed a contract to top her."

"You know as well as I do that a sub has to be strong," Mason pointed out. "I worry that Kitten is here because it's easier than finding her place in the world. She's still having nightmares."

"I'm not sure anyone ever truly gets over what happened to her." She'd had her life taken from her. "She's been in therapy."

"And has she had a job?" Mason asked. "She's what? Twenty-four?"

"Twenty-five, and she worked as Leo's assistant."

Mason nodded as though the answer justified something in his head. "So she worked for her shrink. That must have been a safe place to be."

"I don't think Julian would have allowed her to work outside The Club. He didn't even let her play for the first two years she lived there. Not in the dungeon. He was careful with her." He realized what Mason didn't understand when he raised an eyebrow at Julian's name. "She's Finn's first cousin."

"So she lived at The Club, played there eventually, worked there, and now she's in a twenty-four-seven relationship where you make all the decisions. You have to be worried that she's become used to following orders. She was kept with other women, wasn't she? What happened to them?"

In under a minute, Mason had figured out everything that bothered him. Could he figure out a way to solve the problems? Or would Mason simply cause more? "Gretchen committed suicide."

A grim look came over Mason's face. "I'm not surprised. And the other? Is she still struggling the way Kitten is? Did you think about taking her in, too?"

Cole huffed at the thought. "Oh, I don't think that would work out. She likely would have killed me. No, Natalie married the Dawson brothers."

Mason's jaw dropped. "Wait. Are you trying to tell me that someone was crazy enough to marry Chase Dawson? That man is a walking disaster. Hot as hell but twice as socially awkward."

Cole had to smile. There was apparently a lot of gossip Mason had missed out on. It used to be one of his favorite things. They would attend the Sunday breakfasts at Julian's and Mason would choose to socialize with the subs. They had the best gossip, he would explain. "From everything I can tell, they're happy. Natalie is well adjusted, though I know she struggled. Kitten was with him for longer. She needs more time."

"How often does she go out?"

Cole had to think about that. "We've gone to The Club several times, and Julian's for dinner."

Mason continued to push. "How often does she go out by herself? I'm not talking about The Club. It's obviously her safe place. I'm talking about going shopping and to the movies with her friends. Does she go out when you're not with her?"

He went back over the last month in his head. "With the exception of yesterday, no. She insisted on having a car at her disposal, but as far as I know she never used it before yesterday. I'm not trying to keep her a prisoner."

"I know you're not, but you're also not exactly a social butterfly. You prefer to stay in, to be insular."

"I work all day."

"And a lot of nights."

He hated the guilt that was starting to swirl inside him. "The business requires my attention. You know that."

Mason sat back. "So Kitten's left here with Ms. Hamilton, who will never accept her. She won't accept anyone except Emily. She would greatly prefer you were alone, mourning your lost love."

Guilt washed over him. He was trying to do what was right, but he seemed to be failing again. "What would you do?"

"Spend more time with her. Engage her. She likes to be needed, and not in a wash-the-dishes way. Kitten needs to feel important, but she'd fight it, too. She's been taught to negate herself. I'm sure therapy has helped but she'll likely always have to be reminded that you don't read minds." Mason stilled for a moment. "I could teach her. I could teach her how to be your sub. If there's one thing in the world I understand, it's how to handle you."

Cole suddenly understood what it meant to be Adam, or perhaps Eve, because that was a juicy apple Mason had offered and one he wasn't sure he wanted to resist. Sitting across from Mason reminded him of what a hole he'd left in Cole's life. The years without Mason played through his head. Pure drudgery. Life had become a daily chore. He'd thought signing a contract with Kitten would bring him out of it, and in some ways it had. He looked forward to his time with her, but there was an awkwardness to it. He was worried if something didn't change that she would walk away and he would regret that for the rest of his life.

He might regret this as well, but it was far better to regret than to stay in this numb state. "It's a deal."

Mason grinned and Cole had to wonder if his deal hadn't been made with a devil. A gorgeous, sexy, love-of-his-life devil.

Chapter Eight

"So Mason's back and he's staying here and he's watching after you." Tara frowned as she looked at the men sitting out on the balcony of the Dawson family condo. Ben and Chase were talking to Cole and Mason, each man sitting in their chairs like they were kings on thrones. The Dawson home was one floor under Julian Lodge's, the penthouse suite Kitten had lived in for years. She'd thought nothing could be nicer, but she preferred Cole's home. There was a certain lived-in feel to many of the rooms. Oh, some of them were kept in museum-like quality, but the rooms like the den, with its big TV and comfy couch, were so nice. They felt like the home she'd never had.

"Actually, I've watched after him the last couple of days," Kitten replied, though she knew what the truth was. Mason would top her when he felt well enough. He would be her Master when the Master was at work.

Why did her nipples get hard at the thought?

Nat leaned forward, catching a glimpse of Mason through the window. "But he's a switch."

"Yes." Kitten gave Nat a grin. "He is."

Nat's eyes widened in one of those expressions that let Kitten know she'd been looking for more of a response. Kitten liked to keep things simple.

Nat shook her head. "Come on. There has to be more to that story. You've spent months with Cole and this is the first time I've really seen you smile. That has to be about the new guy. What is going on between you and Hottie McHotterson?"

Kitten sighed as she looked out on the balcony to make sure her Master couldn't hear her. She didn't want to make him feel bad. "Mason is a lot of fun."

It wasn't that Cole wasn't a lot of fun. It was different fun. Cole was quieter, more circumspect. He was serious. Mason made her smile. Constantly. Mason teased her. There were only a few times when she wondered if there was something dark in Mason. Just sometimes, she would find him staring Cole's way with deep intent.

And then he would turn and catch sight of her and his whole face would change and it was like the sun came out again.

"Mason is a lot of trouble," Tara said with a frown. "Don't get me wrong. I like Mason. I always did. You never met him before? He was at The Club while you were there."

Nat shook her head. "Julian kept us out of the actual club portion of The Club for two and a half years. We worked in his businesses, but mostly we went to therapy and got reintegrated into the world."

It had been a frustrating time. She'd only met the closest of Julian's friends, his inner circle. She'd been so curious and he'd forced her to keep her interactions with the lifestyle to a minimum. She'd been allowed to study and had attended a few small play parties, but no Club for her until Julian allowed it. Otherwise, she might have met Cole and Mason before now and she would have known their story.

"Well, Mason's a sweetheart, but there's a nasty history there," Tara explained.

A history that had to do with Emily. She'd tried to be good, but the curiosity was killing her. "They seem to be getting along now."

Nat's eyes narrowed. "Are you serious? You're not going to ask?" She turned to Tara. "Fine, if she won't ask, I will. Spill."

A small smile curved up Tara's lips. "That wasn't exactly asking, but you know I love to help out. Don't tell Darin. I'm not allowed to gossip, but this is something I think you need to know,

Kitten. And you won't ever ask."

"It's not that I don't want to know. It's that my Master would probably like to be the one to tell me." Her mind swirled with ideas. There was always a way around orders. And he hadn't actually ordered her to not talk about this. "Nat needs to know though. I think you should tell Nat. I will simply sit here because I find myself tired."

Tara laughed. "You do that, hon. So Mason and Cole were an item forever. Like they got together as teens. They joined The Club when they were in their early twenties. They almost immediately found a girl."

"They?" Kitten sat up straight because that was a bit of gossip she hadn't thought she'd hear.

Tara stared at her. "Should I answer you directly or will that get you in trouble?"

Nat sat forward. "I'll take this one. They?"

Tara nodded. "Yes. The rumors are they got together as kids but by the time they were in college, they were finding girlfriends, so to speak."

What did "so to speak" mean? Why couldn't she speak without the so? Frustration welled, but she had to stay somewhat close to the letter of her contract and that included no gossip. She couldn't fool herself. This was definitely gossip. But the contract didn't state that she couldn't be in the room with gossipers.

"So they found their first permanent girl in Colorado," Tara continued. "Cole spends about half the year there. They brought her back to Texas and she served as their sub for a year or so."

Their sub? Mason was supposed to top her when Cole wasn't around, but there was something about the way Tara said that word that made her think it was more than topping.

"Is she all right?" Tara asked.

Nat waved her off. "That's her 'I want to do or say something I shouldn't, but I'm too subby to do it' face."

"I have one of those?" She'd been utterly unaware. She tried to appear placid at all times.

Nat laughed. "Oh, you so have one of those. So, what happened to the first chick who got between those hunks?"

Kitten felt her hands curl into fists. Being quiet was so hard, but she really would be gossiping if she blurted out that Nat was wrong because Mason was gay. Maybe Master Mason didn't want anyone to know.

"She left after a while and it became apparent to the rest of us that the core of the relationship was the guys. The girls kind of came and went. Until Cole took in Emily." Emily's name came out of Tara's mouth with an ominous tone.

Kitten stilled. She knew so little. Cole didn't speak of it. Mason hadn't opened up, and she didn't feel it was her place to ask.

"I've heard Chase talk about her in an unfriendly way, though he's kind of a misanthropic bastard, so I discount most of what he says," Nat allowed. "Now, Ben on the other hand, hated her as well. I have to wonder what she was like."

Tara snorted. "She was a righteous bitch. The other subs they brought to the club were all right, but Emily had issues. I think that's why Cole picked her. Somewhere along the way he got it in his head that he could help subs with their problems. It's like he needs to be needed."

She could certainly see that. She had a million questions about Emily. How had she met them? Had they loved her? Did they still mourn her?

Damn it, she hated being good.

"Was she in therapy?" Nat asked, not going to the place Kitten wanted to go.

Tara shook her head. "Oh, no. That was where Cole was plain wrong. He seemed to think that her problems could be cured with discipline and firmly placed boundaries, but she was a crazy bitch. She was the type who would smile and simper around the men most of the time and the minute they turned their backs she would be a raging bitch to the women. The queen bee of the subs. She was also reckless. She had several car accidents during their time together. She would always say she drove like she lived—fast and with no consideration for others. And yes, she would say the last part. That's the kind of woman she was."

She sounded quite dreadful.

"And Cole put up with it?" Nat asked.

"Cole disciplined her, of course. The trouble was Emily was a pain slut. Oh, she cried at all the right times. She was a phenomenal actress, but she liked even the non-erotic discipline and Cole would never withhold affection. The only time he seemed to actually get her behavior to change was when he withheld the credit cards. Then she acted sweet as pie until she got them back. She had Cole fooled." Tara took a sip of her water. "Mason, on the other hand, saw right through her."

"But he slept with her?" Nat asked.

Kitten couldn't help but squirm. She wanted to know the answer to that question.

Tara shrugged. "I have no idea how it worked. They were very circumspect on the dungeon floor. I know that at the end, Cole and Mason fought a lot about her. Mason wanted her gone. Which is why some people worried that he let her get drunk at that party."

Master Mason wouldn't do such a thing. Would he?

Nat leaned in, her voice going low. "Are you serious? They think he killed her?"

Tara shrugged. "There was a rumor. I don't believe it and neither does Darin. Darin's seen the worst of humanity, trust me. He can't buy that Mason would purposefully do it. What I can buy is that Mason was so miserable at the end that he got drunk himself and Emily took advantage of it."

It was killing her not to talk. She had so many questions and not enough answers. Was the relationship between Cole and Mason and Emily similar to the one Cole had laid out for her? Was Mason supposed to be Emily's second Master? Was he supposed to be her playmate? How had Mason handled sharing his lover with someone he hadn't even liked?

"So let me get this straight," Nat began. "Emily died in a car accident and Cole blamed Mason?"

"I believe so," Tara replied. "Again, Cole isn't one to talk. All I know is he returned from Colorado utterly broken. Julian flew up for the funeral and brought him back down and Mason wasn't with him. He holed up in his house for a year or so before he came back to The Club. I know everyone was worried about him."

But they weren't worried about Mason?

"They were worried about Cole and not Mason?" Thank god for Nat.

Tara's expression turned grim. "Not at all. We were all worried about Mason, but he pushed us away. I tried calling him many times and he wouldn't answer. I finally stopped after he disconnected his phone."

Kitten wasn't sure he'd disconnected it. She would bet turning off his phone service hadn't been Mason's idea. As far as she could tell, Master Mason didn't have much money. If he'd lived with Cole, he'd likely gotten used to it, and to be poor again had to have hurt his pride.

He'd likely not talked to anyone because of a wounded ego.

"Do you think he felt guilty?" Nat asked.

Tara sighed. "All I know is Mason seemed unhappy at the end. He was always the type who could light up a room, but fighting with Cole about Emily seemed to dim him somehow. When he walked in this afternoon and he smiled, that was the first time I've seen Mason be Mason in years. I worried he was gone forever. I guess I thought he'd probably moved out of the city."

Nat turned to her. "Come on, Kitten. It's your turn. It's not gossip. It's facts. Did Mason leave?"

It wasn't gossip. She was merely answering a question for a friend. She was supposed to be helpful, right? "I think he's been here in Dallas the whole time."

"But he hasn't been to The Club. He hasn't seen any of his old friends," Tara said. "Marcy and Mason and I used to be close."

This was gossip because she wasn't sure it was true. But Tara seemed upset. Gossip or let a friend hurt? Sometimes being a submissive was difficult, but then she was the one who had to live with herself. "I think he was ashamed. I don't know everything certainly, but I do know he lost his job when he and the Master split up."

Nat gave her a smile of encouragement. "See, I knew you could do it. It's easy."

"I'm only speaking about it because Tara seemed sad," she explained. "I don't think he wanted to lose you as a friend. I believe he thought everything had fallen apart and he likely didn't want to bring you in."

Tara nodded and her eyes drifted to the balcony. "Well, I would have helped him. I loved Mason. He was a sweetheart. I never agreed with what Cole did to him. It was cruel no matter what he thought Mason had done."

Oh, she wanted to know about that, too.

Nat sighed. "What did Cole do? She won't ask."

Tara let her eyes drift back. "Don't judge her too harshly, Nat. We're both comfortable in our relationships. Hers is new. She can't be sure if she'll be spanked or shown the door, and I think that's what she's really afraid of."

If she wasn't good, she wouldn't be allowed to stay. That was how it had always been. It was why she had to be careful. She didn't want to fail again. She wouldn't have anywhere to go.

Was that how Mason had felt?

"Cole was very angry. He got Mason fired and then made sure he couldn't find another job," Tara explained.

"Master Cole wouldn't do that." She said it with certainty. Maybe she hadn't known him for long, but she couldn't see him taking revenge in that way. He could ask Mason to leave, but he wouldn't throw him to the street with nothing to live on.

A single brow arched over Tara's eyes. "I heard all about it. I work for a law firm, and every firm in town was warned away from him. From what I understand there was a letter and it came from Cole's address."

She didn't like that thought, but Tara wouldn't lie. "From his home address?"

"No, it was an e-mail," Tara replied. "But it was from Cole's private e-mail address."

She still wasn't sure. Master Cole didn't strike her as vindictive. He'd been patient with her. He had rules, of course, and if she broke too many, he would end the relationship, but she doubted he would try to ruin her. She'd met truly horrible people in her time, and Cole didn't strike her as one of them.

"Why would he let Mason back in?" Kitten heard herself saying.

She was only thinking out loud. It wasn't her fault if someone actually answered her.

"I don't know. I would have bet Cole would never have spoken to him again," Tara mused. "But then there was always crazy heat between those two. Maybe Cole's calmed down and figured out it was a mistake. What surprises me is that Mason forgave him."

Had he? There was something in the way Mason looked at Cole from time to time. When he thought no one was looking, Mason seemed almost predatory. He scared her a bit in those moments, but he intrigued her far more. And she'd caught him looking longingly at Cole as well. He seemed almost embarrassed at those times. She'd watched him walk through the house the afternoon before. He would stop and touch things and a soft smile would hit his face as though the memory warmed him.

They had such history between them. Could she ever compete with that?

And why did she even think of the word compete? She wasn't competing. She was their sub. She didn't have to compete. She merely had to serve her Masters and then she would belong.

Nat belonged to her husbands even when she misbehaved. She'd seen Master Chase roll his eyes and call Nat a brat and let her get away with next to murder.

But Cole and Mason weren't her husbands and never would be. She wasn't meant to be a wife. She was meant to be a sub and she'd found her place.

She would be happy with it.

She would. It was just another choice to be made. Kitten was happy. She was. *I am*.

And happiness meant accepting things the way they were.

Didn't it?

"What's she doing?" Tara whispered.

Nat held out a hand. "That's her 'I'm reasoning my way through a problem but will likely still come to the wrong decision' face."

She frowned. "I know I don't have one of those, Nat."

"Oh, you so do." Nat slipped a hand in hers. "What were you thinking about?"

She didn't want to say. "I wasn't thinking of anything. I often do that."

"No, you don't," Nat said with a sigh. "You're always thinking, always worrying. I wish you would trust me enough to talk to me."

She shook her head. "As an extension of my Master, I need to watch what I say."

"Yes, you do," a masculine voice said. Mason walked into the room carrying a tray of wine and cheese. He set it down.

"Mason," Tara began, her voice a warning.

Mason wasn't having it. "No. She's my submissive for the short term, Tara, and we're going to clear up something right here and now."

Nat's spine went straight and Kitten knew she had only minutes before Nat got in serious trouble. She'd spent so much time protecting Kitten, it was second nature, but Kitten had to show her she didn't need protecting. Not from her new Masters. She forced back her fear and gave Mason a sunny smile. "Of course, Master Mason. I am eager for your teaching."

"And that's your 'don't rock the boat' face." Nat took a deep breath and she and Tara exchanged disappointed glances.

She wasn't going to cry. They simply didn't understand her. This was the life she wanted. She wanted to please her Masters and that was all.

"Well, I'll rock the boat," Mason said, getting down on one knee. "I don't know how long I'm going to be here, Kitten, but I will teach you this. Look at me."

She'd known she was making a mistake and she'd done it anyway. Curiosity always did kill the cat. She'd done the crime so she would do the time and she wouldn't gossip again. She forced her eyes up to his. "Yes, Sir."

"You are not an extension of me. You are not an extension of Cole. You are Kitten. You are you and this is exactly what scares Cole off. It isn't because he's waiting to see if you behave perfectly. He doesn't expect that. What he does expect and want and need is a woman who can choose. He needs to know that you choose him, and not because Julian sent you off with him, but because he's worthy of your trust and devotion. He can't get that from a robot. He can't get that from a woman who mindlessly obeys."

Now the tears were there, right on the cusp of her eyelids. "I chose to sign the contract."

"Did you? Or were you afraid that there wouldn't be anywhere else for you to go?" He held a hand up. "Don't answer now. I don't know that I want to know the answer at this point."

"What if what I want is to obey? What if I make the choice to obey? Shouldn't you honor that?" She wasn't sure why they had to make it so damn difficult. Irritation welled up inside her.

A sad expression crossed his face. "You can't make the choice once and then never again. A relationship, a real relationship, changes and grows, and you have to make that choice every single day. I'm afraid you're here because it's easy and you want a contract to force the world to make sense to you, but it's nothing more than a piece of paper. It will fail you at some point because it was written by humans and we fail. I don't want you to fall apart when it fails you."

Because he had. He'd fallen apart when he and Cole had.

When her relationships ended with her previous Masters, there had been no grand emotion. She'd simply moved on to the next. There had been no sex and no chance of any, of course, but shouldn't she have felt something? Shouldn't she have fallen even a little?

She was terrified to fall in love and yet what would it mean if she didn't? She'd never been in love. Wasn't it worth the risk? But Mason was right. It couldn't be love if she was merely an extension of someone else.

She had to be more.

She nodded. "Then I'll be me. You should know I have a penchant for gossip."

He brought his thumbs up and wiped away her tears. "I can live with your flaws, gorgeous girl. I can't live knowing I'm nothing but someone to serve, and neither can Cole."

They wanted to know her. The real her. The trouble was she wasn't sure who that was yet. "I will try."

He leaned over and kissed her forehead. "That's all I ask." He got to his feet. "Now what's this about gossip? I have to leave the boring Doms. They don't gossip at all."

Tara had tears in her eyes. “Mason, I missed you.”

She put her arms out and walked to give him a hug.

Mason hesitated for a moment, but then his arms came up. “I didn’t think anyone would want to see me.”

Tara shook her head. “Dummy. We all worried about you. We loved you, Mason. Don’t leave again. No matter what happens. You weren’t an extension of him, either. You’re Mason and whether you’re with Cole or not, your friends love you.”

Mason stiffened and then relaxed, and when he turned back to her, Kitten could see Mason was holding back his emotions. He reached out and held Tara’s hand for a moment. “All right. I won’t lose touch again. Promise. Now let’s do what subs do and drink wine and gossip. I have years of club gossip to catch up on.”

He sat down between her and Tara and within moments every woman had a glass in her hand and they were all fawning over him.

“I think that one’s a keeper,” Nat whispered in her ear as Mason and Tara started talking about mutual friends.

His arm went around her shoulders and Kitten realized she might be getting in far too deep.

* * * *

Chase Dawson whistled as Mason disappeared through the door that led to the kitchen. “Yond Mason has a lean and hungry look.”

Only that pretentious bastard would quote Shakespeare at a time like this. Though he had to admit he’d rather thought the same thing. Mason wasn’t Cassius and Cole certainly didn’t think of himself as Julius Caesar, but he did wonder if Mason wasn’t planning some form of revenge. “He seems to think I had something to do with him not being able to find another job.”

Darin’s eyes narrowed. “Well, we all know that, Cole. You couldn’t expect him not to find out.”

Ben Dawson was his brother’s more reasonable twin. He held out a hand. “Let the past stay in the past.”

“No,” Cole said suddenly. Something was going on that he did not understand. “I want to know why Darin is looking at me like I’m the bad guy here. I understand that I caused him to lose his job. I wasn't thinking particularly clearly at the time or I would have made arrangements. I certainly didn't blackball him from every law office in the Metroplex."

Chase was the one staring at him now. "That's not how I heard it. I find that interesting."

Chase also found serial killers, bombs, and snipers interesting. It didn't make Cole want to delve further. He wanted to look to the future. "What's interesting about it? Gossip is often wrong. You should know that."

Chase's face lit up. "Ah, but I don't think it was gossip."

Ben frowned. "What do you mean?"

"He means the letter exists," Darin explained.

Gossip was going to be the death of him. "Who's seen this letter?"

"Finn got a call from a law firm asking him about an e-mail from you. The man at the firm in question was supposed to interview Mason and he canceled after receiving your e-mail," Darin explained.

"Did Finn see it?" His blood pressure was starting to tick up. "Is this why Julian seems to think I'll hurt Kitten?" It made sense if Finn had been telling tales to his Master. "Perhaps I should have a talk with Julian about his sub's lies."

"I don't think that would go well," Ben said.

He was at the point that he couldn't give a flying fuck if it went well. Mason had heard some nasty rumors about him and he wanted them stopped. If they were going to have any kind of a shot at starting over, he needed for Mason to believe he hadn't ruined him.

Was he truly thinking about trying again? Who was he kidding? It was all he could think about.

Chase held a hand up. "If there's an e-mail out there, I can find it. I can put the question to bed once and forever."

"I thought we were here to talk about Mason's accident." Ben leaned back in his chair. "I don't want Chase running down rabbit holes. We'll lose him and I need him on this. I don't agree with the findings of that police report. I went out and checked Mason's car. I'm with Darin. I think this was deliberate. He was hit at least twice. From the impact points, it's clear the person who hit him had an unobstructed line of sight."

Chase reached for his Scotch glass. "It's going to take Ben a while to run skip traces on all of Mason's clients. They are wide and varied and run the gamut from truly terrible to evil as fuck. The one thing they all had in common was having barely enough money to hire a cut-rate lawyer instead of going with the public defender."

Mason wasn't a cut-rate anything. How had he ended up in that pathetic little building? Cole had visited Mason's workplace the day before while Mason had been sleeping. He claimed he was feeling better but mostly what he'd been able to do was eat and sleep. Cole had to damn near order him to take a couple of Advil so he could rest.

The offices of Benedict and Wright were a dull beige, the carpet weathered and worn. Mason's office was nothing more than a dreary cubicle. Cole couldn't see him sitting there. There had been no plants or pictures or books beyond some legal tomes.

If he hadn't recognized Mason's handwriting, he would have said it wasn't his desk at all.

It was as though all of Mason's light had been negated.

"I want to know if there's a letter." He made his decision quickly once he really looked at the evidence. He'd been going off his own truth, believing Mason had only been trying to hurt him, had either listened to rumors or made them up himself.

But what if Mason honestly believed that Cole had ruined his life? What if someone had purposefully tried to hurt him? It was unlikely, but he needed to know. He suddenly needed to be able to prove to Mason that he hadn't destroyed him. Would never.

"You didn't write that letter," Darin said, looking at him with respect for the first time in years. Had they all believed he would be so cruel?

Why wouldn't they? He'd said he loved Mason one day and thrown him out the next without listening or trying to hear him out. "No, I did not. I didn't write the letter, but I did hurt him. Look, I have to try to make this right and that starts with figuring out if there is a letter and where it came from. I set everything up for Mason when we split. He should have been quite comfortable. He should never have been forced to take a job that put him in danger. He would never have been on that road a few days ago."

"You can't know that," Ben shot back.

Chase shrugged. "But it's a pretty good bet. He was on his way to the office. Which is a hellhole, by the way. He wouldn't have been defending low-level drug dealers. You see the problem with low-level drug dealers is that they know mid-level drug dealers, who know high-level drug dealers."

"Ah, the vice ladder," Darin said. "You think someone was trying to ensure one of Mason's clients didn't cut a deal? Why not simply take the client out? Why go through the lawyer?"

"I can think of any number of reasons," Chase explained. "If they want to keep the asset, but they want to make sure his mouth stays closed, going after his lawyer might teach him a lesson. Mason might know something he shouldn't. He might have pissed someone off. He's lost several cases in the last year."

Ben held up a file. "He lost them because his clients were totally guilty. He managed to get reduced sentences on a couple, but there are some crazies out there who could blame him for the fact that they went to jail."

He hated the entire idea that Mason had been working for criminals. "So what you're telling me is there are multiple reasons to be worried that someone tried to kill him. Do you think the threat is still out there?"

Chase shrugged. "I think he's fairly safe as long as he's on the grounds of your estate."

Cole snorted at the thought. "I've never been able to keep Mason caged. The minute he feels better, he'll want out. I've got a plan in place to take care of his house, and he doesn't know it yet, but he's not going back to his job."

Ben frowned. "Do you think that's a good idea? He just came back into your life. You can't pick up where you left off. You need to take a step back."

If he did, he would likely lose Mason forever. "I did this the wrong way already. I can't back off. I have to make up for what happened to him. I'm not going to push him. I'm merely going to give him a safe place to stay."

"So you've changed your mind about Emily?" Chase asked, his

face a polite blank.

No one had liked Emily. Now that he had some distance, he could see plainly he'd placed Mason in an impossible position. He'd let his stubbornness cost all three of them. "I think Mason made a mistake. He was irresponsible, but I was, too. I still love him. I was wrong to shut him out, but I'm not sure he can forgive me."

"He's planning something," Chase said, his eyes going to the window where Cole could plainly see Mason chatting with the ladies. He was sitting beside Kitten, his arm around her shoulder.

"Yes, I'm worried he is." Mason could hold a mean grudge. "I'm worried he's plotting some form of revenge."

"Best to keep your friends close and your enemies closer, huh?" Darin asked.

"No. It's not that." How did he make them understand? "If we're going to have any kind of a shot at this, one of us has to bend. One of us has to try to have a little faith in the other, and I think that has to be me this time. I burned him before. If he burns me, well, I have to hope I survive the fire."

"And Kitten?" Ben asked. "You're willing to risk her, too?"

"He would never hurt her. He might come after me, but she would be off-limits." He was one hundred percent sure of that. He wouldn't even think of giving this a shot if he wasn't certain Mason would be kind to her. "He might attempt to take her away from me, but he won't hurt her."

"I don't know that she should be placed in a position where she's forced to choose," Ben said quietly.

Cole would have agreed a couple of weeks ago. One of the things Mason had forced him to rethink was his position on pushing Kitten's boundaries. For most subs that meant sexual boundaries, but for Kitten they were all emotional and personal. "She has to start making her own decisions, and I don't mean deciding to sign a contract and then giving up all free will. Mason is going to start to gently push her toward independence."

"And if she can't handle it?" Chase's hands were steepled over his chest and those intelligent eyes of his were laser focused on Cole.

"She can. She's stronger than she thinks. She survived, but

there's more to life than surviving. I like her. I think she's the perfect woman for me and Mason, but she has to be more than our lover, more than our sub. She's smart and capable and kind. There's a place for her outside the walls of my home. We have to push her to find it."

"Thank god," Chase said with a groan. He stood up and held a hand out. "Julian wants to make sure she's safe, but I think she needs more. I didn't think you would be the one to give it to her."

Was he supposed to say thank you? "I'll take care of her and so will Mason. If war breaks out between the two of us, know that I intend to mitigate the damages. I'm not going to make the same mistake again. I hope that spending time with me softens Mason, and finding out who wrote that damn letter might help enormously."

"I'll get on it," Chase said, shaking his hand. "I'll work on the letter from a few years back. Darin is checking into DPD's records on the clients Mason defended, and Ben is lying around looking like a himbo."

Ben shot his brother the finger. "Fuck you. I'm trying to get sun. Just because you want to be pasty white doesn't mean I have to be."

"You're trying to show off your three chest hairs in an attempt to make our wife drool. Ain't happening, buddy," Chase shot back.

Darin rolled his eyes and stood. "They're useless now. Wanna grab a beer? The ladies and Mason are perfectly safe from everything except the Dawson twins' never-ending arguments."

The Club was below, a quick elevator ride away. He hadn't spent time in the bar without a sub in forever, but once it had been a home away from home. When the dungeon was closed, the bar was still available to members. He'd spent many an hour having a beer and talking with friends.

And then he'd been alone.

The Dawsons were getting in each other's space, throwing down smack.

"The quicker, the better, my friend."

Darin grinned. "They won't even notice we're gone."

He followed his old friend into the condo and wondered if—after all these years—he might get his life back.

Chapter Nine

Two days later, Kitten watched her playmate as he dove into the deep end. That was the way she was beginning to think of Mason. He was her playmate. Master Cole had bought her a friend.

She had to keep herself from clapping her hands together because Mason Scott was the best thing to happen to her in forever. Her boredom was gone because nothing was boring around Mason. He had a way of making even the most ordinary of activities thrilling.

"Are you coming in, gorgeous girl?" He rested his arms on the side of the pool, those gray eyes winking at her.

He was the gorgeous one. "I'm not a good swimmer. I think I'll lie here and watch you."

He pouted but it made him more handsome. "Come on. You can't leave me in here all alone."

At least she had an answer for that one. "I'm not sure you should be in there in the first place. The doctor hasn't cleared you for strenuous activity."

"The doctor would tell me that if I feel fine, I should probably be fine. It's been a week. I'm still a bit achy, but the faster I allow myself to get back to a normal routine, the better."

"Does that mean you're going back to work?"

Mason frowned. "No. The Master quit for me. Bastard. That's

going to help me out in the long run when I need another job."

"I'm sure he was polite about it." Kitten couldn't say that with a straight face.

"He was an asshole, though don't tell him I said that because I will get my ass beaten," he said in a low voice that let her know he probably wouldn't mind all that much.

"Well, you know he considered your workplace dangerous."

"He also had my things moved out of my apartment. He promptly took one look at my things and threw them away."

He was missing the point. "He bought you new things."

"What if I liked the old things?"

"Did you?" She knew the answer but she wanted to see if he would be honest.

A single muscular shoulder shrugged. "No, they were crap, but that isn't the point. The point is that you should get that lovely swimsuit wet. Come on, love. You know you want to. Better than that, you know I top you when the Master's not around. Let's go. We can both use the exercise."

She sat straight up. Cole had explained that Mason topped her when he wasn't around, but he hadn't used that power. In the days since she'd picked up Mason from the hospital they'd settled into a pleasant companionship. Even the Master seemed happier. Mason was a bright light and he seemed to illuminate all the dark places. Dinners were livelier. Mason and Cole would discuss business issues and the news. She'd started watching CNN so she could keep up with them. She didn't talk very much, but she understood their discussions. They sat together at night and sometimes they played cards, sometimes turned on a movie.

She felt like she was in a real family for once.

But now one of her real family members wanted her to do something unpleasant. She was torn. It was the first thing he'd really asked of her, but it was something she was afraid of.

"Kitten, I might not have the right to punish you, but I can assure you that Cole will hear about this."

Damn. Damn. Damn. "I can't swim, Mason. I'm afraid of the water. So I would rather stay out here."

There was a whooshing sound as he hauled himself out of the

water. She managed to stop her gasp. Mason was a lovely man. In a few days he seemed to have gained a bit of weight, and it was all muscle. He and Cole hit the gym twice in the last couple of days. She'd stood outside, watching them as they worked. There had been something beautiful in the way they methodically used each machine or weight. They were strong. What would it feel like to be strong? To not be afraid?

Mason stood in front of her. "You can't swim?"

She sighed. She'd avoided talking about her past, but he seemed to be pushing her. She preferred to stay in the now. She didn't like to look to the past. "I never learned. My father thought bathing suits were…tawdry." His exact words had been more like slut suits.

He would hate what she was wearing. Her father should have been born in the middle ages.

"Well, the good news is your father isn't here. The bad news is I don't feel comfortable having a pool on the grounds when you can't swim. I'll teach you."

She heard the door open, and for the first time she was actually happy to see Ms. Hamilton begin to walk her way. She had a tray in her hands.

Maybe she wasn't happy. She could see a hint of green. Why did the woman seem to have a need to serve her poorly crafted greens?

Mason followed her line of sight and a frown came over his lovely face. "Ms. Hamilton, to what do we owe this pleasure?"

Kitten sat up. The last several days Mason had been doing something else at this time of day. He'd had many phone calls about his job and his apartment. He'd been trying to clean up all the loose ends Cole had left behind when he'd cut ties for him. It seemed as though her Master…their Master meant for Mason to stay around for a bit. But it left her with a problem. Mason topped her, but she didn't like the idea of him knowing her conflicts. Ms. Hamilton was troublesome. Or rather Cole's dictates about her nutrition were a problem she'd managed to keep hidden until now. She would either have to eat that crap or let Mason know what a brat she was.

Damn. Damn. Damn. She should have handled this better. She should have thought about the fact that her snack was at this time.

Lunch had been better since Mason was around. It seemed like Cole took his preferences into account.

Ms. Hamilton stopped, seemingly surprised. "I thought you were scheduled for a doctor's appointment."

Mason stared her down. "I was. I rescheduled because the Master wants to go. He seems overly interested in my health, but he had a meeting today. Kitten and I are going into the office at four to meet him. We'll see the doctor tomorrow. What is your purpose in interrupting our time together?"

The older woman looked a little like a fish out of water. Her mouth opened and closed like she needed extra oxygen.

"I'll ask again," Mason intoned. "What is your purpose here?"

"I was bringing Miss Kitten her snack." She set the tray down and then took a step back.

Mason stared at it for a moment. "That's not a snack. Ice cream is a snack. Cheese is a snack. I'll even give you fruit."

"It's fine." She'd choke it down. "It's what the Master ordered for me."

Ms. Hamilton frowned. "Not that you ever eat it, you ungrateful thing. You are the worst submissive the Master has had. With the exception of you." She nodded to Mason. "You're a criminal. Master Cole will wake up and realize what you're doing. Don't think I don't know that you're using him again."

Mason's eyes went cold. "I believe we will no longer require your services. Stay out of my way and you are not to have anything to do with Kitten again. Am I understood?"

Her lips formed a flat line. "We'll see what Master Cole has to say about this."

She turned on her very functional heels and walked away.

Mason moved his focus back to Kitten. "Explain what's been going on here while Cole's away."

He switched quickly. One minute he was all charm and the next he transformed into a Dom, his shoulders back, his eyes like steel.

Kitten averted her gaze.

"Don't you dare. You can pull that crap on Cole, but that's not how it's going to go with me." His fingers touched her chin, raising her face until she had to look him in the eyes. "I am not the bastard who hurt you. I am the man who will take care of you and you will honor me by not lumping me in with him. Cole treats you with kid gloves, but I know you're made of sterner stuff than this. You're a brave woman who survived something terrible. You can look me in the eyes and tell me what's been happening and then you're going to tell me why you haven't taken this up with the Master because he will be horrified when he finds out how she's been talking to you."

He didn't understand. "She isn't nice to me, but I haven't been following Cole's orders. He leaves a menu for my breakfast, lunch, and snack. I am to receive oatmeal for breakfast. I have some form of salad for lunch and then a healthy snack."

"And Cole told you this?"

"He told me I needed to eat my meals."

"But he didn't sit down and tell you what those meals would be?"

"He left a list with Ms. Hamilton. Why else would she…" Sometimes she could be very naïve. "You think she's attempting to punish me."

"I think Cole expects you to eat what you want to eat," Mason said. "He expected you to tell Ms. Hamilton what you would like to eat for those meals. She's here to serve you, and she's paid quite well to do it."

Kitten bit her bottom lip. "It seems rude for me to order her around."

"It's her job. She doesn't top you." Mason took a deep breath and stepped away. "You do understand that only two people in the entire world get to top you, right? Cole, because you signed a contract with him, and me, because we've all agreed. No one else. To allow someone else that power over you dishonors our Master. Your submission is a gift that is not to be taken lightly. Do you want to be known as a sub slut?"

Kitten felt a smile start. "A sub slut? Somehow I don't think you're talking about sex."

When he grinned her heart nearly stopped. "Smart girl. I'm saying that if you want Cole and me to take your submission seriously, we need to know that you aren't giving it away to anyone on the street." He got serious again. "I'm going to ask you a question and I want you to think about it for a while. Is this who you want to be? The woman who won't get in the water because she's too afraid to learn how to swim? Do you want to be the woman everyone steps on because you won't defend yourself? Do you want to be the woman who hides or the woman who figures out her place? You think about that and give me an answer in a couple of days."

She didn't need a couple of days, but when she opened her mouth, he put his finger there to stop her.

"I want you to think about it. Now, I saw some cookies in the pantry."

He was going to be difficult. She shook her head. "I don't want cookies."

His eyes widened. "That's the first time I've heard you say what you want."

She shrugged because if he was surprised about that, then he might be a little shocked by what she was going to do next. What he'd said had gotten to her. Ever since she'd gone to live at The Club, she'd been treated with gentleness. Oh, there had been plenty of spankings and fun floggings, but now she could see that they had treated her like a victim. She couldn't blame them because perhaps that was how she'd acted. Maybe at the end of the day, that was how she'd always acted.

She stepped to the pool and looked down at the water. She liked looking at it because it was pure and blue. She could see to the bottom.

What if she was like that water? Her real self. What if she'd spent years and years being afraid to know herself?

"My mother did what my father told her to."

Mason stepped up beside her, his hand tangling with hers. "Always?"

"Yes." It was funny how moments crept up on her. It wasn't the big moments that changed a person. People could take pictures of prom and their weddings, but for Kitten it was always the little moments that she knew would change her life, and another one was on top of her.

"I was at the school Hawk took me from because my father decided where I would go and what I would do."

"Why do you think he was so controlling?"

"He was always controlling, but I had a brother." She'd seen a few pictures of him, the ones her mother had hidden away, the ones no one was supposed to know she had. Her brother. Jerrod. "I wasn't even born when he died. Overdose. He was seventeen. Supposedly that's when my father went into overdrive. My mom was so broken, she did what he told her to. He wanted another son. He got me. He decided he would do it right this time. He would make sure I never strayed from the prescribed path. I wonder what my brother was like. They won't talk about him. Not ever."

"What do you want to do, sweetheart?" His voice sounded tight.

She was so falling in love with Mason. It was typical that the man who opened up her heart would never be hers, but love was love and she would take it in any way she got it. "I want to learn how to swim. I don't want to be afraid anymore."

He was right. She was hiding, but it was all she knew to do. She was attracted to Cole, but she didn't know how to ask him for what she needed. Watching him with Mason had been a revelation. They were still wary around each other, but sometimes they seemed to forget and then there was a beautiful ease to their relationship. It was like Julian and Finn. When she'd first come to live with them, she'd expected to see a more consensual version of what Hawk had done to her. She certainly hadn't thought Finn would be locked in a cage at night, but she hadn't expected that Finn would seem so…normal. Finn asked for Julian's advice, but he was a well-respected lawyer who made tough calls at his job all day. He simply liked to play and preferred to let Julian make the decision on where they would eat at night or what they would watch on TV. Julian's wife, Dani, was also submissive, but she ran part of Julian's businesses and all three of them took care of their child.

What if that was the type of relationship Cole really wanted? It seemed like such a simple thing to do, to choose for herself, but she'd never done it before.

Mason stepped into the water and held his hand out. His hair was so black that in the sunshine parts looked almost blue. "Come on. I want to get you used to the water first. Hold on to me. I won't let you go."

She hesitated. At the end of the day, she'd known him for a little while and yet she was supposed to trust him with her life. Everything that the world had taught her said he would more likely drown her than teach her.

Kitten took that first tentative step into the water because she'd figured something out about herself.

"Sweetheart, you're crying. You don't have to do this."

She took a shaky breath. "I just figured out what I'm good at."

The water was crisp on her skin as she stepped down the stairs and it came to her knees. He pulled her into his arms. "Wrap yourself around me. We're going to float for a while." He rubbed their cheeks together as she did what he asked. "You're good at a lot of things."

She shook her head and held on. It was nice. The water was cool, but she wasn't cold because his skin warmed her. He bounced as he walked and they talked. She felt weightless, oddly unburdened. "No, I'm not. I like to think the people in my life have their superpowers. Like Finn is incredibly smart and Chase can figure out any mystery and Nat is the bravest person I know, but I have something I do better than any of them."

"What's that?"

"I can get kicked and hurt and tossed away like a piece of trash and I still believe that someone is going to love me. I still hope that someone will. I believe, Mason."

He stopped and then he was staring at her, his hands clasping, holding her so tight that there was no way he would let go, no way he would leave her. "No matter what happens between me and Cole, I need you to understand that I will always take care of you. I know I haven't known you for long, but sometimes we meet special people and we form connections that we know will last. I feel that way with you. I won't willingly leave you. I will hold your hand while you go through this and I will be with you on the other side. I'll stay as long as you let me."

It was easier to act on her instincts with Mason. He was so open, so honest. She leaned over and brushed her lips against his. It wasn't wrong. She didn't mean anything past love and friendship. Until her lips met his and her whole body came to life.

She'd meant it as a sign of affection but heat flared through her. She pulled back, utterly startled.

"Hey, that's not wrong. We're allowed to play a little as long as it doesn't go too far. When the Master's more comfortable, it can go as far as we like. Do you think you might want to play with me, too, gorgeous girl? Or is everything you have for the big guy?" He was so close. His lips were right there, hovering above hers.

"Mason, I…I…" How did she put this? She didn't want him to think he had to return her affection. "I don't want to make you uncomfortable."

He groaned and suddenly she felt something against her belly, something big and hard. "I've been uncomfortable since the minute I set eyes on you."

He was erect. Really quite erect. And it wasn't a small erection. "But you're gay."

His laughter filled the space and took what had been an almost grave moment to something joyous. He twirled her around, but she wasn't scared because he wouldn't let go of her. "I am perfectly bi, love, and when the time is right, I will prove it to you. But first we have to get the Master on board and I have a plan. Do you want to hear it?"

He wasn't gay. And he liked her. She hugged him again, loving the way his cock felt against her. "Yes, Sir. I do."

She relaxed as Mason began to talk. She let the water and the words flow over her and vowed to not forget this feeling.

For the first time, she felt as though she'd chosen correctly.

* * * *

Mason was of two minds as he walked into the gorgeously decorated offices that housed Cole's executives. He was sure it was in the best of taste since he'd been the one who consulted with the designer. Like Cole would even care. He rarely thought about things like design, though he tended to have his preferences. Mason had watched Cole for years, learning him in a way he'd never known another human being. He knew Cole found certain colors of green soothing, but he hated to be surrounded by browns and beiges. He liked clean lines but needed sturdy furniture because he worried he would break something that looked too fragile.

It was precisely why Cole was taking his sweet time with Kitten. He didn't realize how strong she was. Cole couldn't break Kitten, but Mason was starting to worry that *he* would. And there was the rub.

He was starting to love the girl. He was beginning to need her, and not merely for revenge.

He was starting to get comfortable again and that was one thing he couldn't do.

"It's lovely." Kitten turned, looking at the reception area with that joyous air that seemed to follow her. She loved everything, walked around commenting on all the paintings and how plush the rug was.

While Kitten was oohing and ahhing, Mason stepped up to the receptionist. "Could you tell Mr. Roberts that Ms. Taylor and Mr. Scott are here to see him?"

The receptionist smiled up at him. She was a lovely woman who obviously took her appearance seriously. Her makeup was flawless, her platinum blonde hair in a stylish bob. "Are you here for business, Mr. Scott? I haven't seen you around. The boss usually only sees the same people over and over again."

She was looking him up and down. Sizing him up, and he could easily see that she liked what she saw. It made him feel like a piece of meat. He was glad Kitten had started talking to someone across the room.

Kitten hadn't come on to him in the beginning. Not like this. She'd told him how handsome he was and that he should be proud because working out had given him a lovely backside. Innocent. Sweet.

There was a wedding ring on this woman's finger. He couldn't abide that. It was one thing to have casual sex, but there was nothing casual about cheating. He knew he had an odd sex life, but he'd been completely committed to Cole and the women they brought into their lives. Still, he wasn't the morality police. Not even close. "Well, I promise he'll see me."

"I don't know about that." Her fingers drummed along the desk and she gave him a flirty wink. “He’s kind of a recluse, to say the least. Do you really want to talk to him? He’s not that much fun. The boss is uptight, if you know what I mean.”

“I don’t.” Cole only seemed uptight. It was part of his personality. He could be closed off. He only opened up to his subs, and only when he trusted them completely.

Like he used to trust Mason.

The receptionist leaned forward. “It’s almost quitting time. Why don’t you come and have a drink with me? You can ditch the weird chick.”

He turned and sure enough, Kitten was doing something weird. She was on the edge of the couch sniffing the painting. She grinned as she looked back down at her friend.

“It does smell like vanilla. How interesting.” She clapped her hands together and jumped off the ten-thousand-dollar couch. Her shoes had been kicked off at some point. Yeah, she hadn’t gotten out in the real world very much, but then that was part of the fun. He got to show her new things and she embraced them all.

She made him feel young again.

When he looked back, the receptionist was rolling her eyes. “Classy, huh? So what do you say? Do you want to have that drink?”

Oh, he had a lot to say. He was surprised to find his inner predator. He was the guy who laughed off everything, the one who smoothed things over because it didn’t matter. Now it fucking mattered. He let his voice drop to what he knew damn well was a sexy growl. “Do you know what I’m going to do when I get alone in that room with your boss?”

She leaned forward, giving him a good view of the tops of her breasts. “What are you going to do?”

“I’m going to get on my knees and I’m going to suck him off. I’m going to take out his cock and then I’m going to put my mouth all over him, and my jaw is very likely going to be sore because it’s been a long time and he’s got such a big dick. I’m going to suck him until he comes and then I’ll drink that down and hope that it doesn’t take him long to get hard again so he can take my ass. That’s what I’m going to do. And then, if I’m lucky, I get to do it all over again with that gorgeous woman over there because we're both insane about her."

"The boss is not a flipping queer." She rolled her eyes. "We all know he's doing his assistant and has been for years."

"Mason?"

Shit and balls. He turned and there was Cole. It was obvious he'd overheard everything. He damn near stared a hole through him.

He had to force his eyes to meet Cole's. It was his instinct to drop to his damn knees and beg Cole's forgiveness. He'd done something unthinkable. He'd fucking outed him to someone who didn't know. "She was hitting on me. I thought she should know what interested me." He shrugged. "Sorry about lying. Obviously, I'm not going to do any of those things to you. I got mad and you were the nearest target."

Maybe he could save it. Maybe.

Cole frowned. "What else did she do? You're typically discreet. Have the last few years changed you so much?" His eyes strayed to where Kitten was showing her new friend the bracelet on her wrist. "Ah, I see."

What had he done? He couldn't get kicked out at this point. "I'm sorry, Sir. I was rude and I said things I shouldn't. I made it sound like I was going to do something I would, of course, never do. That you would never do."

One dark brow rose. "Come here, Mason."

He was using that voice, the one that got his cock hard and made him breathless. Fuck. He'd screwed everything up. Cole tended to be very discreet at the office. The lodge in Bliss was different, but he kept his private life private here in Dallas. Mason was fairly sure he was about to get kicked to the curb. Would he be allowed to say good-bye to her? He panicked at the thought. Not seeing Kitten would be as bad as not seeing Cole.

He shook off that thought because this wasn't about Cole. All the time they were spending together was about his revenge. It sure as fuck wasn't about getting back into Cole's bed.

"Mason, I asked you to come here."

They were standing in the middle of his reception room. At least it would be civilized this time. There was no more putting it off. Once again he'd been reckless and it would fucking cost him. He never learned. Not ever. He stepped in front of Cole and suddenly there was a hand on the back of his neck.

Warm and big, Cole's hands were so big. Like the rest of the man, his hands were massive and seemed to send a shock of pleasure through Mason's system. Cole stared at him for a moment and Mason was completely shocked when Cole lowered his mouth to his and their lips brushed together for the first time in years.

He was seventeen again. At first Cole had been the innocent one, the one who needed to be led, but the minute he found his feet, he'd been the leader. They hadn't known what to call themselves then. Hadn't understood that Cole was the top and Mason the bottom. It hadn't mattered because that first kiss had been about something more.

Love. It had been the first time in his life that Mason felt like someone loved him.

His cock hardened painfully but then that seemed to be its constant state at this point.

Cole kept the kiss brief, a brushing of lips that seemed all the sweeter for the relief Mason felt.

Cole had never once kissed him in front of people at the office. Never. Now his blue eyes held Mason's for a long moment. With his hand on the back of his neck and their bodies close together, it felt almost like communion, a sacred intimacy he'd missed for years.

"Are we kissing? Is it kissing time now?" Kitten was grinning beside them, her previous conversation apparently ditched in favor of watching them.

He looked at her, studying her face. There was no jealousy, only a happy curiosity there.

Cole leaned over and surprise, surprise, he kissed her, too. "It's always kissing time when you're around, pet." He turned slightly and his eyes went arctic. "Ms. Calhoun, do I look like a man who shares?"

Her eyes went wide.

Mason cleared his throat, trying to point out the obvious.

Cole shrugged him off. "That doesn't count. You're both mine. I can do what I like with you. I'm certainly not going to allow

Mason to run off into a broom closet with someone else. Not while he's under contract to me."

"Contract?" Ms. Calhoun's head shook.

"I believe that is absolutely none of your business," Cole said. "Haven, dear?"

The woman Kitten had been talking to had the biggest grin on her face. She was a dark-haired woman who looked to be somewhere in her early thirties. "Yes, Sir?"

"Would you mind taking Ms. Calhoun's place? This isn't the first time I've heard she's hit on my guests. She's fired and will be escorted from the building very soon. Unless you would rather hit on my subs."

Haven shook her head and seemed amused by the situation. "I would never do that, Sir." She sighed as she looked over at the receptionist. "Out, skank."

"Haven." Cole barked her name and she seemed to need no other explanation.

"Sorry," she said, her eyes on the floor. Mason got the feeling she wasn't really sorry. "It's just she's kind of horrifically awfully painfully mean to all the other women and we're going to have a big old party to send her off. One that she's not invited to."

"You'll hear from my lawyer. And I fully intend to out you for the pervert you are, Roberts. Don't think I won't." The receptionist wasn't waiting around for her escort. She grabbed her bag and strode from the room.

Cole stared after her, a quizzical look on his face. "Why does she think I care if she tells someone?"

Mason seemed to be the only one who realized there might be consequences. "You've always been circumspect at the office."

"No, I'm not. I remember a time when I locked all the employees out of the great room at the lodge because we were celebrating your birthday. They knew what was going on. I actually found a couple of them listening outside the doors like five-year-olds."

Kitten bounced on her toes. He'd noticed when she was truly happy she struggled to sit still. "That sounds like such fun!"

Mason kind of thought they were both missing the point. When the hell had he become the voice of reason? "That's the lodge. This is the office. You know that place where you make a lot of money in a traditional way. Here you've always kept it hidden."

Haven was giggling. "He doesn't keep much hidden. Do you know how many subs from The Club he's hired in the last few years? And a couple of Doms work for him, too. And Mistress Anne, but she scares the holy fuck out of me. I think she Tasers people who irritate her."

"She's the head of my security team," Cole explained. "After…Well, in the last couple of years, I started hiring friends who needed jobs and were qualified. Don't get me wrong. The board probably wouldn't like it, but I'm still in charge here. I find it's much easier to have employees who have Doms to take care of discipline problems. Honestly, the threat of a non-erotic spanking has handled many of my staff issues. It looks like we need to hire a receptionist."

"I can do it." Kitten held up her hand.

Kitten liked to answer the phone, put people on hold, and then sing pop songs as the waiting music. She'd done it several times on the house phone. She seemed to particularly like Katy Perry songs. Yeah, no. "I think we have plenty to work on back at the house, love. Your swimming lessons will take up some time."

Cole sent him a grateful look. "Yes, I want you working with Mason. It's why he's here."

Was it really? What the hell had that kiss meant?

"Come with me, you two. I have a few things to get through before we can leave. Do you mind waiting in my office?" He nodded toward the back of the building. Mason knew the way. "Kitten, pet, don't forget your shoes."

Because she would. Mason had taken to organizing her closet and ordering her to keep things in specific places because otherwise she couldn't find a thing.

She ran back and hugged Haven before grabbing her shoes and rushing to slip her hand into Cole's. He stopped and stared at her for a moment before squeezing her hand and looking back at Mason.

Thank you, he mouthed.

Mason nodded because he was pretty damn sure Kitten hadn't

been so openly affectionate before he'd come around.

Cole was getting everything he wanted. Again.

And Mason was going to make damn sure he got what he wanted this time. The trouble was his stupid-ass heart was starting to war with his head, and he wasn't sure what he truly wanted anymore.

He followed, trying to tell himself that his heart didn't matter. Not anymore.

Chapter Ten

What the hell had he done? The question was running through Cole's head as he closed the door behind him, leaving Mason and Kitten in his office, though he didn't want to. He wanted to close himself inside with them. Or even better, get the hell out of here and find someplace quiet where he could have a drink and let them undress him and then, oh, then, he would tie them up and work them over and worship those gorgeous bodies of theirs.

When he'd invited Mason in, he'd fooled himself into thinking it was all about Kitten and helping out an old friend. What bullshit.

He had to deal with the board again. They were rapidly becoming a pain in his ass. He didn't even know what they wanted with him this time. They'd had a freaking meeting earlier in the day. He'd spent the last several years burying himself in work and now he was annoyed as hell at having to stay until five.

Because of them. As much as he wanted to deny it, his contract with Kitten hadn't been working until Mason walked back through his doors. In the last several days, he'd become immersed in their lives, eager to get home and be with them. With Mason to smooth the way between him and Kitten, they were finally getting close. He was ready to move on to sex.

It was time to consider forgiving Mason. He'd changed. He was obviously not as reckless as he'd been.

Kitten liked having him around. That was another reason to think about it. Kitten and Mason seemed to bring out good traits in each other. Unlike other women who brought out the worst in Mason—either in his jealousy or his self-destructive tendencies.

Who the fuck was he kidding? He didn't want Mason around to please Kitten. He just fucking wanted Mason. He wanted them both. It felt right. So fucking right.

"Why is Mason Scott here? And what is this I hear about you firing Alli Calhoun?" Lea strode down the corridor, a frown on her face and her ever-present cell in her hand. "I got a call from her. She's threatening to sue. She says you created a hostile work environment."

"Not for her. I fired her so she doesn't have to worry about me being hostile." He'd kind of already forgotten about her. Since he'd realized that the work environment was so much nicer when he was surrounded by lifestylers, he'd very quietly replaced the people in the office who left with subs and a few Doms. He would never fire someone just so he could replace them, but he had breathed a few sighs of relief. If only he could control the board as easily.

He rather thought the time was coming for Lea to find new worlds to explore. He'd been passive the last two years. Now he realized he'd been mourning Mason.

Not Emily. God, he hated it about himself, but it was true. The person he'd mourned those years had been Mason.

"Mason is here because I invited him." It occurred to him that he really would rather be back in the office with Mason doing exactly what Mason had said he would do. He could close his eyes and let Mason suck him off. So much nicer than being here. "I fired Calhoun for unprofessional behavior. She was hitting on clients."

"On who?" Her eyes narrowed. "Ah, I see. Is that what Mason told you? He's gone for years and then two minutes after he's back, suddenly the office is in an uproar. I have to call the lawyers about this."

He was getting tired of defending himself. "Mason didn't tell me anything. I overheard the conversation. I made the decision myself. If anyone is in an uproar, there's a simple solution to that. They can let me know they want a pink slip and the problem is solved. I do mean anyone, Lea."

She knew his business inside and out and anyone else he brought in would take years to get to her level, but he suddenly didn't care anymore.

She seemed to understand she'd gone too far. "I'm sorry. It's been a stressful day. I was surprised to see him here. It's been a long time. Is he working for you again?"

Not in any way she would understand. "We're talking again. It's not about business so it doesn't concern you in any way. Tell me what they want to talk to me about."

She went a little pale. "The board wants to use the property in Colorado for the new mall project."

"I already vetoed that."

"They're going to outvote you. They already did. They used a loophole in the company bylaws to do it. I'm worried that if you cause trouble now, they might get rid of you as CEO."

"It's my fucking company." But he knew they could do it. It might be his company but his father had gone public. A little spark of panic threatened. "I want a shareholder's report. I want to know each and every person who owns even a single share of stock in this company."

"Already sent it to you. It's sitting in your inbox." She frowned. "You're not going to like it. The Holmes Corporation has been buying up your smaller investors. They've done it through shell corporations and subsidiaries and friendly companies. They could sell to the main company at any time. That's why we haven't caught it until now. Your personal stock is only forty. You're still the majority holder, but you know that doesn't mean a thing if they band together and vote you out. I think they're moving, Cole."

A takeover. He let it sink in for a moment. This company had been something his grandfather had built and had been passed down to him. This company had been his responsibility for most of his adult life. He'd given everything to it.

Hell, it might be a relief. Being booted out of his own company might not be so bad. He would make a shit ton of money in a buyout. He could move to the lodge and be an innkeeper full-time. He could take all that money and do what he should do—build resorts that respected the land around them, that gave back to the community. No stockholders. No board meetings. It would be him and Kitten and Mason making the decisions.

That was taking things a bit fast, but it was where his brain went.

Then his brain came to a squealing halt. If he was ousted, the corporation would get all that land in Bliss and they wouldn't care that they would be protested. He had a sudden vision of being the one who caused it all to go away. He hadn't thought that way in the beginning, but he'd seen the light. His original plan had been wrong. It was a massive plot of land. They would turn all that gorgeous nature into tacky malls and cheap housing. Hell, they could sell to industrial companies for all he knew. If he lost control of that land, everyone in Bliss would suffer, including his resort. Right now it overlooked gorgeous terrain. His grandfather's legacy to him could be washed away and all because he hadn't paid enough attention. He'd had his head in the sand. "How has this happened under my nose?"

Lea shrugged. "You haven't been on your game for the last couple of months. You've been distracted. They're starting to talk about it. Even here in the office."

"Talking about what?"

"You going soft," Lea accused. "You losing focus. For the last several years you've been a shark and everyone knew it. You made more money for the investors in the last two years than in all the years before. They looked up to you. You even stopped spending so much time in Colorado. You became everything they needed you to be and now they're losing faith in you. You've been distracted."

He could read between the lines. He'd been distracted since he'd first started thinking about finding a new sub. When he'd begun courting Kitten, he hadn't merely thought about work. "I've done my job, damn it."

He had to find a way to save that land.

"Has Mason been in the office lately?" Lea asked, her eyes narrowing.

"No. This is the first time he's been here. Why?"

"Because I'm wondering how The Holmes Corporation knows

so much about us. I find it odd that Mason comes back and suddenly we're having all these problems."

"It's not Mason." He wasn't going to believe it. He would put that shit right out of his mind.

"Mason has always been jealous of your success."

"Stay out of this, Lea."

"It's hard to because I see that you're making the same mistakes again. You need to surround yourself with people who understand you but you bring Mason back and that odd girl who dances around half the time. I'm saying this as a friend. I'm worried about you. Have you considered the fact that Mason came into your life to get revenge on you for dumping him?"

He considered it all the time. He wasn't sure he cared. "He was in a car accident. I scarcely think he set that up himself."

She huffed. "Why not? He's done it before."

Cole stared at her and seriously thought about firing her then and there, but if he was going into a fight, he was going to need her. She knew more about the bylaws of the corporation than he did. She knew the ins and outs. She knew the power players.

If not for that piece of land, he would say screw it all, but the valley was important and he was the one who had put it in danger. He was the one who had scooped it up from under Stef Talbot's nose, and he couldn't be the one who ruined that place. He couldn't.

A sick feeling started in the pit of his stomach. He ignored what Lea had said because now was neither the time nor the place to deal with her. "Let's get this party started."

He strode toward the conference room.

If they wanted a fight, he would give them one. And they would find out he didn't play fair.

* * * *

Mason stared out the office window and wished he had a better way to while away the time. They'd been sitting in this damn office for an hour and a half. Kitten seemed perfectly happy. She was curled on the couch with her tablet crushing candy or playing another mindless game.

But he knew there was something going on. Cole wouldn't leave them alone unless it was very important.

He hated being out of the loop.

He stared at Cole's computer and wondered if his passwords were the same. He wouldn't do anything. Just take a quick look at his e-mail to see what was going on.

And that would get him shoved out of his home again.

Damn it. He was already thinking of it as his home, and he couldn't afford to do that. It was a temporary way station where he could milk Cole for cash and make inroads with Kitten because he was getting the girl this time.

She giggled at something on her tablet and he wondered if she would leave with him or she would be smart enough to know he could never give her what Cole could. Not really. There would always be this perverse part of him that needed to submit. Why he couldn't simply be one thing was the bane of his existence. He wasn't straight, wasn't really gay. He wasn't all Dom and he couldn't be happy only submitting. He'd always wanted it all and it always fell apart.

"Do you want to take a walk, Sir? I think I saw a snack machine downstairs if you're hungry." Kitten sat up, putting her tablet away. "If you prefer to wait, I could get you something."

Such a sweet thing. He crossed the space between them and sat next to her, swinging his arm over the back of the couch. Being close to her soothed him in a way. "At this point it's almost dinnertime. I'm going to give the Master another ten minutes and then I need to feed my girl." He couldn't do a damn thing with Kitten in the room. He wasn't going to bring her into this any more than he had to. Besides, Cole often brought his laptop home and he liked to sleep in on Saturdays. Or there were always the nightly sessions with Kitten. He could sneak away and figure out what was going on.

The door opened and Cole strode in.

"Do you know how long…" Mason began and stopped immediately at the look on his face. Or rather the complete lack thereof.

Cole's face was utterly shut down. There wasn't a hint of

emotion in his eyes. They were stony as he turned and stared.

Mason was on his knees before he could even think about it. He found his position on the floor and lowered his head submissively. Pure instinct took over. When the Master was that upset, there was only one thing to do. Anger, sorrow…it didn't matter. What Cole needed was to be in control because only being out of control could put him in this state.

"Join me, gorgeous girl."

He could only see Cole's shoes. He hadn't changed those. Prada loafers. Mason used to buy them for Cole. One pair a year because that was how long it took before Cole broke down and let him buy another. Mason had bought all his clothes because Cole didn't care about them. He'd literally gone from his mother buying his clothes to Mason buying them. Who was buying them now? Or did he hire a shopper?

He felt someone move beside him and suddenly he wasn't alone on the floor. Kitten dropped to her knees and he felt the warmth of her hand brush his before she placed her palms on her thighs. They were still touching though. Their knees rubbed together.

He wasn't alone. It felt so good to not be alone.

There was a long sigh from above. "I'm sorry I left you here for so long. Something came up that required my attention. I should have sent Haven to warn you, but I got in the middle of the meeting and I forgot. There's no excuse. Unfortunately, the problem isn't over. I'm afraid I'm going to have to ask you to take Kitten home."

"I would rather stay and wait for you, Sir," Kitten said. "I can be very quiet."

There was a stony tone to Cole's voice. "I'm going to be late. Please get your things and go. Mason will take care of you."

Something was definitely up. If he took Kitten home, he would likely lose valuable ground. He'd spent a week getting Cole into the mood to share.

And he didn't like the hollow look in his Master's eyes. In Cole's eyes. Damn, he was walking a thin line, but he couldn't go back now.

He looked up. "We'll leave, but not until we've served you."

"Mason," Cole began.

"Or you can talk to us." He brought his eyes up. "It's obvious to me that something's happened. We're supposed to be here for you."

"You're here for Kitten," Cole said harshly.

That was a kick to the gut. He lowered his head again.

A long moment passed and Cole's hand found his chin, bringing his gaze back up. "I'm sorry. I'm anxious about something, and you know how I get when I'm anxious. I think I can be honest enough to say asking you to stay was an excuse. I've missed you."

He'd missed Cole every day, and twice as much in his dreams. His revenge could wait awhile. If he really thought about it, having sex with Cole was a part of his revenge. He could remind his Master of everything he missed, everything he would miss.

God, he wanted Cole. His cock was already hard. His heart was pounding and his clothes seemed far too tight. "And I've missed you."

"I miss everyone," Kitten said.

Just like that the horrible tension was eased.

Cole barked out a laugh. "I wouldn't want you to miss me, pet." He sobered a bit. "But I also have more work to do tonight. I might have a lot to do for a few weeks. I think it might be good for Mason to take you home."

"I could stay and sit at your feet," Kitten offered.

That wasn't Cole's style. Not when he was worried. When he was worried, he needed comfort and he got that from sex.

"I'll take Kitten home and make sure she's fed and comfortable, but let us relax you before we go. We have to be something more to you than companions, Cole. You brought me here to help teach Kitten how to be your submissive. Let me show her how your sub takes care of the Master."

Longing swept over his features before Cole stepped back. His shoulders squared and it was easy to see the worry slide from his body. "My submissives certainly don't greet me like that. Undress."

He was on his feet in an instant. He reached down to help Kitten up and suddenly it wasn't enough to just be with Cole. He wanted to belong. Even if it only lasted for a little while. He stared at her, taking in the graceful lines of her form and the way her hair framed her face. "Cole, you told me I topped Kitten."

"You do."

"I need to know what that really means."

He stared for a moment as though assessing them both. "Can we put the past behind us?"

Mason wasn't sure he could ever let it go, but he would say anything to not end this moment. "Yes, I would like that. You have my solemn word that I will protect her. I'll cherish and keep her comfortable. I'll be your partner in taking care of her and I will give you what you need, Sir."

"Call me Master, Mason. I need to hear it. And Kitten, you as well. Undress Mason and then yourself and then you will find your position in front of me. I want you to watch. I want you to learn."

Kitten's eyes were wide as she turned to Cole. "What do you want me to learn, Master?"

It was time to get down and dirty, and Mason's whole being tightened. This was what he'd been waiting for. This was why he was here.

God, how long had it been since his blood heated and thrummed through his system like an out of control river? How long since his dick pulsed and thrummed and knew it was going to get well fed?

"He wants you to learn how to suck his cock," Mason explained, his voice hard with arousal. "And I'm going to show you."

Chapter Eleven

Cole watched as Kitten undressed Mason and worried that he was fucking up again, but he couldn't help himself. The afternoon had gone…poorly.

If he didn't do something and fast, he would lose the company and he would lose his damn honor all over again because people he loved would suffer for his mistake.

He viewed it as his mistake. He should have been more careful, should have had more control, should have seen what could happen. It was exactly like what had happened with Emily. Now that Mason was back, Cole could see he'd been wrong to blame him. It had been his own fault. He knew Mason's nature. Mason was reckless and wild and needed a firm hand. His Master should have been more in control.

Kitten took her time, unbuttoning each button on Mason's brand-new dress shirt after pulling his tie off. It was new because he'd taken one look at the shithole Mason had been living in and decided nothing would come with him. He'd turned Mason and Kitten loose at NorthPark with his AmEx and Ben Dawson as a bodyguard and now Mason looked like Mason again. Mason and Kitten had taken to each other so quickly. Mason had scheduled spa days and lunches and had them attending a cooking class together. He was getting Kitten out in the world and it was doing wonders for her.

Hell, it was doing wonders for him. Cole hadn't felt so settled in years. Until this.

So why hadn't he moved them toward sex? Why had he made a big show of teaching Mason how to flog Kitten when he already knew what the hell he was doing? He'd sent them all to lonely beds at night when it was so obvious what his subs wanted.

Because he was scared. He was fucking scared that Mason wasn't being truthful.

It was time to move past that. He needed this more than he'd imagined.

He stood and crossed the space to the door, locking it with a decisive click. His decision was made. It was likely one that would haunt him, but there were things he couldn't help and loving Mason was one of them. He'd been a fool to try. He'd been wrong and he needed to start making it up to Mason. Maybe then he could get the nasty look out of Mason's eyes he thought Cole had missed. Mason was planning something. He wasn't stupid. Mason could hold a grudge. Cole had to hope that he had a few weeks to remind him of how good they could be together.

Kitten slowly pushed the dress shirt off Mason's shoulders. Even a couple of days of regular meals had put some meat on his bones. Mason's shoulders were perfectly sculpted, his chest lean and muscular.

"Do you like what you see, pet?" It had been forever since he'd indulged this particular kink.

Kitten bit her bottom lip as though wondering which way to answer.

"Mason, help her," Cole encouraged.

A slow, infinitely sexy smile crossed Mason's face. "The Master likes to watch people fuck, gorgeous girl. It's a kink of his."

Cole stood a few feet away because he wanted to see them together. "He's wrong. I don't just like to watch anyone. I like to watch Mason fuck. He fucks like a god. I like having my subs put on a show for me. It's been a spectacularly shitty day. I want you to undress and then you'll suck me off and then I'm going to sit back and watch Mason fuck you on top of my desk. I'm going to watch and then every time I have to sit there, I'll see him on top of you, fucking you for my pleasure."

The thought got him hot.

Mason turned, his eyes going wide. Yeah, it felt good to be able to surprise him. "Cole? You haven't slept with Kitten yet."

"But you have." Cole pulled his own tie off and realized how much he hated it. It was a boring brown, nothing like what Mason would have selected for him. He was due a new wardrobe, too. He would send his subs out next week and let them select his clothes. He would wear them knowing it was how they thought he looked best. "Don't think I don't know Kitten sneaks out to the pool house."

Mason's hands came up. "She has bad dreams. We've done absolutely nothing."

Did Mason think he was accusing him of something? God, their trust had been shattered, and he had to find a way to put it back together because he needed Mason and so did Kitten. He needed them both. Now he realized his life simply didn't work without Mason. "I know that. I think we should all move into the big bedroom. I'm tired of sleeping alone."

He was the one being reckless but he was done playing it safe. Playing it safe had gotten him nothing in the last few years. Nothing but loneliness. He would have them in his bed for as long as he could and he would deal with the ramifications.

Mason's face had softened. "But Cole, she's yours."

"I don't mind." Kitten looked between them like she was afraid one of them would disappear.

Now he could see that his distance hadn't helped her. He'd thought he was giving her time, but she would rather have a Master who made a few mistakes than one who was too afraid to touch her. Although he was definitely afraid to touch her tonight. "Kitten, it's not that I don't want you."

Her shoulders swept back and there was a pride in her bearing he hadn't seen before. "I am ready, Master. I want a lover. I want to know what it means to make love. I'm not a virgin."

This was what she didn't understand. He moved toward her, taking her face in his hands. "Yes, you are."

Tears pooled in her eyes. "I'm not."

"Love, you hadn't been kissed before a few nights ago."

"But I have had sex."

"You've been raped."

Mason moved on the other side of her, his hands on her waist. "The Master's right. You're a virgin and the reason he wants me to take you is that he's worried he'll be too rough. He's on edge tonight for reasons he won't talk about, but he wants to make sure you get what you need. And he wants it to happen here. He wants to sit at his desk and remember your every cry of pleasure, the way I'm going to make you moan. It will give him comfort. It will also give him a memory to masturbate to."

Kitten smiled. "The Master doesn't need to do that."

She had some misconceptions about him. "Yes, he does. The Master has done nothing but masturbate for six damn months, and to be honest my sex life was nothing to write home about for the year before that. I had a few casual hookups with women at The Club and nothing more." He stared at Mason. "Nothing more."

No men. Not for him. The women had been there to scratch an itch that he'd finally decided he could live with.

"I haven't been celibate," Mason said. "There were two women. Like you, they were casual. No men."

"Is it different then?" Kitten raised her hands, putting one on both their shoulders as if she needed to touch them both, to be the connection between them. "Is it different with someone you love?"

Emotion welled inside him. He could teach her because he was fairly certain he was going to love her forever. Like he did Mason. "Sex, when it's consensual, can be amazing. And it has absolutely nothing on making love with your soul mate."

Mates. He'd always known he needed two. He and Mason weren't happy without a woman. They'd tried so hard to complete their trio, but Cole could see now that they hadn't found anyone who fit them both. Emily had been a mistake. The others had served one of their needs but not both.

Kitten was their perfect mate. Sweet. Vulnerable. Open to the world. Ridiculously lovable.

Could he have this? Or had he ruined it when he'd chosen his honor over Mason's needs?

"I want to share her with you, Mason. Will you be my partner in her pleasure?"

"Just hers?" Mason asked.

Cole put a hand on the back of Mason's neck. It was something he often did to show his possessiveness, to make Mason feel surrounded. "I'll take anything you'll give me. We both made mistakes. I'm willing to look past them. Can you?"

Something flickered deep in Mason's eyes, but then it was gone and a smooth smile crossed his face. Oh, his boy was hiding his rage, but this wasn't the time to confront it. If he did, he would lose Mason. A storm was building, but then maybe he deserved to get battered by it.

"I want to be here and I definitely want her," Mason said.

They were set. Whatever would happen in the future, Cole didn't intend to think about it tonight. He wanted his comfort and they were here to provide it. "Finish your task, pet."

Kitten's hands went to the buckle of Mason's belt, struggling with it a bit. Even her clumsiness was charming. Cole shrugged out of his shirt and sat back on the couch. His office was certainly big enough for this impromptu play. He had the corner office, the biggest in the building, though it wasn't soundproofed. That was an oversight. Outside he could hear people shuffling by, but he didn't care. The door was locked. It was their own world. He could see that night was falling and a light rain had begun. It streaked across the big bay windows. The lights of downtown twinkled like stars and he watched Kitten drop to her knees in front of Mason as she smoothed his slacks off. Mason hadn't changed. No boxers for him.

Cole felt his pulse tick up as Mason's big cock broke free of the constraints of his clothes.

Mason hissed a little as Kitten's face brushed against his dick while she dragged the slacks down. He kicked off his shoes and stepped out of the pants.

Mason was damn near perfect. Every inch and line of his body was honed and crafted like a classical sculpture. Elegant muscles covered his body. Broad shoulders led to a tapered waist and a cock that almost reached his naval. Big and thick, with a luscious purple head.

"Stroke yourself." He settled in. This was where he needed to be. He needed to watch them, to direct them and gain his own pleasure. A pleasure that would be more than momentary. A pleasure he wouldn't forget the minute he rolled out of bed.

Mason's hand held his cock and stroked from bulb to base, his eyes on Cole. How many times had he had that big cock in his hand? In his ass? He'd been so fucking empty without it.

Kitten finished folding Mason's clothes and started to work on her own.

"Mason, help her. She's going too fast."

Mason turned, his eyes going straight to their girl. "Stop. Allow me."

Kitten turned her face up to his as Mason stared down at her. They were gorgeous together. Kitten was the picture of innocence and Mason of decadence. His. They were fucking his.

His to command. His to protect. His to fuck and pleasure. His to love. His to lose.

"You have to go slow." Mason's hands found the buttons on her dress, leisurely unfastening them one by one, each move another seduction. His mouth hovered above hers. "You have to tease the Master. Show him what you're offering him. Show him what belongs to him. Your breasts. Your lips. Every inch of your sweet skin."

Mason knew exactly what he was doing. Cole's cock was aching as he watched Mason's hands move across her body, preparing her, showing her off.

Mason moved behind her as he smoothed the top of her dress down. Kitten wasn't wearing a bra. She rarely wore them. Her breasts were petite, like the woman herself. Delicate and tipped with little nipples that had already tightened up. Mason leaned in.

"Show the Master your breasts. Ask him if he's pleased with them."

"He's seen my breasts before," Kitten replied.

"Mason," Cole urged.

Mason knew exactly what to do. He reached around and took a nipple in his hand and twisted hard. It wouldn't hurt her, but it would remind her where she was and what she was supposed to do. She was supposed to obey, not prove how good she was at stating the obvious.

Kitten squealed, but her eyes had darkened, her skin flushing. "Oh, I quite liked that."

Mason frowned and looked Cole's way. "It's supposed to be a punishment."

"Kitten's a bit of a pain slut," he admitted.

Kitten was breathless. "Oh, Master Mason, could you do it to the other one? Please?"

"Perhaps it's better to withhold as punishment," Cole said with a chuckle. He didn't have to worry she would frown on his darker impulses.

Though it would be his responsibility to ensure she didn't let him go too far.

"You get nothing more until you obey," Mason commanded in her ear. "I want you to show your breasts to the Master and I want you to ask him if he's pleased."

She hesitated for a second and Cole wondered if she thought he would reject her. She was going to find out that his games always led to her pleasure. It was proof that she trusted him that she quickly recovered and her hands cupped her breasts. "Master, do my breasts please you?"

Silly thing. She looked worried. And the masochist inside him thrilled a little at what he did next. "Not yet they don't. Mason, our submissive's nipples should be a bit tighter, don't you think?"

Mason's hands came around and he rolled those pert nipples between his thumbs and forefingers, capturing them and tugging and twisting.

Kitten gasped and then her whole body flushed. "Oh, that's very effective, Sir."

"Master, please."

"Master," she panted. "Mason is a very good pincher."

How did she always manage to make him laugh? He looked at Mason and even though he had his hands all over her breasts, there was a grin on his face that made him look years younger than he had. Somehow their crazy girl managed to bring out the boy Cole had fallen in love with.

"I try," Mason said with a grin. "Now, Master, how are her

breasts?"

There was a sweet pink to her nipples that hadn't been there before. "Lovely. They're a gift. Let me see what else she has to offer. And you should remember, Mason, that I like my gifts to be of a certain shade."

That would please his Kitten. He watched and wondered how hard it had been on her to have her every pleasure scheduled, as if it was a burden to the one bringing it to her. She'd gone for years knowing exactly when and how she would be disciplined. Her play had been a rote activity because no one believed she could truly want it. No one believed she could go through what she did and still want to play.

It was time for him to toss that thinking aside and allow Kitten to figure out what she wanted. She was ready. She was strong.

Mason tugged her dress off and turned her around to show her backside. Even though she was slender, she had a beautiful ass with round cheeks he loved to spank. Her skin flushed so quickly. "Lean over a bit. I think the Master will adore this. Such a lovely ass."

The minute Kitten leaned over, Mason's hand came down in a short, sharp arc. The sound cracked through the room and Cole was certain anyone in the hall could hear them, but he didn't give a fuck. His board had recently done the unpleasant equivalent to him. Mason didn't hold back. He smacked that pretty ass like he'd been waiting to do it all his life. Cole counted it out. Ten and then fifteen and twenty. Kitten was shivering, her whole body shaking, but she planted her feet and legs and didn't move them an inch. She didn't struggle to get away or scream out for him to stop. Her back arched and her eyes closed but not before he caught a look of pure bliss in them.

He'd held back because of everything that had happened to her, but her words came back to him.

Was something less beautiful because of the way it was born? Why was it wrong for Kitten to enjoy this as much as she did? If she were any other woman, he would say it was beautiful because she was so comfortable with her sexuality.

When Mason stood up, he helped her, taking her into his arms and balancing her. "Are you all right?"

She gave him a happy smile. "I think you're a great Master."

"Get used to praise, Mason. She's liberal with it." Because it had been withheld from her. He wondered if he would have been so kind to a world that had been unkind to him. All the Doms joked about Kitten's proclivity to over praise, but Cole wondered if any of them could find a tenth of the grace she'd shown. "Kitten, do you know how beautiful you are?"

He'd spent all of his time trying to mold her to his way, but maybe her way was better. He was starting to wonder if she wasn't the one who should be teaching him.

Her face lit up. "Thank you, Master. I think you're beautiful, too. My Masters are the loveliest men in the world."

Cole opened the fly of his slacks. His cock was painfully throbbing now. It was time to let go of the millions of ideas running around his brain and get down to some serious business. "I'm becoming impatient. Kitten, you're the most beautiful woman I've ever seen. I accept everything you have to offer me. Now come and get your first lesson in pleasing your Master."

Mason caught her mouth with his in a light kiss and Cole heard him whisper. "We must be doing something right because the Master is never impatient."

But he was tonight. He couldn't wait to feel their mouths on him. "I would hurry or you'll both find yourself counting it out and I'll still get my blow job."

"He means that." Mason was already in motion. He reached down and picked up her dress, folding it across the back of Cole's chair. "If we don't take care of him, he might not allow us to have our fun, and I want some fun."

He tugged on her hand and then both of his subs were on their knees in front of him. Sheer perfection. He had to sigh at how stunning they were in contrast. Kitten was delicate and feminine, her hair shimmering in the low light of the office. Her knees were spread wide and he could see how the spanking had gotten her aroused. Her nipples were hard, her pussy soft, and he would bet his life that she was already wet.

And Mason. Mason's spine was ramrod straight, his shoulders back. There was nothing submissive about his pose with the singular exception of his head being low. The rest of his body was displayed with pride. Cole took in that body he'd loved so long. Tan skin covered a body honed with years of working out. Mason's knees were splayed wide, showing off a cock that was already rigid and erect.

Like his. His subs were more than ready to play. "Come here, pet. I want you to touch me. To get used to me. I intend for you to play with my cock often from here on out."

Kitten came forward with an eagerness he'd never seen from her before. Had she been waiting for this all along? Had he kept them apart for nothing more than his own fear since Kitten didn't seem to have any? She settled herself between his legs.

"Take out my cock."

Kitten took a long breath and gently reached into his pants. The fly was already open, so she smoothed the sides down and rolled the waistline of his boxers, freeing his cock. It bounced out, eager to get to the good part. She stared for a moment and he gritted his teeth, determined to let her explore as he had with their kiss. Her fingers brushed the head of his cock and a bead of arousal pulsed at the tip.

She rubbed her forefinger over it, seemingly fascinated.

"He tastes good." Mason hadn't left his place, but his eyes were on them.

If there was one thing he knew about Mason it was that he hated to feel left out. It was one of the things that had been difficult about being his Master. Mason ached when he thought he was on the outside.

"Come over here and show her," Cole said. He'd never been able to deny Mason. When Mason and Emily so obviously didn't enjoy each other's company, it had proven a difficult balancing act. At the time, he'd been so angry he'd simply lumped Mason in with Emily and called them both jealous. But it wasn't about jealousy with Mason. It was about belonging.

He belonged with these two. God, it felt so right. How could he find this slice of heaven at the precise moment that everything else was falling apart?

Mason took his place, his hand on Cole's thigh, but Cole's brain was whirling. What the hell was he doing? He was headed into the fight of his life and he was sitting here with his dick out. He was drawing in two people he cared about, and he might not be able to take care of them in the future. He had huge decisions to make. He would have to weigh their comfort against a whole town's existence, against his place in the world he'd always loved.

"Lick him. You have to bring him back to us. He worries. Always. His brain is constantly coming up with worst-case scenarios, so it's up to us to make him forget for a while."

He could hear Mason speaking, but he wasn't listening to the words. He was seeing a world where he used every last bit of money he had to fight this takeover and he lost. He could lose their home, their income, their future.

"I know he doesn't look worried. That stony face, the one you're looking at right now, that's when you have to know bad shit is going through his brain. He won't cry, Kitten. He won't ask for help. He will very rarely even talk about it, but he's upset."

It was the word "their" that scared the fuck out of him. If it was just him, he might relish the fight, but he had subs to take care of, subs who needed him. He'd brought people he cared about into this company, and what would happen to them if he lost it? Would anyone want to come skiing at a lodge that looked out over a parking lot? What would happen to all his employees there?

His eyes nearly rolled to the back of his head as his cock jumped. Something warm and wet ran across his dick. He blinked, finally coming out of his thoughts a bit and when he looked down, Kitten was bent over, her tongue a delicate instrument across his flesh. She lapped at him like the cat she was, running her tongue up to his cockhead and then moving slightly so she could taste another part of him. She concentrated on her work, making sure she didn't miss an inch.

Heat sizzled up from his balls, and he couldn't think about anything but his cock.

"That's it." Mason's hand smoothed over his thigh, and Cole wished he'd taken off his slacks. He wanted to feel skin to skin, but he wasn't about to stop Kitten now. Mason had one hand on his thigh and the other on Kitten's back. "Lick the head. Don't miss a drop."

Kitten's tongue darted out, scooping up the fluid seeping from his slit. Fuck. She felt so good, but it was a teasing, tantalizing pleasure that made him want so much more. He watched as she licked around the head of his dick, rubbing her tongue over the ridge before starting on the stalk again.

"Talk to her, Cole. Tell her how it feels," Mason said, encouraging him to speak.

He'd missed this. He'd missed being in the same room as Mason because Mason reminded him of all the things he needed to do. Sometimes he wondered if he would have ever found himself if he hadn't had Mason to remind him there was something beyond books and business. "Her tongue feels so fucking good. God, do you know how long it's been since I sat and let a sub suck me? For fucking ever. Keep it up, pet, but don't forget my balls."

"He likes to have his balls licked and played with," Mason said with the sexiest groan. His hands kept stroking, like he couldn't stand to not be in on the action. Mason didn't like to watch. He always wanted to do. "They're so big though. When you suck on them, you'll have to take them one by one. Let me hold his cock so you can get to them."

He was happy he'd kept up his grooming ritual. His cock jumped as Mason's big hand surrounded him. Kitten couldn't get her fingers to touch when she stroked him, but he was surrounded by Mason. Mason took him easily, beginning to stroke him long and hard. Rough. Mason hadn't forgotten.

He caught Mason's eyes, the full weight of their history between them. They would be gentle with their woman, but he had a sudden vision of throwing down with Mason. They would be rough and tumble together. As if agreeing, Mason's hand tightened to almost the point of pain and a flash of pure energy shot through Cole.

"Fuck. Stroke me, Mason. Don't hold back."

Kitten licked his balls while Mason worked his dick, and it took everything he had not to come then and there. His fingers sank into the plush cushions of the couch, needing something, anything, to keep him balanced.

He wouldn't last long and he didn't want to come all over his slacks. "Mason, finish me."

Kitten would have to work up to taking his dick all the way, but Mason was an expert.

Kitten moved to the side, grinning up at him. "I liked that, Master. It was fun and Master Mason was right. I love how you taste."

His heart swelled because no sub had ever said that. He'd gotten many "thank you, Sir, may I have anothers" and gratitude for the way he handled a whip, but never a simple "I like the way you taste."

He hadn't tasted her yet.

"Come here and kiss me."

She practically jumped on the couch beside him as Mason settled between his splayed legs. Her lips were on his in a sweet kiss. How did the little imp make something that should be dirty and tawdry into something almost innocent? "I like kissing, Master."

"And I like kissing you," he replied. He almost never kissed his subs. He couldn't get enough of kissing her.

Then he couldn't breathe because Mason swallowed his dick in one long suck.

Kitten's eyes went wide. "Master Mason is good at that."

Fuck. Master Mason was a fucking genius when it came to oral. He didn't play. He didn't prevaricate. He sucked and he sucked hard. Cole gritted his teeth because he wanted a minute or two of this pure pleasure before he gave in. It was a fight with Mason, a battle to see how long he would last under that gorgeous bastard's teeth and lips and tongue.

Cole thrust his pelvis up, wanting to go as deep into the furnace of Mason's mouth as he could. Mason's tongue whirled around his cock, leaving not an inch unexplored, unconsumed. He bit back a moan, but then Kitten was there, covering his mouth with hers. He took the distraction, letting his tongue play against hers, but it couldn't last for long.

Mason was devouring him in the sweetest way, and it had been so long since he'd felt like this. Somehow Mason always managed to make him feel right—like he was in control when he knew damn well he wasn't. Like he was a king when he was really the one who worshipped at Mason's feet.

His balls tightened, threatening to shoot off at any minute.

He looked down his body, watching Mason's head working over his cock. Up and down. Up and down. Mason would bring his dark head up until he almost lost the crown of Cole's cock, and then he would suck his way back down again.

"He's so beautiful, Master." Kitten watched the whole scene with a lovely, angelic grin on her face.

"Yes, he is."

Mason's eyes came up, catching hers, and Cole could feel the connection between them. Mason's hand reached out and Kitten held it. Never once did Mason falter, simply kept up his work as he threaded his fingers through hers. Kitten's arm came around Cole's shoulder and for a second they were so connected. For just a minute he was part of a family again.

And then he couldn't take another second. His balls drew up. "I'm going to come, Mason. It's your choice if you want to swallow or finish me with your hand."

It was too early to truly demand that of Mason. He had to be careful with him. Mason was like a dog who'd been kicked once too often. He wanted love and affection, but he could bite at a moment's notice.

A huff tingled along his dick. Even with his mouth filled with cock, Mason could sound sarcastic.

"He won't finish you with his hand. He's going to suck you down and then he's going to kiss me so I know what you taste like, too," Kitten said. Cole had heard many women talk dirty to him, but with Kitten it wasn't about the sex. It was about being close to them, and that did something for him.

Mason groaned and that was all it took. Cole shot off like a cannon. His eyes rolled to the back of his head as sweet relief flooded his body.

Sure enough, Mason sucked him dry. He pulled and nursed his cock until there was nothing left. As he finally released him, Cole let his body sag against the couch and realized he would do anything to keep them safe.

He'd gone over the edge and there was no going back.

Chapter Twelve

Kitten's heart was pounding in her chest as she watched Mason lick the Master's cock. His tongue ran all over Cole's erection which—though softer than before—was still impressive. He lapped at it, gathering every ounce of semen that coated it.

Was this really going to happen? Would she be able to erase all the bad things from before with this moment?

She looked at the two of them and realized she didn't actually want to. What had happened to her had also brought her here, and this was where she wanted to be.

Maybe bad things happened, but that didn't mean she couldn't find some ounce of good in them. Without her captivity, she wouldn't have found this. She likely would have married her boyfriend and settled into a relationship where her submission was expected but not honored.

Mason sat up, staring at her. His lips were a deep ruby red, his hair tousled and all the more lovely for it. "Kitten, you don't have to be afraid. If you don't want to, it's all right. I'll need a very cold shower, but I would never push you."

What was he talking about? "I'm not afraid."

She was terribly, righteously horny though. And she was fairly certain she'd never been as wet as she was in that moment. She was grateful the Master had chosen leather for the furniture. He'd been very smart to do so.

Cole's face was flushed, his body relaxed, though he reached up to touch her cheek. "You're crying, pet."

Was she? "Not because I'm afraid." How did she tell them and not sound like the crazy person everyone thought she was? "I'm happy. I don't know if that's the right word. I'm ready. I want to be here. I'm excited, but I also think that it's not just sex. I kind of thought it would just be sex. So I guess if I'm scared of anything, it's that it's just sex for you two. I think that would make me sad."

For years she wanted exactly that. She'd wanted sex because it would prove that what happened to her had truly been abnormal, a twist in her fate that didn't have to lead to something bad. She'd simply wanted to know that sex for her could be something fun and pleasurable. She wanted to truly know why Nat smiled and her whole body softened when Ben or Chase walked into a room.

But she'd realized that simple sex wouldn't answer that question. What Nat had with Ben and Chase went far beyond sex.

Dear god she wanted to be loved, and she was fairly certain she would die if they turned her down, but she couldn't stay quiet.

She was becoming again. As she had become something different after Hawk. After meeting Julian. It was odd how she'd found these moments when she knew she wouldn't be the same. The moment that Hawk had taken her had been a turning point, and the Katherine she'd been had died. The moment that Nat had reached for her hand in the cage had been another. When Nat had been taken again and she'd realized she would go back into the cage to save her friend—that was the moment she'd known she was really ready, the moment she'd realized she could be strong, too.

And this…

"I don't want to sleep with either of you until you know you want to stay with me." She took a deep breath. "I'm sorry if I've been leading you on. I didn't mean to and maybe if it weren't the two of you, I could see it as mere sex, but I want more. I want to mean more than that. I want to be special."

She'd never been special. She'd been the unworthy replacement for the child her parents had lost. She'd been one of many in the cage, useless, replaceable. She'd been an object of pity at The Club.

She didn't blame them for that. They were trying to help her, and though she'd often been angry with Julian for not allowing her to explore, she was happy now because she'd realized that sex was something in between what she'd learned from her parents and what she'd learned in the world.

It was a gift, but not one she could only give once. There was no real prize to a person's virginity. There was something beautiful in sharing her soul, and that's what she wanted sex to be for her.

Mason stood, his gorgeous body proud and tall. "I have no intention of leaving you. It's early to say things like 'I love you,' but I've come to truly care about you. I think it's heading to love, and I kind of thought I wouldn't do that again. I want you more than I've ever wanted a woman and if you let me, I'll show you, but I won't stop caring about you if you want to wait. I won't walk away."

Cole stared at her. "We have a contract, Kitten."

Yes, they had a contract that lasted for six months, a contract that stated all the rights and responsibilities of each partner, and it contained not a word about love. At the time it seemed like a comfortable thing, but she was starting to wonder if it wasn't a cage, too. "I know, Master."

"I don't want you to leave me after six months." His expression didn't change, but she could hear the vulnerability in his voice.

They didn't view her as replaceable. It was all she needed to hear. She wrapped her arms around her Master's strong body and planted a kiss on his cheek. "I don't want to leave either. I'm happy here."

Cole turned slightly and she found herself in his arms. He easily hoisted her onto his lap. She could feel his cock stirring to life against her bottom. She'd been naked in front of him many times and he'd given her several orgasms, but this was different. This was far more intimate, went beyond service. "I'm happy with both my submissives. I think we work well together, don't you?"

His arms bound her to him, but his eyes sought out Mason's. There was a wariness to the question. Her Masters were still circling each other, deciding whether to fuck or fight. Kitten knew what she would vote for, but this was something they had to work out. She'd tried to play the go between, but at the end they had to make the decision to love each other again.

"We do," Mason said gravely.

"Then you'll sign a contract?" If there was one thing she'd figured out about her Master, it was that contracts were necessary. He needed them to feel safe. "We haven't made it formal."

Something passed over Mason's face, something dark, but it was gone in a moment. "Of course. I want rights to our woman. I want to formally top her. I want rights to discipline her, to fuck her when I want, but most of all I want rights to protect her."

Cole nodded. "I'll put them in the contract. And I'll write another for all three of us. One without an end date. We'll go to The Club tomorrow and Julian can negotiate."

Mason turned the sweetest shade of pink. "I don't know that I'll be welcome there. I might have told Master Julian to fuck himself the last time we talked."

Cole chuckled and kissed her shoulder, his hand starting to play against her thigh. It was inching closer and closer to her pussy. "Then we should expect a bit of public punishment before Julian concedes. I'll bring the single tail."

Kitten sighed. He hadn't used the single tail on her yet. Mason got to have all the fun.

Cole's fingers teased at her. "So is that settled enough for you, pet? Because I worry that Mason might expire if you don't let him touch you soon."

She looked up at Mason and his cock was straining. The thought of public punishment had done something to him. It was all right because she could ease him. She could finally have something of her own. Master Cole took his contracts seriously. He wanted her to stay and he wanted Mason with them.

One big finger slipped over the petals of her sex and Kitten couldn't help but squirm.

"No moving unless I tell you to." Cole growled in her ear, the sound rumbling along her skin. "This is my playtime. Mason can have you in a minute. I want to watch him fuck you, pet. I want to watch that big cock of his take this sweet little pussy and split it wide."

She laid her head against his shoulder and tried not to move. It was so hard because Cole's fingers were teasing her, playing in and around her pussy, never quite touching her clitoris.

"Master, could you spread her legs for me?" Mason asked.

"You want a taste of her, too?" Cole shifted her, spreading her legs with his own. She was laid out on his body, offered up to his partner for their pleasure. "I think Mason wants to play. You're awfully wet, pet."

She couldn't help it. She was going to go crazy under Cole's torturing hands. "I've never…" It was hard to talk. She watched as Mason got to his knees between Cole's legs. He was staring at her pussy, watching the way Cole spread her and showed her off. "No one has ever…"

"Eaten your pussy?" Mason licked his lips, beautiful full lips that were about to touch her tenderest flesh.

She shook her head. "No. Oddly enough my pleasure didn't mean much to my captor. I am very good at giving however."

Mason stopped and frowned.

Kitten groaned. "I'm supposed to talk about it. Leo says I should say what I feel when I feel it rather than bottling it up."

Cole's hands softened on her skin. "What are you feeling now? We don't want you to be afraid."

"I'm feeling frustrated because you're both treating me like I'm breakable and I would much rather you treat me like I'm edible, and if Mason doesn't lick me soon, I'm going to throw a bratastic fit to end all fits." Her friend Georgia had told her sometimes a fit could turn the tide. It might lead to a spanking, but they had to stop treating her like she was made of glass. She needed to talk about it. It was her only real experience. She didn't cry every time a memory came up. It was nice to be able to talk about it.

She couldn't pretend it hadn't happened. She couldn't act like that was a blank space in her history.

Cole's fingers came up to pinch her nipples hard. Pain flared and it seemed to go straight to her pussy. The pain fed her arousal. "You be polite to the man who's going to eat your pussy. Mason, I think what our sub is trying to say is that she wants us to stop treating her like she's damaged. She's strong. She knows what she can take and what she can't. Let's start to trust her."

Mason looked up at her. “I can do that.”

He leaned over and then Kitten couldn’t think anymore. His tongue swiped across her pussy. Warm, wet kisses lit up her system, sparking across her skin. Only Cole’s strong arms kept her where she was. She felt like she was melting.

Mason’s tongue moved over her labia, not missing an inch of her flesh. Long strokes of his tongue had her panting. It was unlike anything she’d ever felt before.

Pure pleasure swamped her senses. Mason’s fingers parted her labia as he worked her flesh.

She wanted to thrust her pelvis against him, to sink her hands into his hair and force him to fuck her harder. She couldn’t because Cole held her tight. He tethered her, keeping her connected when she might float away. Mason was playing, teasing her. A single finger taunted her as Mason sank it deep.

“You’re so tight.” Mason said the words against her pussy, his voice vibrating on her flesh. “You’re going to hug me so tight when I get inside you. Do you know how much I want to shove my cock inside you?”

“He’s going to fuck you so well, pet. He fucks like a god. It’s his true talent in life,” Cole whispered against her ear. “He takes his partner’s pleasure seriously.”

“She’s more than my partner,” Mason said, shoving his nose into her pussy and taking a long whiff. “Fuck, you smell good. You’re my sweet sub. You matter to me. Everything about you matters to me. Don’t think this is one in a long line. You’re important to me.”

And that was all she could ask for. Well, that and an orgasm that was shared for once.

Mason went back to eating her like she was the best dessert he’d ever tasted.

Cole’s hands wandered once she settled down and managed to do what he’d ordered her to. His legs held hers open wide while his hands came up to cup her breasts, playing with her nipples and pinching them to the right point of pain. “Do you know how much I love those sounds you make? I love to hear your whimpers and cries. They make your Master hard.”

His erection proved his words. Cole's cock had come back to life and he was rigid against her spine.

"Give her one, Mason. Give her one and then I want to watch her take that cock of yours," Cole commanded.

"With pleasure, Master." Mason sucked her clit hard and she came apart.

"Don't be quiet. No more of that. I don't give a fuck who hears," Cole growled in her ear. "I want all your sounds. I want you to scream for us."

She'd had to be so quiet before. Hawk punished any sound she made. She'd taken some of the worst beatings and never made a peep. It was hard to change that behavior. It was her nature to be quiet, to hide what she felt.

She managed to let a moan out. It was small, almost a whisper.

"I'll have my scream," Mason promised. He stood up and she couldn't help but see his cock. It was weeping with arousal, nearly pulsing in front of her. He was going to use that big, gorgeous weapon on her and it wouldn't hurt. He wouldn't let it. He cared about her.

He reached down and for a moment, Cole held her.

"Have you changed your mind?" Mason asked, his voice tight. "If you have, I should leave. I can meet you two at home, but I don't think I can sit by and not be involved."

Cole kissed her ear. "No, I haven't. I'm nervous. She's precious to me."

"It's a gift you're giving me," Mason allowed. "I promise to take care of her."

Cole whispered. "Don't think my allowing Mason to have you first means anything but the fact that I'm bigger than he is and you're quite small. I don't want to hurt you. I think Mason will handle it better than I would. Besides, he's quite good at taking a lover's virginity. I should know."

"You weren't the only one who was a virgin, you know," Mason said. It was all there, their shared history laid out and filled with love and longing, and if she played her cards right, she could be a part of their future.

She took Mason's hand and he helped her up and then she was

in his arms.

"This is how you taste. You and Cole, you're still on my lips. Together." His mouth covered hers, devouring her lips as surely as he'd taken her pussy.

Heat flared again. Her body, languorous a moment before, sparked right back to life. Greedy. She was greedy for pleasure, greedy to feel his body on hers. He licked across her bottom lip before plunging his tongue deep. She could taste herself on him. Salty and the slightest bit sweet. She let her tongue rub against his. They were all there. She and Cole were on Mason's tongue, mixing together.

Mason held her close, fitting her to his body. He was so big. Not as tall and broad as their Master, but Mason was at least five inches taller than her. He made her feel delicate and fragile. Oddly though she knew she should be scared of that, she found it arousing. Mason had all that power in his body, and she knew how he could use it, but his hands were gentle. His mouth dominated, but she knew she could stop him at any moment.

She was in charge. Though she was submitting to him, to both of them, these were men who would stop at a single word.

Big hands cupped her breasts and she felt Cole at her back. Surrounded. She couldn't turn without one of her men blocking her way. She was safe here in their arms. Safe in a way she'd never been before. Julian had protected her, her Doms had watched out for her, but these men wanted her. They wanted to know her inside and out, and she had to figure out who she was because they wouldn't let her play the games she'd played before.

She'd tried to break it down to sex, just sex, no emotions involved. Simple pleasure was all she'd wanted. She thought it would empower her, but now she saw what she'd been doing. It was safer to not care, to not need. She was on a ledge with these men. They could do what Hawk hadn't managed. They could destroy her. They could rip her up, but they could also free her.

Cole's hands played with her nipples, his cock a presence against her ass. She had a sudden vision of that first time.

Pain. Horror. She hadn't even known that was possible. It wasn't something she'd ever thought about, ever heard of. She'd felt the pressure and humiliation and she'd screamed. The one time she'd screamed. Such pain followed.

"Don't." Mason was staring at her. "Don't you leave me. Don't you dare leave. I need you, gorgeous girl. Don't go there."

Mason shook her, his gray eyes wide.

She came out of it, focusing on him. He needed her. He'd been hurt, too. She let her hands drift up. "I'm sorry."

His head shook. "No. Just…stay with me. Be with me."

She shoved her fear down because there was no need for it here. "I want to be with you. I don't want to be anywhere else."

She put the past aside. There was a future with these men.

"Perhaps we should slow down." Cole took a step back. "Maybe we should sit and talk."

And end the physical side? Her Master was overly cautious. If he decided she was too fragile, it might take weeks and weeks to get back here. She threw her arms around Mason's neck. She didn't need to talk. She needed to kiss and rub and love. She needed to do what she'd said she wanted—be with them.

She kissed Mason, for the first time in her life really taking control. She couldn't let this moment pass, couldn't go backward instead of forward. She needed to know what it felt like to be precious, and Mason could show her. Mason cared. Mason wanted.

She pressed her body against his, comfort flooding her when his arms wound around her again.

"I want you so much," he groaned against her lips.

He hauled her up and into his arms, her feet dangling. She held on to him as he started walking across the office. He held her easily, making her feel light and dainty.

"I won't tie you up. I won't. I want you with me. All the way." He found his way to Cole's desk. It was neatly appointed and he set her down on it, spreading her legs and making a place for himself there. He crowded her but she didn't mind.

She nodded, giving him permission to continue, to take her any way he wanted. There didn't have to be a protocol for this. Kitten allowed herself to simply act and feel.

She ran her hands along the muscles of his back as he eased her down. He covered her body with his, giving her his weight. She didn't need to be tied down. Master Mason's magnificent body managed that without a single rope. She loved how he felt against her, how hard his cock was as it rubbed against her pelvis. Mason's mouth came down on hers again, brushing their lips together, letting his chest rub against hers. He'd lost that smooth sensuality of his. Mason was always such a decadent-looking thing, always with the right moves, but now he was just a man who wanted, and that made him all the more attractive to her.

"Condom." Cole's voice broke through her pleasure.

She turned her head and Cole had sunk into the chair in front of his desk, his eyes intently on them. He looked a bit like a king sitting there. He was still in his slacks but he'd taken that magnificent cock of his out and stroked it in his big hand.

Mason's eyes widened. "Of course."

With his free hand, Cole tossed him a little packet. A condom.

"I'm on birth control." She took a shot three times a year.

Mason shook his head. "Not until I've passed the medical tests. I won't put you at any risk." He quickly rolled on the condom.

"I'll arrange to have my doctor get the results of the blood work you recently had done at the hospital. I'll call him tomorrow and then we can dispense with the condoms," Cole said. "Do you know how beautiful the two of you are? I really will think about this every day from now on. When I need to relax, I'll bring you two to the office and you can perform while I get my work done."

Mason stared down at her, his eyes soft as he ran a hand down the length of her body. "I think we'll be happy to oblige, Master. Your subs wouldn't want you stressed. We're here for your pleasure."

And their own. Cole was gaining pleasure from watching theirs. It was right there in his eyes. He wanted them to be happy.

Mason put his hand on her breast, right over her heart. "Are you sure? Because there's no going back. I'm not the best man in the world. You could choose better."

She shook her head. "I want you. Please, Mason."

His lips curved slightly. "Your mistake is my gain because you're mine now and I won't let you go."

He placed the head of his cock against her pussy and for a

second, she was scared.

"Stay with me. Look right in my eyes." Mason was holding her. Not anyone else. It was Mason, and Mason cared about her. Mason wanted her for who she was.

Suddenly Cole's face loomed large over hers. He'd taken a place beside the desk and he leaned over, brushing his lips against her forehead. "Stay with us. There's no room for him here. Only us."

Her sweet Masters. Tears pricked her eyes, but they were happy tears. "Only us."

The three of them. Together. Her men blocking out the rest of the world so she was safe and happy.

Mason pushed forward with a low moan.

"She feels good. Doesn't she?" Cole asked.

"So fucking good. God, you're tight." Mason gave her another inch, tension plain on his face.

It felt right to have him inside. Good and right. She bit her bottom lip as she spread her legs to take more of him.

Cole's hand worked its way in between her and Mason and his fingers started teasing her clit, sending sparks of pleasure through her.

"Thank you, Master," Mason said as he worked his way into her pussy in short thrusts. "I won't last long. It's been forever. So fucking long since I felt this way."

She'd never felt this way. Never. Mason's big cock was invading but there was no pain this time. No humiliation. She'd almost feared she would need to be humiliated. Mason banished that fear. Between his loving thrusts and Cole's dark voice whispering in her ear, she realized she could enjoy this without any reminders of what had happened before. Her sexuality hadn't been written by violence. That was something that had been done to her, but this…this was something she chose. This was who she was. She got to choose.

"You are so fucking beautiful, my pet," Cole whispered in her ear. "Do you know how happy I am that you're mine?"

"Mine, too." Mason held himself against her body. "Ours. All ours."

Mason drew out and then thrust hard back in and she couldn't think about anything but the feeling of his cock sliding in and out of her body. Mason dragged his full length in and out while Cole kept up the hard pressure against her clit.

She reached up and touched Cole's cheek while wrapping her legs around Mason's body.

Pleasure unlike anything she'd ever known bloomed inside her. She'd thought she'd had an orgasm before, but this was a bomb exploding, sending wave after wave through her system. This was past anything else because he was with her. Mason's gorgeous face tightened even as she cried out. He groaned and then his thrusts lost all grace as he came. Over and over he pounded into her, shooting aftershocks all along her skin. She loved the way his face flushed and his head dropped back.

She'd given that to him. She'd been the one to bring him pleasure as surely as he'd given her hers.

Mason let his body fall on top of hers, giving her all of his weight, and she wrapped herself around him, holding on to the moment for all she was worth.

Cole had a hand on them both. Kitten turned and saw that Cole's cock had swelled again, straining up to his navel. Still, there was a tender look on his face as he stared down at them. "That was beautiful."

Mason's grin was devilishly sexy. "You seem to have a problem again, Master."

Cole shook his head. "She'll be tender and you've already helped me."

"I can help you again. Kitten, love, do you mind if the Master uses you for a little target practice? I think he would love to decorate your breasts."

Cole's eyes closed as he cursed and his cock pulsed.

Mason kissed her and climbed off, wrapping his big hand around their Master's cock.

Kitten offered up her breasts, her whole body and soul satisfied.

An hour and one very hot shower later, Cole kissed her as he opened the door to his office.

"We could stay the night with you," Kitten offered. His office boasted a full bathroom and the couches were big enough to snuggle on. "We could order dinner and then we could keep you company."

Cole smoothed back her hair and laid a kiss on her forehead. "I have some difficult phone calls to make, pet. I promise as soon as I handle this situation, we're going to take a nice vacation anywhere you like."

She nodded. "All right." It was so much easier to step up to him and wrap her arms around him. She would have hesitated before but he was her Master and she needed a hug.

Mason stepped up and it was easy to see that despite their intimacy during sex, they were awkward again. Mason held out a hand and Cole quickly took it. "I'll make sure she gets home all right. We're going to grab some dinner on the way."

Cole frowned. "Mason…"

"Drive through," Mason said quickly. "Until the Dawsons come back with news, we're going to keep a low profile. I promise. I don't want to put her in any danger."

Cole nodded and there was an awkward pause. Mason turned away before Cole spoke. "And you. Don't put yourself in danger, Mason. Set the alarm when you get home and call me if you need anything at all. I'll get home as soon as I possibly can."

"Do you want to talk about this?" Mason asked.

Cole shook his head. "Not yet. I need to get a handle on it."

She wished the Master would be more open, but she had other things to think about. Mason took her hand and started down the hallway. It was quiet at this time of night, though they were hardly alone. There were plenty of offices with lights on, and several of the secretaries were still at their desks.

"Do you think they know?" Kitten asked.

"I don't care." Mason brought her hand up to his mouth, kissing her as he pressed the button to the elevator. The doors came open and he led her inside. "And apparently the Master doesn't either. He's always been circumspect with his behavior around the office, but I think that's changed. And you should know he'll never hide you away. He'll take you to business dinners and parties. He'll expect you to be his hostess eventually."

The doors closed and she couldn't help but get a little scared. She wasn't some hostess. She didn't know what to order or how to run a party. She'd never done any of those things. She wouldn't be good at it. She would fail.

"Hey, calm down. I'll help you." Mason stared down at her. "I can show you the ropes, but you'll have to find your own style because Cole has none. I mean none. He would go to work in sweats and a T-shirt if I let him. I had to teach him how to dress. I can certainly teach you how to select a good wine. It'll be fun. Maybe we can start tonight. We'll do an impromptu tasting."

"I don't know that the Master would like that." Her mind was still whirling. She hadn't thought about doing anything but pleasing the Master in a D/s fashion, but now she could see that this might please him, too. What if she couldn't handle it?

And there was something else playing in her head. Something that threatened to blow away her peace of mind.

For the first time in her life she'd felt an emotion she never had. She'd always been happy to share what toys she had. She'd grown up with so little, but sharing had always felt like love to her.

While Mason worked over her, she'd known something new about herself. When Cole had kissed her, she'd been very sure of it.

She couldn't share her men. They were hers. Only with each other would she be willing to allow them to take another lover. A wild possessiveness ran through her.

She'd filled out the original contract—the one she'd signed with Cole—but now she could see she wouldn't be able to go through with it. She'd marked that Master Cole could play with other subs, and Master Mason would likely want the same freedom. She'd actually said she would like a sister submissive.

Panic welled inside her at the thought of watching Mason touch another woman or Cole kiss a sub like he couldn't stand to wait another minute to have her.

The doors opened and they stepped into the underground parking garage. The lot was quiet at this time of night, but there were still several vehicles on this level. "Are you all right? Are you having a flashback?"

More like a flash forward. What had she done? That contract was meaningful and she couldn't take it back. She'd signed it. She had to go through with it.

She forced a smile on her face. "No, I'm fine."

Mason stopped her. "If tonight brought on bad memories, I would rather talk about it. I can't stand the thought of you being alone in that place."

Because he was so kind. Her heart skipped a beat as she thought of how beautiful he was. Perhaps she should talk to Nat and figure out how to keep subs off her Doms. She could find a way around that clause, surely. Nat could put out the rumor that they both had some form of horrible disease. That could work.

She turned her face up to Mason's and thought about what Cole had said as he'd kissed her goodnight. "I had a lovely time this evening, Master. I wish it hadn't ended. I know the Master said he would be in late and doesn't want to disturb us, but I don't want to sleep in my room tonight." Cole had promised they would all move into the big bedroom in the morning, but it wasn't soon enough for her. "Please can't we sneak into Cole's bed and be waiting for him? I want us to sleep together."

He searched her face and seemed happy with what he found there. "All right. He might punish us though. I doubt it and, anyway, punishment can be fun. Now let's pick up some tacos and we'll turn on the TV and cuddle and eat and drink wine. How does that sound?"

It sounded beyond perfect. She didn't have to think about tomorrow. She shoved her worries aside. They were for another day. Tonight was for reveling in her Masters' affection. Her whole body ached in a good way. She didn't usually drink wine. She feared it a bit because Hawk would drug her, but Mason would show her the pleasures of it.

Her Masters were rapidly showing her that life could be lovely.

And scary because they wanted more than she had previously thought she could give, but tonight she'd moved past that. She'd given them pleasure and taken her own. She was Kitten, and Kitten was rapidly figuring out what she wanted out of life.

If her Master wanted her to throw a party, then she would, and it would be good. She could try because he wouldn't make fun of her. He would give her room and the tools she needed.

Like he'd given her Mason. She slipped her hand into his as they walked down the aisle of the parking garage and felt him squeeze her hand reassuringly.

"I'm crazy about you, gorgeous girl. I think meeting you is the best thing to happen to me in a long time." He took a deep breath, as though banishing some unnamed emotion. "Now where did we park? I wasn't paying attention. I was watching you walk. Your ass is fucking delicious in that dress."

She laughed, her heart light. "Click the beeper thing, silly."

She turned and her laughter died.

Standing there in the middle of the aisle was a man in a black jacket, the hood pulled over his face. Silent as the grave, he raised his hand and Kitten caught sight of the gun aimed right at her head.

Chapter Thirteen

Mason saw the gun right before it went off. The person holding it was at the opposite end of the parking garage, but there was no way to miss the glint of metal or the way his hand rose with perfect intent. He was dressed in all black, the grim reaper in a hoodie. Mason's heart had a mere second to tick up before he was forced to react. He planted his feet and shoved Kitten out of the way, toward the row of cars on the left side. Cole's Navigator was there and it was big enough to give them some form of cover. He only needed a few minutes to figure out how to get Kitten out of here.

The gun barely made a sound. He almost thought he'd overreacted but then he felt a pain in his right shoulder, a burning sensation as the bullet clipped him. He dove for cover. The motherfucker had to be using a silencer. Mason hit the hard ground and heard the sound of boots slapping against the concrete. Damn it. He couldn't catch a fucking break.

He'd driven Kitten back toward where they'd come from. They were still close to the elevator. If he could distract the shooter, she might be able to get away. Of course, he would have to distract the shooter by dying, but he wasn't sure there was another way out.

His brain raced. If the man was using a silencer, he was serious. He very likely wasn't some thug who snuck in and was trying to jack a car. Those boots weren't running away. They were getting closer. *Fuck.* Someone was after him and he couldn't allow Kitten to get caught in the crossfire.

The shooter had been standing maybe a hundred feet away. He would be on them very quickly.

"Move," he ordered in a harsh whisper. "Put yourself between the front of the car and the wall. You can fit. Work your way around it. When he finds me, you run as fast as you can. Get to the elevator. Call the police and Cole. Do you understand?"

He had to hope the shooter would be satisfied with killing him. If Kitten was quiet, she might have a chance to get away.

Kitten was reaching for her bag. She dumped it on the ground and pulled out what looked like an air horn.

"What are you doing?" Mason demanded. "I told you to hide and run."

"I don't think that will work. I'm sorry, Master. This is going to be loud." She depressed the button and, sure enough, the loudest damn sound he'd heard in forever blasted through the air. It wasn't more than a second or two before the car alarms up and down the aisle began blaring, the vibrations from the air horn setting off the more sensitive ones.

"Pepper spray or stun gun?" Kitten asked loudly, her voice rising over the cacophony.

"I told you to run." Why the hell wasn't she obeying him?

"You can spank me later, Master," she said before blowing her air horn again.

He grabbed the pepper spray. It was a lovely pink container and it looked like Kitten had bedazzled the damn thing. He flicked the safety off. His woman was a walking arsenal, even if most of her weapons had tiny rhinestones glued on them. "Call the police and run when you can. I mean it."

Mason got to his knees, his arm aching but usable. He picked up the stun gun with his other hand. He hoped the pepper spray worked since he'd have to get really damn close to use the stun gun. He placed his back to the Navigator. Damn it. He couldn't see the guy coming.

Except suddenly he could because Kitten had a mirror and she was on the ground beside him, using it to try to get a line of sight.

The car alarms were really fucking annoying. There had to be three of them going off, including Cole's. He could feel the vehicle vibrating against his back. It was loud enough that security should be on their way.

"I told you to go." He got the pepper spray ready because he could see the shooter through Kitten's little mirror. He was walking carefully up the aisle of cars, his gun at the ready. Sure enough there was a silencer on the muzzle. He moved with the efficiency of a professional.

Kitten held the mirror steady as she looked up at him. "I can take the spanking. I can't leave you."

And he couldn't fail her. It suddenly wasn't a case of using his body to buy her more time. She was forcing him to fight because if he didn't win, she was dead. Two more seconds. He had to be patient. If he moved too quickly, the guy would be too far away for the pepper spray to be effective. Mason forced himself to breathe. Perhaps she would be smart enough to run when he actually confronted the bad guy. He had to hope the asshole would be happy killing him and let Kitten go, but the way some of his former clients behaved, he doubted it. He swore to himself if he got out of this, he would figure out who was coming after him and he would make them pay. Criminal law sucked. No one had tried to kill him when he'd been writing contracts for corporations.

Almost there. Mason stood and turned and sprayed the pepper spray.

"Shit!" The figure in black took a step back as Mason sprayed the chemical in a back and forth motion.

A direct hit.

The shooter staggered back, cursing again. His gun went off, striking a car to Mason's right. "This shit ain't worth it."

He turned and started to run, a hand against his face.

Mason started to jog toward the fleeing shooter. He'd gotten nothing but relative height and build and the fact that the guy was a white dude.

"Master, he still has a gun. Please. Please stay with me," Kitten called out.

As if to prove her point, a third shot pinged through the air. The shooter was firing blindly and there was no way to know what he would do. If he kept shooting, he could get lucky and hit Mason. Or at this point, Mason wasn't even sure Kitten would stay down. She might jog after him and try to offer him aid in the form of lipstick that turned into a jewel-encrusted knife.

He needed to get them out of here. He reached down to help Kitten up. "Let's go back to Cole's office."

God, he was going to have to talk to the police again. His hands shook as he started to pull her toward the safety of the elevators.

"What the hell is going on in here?" a new voice asked.

Mason turned and saw the security guard running from the elevators. He had his gun out, his eyes widening at the scene in front of him. He looked all of twenty, but in that moment Mason would take him. He would take anyone with a gun.

Kitten stepped up, seemingly unfazed. She practically had to shout to be heard over the car alarms. "Someone attempted to shoot my Ma...Mason. My boyfriend. Someone shot at him and I need you to call Detective Darin Craig with the Dallas Police Department. He'll be handling this case for the police."

The security guard stopped and stared at Mason, who realized he was still holding a pink can of pepper spray. "He will?"

Kitten collected her diamond-coated armory, gracefully putting it all in her sunny yellow bag. "He will."

"I'm confused," the guard admitted. "And why are the car alarms going off?"

"Mason? Kitten?" Cole yelled over the never-ending car alarms. He ran out of the elevator, his face tight.

"We're over here, Mas...Cole." She grinned at the security guard. "He's my other boyfriend. He didn't get shot at, but he will be very distressed about the incident. You should understand that the yelling he's about to do is more about his emotional state than your competence. I'm sure you're doing an excellent job."

The noise level went down by at least twenty percent as Cole clicked the button on his key fob and his SUV stopped screaming. Mason was pretty sure he should be running after the shooter, but his arm ached something fierce.

Kitten threw her arms around Cole and held him tight. "It was very frightening. I'm so glad you're here."

Cole was all over her. He gave her a squeeze before setting her on her feet and inspecting her from head to toe. His hands found her shoulders, his eyes looking her over for damage. "What the hell was that text? What did you mean? You damn near gave me a heart attack. Why are the alarms going off? What scared you?"

Mason walked up to the security guard. The poor guard was about to be in serious trouble. Kitten wasn't wrong about that. He leaned in. "We were shot at. Guy in all black. I hit him with pepper spray. You should check and see if he's passed out somewhere and then I would make sure all the cameras were working. That man is Cole Roberts. He owns the building and he's about to be up your ass, if you know what I mean."

"Shit. I'm going to get fired." The young man was immediately on his walkie-talkie, running the way Mason had told him the shooter had gone.

"You can't send me a text like that," Cole was insisting.

"You managed to send Cole a text?" When the hell had she done that? When had scared little Kitten turned into a superhero?

"Oh, yes. I'm very good at texting with one hand," Kitten admitted. "I texted our Master when you pushed me behind the car. I had my phone out because I texted Nat that I finally lost my consensual virginity. I wanted her to know first. I was planning texts to Haven and Tara and Marcy as well." She frowned suddenly. "That was not gossiping, Master. That was informing my very close friends of a miraculous life event. These things are more meaningful when they're shared with loved ones."

"We'll talk about that later." Cole frowned fiercely and held out his phone to Mason. "I got this two minutes ago. What the hell is going on?"

Mason looked at the screen of Cole's phone. *Death. Parking garage.* And then a kissy face emoticon. He had to shake his head. She was cool in a crisis. He would give her that. "We had an incident, that's all. It looks like Darin was right. Someone isn't happy with me. We're fine now."

Except they weren't fine and they wouldn't be until they figured out who was trying to kill him. His arm might ache, but his stomach was in knots because he couldn't stay with her. He was the reason she was in danger. Cole had every right to send him away. The idea of not seeing her again made him sick. Hell, the idea of not being near Cole made him ill, and he was too close to being shot at to fool himself that it was all about losing his chance at revenge. He could tell himself that later when his heart wasn't racing.

"Is that blood on your sleeve?" Cole reached for him.

Mason winced slightly. "It's nothing."

Kitten shook her head. "Master Mason was shot. He shoved me out of the way and then he was shot. That was going to be my next text, but I had to help him disable our attacker first. I used my mirror to track the man and then Master Mason cleverly sprayed pepper spray right in his eyes. He was so good at it. It was very heroic."

"I told her to run." Damn, Cole was going to kill him. "I tried to get her out of harm's way, but everything happened so fast. One minute we were talking about takeout and the next some asswipe was shooting at us, and I told her to hide but she was thrusting rhinestone-studded weaponry my way. Have you seen what she has in her bag?"

"Oh, yes. It's quite a collection. She used to have a rape whistle but she played with that too much," Cole admitted. "It was obnoxious. I replaced it with the air horn."

Now that his adrenaline was flagging, he was starting to get mad. "She directly disobeyed an order given for her health and safety. You'll have to punish her for that."

Kitten nodded. "You should, Master. I was a bad girl. I should at least get a thorough spanking."

Cole closed his eyes for a moment and took a long breath before turning to her. "Why didn't you obey Mason?"

Her smile dimmed. "Because if I had hidden, he would have died."

"That wasn't your choice to make," Mason insisted. She was his responsibility.

She turned to him. "You can't have it both ways. You say I'm not an extension of anyone, that I have to make choices. If that's true then I have to live with those choices and I will always choose to help instead of hide when it makes sense. I used to be scared of everything. I was so scared when Shelley was kidnapped I could barely talk. But then Master Chase forced me to take self-defense classes and I learned how to deal with my fear by being prepared. I've been in worse situations and I know things you can't possibly know. I know that cowardice is far worse than dying. There is a time to hide and a time to fight. This wasn't a time for me to hide. We were stronger together than we were apart."

Cole pulled her into his arms. "I'm proud of you, pet. You did wonderfully. I'm certainly not going to spank you for being brave, but I might give you a celebratory flogging."

"Thank you, Master." She squeezed him right back. Mason was fairly certain corporal punishment didn't work on Kitten.

"Cole, this is serious." She could have been killed. God, he would likely never get the image out of his head. He could have gotten her killed.

Cole's eyes came up, meeting his with a steady stare. "I know. I'm well aware of how serious the situation was. I can see the blood on your arm."

"Like I said before, Mason shoved me out of the way. I think I would have gotten hit without Mason's action." Kitten had her head turned up toward Cole. "I believe he deserves a celebratory flogging as well, Master."

"He certainly deserves something nice," Cole agreed, but then he would agree with Kitten now. Mason wasn't so sure he would still agree later. No matter how it had turned out, the truth was Mason had placed her in danger and that was unacceptable in his mind.

The security guard came jogging back up. "I think the intruder's gone."

Cole stepped away from Kitten and his eyes narrowed. Mason sighed. Yep, Cole was about to blow. "You think? You think he's gone? I'm not sure you think at all, young man. What's your name and who the hell is your supervisor because this is a goddamn secured parking garage so I would like to know how the fuck some punk with a weapon managed to get by the gates, guards, and security cameras I spend a god-awful amount of money on. Those security cameras are supposed to be monitored. Are you going to tell me this guy didn't show up on them? Did he magically appear in the middle of the parking garage? Have we been taken over by ninja warriors?"

"I don't think he was a ninja," Kitten said with a shake of her head. "He was wearing a hoodie. Ninjas tend to dress better."

"You're going to have my job for this, aren't you?" The young man had gone a little green.

Cole's body seemed to swell and he loomed over the kid. "Your job? I'm going to have your fucking soul."

"Remember what I said about the distress," Kitten said, giving the young man an encouraging smile. "Don't let it harm your self-worth. It's only his worry talking."

"My worry is going to eat him alive," Cole shot back between clenched teeth.

The elevator doors opened and Lea Schneider walked off with three other executive assistants and Bob Hays, one of his board members. Bob's eyes widened as he took in the scene, but Lea frowned.

"Why are the car alarms going off? What the hell is happening?" She looked Mason's way as if she knew exactly who she blamed. "You can hear it from five floors up."

Bob held up his key fob and another alarm went silent. "I got a security notice and I thought I'd come down to see what was happening. Good god, did we have some kind of break-in?"

"What we had was a complete breakdown in security," Cole explained.

Lea frowned. "Our security has always been excellent."

Bob's eyes were fixed on Mason's shoulder. "Do I need to call an ambulance?"

"Yes," Cole said.

"No," Mason said at the same time. The last thing he needed was another hospital bill. He already owed far too much. He knew Cole had paid the bill, but he was going to pay him back.

Cole turned and it wasn't his friend or lover looking at him now. It was his Dom. Mason's eyes slid away.

"Make the call," Cole commanded. "Mason's been shot. Some asshole broke in and attacked him. He almost hurt Kitten as well. I want the police here five minutes ago."

Mason didn't argue with that.

"I already called both the police and an ambulance," the security guard said. "Please don't take my soul."

He should have kept quiet because Cole seemed to remember that he had a target he could scream at and he started in on the young man again. Bob stood by Cole, staring down the poor dude.

Lea crossed her arms as she approached Mason. "Is this some kind of stunt to get Cole's attention? He has to work late, but you always did like to make it hard for him."

God, why did Cole surround himself with vicious bitches? "This isn't any of your business."

"Oh, I think it is." Her eyes narrowed in obvious distaste. "It's everyone in the company's business because you always distract him. You know he used to be the smartest man in the game. He was ruthless and he knew when to go for the kill. He could have made this company the biggest in the country. He was well on his way again, but then you showed up. He always picks the wrong partners. He picks people who drag him down."

By dragging him down, he was sure Lea meant Cole picked people who loved him and forced him to relax from time to time. "I don't care what you think."

"You don't care what anyone thinks, Mason. You never did. You also never cared about who you hurt. You want things your way, and you'll do anything to get what you want," Lea shot back. She looked toward Kitten. "Are we sure whoever this person was, he was after you? I seem to remember the last time Cole got close to a woman, she was mysteriously killed, too."

She turned and walked away.

Kitten walked up to him and slipped her hand into his and gave him a reassuring squeeze.

He would be dead without her quick thinking and preparation. He owed her everything.

He owed it to her to walk away.

Chapter Fourteen

Cole sat in the study, slowly letting the Scotch begin to work its way through his system. Hours after the police had finished up the interviews and the ER doctors had sworn Mason didn't even need stitches, Cole's hands were still shaking.

He'd almost lost Mason. Again. If Mason hadn't reacted so quickly, he likely would have lost them both. They would have been dead in the parking garage, their bodies left there like so much refuse.

He closed his eyes for a moment as he let that settle in. He'd been a stubborn fool. He'd cost them years they could have spent together, and he had to wonder why.

After a few weeks, the first year after the accident had been almost easy. He'd gone cold, arctic even. He'd thrown himself into his work. He'd felt driven, a bit like the first years after his father had died. He and Mason had both been starting their careers. They'd worked long hours and stolen whatever moments they had together as Cole rebuilt his father's company and Mason built his career. They'd played at The Club and cuddled every night.

Cole hadn't done anything but work in the first year after they'd broken up. He'd ruthlessly taken down his competitors and made more in that first post-Mason year than his board members could have imagined. He'd even stayed away from the lodge for a while.

His bank account and that of his investors and board had grown substantially. He'd been praised as a true captain of industry.

And then he'd slowly realized how empty he was.

He wasn't a man who lied to himself. It did no good. He was a man who often didn't understand his own emotions. He struggled with them. It was easier to ignore them than it was to analyze them, but he couldn't do that anymore.

So much came back to that one night—when Emily died. How had he really felt that night? When Emily died he'd felt horribly guilty because of the relief that it had been her and not Mason. But deeper, way down in his gut, he'd been terrified.

He had to wonder now if losing his parents in such a short period of time hadn't affected the way he'd handled Emily's death. The truth was he'd known he couldn't handle another loss.

He couldn't handle losing Mason and it was easier to push him away than to hold him close. It had been far more comfortable to sink into work and tell himself that it had been about honor and trust when it was all about… Fuck, it had been about cowardice.

He'd taken Kitten in because he'd been so sure he could teach her, train her, and the little thing had already taught him more about life and how to really live it than he could have imagined.

Master, I've been in worse situations and I know things you can't possibly know. I know that cowardice is far worse than dying.

She'd stayed at Mason's side, risked herself. Hell, she couldn't know that the man stalking them wouldn't take her again, wouldn't put her through hell again. What she had known was who she wanted to be. Brave. Strong. Kind.

Kitten might struggle to figure out her own wants, but she knew who she was at the core of her being.

It didn't matter if someone wrote a nasty letter and got Mason blackballed. At the end of the day, Cole himself had been the one to ruin things.

The trouble was he didn't know how to make things better between them.

There was a sound from the hallway that caught his attention. Just a little creak, but it was enough to let him know he wasn't alone. He'd left Mason and Kitten in his bed, both seeming to fall asleep easily, but he hadn't bought it.

Cole opened his eyes because there was a reason he'd been sitting in his study in the dark. One that didn't have to do with insomnia and a need for Scotch. He wasn't stupid. He'd watched Mason carefully during the police interview and while the doctors had examined him. He'd been helpful, forthcoming, giving the police everything they could need. Darin had even remarked that Mason seemed remarkably unfazed for what had happened.

Mason wasn't unfazed. Mason was plotting, planning. Mason had come to some proper conclusions, but Cole had been almost certain that Mason found a solution that was utterly unacceptable.

He remained still with the light off, waiting to see if he was right. He almost hoped he wasn't. There was a little piece inside him that wanted to see Kitten walk by on the way to the kitchen.

A much larger figure than Kitten's walked slowly by the open French doors. Mason had a bag in his hand and he was obviously trying to be as quiet as he could.

Cole reached up and turned on the light. "How are you planning on getting around the alarm?"

Mason stopped and Cole watched his shoulders slump slightly before he took a deep breath and then turned. His face was smooth, placid. It was a pretty mask, but Cole knew what Mason looked like when he was trying to play it cool.

Yes, there had been a piece of him that hoped to avoid the confrontation, but he was suddenly happy to have this chance. They'd been treading warily, each move they made carefully thought out. With the singular exception of the earlier blow job, they'd concentrated every moment of their time on Kitten.

It was easier than dealing with their own issues, but he was done with easy. It was time to step up and take charge. He'd been a prick, but Mason still needed him. Mason had never stopped needing him. He'd failed Mason once. He certainly wasn't going to do it again.

"I know the passcodes you use," Mason said with a casual air. "Are you going to tell me you actually changed them?"

He tended to forget codes. The codes only got changed when

Mason changed them, and even then Cole tended to have to carry them in his pocket for months before they finally got ingrained in his brain. "No."

Mason huffed, an arrogant sound. "I'm surprised. I would have thought you would have changed the locks to keep the riffraff out."

Ah, so that was how he was going to play it? Mason tended to go one of two ways when he was caught doing something he shouldn't. He either played the seductive sub or the righteously arrogant brat. It looked as though Cole would be getting the brat this evening. His cock twitched in his slacks. He kind of liked Mason's brat. He definitely liked showing Mason's brat who the boss was.

"We need to clear a few things up. Why don't you take a seat?" If they could get through this civilly, he would give it a shot.

"Why don't you shove that seat up your ass, Cole?"

Ah, yes, the brat. Mason was scared and believed he needed to make a sacrifice he didn't want to make, and now he would lash out until Cole placed some much-needed boundaries. Cole set his glass down. No more alcohol for him. He would move on to his drug of choice. Dominance. "You're not going anywhere."

Mason laughed but it was a bitter sound. "You know you can't keep me here. We like to play at Masters and slaves, but in the real world, I can tell you to fuck yourself and walk away. Even if I'd signed a contract with you already, it wouldn't hold me. You should know better than anyone that a contract isn't worth the paper it's written on."

He wasn't about to argue contracts with Mason. Not when they had so much else to argue about. "I didn't blackball you."

"So you say." Mason shrugged as if to tell him to try again.

He wasn't going to stop trying this time. "I've never lied to you."

"Oh, I disagree." Mason's voice took on the same smooth, intelligent tones he used in the courtroom. "Let me see. 'I'll love you forever, Mason.' That was a lie. 'I'll always be here for you.' Another lie. I could go on, but I would be dredging up a history that doesn't matter anymore. You're quite a good liar. Practically a professional, but I see through you now. If you honestly think I'll buy into anything you say at this point, you're a fucking idiot."

Only Mason could push his every button. He felt his blood pressure start to rise. "Stop cursing at me or we're going to have trouble."

Mason dropped his bag and stalked into the room. "We already have trouble."

Tension sizzled along Cole's skin, making his heart start to pound. If Mason wanted a throw down, oh, he could give him one. "Do we?"

Mason got into his space, every plane and angle of his body rigid. "We do. We have so much trouble, but I'm going to make it all better by walking away. Look, I came here to see if there was anything I could do to fuck you up. I was going to walk in here and have a very tasty revenge on you. I thought I could make your life miserable. I can see, though, that you're doing fine on your own."

Cole managed to not chuckle. The last thing he needed to do was irritate the beast in Mason. Part of the job of being Mason's Dom was calming him down from time to time. He tended to enjoy drama and played some of them to the hilt. And in this case, he was right. "Oddly, I don't think you caused that accident knowing Kitten would come and get you. You're a planner, but you're not that good. You are right about one thing. I've been utterly miserable without you."

Mason stopped as though trying to figure out if he was being sarcastic.

Cole wasn't going to let him even think that. "I missed you every day, and I only have myself to blame. I was wrong, love. I was a rat bastard who got caught in a storm and didn't know how to find my way back out. When I should have held on to you, I shoved you away and you paid the price. I've lived a hollow life since I did it and if I could take anything back, it was that moment I turned away from you. I sincerely hope that you're going to be smarter and have more grace than I did."

Stormy eyes narrowed. "What the fuck game are you playing?"

"It's not a game. I need you." He took a deep breath because he was ready to say it. "I need Kitten. I made a mistake with Emily. I never should have brought her into our relationship, but you know Kitten is right for us. I want the three of us together in all ways."

"You honestly think I would come back to you after everything you did?"

His whole life depended on it. "I think you can't stay away. I think you need what I can give you. I think you've been as lost as I have."

"You can give me absolutely nothing. I want nothing from you."

Cole put a hand around Mason's neck and drew him in. His lips might lie, but the truth was right there in the press of his cock against Cole's. Their cocks were hard against each other, both rubbing and pulsing. "I think you do."

"I can get that anywhere," he spat back. "Any dick will do."

"Then you won't mind taking mine." If he could get Mason in bed, everything would be all right. Mason was a softie at heart. Intimacy was what they needed.

Mason pushed away. "I think I'll pass. Been there, done that and all."

Oh, his boy was trying his patience. "Mason, you're not leaving this house."

Maybe never again. If Chase couldn't figure out who was trying to kill him, Cole might build a nice medieval wall and moat around the place and Mason and Kitten could be permanent residents.

"Try to stop me."

It was time to try logic. "Where the hell do you think you'll go?"

Mason threw up his hands in disgust. "I don't know. I could have gone home, but you made sure I don't have one. I could have gone back to my job, but…oh, yeah, I don't have one of those either."

"Poor Mason. I'm always the bad guy. I will admit I made a mistake, but I'm not making the same one again. I got you out of that hellhole. I'm not about to let you slide back in. You will stay here where you're safe."

Mason squared off against him. "Are you not listening to me? I don't want you. I don't want any of this. I thought I wanted revenge, but I'm so disgusted by you that I don't even want that from you anymore. If you try to keep me here, I'll call the police. If you try to touch me again, it will be against my will. I don't want you as my Master. I don't want you as my lover. I don't want you in my life. I hate you."

"Do you hate me, too?" a soft voice asked.

Kitten stood in the doorway, her eyes wide as she looked on.

Shit. Cole knew exactly what Mason was doing. He'd lived with him for a long time, loved him almost his whole adult life. Mason was being a self-sacrificing idiot and he would do or say anything he thought he had to in order to get the job done. He would spew vile shit until Cole made him stop. But Kitten wouldn't know that and she'd just slept with Mason. She'd had her first real experience with intimacy, and now that man who had given it to her was walking away.

Mason turned a chalky white at the sound of her voice. "Kitten, this doesn't concern you."

"I think it does." She walked into the office, her bare feet moving across the floor. She was in a white sheath gown, her slender form outlined against the fabric. Her hair was down and she looked young and tender and vulnerable. "If you leave Master Cole, you leave me, too."

"It's not about you though," Mason insisted. "It's about him."

"You hate him more than you could ever care for me. Is that what you're saying?" She asked the question in a quiet voice, her tone shaking slightly as though she was trying to contain her emotions.

"No." Mason wouldn't look at her.

"He does care about you," Cole said.

"I can tell her that myself," Mason shot back.

"But you're going to leave me." Kitten stood in front of Mason.

Mason's head shook. "I didn't come here to stay. You knew that."

"You promised to sign a contract with Master Cole," she pointed out.

Mason shrugged. "And I'm breaking that promise. It's for the best."

She turned and her breath hitched. Cole could see her face, but Mason couldn't. Her shoulders slumped forward. And she winked at him before saying, "You had me once and now you don't want me."

Little brat. Oh, she was in for such punishment. Or reward, because her manipulation seemed to be working in a way his reason hadn't. It all sort of looked the same to Kitten. Her real punishment would be withholding affection and attention, and he found he couldn't do that to her. Their relationship had taken a turn he hadn't expected. He couldn't deal with her the way he had other subs. If he'd asked himself if he wanted this type of relationship, he would have said no, but then he hadn't met her yet. She was changing his mind about a lot of things.

Mason moved in behind her. His hands went to her shoulders. "Of course I want you, but you can't go with me."

"I want you to stay," Kitten said. "I don't think you truly hate the Master. I think he hurt you and he wants to make up for his foolish mistake. Even Doms make mistakes. Many. We have to forgive them. They forgive us."

Yes, the minx was already asking forgiveness for this stunt, and he softened his expression to let her know it was freely given. Kitten would never be the woman to throw up a challenge. She would quietly and with as much kindness as she could find, try to convince her lovers that she was right. It was her nature. It had probably been her nature before her capture, too. Cole blasted through things. Mason blustered through. And Kitten gently turned the tide until her lovers believed it was their idea in the first place.

He was starting to think that Kitten didn't need more than a steady hand to force her into the world. The core of who she was hadn't really been touched by the evil that had taken her.

Kitten would never have turned Mason away that night. She would have reached out to him. She would have been brave.

Mason wrapped his arms around her shoulders and dragged her back against him. "I don't want to leave you behind. I don't want to leave you at all, but…"

"Then why can't you stay?" Such a clever girl. She was going to make him say it, to bring it all out in the open.

"Because someone will hurt you if I stay here." There it was—the root of the problem. Oh, Cole believed that Mason meant what he'd said. He very likely had plotted and planned a revenge he wouldn't have had the heart to go through with.

"And someone will hurt you if you leave." Cole stepped up, unwilling to stand apart any longer. It was funny. So often the women they brought in had served multiple purposes, including his own voyeur kink. He liked watching Mason with their women, but he'd always held himself apart in those moments, watching as one would watch a work of art. He hadn't been able to do that while watching Mason and Kitten. He'd had to move in, to be a part of them. He'd felt an ache at the thought of being on the outside.

"It's not your call, Cole," Mason said quietly.

They were close to a breakthrough. "It is. I'm the head of this family. I'm willing to loosen up. I'm willing to relax my rules because I want the two of you to be happy and I want you to feel secure, but this is not negotiable. You're in danger. You're not going to leave without a bodyguard."

Mason stepped back. "You have got to be kidding me."

Kitten gave Cole a quick hug as she got on her tiptoes and whispered in his ear. "He's afraid he'll hurt us, Master. Please don't let him leave."

"It's going to be okay. He isn't going anywhere." He kissed her forehead. "But now you have to let this be between me and Mason. You understand?"

She nodded and took a seat on the sofa. "May I have a drink of the Scotch, Master? I'm going to be sad watching you fight."

Mason pointed a finger her way. "You are not going to manipulate me into staying."

Kitten's eyes went wide. She had the innocent look down. "I would not do that, Master Mason. But I would be heartbroken if you left. I can't imagine not being able to see you, to not know if you are safe." She sniffled.

"You can finish my drink. Sip it slowly." He might need another bottle after having to deal with his subs. "Mason, do you want to sit and talk?"

He was right back in Cole's face. "You can't keep me here."

Cole turned to Kitten. "Pet, this might get dirty. I might be forced to show your other Master that he is not the top here. If you're going to cry, you should do it in your room. You can go and wait for us in your bedroom or mine. We'll join you shortly."

"Yes, you should probably go, sweetheart." Mason was practically snarling. "You don't want to see this."

Her eyes went between them as she held the tumbler of Scotch in her hand. "I would rather stay and watch."

"Go to your room, Kitten," Mason commanded.

"No, I'm her Dom. If you're walking out, then you get no say in what she does." He thought her presence might keep them civil. Might. "She can stay if she wants to."

"I would like to because I think it could be beautiful." She took a whiff of the Scotch and frowned. "This smells horrible."

"Have you ever had a drink before?" Scotch was probably not the way to go.

Mason moved between them. "It's not going to be beautiful, Kitten. It's going to get ugly."

She stared up, her eyes on Mason though she answered Cole's question. "I haven't had a drink that wasn't drugged and meant to make me pass out, but then until today I hadn't made love. That was what we did, Mason. We made love. I thought it would be sex, but it was so much more than that. Of course, if you walk away then I will likely come to the conclusion that it was merely sex to you, and then it will be less beautiful. Do you think the Scotch will help me get past the pain of knowing you simply used my body and didn't touch my soul?"

Mason's jaw dropped open. "Are you going to let her get away with that shit?"

It was kind of fun to be on the other side. So often it was Mason and their woman against him. It was good to watch Mason have to deal with being the one on the receiving end. "She's only telling you how she feels."

Kitten nodded. "I'm supposed to talk about my feelings. Leo says if I don't talk about them they get stuck inside and one day I'll be on the news and everybody will shake their heads and say, 'But she seemed so quiet and nice.' He doesn't say that in front of me, though. I had to eavesdrop to hear that. What do you think I'll be on the news for?"

Very likely Leo had thought she would end up losing her shit on someone, but Cole was certain that would never happen because Kitten was stronger. "I think it will be for something lovely."

"What the hell is wrong with the two of you?" Mason growled the question. "Do either one of you care about what happened tonight?"

"I care. I care quite a bit, and that's why I'm not allowing you to walk away," Cole replied.

Mason pointed toward the door to the office. "Then send her to her room. This could get nasty and I don't want her to see it."

Kitten sat up straight. "How much nastier could it get? You've already said you hate Cole more than you love me and you would rather leave than stay. I thought we were falling for each other, but it seems like you were using me to pass the time."

"It wasn't like that," Mason began.

He didn't seem able to see past Kitten's manipulations. "Mason, she's playing you."

"Maybe you're the one who's playing me, and I'm done with this game. There's nothing you can do. There's no way for you to stop me from walking out that door." He turned and started out again.

"Master," Kitten began, a worried look furrowing her brow.

He held a hand up to let her know all would be right. He'd had hours to figure out what to do. "Mason, if you step one foot out that door, you will be arrested."

He stopped and turned. "For what?"

"I don't know yet," Cole admitted. "I'll come up with something good. Corporate espionage. Maybe real espionage. That could get you in a federal prison. I would feel safer if you were behind bars."

"That is smart thinking, Master. Although you could get him for theft," Kitten mused.

"Don't even say it." He groaned because he was almost certain of what she would say next.

"He stole my heart," Kitten said.

"We have to work on that, pet. Sometimes you can be a bit syrupy." He'd calmed considerably and he suddenly realized that it was Kitten's doing. He'd been alone in dealing with Mason, but the minute Kitten came in, he'd had an ally, and an amazingly devious one at that. It was nice. He would never in a million years have allowed another of his and Mason's subs to witness a fight. He would have sent them away, but Kitten belonged with them.

Even when she was being clichéd.

"You wouldn't dare," Mason said, his jaw tightening up nicely.

Oh, but he would, and he would have an ally. "Try me. I can have Chase Dawson dummy up evidence on you in a heartbeat. He enjoys that sort of work so much he won't even charge me. Once you're in jail, I'll make it plain that you're in danger from all other inmates and you'll be placed in solitary confinement."

Kitten's nose wrinkled as she took another whiff of the Scotch. "Master, I don't think orange would go well with Master Mason's skin tone. Perhaps he should stay here."

"You better hope that I end up out of this house because I swear that I will punish you. He might top me, but I top you, and I will take this out on your ass." Mason was practically vibrating with rage. "I am a kind Master, but I won't let you manipulate me like this."

Kitten smiled. "I'm not doing anything. Master Cole is handling everything beautifully." She took a drink of the Scotch. And promptly coughed it back up. "Oh, that is horrible. Why would you drink that?"

He took the glass out of her hand. It was an eighteen-year-old single malt. It wasn't for virgins. "I'll be sure to note your preferences." He would buy some fruity wine and the makings of piña coladas to introduce her to the pleasures of an after-dinner drink. "Mason, I mean to do everything I said. I will ruthlessly use every asset I have to make sure you don't walk around with a target on your back. I have to ensure that you're alive tomorrow and the next day and the next, so don't doubt my will in this."

There was a long moment and Cole was almost sure Mason was going to run, but he finally clenched his fists at his sides. "Damn it, Cole. Can't you see I'm doing this to save her?"

"You don't have to save her." Cole stepped in. It was time for some physical comfort. He reached out and Mason didn't swat him away. "You just have to play this safe. Do you think I would risk her? I won't risk either one of you."

His eyes came up. "She's different. We can't play this the same way we did before."

"I'm not." His heart clenched, a weird feeling that made him the slightest bit anxious, but he was done with being scared. "This is about you and her. You two are my responsibility. I'm not putting you above her. Mason, if it came down to a decision between you and Kitten…"

"You would choose her," Mason said firmly.

"And so would you," Cole returned with gravity. It was a covenant between them. This was why Kitten was the one. She was the only woman they would put first. Her life, her needs, her pleasure—they came first before anything else. They would work for her happiness, and she would bless them with her joy, her unique feminine soul.

Mason's voice was tight, every muscle rigid. "I really do want revenge."

Of course he did. Cole moved in. They didn't need space. "I know, love. I know you do. I'm asking you to be better than me. I'm begging you to forego it."

"I don't know that I can."

At least he was being honest now. "Can you let it go tonight?"

Mason sniffed and then laughed. "Apparently I don't have a choice unless I want to know what solitary confinement feels like. Damn it. That man almost killed her tonight. I almost got her killed."

He was missing the point. "You saved her."

"I don't know that he was after Master Mason," Kitten said. "I think he was aiming at me."

She'd told the police that, but Cole wasn't sure. Mason certainly had made his position clear. He believed this was all about him, and it made sense. Kitten had lived in The Club. She had no friends outside of it. There was no reason to hurt her.

Unless someone wanted to hurt him, and then it would be perfect.

No. The simplest explanation was the best. Someone had tried to kill Mason. He had unsavory connections that Kitten didn't have.

The only thing that connected Kitten and Mason was Cole.

He pulled Mason close, ignoring how stiff he remained. "I won't let you put yourself in danger. I won't let anything take the two of you from me. Not even my own idiocy."

"Nothing you do is going to make me love you again."

Mason's words made him ache, but he was done talking and let his hand draw Mason in. Cole pressed his lips to Mason's and felt as though he could breathe again. He hadn't realized it, but he'd been holding everything in for years. He wasn't whole without this man and they weren't complete without her. Kitten made everything possible. It was possible to let them both in.

He kissed Mason, slowly at first, almost afraid that Mason would shove him away and force the issue to a nasty conclusion. Mason stood still, so still. It was almost as if he were made from stone. Cole let his lips play along Mason's unmoving ones.

"See, I told you it would be beautiful," Kitten said quietly.

Cole turned and she was looking up at them with such longing. "I think we should move this to the dungeon, don't you?"

"Master Mason did attempt to sneak out. He should be punished or we'll all run wild," Kitten said sagely.

"Yes, I do believe a bit of discipline is in order. Mason, follow me, but know that this is your choice."

"You're giving me a choice now?" Mason asked with a huff.

"Yes, in everything except what would be a suicidal move, you have a choice," he said. "I want the three of us together. I want to start making love again, but you broke trust tonight."

Mason's gaze hardened again. "And you broke trust years ago."

"This can't work unless we forgive each other." It had been a long time since he'd felt so vulnerable.

Mason shook his head. "I didn't do anything that needs forgiveness."

He'd been thinking about that one question a whole lot lately. Cole's guilt might eat away at him, but he hadn't been totally alone in causing the problem. "Didn't you? Did you tell me everything? Did you sit down and talk to me about your problems with Emily? Did you trust me enough to tell me what you wanted? What you needed from me?"

Mason seemed to think about that for a moment. “No.”

“Then follow us to the dungeon and let’s start over.” Cole turned and held a hand out for Kitten. When they walked out the door, he prayed Mason would follow.

* * * *

Mason stopped and realized he had no idea what to do. He always had a plan. Always. They might not be good plans, but he always knew what he wanted.

Now he wasn’t sure.

What the hell kind of game was Cole playing? Start over? Did Cole honestly believe they could toss the past aside and…do what? Pretend it didn’t happen? Play like everything was the same?

It didn’t feel like the same. It felt wildly different. It felt weirdly right, and the reason for that had a name and a date with Mason’s crop. Kitten.

Yeah. That was why he was going to follow them. He was going to walk into that dungeon because he owed Kitten some serious discipline. Did she think he would allow her to manipulate him like that? He strode out of the office and down the hallway, leaving his backpack behind since it didn’t look like he would need it. Fucking Cole had everything planned out, of course. It had been foolish for him to think he had any say in what went on in his own life. He would have to stay until Cole decided to chuck him to the street again.

And forgiveness? Who was he kidding? There was no reason to ask for forgiveness. He was the one who had been wronged. Not the other way around.

He didn’t owe Cole a damn thing.

So what if he hadn’t really talked to him about Emily? So fucking what? Cole should have been able to see that she was a crazy bitch who constantly put down anyone she thought was beneath her, and that included everyone with the exception of Cole and any Master with money.

If Cole wanted to pretend like they could forgive and forget, more power to him. Mason stalked down the hall, watching them as they turned down the corridor that would take them to Cole's private dungeon. Maybe it would be even sweeter to ruin Cole's life knowing he was counting on Mason's soft heart to not allow him to go through with it.

He didn't have a heart anymore.

Who the fuck are you kidding? Can you hear yourself? Don't be an idiot. You're half in love with her already, and you never stopped loving him.

He shook his head as if he could shake the thoughts off. He didn't need his inner voice to be reasonable. He needed it to get in line with the current mode of thought, and that was all about revenge.

Or it could be all about getting your damn life back, but better this time because she's here. Damn. She's finally here and you and Cole can be complete. This could be it and you're thinking about throwing it all away because he hurt you?

Cole hadn't merely hurt him. Cole had destroyed him.

He also saved you when you needed it. Don't the two cancel out? Don't they make it possible to move on?

No.

He ruthlessly shut down the part of him that kept trying to open up. He didn't need that part of himself anymore. Cole hadn't taken the opportunity to save himself. He'd ruthlessly shoved that opportunity back in Mason's face so now he had a clear go signal.

He could take Cole's protection and care and use it all to gain the revenge he'd come here for.

Dumbass. No, you won't.

He pushed through the door and damn near lost his breath. Kitten had gotten out of her pajamas and every glorious inch of her skin was on display. She gave him the sweetest smile. How could she look so damn innocent naked and surrounded by every sex toy known to man?

Cole was shrugging off his dress shirt, his big, muscular chest being revealed with every movement.

Graceful femininity and the powerful alpha male who could top him without breathing hard. They both looked his way and his cock hardened to the point of being painful. Kitten gave him a wink, but the look in Cole's eyes was almost enough to make him come then and there.

Yeah, you're going to give up all that for the momentary pleasure of revenge over something you had a hand in since you wouldn't even tell him Emily was running wild because you thought he would question your rights to play the Dom. You thought it would mean he would see you as something less.

Fuck all. He was still doing it.

"Kitten's been lying to you. Ms. Hamilton has been cruel to her. Kitten's not eating at all during the day because Ms. Hamilton only feeds her oatmeal without sugar and salads with no dressing."

Kitten's jaw dropped. "I haven't lied."

"It's called lying by omission." If he was staying, he should play his part. This was what he didn't do with the other subs. He tried to be Cole when Cole wasn't around, but he was never going to measure up and Cole didn't expect him to. Cole did expect him to watch out for their woman and himself. Mason had done neither when it came to Emily.

Maybe he wasn't completely innocent after all.

"You told." Kitten's eyes were as wide as saucers. "You weren't supposed to tell. It will make Cole feel bad. Why would you do that?"

Cole's eyes narrowed as he turned to their sub. "He'll do it because it's his job. What the hell has been going on and why am I only hearing about it now?"

Kitten's eyes found the floor. "Master, she was only following your orders. Maybe you didn't know I don't like kale."

"What the fuck is kale?" Cole asked. "Kitten, I left no instructions except that you were to be given anything you wanted."

Ah, the communication breakdown. It caused chaos. "Ms. Hamilton hates her the same way she hates me. The only difference is she's scared of me and she kicks Kitten around because she won't stand up for herself. Kitten thinks she's not allowed to eat anything Ms. Hamilton doesn't put in front of her. She's gone hungry because that woman convinced her it was your will."

"She'll be gone in the morning," Cole said, his voice tight.

"What?" Mason was floored. Cole had kept the woman around because of his promise to his father. He'd put up with her gloom and doom for years. "You can't do that. You'll feel guilty."

"I'll feel worse knowing I did nothing. She'll be given a pension and plenty of time to find new lodging, but I won't have my subs abused in their home. You two will always come first," Cole explained. "You two are my primary responsibility. You can hire a new housekeeper. One who pleases both of you."

Somewhere in the back of his head, he'd always expected to lose that fight. Any fight, really. He was still the stupid teen who realized his parents love wasn't unconditional. Deep down he always expected Cole would drop him the minute he complained.

That fear hadn't made him a good partner.

Cole turned to Kitten. "None of this works if the two of you won't talk to me, damn it. How can I do my job if I don't know anything is wrong? I'm not particularly good at reading the signs. It's a flaw, but one I try to make up for by having open lines of communication. As for you, pet, you're going to get your every wish tonight. Spanking bench. Ass in the air."

Kitten gave him wide, innocent eyes. "Please don't fig me, Master. I would hate it if that happened."

"Yeah, I'll make sure to do that, you little brat." Cole had gone a nice shade of red. He turned back to Mason. "You're not off the hook either."

Mason's blood began to thrum through his system. In the days he'd been in this house, he hadn't been the focal point of Cole's dominance. He'd watched Kitten take Cole's discipline, but had received none, and now he knew what he wanted—even if only for a night. He wanted to be topped by that magnificent man. He wanted to feel the pain as it sparked pleasure all through his system. He wanted to give up control if only for a little while.

Kitten walked to one of two spanking benches. They were side by side and Mason had to wonder why Cole had left the extra.

"I couldn't move it." Cole was staring at him as though he could read Mason's mind. "I couldn't put it away and I couldn't get rid of it. I never used it, but I couldn't bring myself to haul it out."

It had sat there, a visible reminder to Cole that Mason was gone. Why would he do that? Unless Cole really had missed him. Unless he'd been telling the truth about the ache in his gut—the same one Mason had felt every day of their separation.

"This doesn't mean I'm coming back to you. It just means it's been a long time and I need to play." The words were out of his mouth before he could take them back. He was supposed to play it cool, but that was a state he couldn't attain around Cole. Around Cole, he was always hot as hell.

Cole stepped in, crowding Mason and sending his eyes right to the floor. Cole's hand came up, winding into Mason's hair and tugging his head back with a pull that lit up his scalp. "You should understand I'm going to make it impossible for you to leave me. After this is settled, I won't hold you, but I intend to love you so long and so well while you're here that you won't ever leave me again."

"I can't trust you," Mason said, but his stupid heart was already pounding at the thought of being with him. It was like the world had been dim and suddenly the sun had come up.

"I intend to dream up several plots that will make it very difficult for you to leave us, Mason," Kitten admitted solemnly.

"You should listen to her. She really will do it, and I'm rapidly coming to believe that under her sweet smile lurks the heart of a super villain." Cole sobered as he looked down into Mason's eyes. "We need you. We aren't whole without you."

Cole should have thought about that when he'd tossed him out. That's what he meant to say. His mouth wasn't listening to his anger anymore. "I've been so fucking lost."

"Then let's find each other again." Cole's mouth came down on his, and Mason couldn't hold back this time. His hands found Cole's waist, the skin warm against Mason's fingers. He'd touched Cole a thousand times but this felt fresh and new, like they were kids all over again. Like they had another shot to learn the valleys and hills of each other's bodies.

Cole's tongue surged in and Mason nearly drowned in the sensation. He hadn't kissed in years and now he'd spent all evening sinking into the act. He'd loved kissing Kitten, loved being the forceful one with her, but god, he needed this, too. It had always seemed so wrong to need both. It had been one more way he was a freak, but there was no denying it.

Cole took his mouth, his tongue dominating Mason's as his hands dragged their bodies together. He could feel the hard press of Cole's cock against his belly. It had been so good to have that cock in his mouth, but Mason wanted it in his ass. He wanted to feel Cole there, tearing him up and bringing him the most insane pleasure while he did the same to Kitten's little pussy.

Fuck, he wanted to be in the middle. He wanted to be surrounded by them, to not be able to move without touching them. His lovers. His man. His woman. Fucking his.

Cole growled as he stepped back. His eyes went straight to Mason's mouth. "I missed kissing you."

I missed everything about you. I missed her, too, and I didn't even know her.

Cole stared at him as though he could hear his inner thoughts and was disappointed he wouldn't voice them. He sighed and then pressed another kiss on his lips, this one sweet and simple. "Tie her down for me. Leave access for yourself. I'm in the mood to torture you both."

He barely bit back a groan because Cole's torture had a way of turning into the sweetest pleasures he'd ever had. Cole turned and started for the wall. The eastern portion of the dungeon was one large wall showcasing all of the Master's favorite toys. There were crops and whips and canes and paddles. A veritable toy store.

Mason refocused his attention on the gorgeous brat who had spent her entire evening manipulating him. He frowned her direction, not at all fooled by the way her eyes slid to the floor and her whole body took on a submissive posture. He strode to her and lifted her chin up, forcing her to look him in the eyes. "You and I are going to have a talk."

"Of course. What do you want to talk about, Master? You're very good at conversation."

And she was very good at deflection. "Could I have clamps, Cole? If I'm going to top her, we need to come to an agreement."

"She likes clamps," Cole warned.

"Oh, clamps make my poor nipples ache," Kitten said.

And she loved it. How did one go about punishing a masochist? It didn't matter because punishment wasn't his goal. Making himself feel better was and that could be accomplished easily. He grabbed the alligator clamps Cole handed him. "The talk is the most important thing."

He got to his knees so his eyes were level with her tits. Damn, but he loved her tits. He let his hand cup one, feeling the silky perfection of her skin as his thumb and forefinger rolled her nipple hard. "You manipulated me all day."

"I prefer to think of it as herding you in the right direction, Master. You're so smart. You came up with the right answer every time."

He pinched down hard, his cock twitching at the sound of her groan. Yes, they were nicely suited. He loved rough play but always worried about hurting his partner. It was only fun if it made her hot, too. "I will not be manipulated."

"Of course not." She gave him an encouraging smile, as if he was a toddler and he'd taken his first steps.

Damn but she was going to kill him. He leaned over and gave one perky nipple a lick before sucking her hard into his mouth. She gasped and her body leaned into his. At least there was one place he had a firm grip on her. When she made him insane, he would fuck her and remember he was the boss in the bedroom. He gave the little bud a sharp nip before sliding the first clamp on. "If we ever find ourselves in danger again, you will obey me. You will absolutely do as I say."

"Yes, Master." She gasped as he tightened the clamp, her whole body flushing. "I will obey you in every way except the ones that get you killed."

He took the bare nipple in hand and gave it a wicked pinch that had her moaning. "That's not what I said, but you're going to keep twisting my words so I'm going to make sure you can't talk anymore, love." He slipped the second clamp on, loving the way her nipples turned a dark, rich red. They were likely going numb, but she would squeal and squirm when he took them off. "Now turn around because you'll get my discipline first. I'm the one you disobeyed today. I'm the one you disappointed."

"I'm very sorry, Master." There were real tears in her eyes now. "I didn't mean to disappoint you."

So much of his rage deflated in an instant. This was why he had to be careful. Kitten could handle all the pain his inner sadist wanted to give her, but she broke down at the thought of his disappointment. He took her face in his hands and looked deep into those innocent eyes. "I chose the wrong word. I was scared. I wasn't disappointed. You were very brave, but you scared the hell out of me and now I want to take it out on your pretty backside. Do you understand?"

She nodded.

"I couldn't possibly be disappointed in you." He let the words hover above her lips, his mouth waiting to swoop in. "I used the wrong word. Please forgive me."

"Always," she replied.

Mason kissed her, hoping she could feel his emotion for her. She was a safe place. She really would forgive him all his flaws. She would give and give and do her best to make him feel good about himself. He owed her the same. "You're the most beautiful woman in the world, you know." He let his fingers gently tug on the clamps. "You make my cock hard, but you always make me want to be a better man."

She leaned into him. "My Masters are the best men."

"Only you would think that, pet." Cole was standing behind him and Mason felt the warmth of his Master's hand on his shoulder. "She'll keep us on our toes. Master Mason is right. You're always beautiful but you look stunning in your clamps. Look at how they hold your nipples tight. I think she needs rings, Mason. Don't you think our sub would look gorgeous with pierced nipples?"

"I have always wanted them, but Master Julian said no." Kitten practically vibrated with excitement. Mason was fairly certain he would have to watch her to make sure she didn't do the deed herself.

"Well, I agree with Master Cole. You would look lovely. I'll find the best piercer and make an appointment that doesn't conflict with your schedule, Master." It really would be fun to be able to tweak her little rings whenever he got the mind to. He needed to find a job, but he wanted to work from home. He wanted to work with

Kitten at his feet so he could pet her from time to time, and when the stress got to him he could take out his cock and she would suck him until his eyes rolled to the back of his head.

Mason gasped as Cole's big hand covered his dick. "The thought got you hard as a rock, huh? Somehow I can't imagine the idea of scheduling Kitten's appointment really did this to you. Tell me what you were thinking."

Deep breath. He had to tell himself to breathe because all he could think about was that hand on his cock and how he wished he'd gotten rid of his damn slacks. "I was thinking about never letting her wear clothes again. She doesn't need them in the house. We'll find a housekeeper who's lifestyle friendly and then I can take her when and where I want her at any time of the day or night because she's mine. She's mine in a way the others weren't and never could be."

He'd been Kitten's first real lover, the first man to bring her pleasure, and she was the first woman to make him feel safe. The rest had been playthings. Oh, he'd enjoyed them, but they all had known it was a temporary thing. He'd been their plaything, too. It had been sex and experimentation, and in Emily's case a lesson in survival, but Kitten was different.

And he realized why his household fantasy would never really come true. "I was also thinking about keeping her with me when I work. She could sit at my feet and rest and I would find it so peaceful to have her there."

She lit up. "I would love that, Master."

Cole's hand came off his cock. "We should talk about that, Mason."

Mason shook his head. "No. We don't need to. I think we'll be in agreement that she is far too smart and has too much to give to lock her up and keep her for ourselves. When this is done, if I have my way she's going back to college and she's going to find her passion."

Fear crept into Kitten's eyes. "I don't want to go to college. I want to stay here. This is my passion."

Cole stood beside him, forming a wall Mason believed not even Kitten could breach. "You're scared, but we'll help you. You won't be allowed to hide from the world. On the bench, pet. This is a conversation for a later time, but know there will be no getting out of this discussion. Mason, you had some discipline to administer, if you recall. She's not tied down as I asked. I'm afraid that's going to come out of your ass."

Damn it. He'd gotten distracted and forgotten what Cole had told him to do. A flutter hit his belly. "I'm sorry, Master."

"Fix the situation and then we'll discuss how to remind you who is the boss in this dungeon."

That didn't make his cock pulse or anything. Mason let go. All the other crap could wait. Revenge could wait. Decisions could wait. He didn't have to think about the fact that if he went through with his revenge plans, he likely wouldn't be the one making decisions about Kitten's future. He wouldn't sit down with them as a family and talk about what they all wanted. He wouldn't have any say at all. He would have his revenge to keep him warm while Cole had Kitten and their kids.

Fuck. He wanted kids. He wanted babies and a stupid white picket fence.

Cole put his hands on either side of Mason's face and forced him to look up. "Don't. Not right now. Stay with us tonight. You can worry and make decisions later. For now, just be with us."

Cole laid his head against Mason's and Mason nearly melted. He could lie to himself but deep down he knew the truth. This wasn't sex. It wasn't play. They could call it by a thousand different names but it only had one in his heart—communion. This was a communion of souls, a merging, a language of its own only spoken by three people.

Mason forced himself to move. He had a job to do but he couldn't help pressing his lips to Cole's. Kissing Cole felt like coming home. Emotion welled inside him. No matter what happened, he would hold this night close to his heart. He would remember how Cole had taken over, how Kitten had risked herself to stay with him. How just for a moment he'd mattered.

Kitten had placed herself over the spanking bench and her ass was in the air, but somehow she made it look utterly graceful. She didn't need to be tied down. She wouldn't move. She had perfect discipline, but she liked the feeling and that was why he did it. He did it because she wanted it, needed it. She needed it the way he needed her. He dropped to his knees and Cole handed him the rope. Jute. Cole would have had it handcrafted, made for her comfort and pleasure.

Mason worked the rope over her, his hands remembering the rhythm of bondage. Over and under and all around. Just enough pressure to let her know she was held in loving bonds but not enough to cut off her circulation. He made a pretty pattern that would stay on her skin for a while and remind her that he'd tied her down. Kitten's eyes closed and she sighed as he worked.

He couldn't help it. She was so peaceful and his cock was driving him insane. Her breasts hung on either side of the bench. It was an easy thing to reach up and tweak her.

A strangled scream came from her mouth, and Mason couldn't help but love the sound.

"No subspace for you yet, gorgeous girl."

Her shoulders shook slightly as she managed to turn her head to look up at him. "Whatever my Master wants."

Yeah. Whatever her Master wanted as long as Kitten thought her Master wasn't misleading himself and she could bring him back to what was right. She was a brat and he wouldn't take her any other way. "This Master wants you to scream for him."

He got to his feet, her limbs secured, and gave that gorgeous ass a smack that meant business. Her skin immediately pinkened. It was so pretty. She let out a squeal, but nothing compared to what he wanted.

Cole knelt down beside her. "That was next to nothing. We can't tell how we affect you when you keep it all in. Unless I tell you to be silent, and I will only do that if we would disturb others, I want to hear your every moan and groan and cry. I want to hear it because I want to know how my discipline affects you, and I'm sure Mason feels the same."

Mason slapped her ass again, but she was silent. "I feel empty without the sounds of her pleasure."

"It's hard," she managed to whisper. "I was always told to be quiet. Even before."

Before she'd been taken. He'd started to wonder how many of

her problems began even before her capture. He smacked her again because he knew it made her feel good. "I want your sounds. I want to know how I'm making you feel."

Another hard smack and she groaned, much louder than before.

"More," Cole commanded, his big hand coming down on her ass with an audible smack. "I want to hear you." His hand came up and down again.

Kitten groaned, the sexiest sound he'd ever heard. "Please, Master. Please give me more."

That was what Mason wanted. He wanted to hear her asking for what she needed. He gave her a quick five slaps, moving across her flesh for maximum impact. He couldn't miss the way she tensed and then relaxed. Three strokes in, she finally shuddered and groaned, the sound going straight to his dick. She might never scream the way he wanted her to, but she was trying and it was all he could ask.

"She likes the crop." Cole moved quickly, taking one off the wall and offering it to him.

Kitten squirmed against the bench. "Please. Please, give me the crop."

How could he possibly refuse her? He took the crop and tested it against his hand. It gave a nice smack to his palm. Just hard enough. He brought it down on the fleshiest part of her ass and she gasped and pleaded. He wielded the crop like he'd never been apart from it, like those years that had passed without play had never existed. While Kitten cried out, he could smell her arousal. The way he'd tied her down had left her pussy on full display, and he could see the way it glistened, her arousal pulsing every time he gave her what she needed.

Mason stopped and looked at his work. Her ass was a glorious hot pink, and she would definitely feel the session tomorrow. She would sit down and a sexy ache would suffuse her body and she would remember.

"That is beautiful." Cole's hand came out to touch her flesh and she shivered and sighed.

"I feel beautiful, Master," she whispered. "Do you know what would make me even lovelier?"

Cole winked down at her and proved he knew her fairly well.

He had a small ball gag in his hand. "She loves the ball gag. Here's a treat for being so brave, pet."

He placed it against her lips and she enthusiastically worked the ball into her mouth.

Kitten might have found D/s in the worst way possible, but it was obvious to Mason that she needed it. The way he needed it.

Cole's hand found his shoulder. "It's your turn. Undress for me and find your position. Let's get the discipline out of the way. I fully intend to allow you to fuck her again, but I won't sit on the sideline this time. I might be nervous about hurting her, but I know you can take me."

His body clenched in anticipation and he pulled his shirt over his head. He felt Cole's eyes on him the whole time he was undressing.

Mason held Cole's eyes as he toed out of his shoes, slipped off his slacks. His cock was already thick, desperate, and he wasn't sure he would even last through the discipline portion of the evening. It wasn't where he'd expected to be. He'd thought he would be walking down the street, waiting until he was far enough away that he could call a cab. He didn't expect to be standing here, watching as Cole dropped his pants and stepped away from them, his massive cock in his hand. He stroked himself once and then again, his erection swelling with every pass from his hand.

Mason's mouth watered at the sight.

"Fuck it," Cole said, stalking toward him. "I can't wait."

He reached out and slammed their bodies together, meeting skin to skin. Mason gave over. Nothing else mattered in the moment. Nothing could possibly feel better than being in Cole's arms, in knowing he would be inside Kitten's warm body in mere minutes.

Cole kissed him, their tongues tangling in a fight for dominance. Mason knew damn well how that fight would end, but he loved it anyway. Cole ran a hand down Mason's chest, across his abs to grip his dick in a hard hold that had him panting.

"I'll remind you who the boss is," Cole said against his lips. "You won't forget who your Dom is after tonight. I'm going to fuck you so long and so well you won't be able to forget."

He'd never forgotten. He'd spent years lying in lonely beds

remembering the feel of Cole's cock sliding inside his body. He'd longed for those nights when he submitted to Cole, giving his Master his body, his love, his trust. He'd knelt at this man's feet and felt more love than he'd imagined.

Cole stopped, his face turning serious. "Don't, baby." His fingertips touched Mason's face, brushing away the tears Mason hadn't even known he was shedding. Cole leaned in and kissed them away. "Don't hate me. Not when I love you so much. I'm sorry. I will prove it to you. I'm never letting you go again."

"I didn't go."

Cole placed his forehead against Mason's. "I pushed you away. You have every right to hate me, but I'm begging you not to. I'm begging you to stay with us and make the family we always wanted. Kitten would beg, too, if I hadn't gagged her."

There was a groaning sound from the spanking bench and Mason couldn't help but laugh. God he was falling in love with that woman, and he'd never stopped loving this man, but he was so fucking scared of getting hurt again.

"Just be with us. Just for a while. Give us some time," Cole pleaded.

Mason couldn't help but nod.

"Come here." Cole pulled him slightly and Mason realized what he was doing. He was making sure their girl could watch them. Kitten's eyes were wide with love and lust as Cole got to his knees. "Let me get you ready to fuck her."

Before he could say another word, Cole gripped his cock and Mason's whole body lit up. His Master leaned over and licked at his cock. Pure pleasure tore through him, making him shake, but Cole wouldn't stop. His mouth drew on Mason's cock, sucking him down in one long pass.

His Master remembered so well. Cole knew exactly how to suck his cock. He drew on Mason's dick, sucking hard and then giving him the barest edge of his teeth. Cole tugged on his balls gently, a reminder that the Master was always in control.

His big tongue whirled around the head of Mason's cock before sucking him down again.

Heat suffused him, and he wasn't sure how long he would last.

"Master, if you want me to be able to fuck her, you have to stop." He couldn't last. His balls were already drawing up, preparing to shoot off.

With a swift, hard tug, Cole took care of that problem. Mason gasped at the sharp snap of pain as Cole pulled at his balls. "You'll take what I give you. And you're not allowed to come, Mason. You come and we're going to have a problem. I'll be in a bad mood, love."

Torture. The sweetest kind. He gritted his teeth as Cole's tongue bathed him in heart-stopping heat. He looked down and watched his cock as it disappeared and reappeared, Cole controlling everything. All Mason had to do was obey. He could let everything go. This was what he'd missed. He'd missed these blessed moments of peace. His head was always working, but when Cole took over, Mason could go silent and let himself simply feel.

He hissed as he felt the drag of the edge of Cole's teeth, the minor pain lighting him up and causing the pleasure to be so much more intense.

Mason let his eyes find Kitten's and he was humbled by what he saw. He'd expected lust, but there were tears in her eyes. She winked his way. From the infinitely soft look on her face he rather thought she was back to watching something she thought was beautiful.

They could be beautiful together. All he had to do was let go.

Cole gave his cock one last hard suck and then got to his feet. "Put a condom on and get inside her."

Kitten's eyes lit up.

Oh, he couldn't wait to get inside her again. The first time he'd been so careful, and he planned to be again, but he knew he wouldn't hurt her now, wouldn't dredge up any terrible memories. He intended to build new ones with her, for her. For as long as they had together, he intended to build enough good and sweet times for her to begin to make up for everything she'd gone through.

He grabbed a condom from the box and eased it over his cock. He caught sight of Cole grabbing a bottle of lube and nearly came again.

He had to get himself under control or he wouldn't last a

second, and he intended to spend time inside her.

Kitten didn't move as he positioned himself behind her. The height was so perfect, he had to wonder if Cole hadn't planned everything out. It would be like him. Once Cole decided on a plan, he would ruthlessly and without deviation move forward. He would move mountains and blast through barriers to get his way. It could make a man feel so wanted, like he was necessary and special.

He wanted to make sure Kitten knew how that felt.

"You are the most beautiful thing on the planet, gorgeous girl." Kitten. He would focus on her and then he wouldn't have to think about anything but the sexual connection with Cole. That had never let him down. Cole's cock was something he could trust. It had never brought him anything but pleasure.

He felt her sigh as he traced the graceful line of her spine. He let his hands run under her so he could play with the clamps. They would have to come off soon, but he liked the idea of her having rings he could twist and play with and never have to remove. She shuddered as he lightly tugged on the clamps.

"She's going to be sore in the morning and she'll love it," Cole said as he moved behind Mason. "I need to stop questioning her and let her be who she is. She loves this and it's not because she was brainwashed."

"No," Mason murmured. It had to have been frustrating for Kitten. Likely everyone had questioned her for years. No one would have believed she could have true love for the lifestyle. Not when she'd been introduced to it so brutally, but if there was one thing Mason had learned about his girl, it was that she managed to find beauty and strength in the strangest places. If anyone could take something wretched and twisted and make it lovely, it was her. It was why she blinged out her can of pepper spray and attached little jewels to her air horn. They were reminders that the world could be cruel, but Kitten had taught herself that even the darkest things could be made into something pretty. "We need to trust her on this and she needs to trust us when we say she needs to be out in the world."

She was scared of finding her place. That was plain to see, and Mason thought it likely came from long before her capture. It came from being a replacement child, never as loved as the one who came before.

He could show her how loved she was. He let the clamps dangle again as his hands traced her slender curves and his cock throbbed, desperate to get inside her. Her pussy was a deep coral, already succulent and juicy with arousal. Her plump lips beckoned him inside. He held on to her hips and let his dick have its way.

Mason breathed deep as he thrust in, letting her tight heat surround him.

"Get inside, Mason. Get all the way in because you're next." Cole put a hand on his back, gently forcing him down. "Spread your legs."

He did as his Master ordered, holding himself deep inside her body while Cole moved behind him. Mason let his hand run across the silk of her skin to distract himself from the desperate need to thrust in and out of her hot little pussy until he exploded.

Cold lube hit his asshole and he couldn't stop a shiver. Kitten reacted with some shaking of her own. She tried to shove against him, to force him to fuck her. He brought his hand down, smacking her ass hard.

"I love that you want to fuck, but you're on the bottom. You're supposed to be submitting, and that means you don't steal your orgasm from me. You take what I choose to give you," Mason said.

A loud smack cracked the air and Mason was the one moaning. He was likely going to have Cole's handprint on his ass in the morning. "And don't forget who the top is. Just because I couldn't wait for the sex doesn't mean there won't be punishment for attempting to sneak out tonight. You'll feel it soon."

All Mason could feel now was a hard finger pressing against his asshole. Cole rimmed him, using one hand to spread his cheeks wide while the other began circling Mason's hole.

Pressure and a jagged pleasure began to build.

Cole proved he was impatient because it wasn't a moment or two before that finger was replaced with the broad head of his dick, and Mason had to moan because it had been so fucking long and Cole was a damn monster. Cole gripped his hips as he started to breach his asshole.

So fucking big. God, he was going to be torn apart and there wasn't a damn place else Mason wanted to be. Cole's movements shoved Mason's dick deeper inside their girl.

He was caught between her softness and the hard, relentless length of Cole's stiff dick. He didn't play around. He pushed his way inside. Mason flattened out his back, bringing his chest against Kitten to give Cole more room. He was the one who needed more fucking room. Cole's dick was taking up all the space. He tunneled in, giving Mason not an instant to protest—not that he would. He took every second of discomfort because he knew what came next.

Cole groaned behind him as he finally thrust that cock all the way in. Mason could feel Cole's strong legs against his, holding him up. He was totally surrounded. There wasn't any way to move that he didn't feel either Kitten's softness or Cole's strength.

Caught. He was trapped and he was pretty sure he didn't want to change that in any way.

"Relax and let me move you. I'm steering the boat." Cole flexed inside him, nearly making Mason's eyes cross.

Every cell in his body sang as Cole dragged his cock out, rubbing over the sensitive nub of Mason's prostate. The motion caused Mason to move. Kitten's pussy clamped down around his cock as he was dragged back. Pure sensation swamped him. She was strangling his dick and it felt so right. He let Cole lead him.

"You have my permission to come, both of you." Cole's hands tightened as he thrust inside again, shoving Mason deep into Kitten's pussy. "Mason, I want to hear you. Kitten's in her happy place so I want to hear you roar."

Cole set a brutal pace. In and out. Over and over. Mason couldn't think about anything but how good it felt. It felt good to have Cole fucking his ass, and damn it was heaven to be in Kitten's tight pussy. Every motion was a pure pleasure, every second bringing him closer and closer to climax.

He couldn't take another minute. His balls drew up, tucking in close to his body as Cole fucked in and out of his ass. Kitten groaned around her gag and her head thrashed in obvious pleasure as she clamped hard around Mason's cock.

Mason gave up and let go. He growled out his orgasm, letting

Cole hear him, letting him know how fucking good it was to shoot off every ounce his balls contained.

Cole's hands tightened and he drove in one last time, roaring out his orgasm and filling Mason with heat and pleasure. In those brief moments, Mason knew who he belonged to. He belonged to his Master and he belonged to his sub.

Mason fell forward, covering Kitten and letting the pleasure thud through his veins in a glorious rhythm. All the terror from earlier in the day floated away because he was safe in between them.

"Help me get her out of the bindings and the clamps," Cole said, his voice out of breath. He leaned over and Mason felt a kiss laid on his shoulder. "We're going to bed. My bed. We don't need separate bedrooms. Not anymore. We'll move your things in tomorrow."

Cole reached down and eased the gag from Kitten's mouth. "Are you all right, pet?"

She turned her head and smiled, her gorgeous face beatific. "I told you it would be beautiful."

Mason couldn't argue with her. It had been everything. He just hoped he could trust it would last.

Chapter Fifteen

Kitten came awake slowly to warmth and the most delicious ache. That ache was in her backside, a reminder of the masterful way Mason had disciplined her. It was in her pussy, too, and that reminded her that Mason had done far more than smacked her ass and sent her on her way.

She felt her lips curling up in a smile. That's because Mason was hers. Cole was hers. Her Masters.

And she had a problem because they were going to play this afternoon.

What would she do if her Master ordered her to service another Master? She wasn't even sure who was attending the party. She had simply been told there would be a meeting and likely some play at The Club.

She'd heard about crazy play parties. She hadn't been to one herself because Julian wouldn't allow her to go. Julian himself would never share his subs, but Kitten was fairly certain Dani and Finn hadn't written into their contract that they wanted to be shared so they could feel beautiful and sexy and loved.

They hadn't been silly enough to think that a group of strange men wanting to fuck them would mean they were beautiful and worthy of love.

"I can hear you thinking from here, pet." Master Cole turned over and Kitten watched through heavily lidded eyes as he stretched out next to her.

"Think more quietly, gorgeous girl." Mason yawned behind her and his body cuddled against hers. "It's too early to get up and Cole fired Ms. Hamilton last night so one of us is going to have to cook, and it probably shouldn't be me. I burn toast."

Cole chuckled softly and settled against her. She was in the middle, surrounded by warm, masculine flesh.

This was what made her feel beautiful but only because she knew these men, trusted them.

Oh, she loved them. She loved how careful Cole was and how Mason lit up a room when he walked in. She loved that Cole thought things through and that he'd gotten on his knees in front of Mason and given him what he needed the night before. He hadn't been cold and in control. Some Masters would never get on their knees in front of their subs even for sex, but Cole loved Mason. If only she could make Cole love her, too.

And Mason wasn't merely a playmate. Mason thought of her. She wasn't a convenience to him. She meant something. He'd been willing to leave so he wouldn't put her in danger.

"She's still thinking, Cole," Mason murmured.

A big hand slid over her breast. The nipples were still tender, still so sensitive. "We need to do something about that. And I'll make breakfast, but you have to find a new housekeeper. I'm letting Ms. Hamilton stay in the guesthouse for another two weeks out of deference to the work she did for my parents, but she's been warned to stay away from the two of you. Put the new housekeeper in the pool house until then." His fingers found the tips of her nipples and she couldn't help but gasp.

Mason propped his head in his hand and grinned down at her. "Oh, are my poor sub's nipples aching today? Look at them. They're still a little red. Poor sub. I wonder what we should do about that."

"That depends." Cole's hand moved over her belly until he covered the mound of her pussy. "How sore is our sweet pet?"

She liked being sore. She even liked it when she was sore from exercising. It was a reminder that she was using her body as it was meant to be used. Her body wasn't something to hide and be ashamed of. It could be a beautiful thing. The soreness in her limbs reminded her how much she'd pleased her Masters and how hard they'd worked to bring her pleasure. It was a reminder that they were together.

Would she like being sore from someone else's use? Suddenly she was sure she wouldn't.

"Tell me." Mason had gone serious, staring down at her like he could read her mind.

How could she tell them she'd changed? Master Cole had signed a contract with her under the impression that she wasn't possessive. From what she understood, he and Mason had subs they'd shared with other Doms before—including the woman who had come between them. When Nat had pressed Tara, she'd talked about how Emily enjoyed being shared and had encouraged Cole to play with other submissives.

It was their lifestyle.

"I'm scared you're going to leave." It wasn't a lie. She was still scared of that. She couldn't stand the thought of Mason walking away. She'd followed him the night before, praying she could figure out some way to make him stay. Luckily the Master had already been there and waiting.

Mason's lips turned up in a heart-stopping grin. "If I leave, I get arrested and put in solitary confinement. If I stay I get sexed up. All in all, there's really no choice." He leaned over and gently licked her nipple.

Oh, she wasn't so sore. No. Not at all. She'd thought she would enjoy sex, but she was very addicted to making love. Much more than she'd thought she could be.

"See, he learns, pet." Cole's fingers started playing in her pussy, parting her labia and slowly drawing out her arousal. "The key with Mason is to make sure his choices are very clear."

"Yes, orange jumpsuits and unfun strip searches or waking up next to the softest piece of femininity in the world." He sucked her briefly. "I know what I'll take. He's a bastard, but he knows how to play me."

"You're adding to your punishment, love," Cole said as he licked her other nipple. "You should know you're in for a rough afternoon."

Mason kissed her ear and whispered into it. "He knows I'll like that, too. And you'll like watching me. You'll like watching Cole smack my ass and torture my cock."

She shivered because she would.

"How sore are you, pet?" Cole asked in all seriousness. "Because I would love to make love to you."

"He needs two of us because he has always had the sex drive of a teenaged bull," Mason chuckled.

"And you don't." Cole began to kiss his way down her belly. "Don't let him fool you. We're both highly sexed, but neither of us wants to hurt you. If you're too sore, I can make do with a hand job."

Like she would allow that to happen. "I'm fine. More than fine. If you keep teasing me, I might cry again, Master."

Mason was suddenly frowning down at her. "Yes, I believe when we play this afternoon, we might have a discussion about those tears of yours. You seem very good at making them show up at the most opportune times."

Cole's mouth was hovering right over her pussy. A restless ache began deep inside. "He can't seem to wrap his head around the fact that you manipulate him so easily. He's never been in that position before. He's always been the one in the driver's seat with our women. He'll have to face the fact that you're awfully good at it."

"I don't mean it to be harmful."

Mason stared down at her. "I would prefer you simply ask me for what you want."

That was easy. "I want you to stay with me."

"That was a well-laid trap." Cole's tongue came out and licked her clit, making her squirm.

"Fuck, you're going to kill me," Mason said as his mouth descended on hers.

Mason's tongue invaded even as Cole's began to slide over her pussy. Just like that she wasn't thinking about anything but her men. She let it all slide away because there wasn't a place for worry in those moments when they took over. There was only submission and pleasure and love.

Mason kissed her sweetly before turning his head down to watch. "Look at that. That is a true Master. The man can eat a pussy. I think he deserves some praise for that."

If she could breathe long enough to talk. Cole was making it hard. With every long, lavish stroke of his tongue, he brought her closer and closer to the edge. "My Master is the best. He gives the best kisses."

Cole's head came up, his eyes narrowing. "A kiss is what I do to your mouth. A kiss is a sweet thing. Is that all you want?"

He stopped his sweet attack on her tenderest flesh and laid a very chaste kiss there instead.

Mason's voice was smooth as honey. "Now you've done it. Don't you know the Master likes to hear his subs talk dirty? He likes to hear how much I love it when he takes that monster cock of his and fucks my ass. It felt so good. I still feel it this morning because I haven't taken a cock there in years. When he fucks that tiny pussy of yours, he's not going to last long because it's going to squeeze him so tight. Well, if he fucks that pussy of yours. He might keep giving you what you say you want. Little kisses."

"Fuck, baby, you have the dirtiest mouth," Cole groaned against her flesh but he kept up the slow torture of simple kisses along her pussy. "You need to work on our girl."

"My Master is the best at eating my pussy," Kitten got out quickly because the little kisses thing kind of sucked. Or didn't. And that was the problem. And then she saw another problem. "Except for my other Master. He is also the best."

Mason had been excellent at it as well. She didn't want to hurt his feelings. It had been just as good.

Cole brought his eyes up and grinned at her. "I think we can share the crown." His smile faded and he looked up at her, his face becoming serious. "Tell me you want me."

He was still afraid and her heart softened. He was so careful with her. "I want you more than I can say. I want you, Cole. I don't want you because you're some faceless Master who gives me what I want. I want Master Cole because he's kind and caring and tries to make up for the things he's done wrong. I want Master Mason because he brings such joy to my life. I want you both and I want to be a part of this family."

It was another plea for Mason to stay. They weren't complete without him, and knowing what it meant to feel whole was a revelation, a sensation she wasn't sure she could live without.

Cole pushed himself up and suddenly she was covered by him, taking his weight as his legs spread hers wide to make a place for himself. She felt the press of his cock against her. "Then take me."

She closed her eyes, ready to feel her Master enter her body, but instead she found herself being flipped over, the world upending as Cole turned until she was on top. She opened her eyes and stared down at him. "Master?"

"I want you to take me. I want you in control this time. I want your eyes open," he said, his hands finding her hips.

"He wants you with us." Mason was watching them, one hand stroking his magnificent cock. "We need to know you're right here and not off someplace else."

Because she sometimes went to dark places in her mind and sometimes she used submission as a way out of thinking at all. Her Masters wanted to mean more to her than a way out. She could understand that. She never wanted them to feel that way.

She studied his body. Cole's big form was laid out for her. "I'm in charge?"

Cole gritted his teeth. "For now."

She was in control. It was an odd place to be. "Master, I might not be good at this."

Cole's hands tightened on her as though he was trying to keep her there with him. "You'll never know until you try. I think you're terrified of trying, and that's why you want to stay in this house. The world isn't a safe place, but there are marvelous things out there to be had. You have to trust me—not to always keep you safe. No matter how hard I try, you can still be hurt. Accidents happen. Harsh words can cut. You might fail to achieve the things you want. I can't protect you from that. I can only promise to pick you up when you fall and make sure you know how much I care."

"Take him," Mason commanded, his voice going hard. His mouth was tightly set and it was easy to see Cole's words had gotten to him, too. "How can you be good at a thing if you don't practice?

We'll practice a lot. We'll make you the queen of taking your Masters and making them scream."

She turned her eyes back to Cole, taking in every glorious muscle. In most of her encounters, she'd been tied up or down, and it had been Cole exploring. She'd loved how he touched her, felt close to him in those moments when he worshipped her. Did her Master need the same affection? It was easy to forget sometimes that he was just a man. "You are so beautiful."

Laying her palms on his chest, she stroked her way down his body. His cock was hard against her, but she didn't pay it mind yet. It might be the only time she had such freedom with the Master's body. She wanted to learn it, to memorize it so even when he wasn't with her she could feel his skin beneath her palms. She would be able to close her eyes and smell and see him as though he was right there.

She leaned over, letting her chest touch his. Her nipples, still so sensitive from the night before, rasped over the light dusting of hair that covered his muscles. So masculine. She buried her nose between his neck and shoulder. He smelled like soap from the shower he'd taken before he'd come to bed. She let her cheek rub against the smooth muscle of his neck.

When she brought her face up, she could feel the rough edge of his whiskers. He would shave as soon as they got out of bed so she allowed herself to revel in the feel of them bristling against her skin.

"Do you know how good this feels, little cat? That's what you are. You're a sweet kitten rubbing herself all over me."

She could never forget how she'd gotten her nickname, but she shoved that aside. Bad things had happened to her, but now Cole and Mason were here and bad things might happen again, but they would catch her.

And she was a cat. A sensual kitten, purring against him. Their Kitten. She chose.

She stared at his face for a moment and despite the insistent cock nesting against her pussy, he seemed more than happy to let her explore. His hands held her hips, but he didn't move, allowing her the freedom to do as she chose.

She lowered her mouth and kissed him, licking her tongue

along the seam of his plump lips. She drew the bottom one inside and sucked on it for a moment. Men shouldn't have such gorgeous lips. She rubbed their noses together and let her hands sink into the silk of his sandy hair. There was the faintest hint of gray at his temples. Her Master's eyes had the tiniest of lines showing through. They'd seemed deeper before. It had been Mason's return that lifted the age off her Master. It had been Mason who brought him back to life.

She turned her head slightly and Mason was watching them. "Later, I want my time with you. I want to memorize you, too."

"Is that what you're doing?" Mason asked solemnly.

If there was one thing she knew it was that fate didn't always play fair. She wanted this memory. Forever. "Yes. I want to memorize you. Every inch."

She kissed her way down Cole's chest, exploring the hills and valleys of his magnificent body. Cole let her hips go, giving her leave to do her worst. Here she could still smell the soap he'd used, but another fragrance was stronger. Musk. The scent of his arousal. Clean. Masculine. It was evidence of his need, as was the pearly drop on the head of his cock. Cole's hands had shifted to his sides, but he didn't leave them there. She watched as Cole covered Mason's hand, their fingers threading together as though Cole could draw him in. Never leaving Mason on the outside again. She hoped that was true.

Cole's cock was a thing of pure beauty. While he left a light dusting of hair on his chest, there was none on his pelvis. He was shaved clean.

Kitten let her fingers stroke the thick stalk. Rigid and erect, the skin was still so silky smooth against her fingertips.

"She's going to kill me, Mason," Cole murmured.

Mason's face split in the sweetest grin. "It will be a good way to go, Master."

"We'll see if you feel the same way when she's memorizing you," Cole murmured. "Please have mercy on your poor Master. Memorize my legs and feet later."

She was fairly sure she would have to since she couldn't take her eyes off his cock. She hadn't gotten enough of a taste of it before. Mason had been very determined to suck their Master off. She wasn't going to do that. He'd been explicit that he wanted her to take him in her pussy, but she could play for a moment or two.

Leaning over, she allowed the flat of her tongue to gather the cream on the head of his cock.

Cole hissed and out of the corner of her eye, she saw the way he squeezed Mason's hand. Power rushed through her. Her Master was giving her the power, allowing her to feel how good control could be. She would never want to be totally in control, had no need to top anyone, but she liked the fact that her Master could give up his place to let her experiment.

She let her tongue run all over the head of his cock, noting the way his stomach muscles bunched up as he held himself still. It must be so hard for her Master. She sucked the head into her mouth, finding the deep ridge that separated it from the stalk of his cock. She closed a fist around it as much as she could. He was big, her Master. She couldn't quite make her fingers reach, but it was more than enough to stroke him.

"He's not fragile," Mason said, his voice deep and low. His head was close to Cole's, their hands together as they both watched her. "Stroke him hard. He wants to feel it. When you take your Masters' cocks in hand, use a firm grip. We'll love it."

Her worry melted away. They would tell her what they needed. They would give her direction and she could learn how to please them. They wouldn't let her fail in this. They would be patient and kind and give her time. She tightened her grip as she stroked up and was rewarded with a groan and a little twist of Cole's hips, as though he couldn't stay completely still.

Another drop pulsed out, but she was there to catch it. Salty sweetness lit her senses and she played with the slit of his dick as she stroked him, her tongue delving in slightly.

Her body was humming. She couldn't help but move along the strong muscle of his thigh, bumping her clit against it and riding it as she sucked Cole's cock. Every twist and motion of her hips got her wetter and more ready. Mason had been big. He'd barely fit inside her and Cole was larger, but she was determined. And just about as aroused as she could get.

She gave his cock one last lick and then got on her knees.

"Do you have any idea how fucking gorgeous you are right now?" Cole asked, his free hand coming up to cup her breast.

"Not as gorgeous as my Masters." They were decadently beautiful lying there together. This was what she'd longed for when she'd filled out that stupid questionnaire. She thought she'd simply wanted to not be alone, but no sister sub was going to fill the void. Mason and Cole. They were all she needed. They were everything.

She settled over Cole, gripping his cock to bring it to her core.

"Go slow," Cole said, his voice tight. "Only take what you can."

She intended to take it all. She wanted everything he had to give her. With a long breath, she began to lower herself onto his cock. Inch by inch, she took him inside.

"Don't close your eyes," Cole commanded. His hands were again around her hips, helping ease his penetration. "Stay with me. Let me see you."

So hard. It was hard to open her eyes because she'd always kept them closed before. She hadn't wanted to see the man who took her. It hadn't always been violent with Hawk, though she'd never had a second's pleasure from him. Sometimes it had been something to get through so she could go back to her cage and feel safe again.

Cole was trying hard to open her cage and force her out into the world.

"Don't let him in," Mason said. His fingers came up and she realized she'd started crying again.

"Hush." Cole's voice was soft, his hands strong and soothing as they rubbed her back and hips. "He's always going to be there, but we're stronger. She knows I would never hurt her."

No. He never would. He would protect her, but he was also determined to set her free. She'd thought she was free. When she'd had the tattoo Hawk forced on her removed, she'd declared that she was free and didn't need anything else. But she was still hiding.

Mason had taken her out into the pool and showed her she could learn to swim. Could she learn to want more from life?

She knew the first step. She kept her eyes steady on Cole's as she sank onto his cock. "I'll start looking at schools today. I don't know what I want to do."

His smile lit up the room. "You don't have to know yet, pet. You just have to explore."

Like he'd allowed her to do with his body. He was giving her a safe place. She could try and fail and he wouldn't shove her aside. He wouldn't throw her away.

So full. She was full of him. She rocked her hips back and forth, allowing herself the time to get used to how big he was. She was stretched, but she loved it. She could handle her Master. She could do it.

Slowly, she brought her body back up, clenching around the cock splitting her in two.

Cole's eyes went dark, his hands hard on her flesh. "You feel so right. Ride me. Do your worst."

She concentrated on moving up and down, on finding the perfect rhythm. Up on her knees until he almost slid out, and then she would greedily plunge back down, taking the whole of him to his root. Her Master groaned and twisted his hips as though he couldn't stand not being a part of her even for those seconds she was moving up.

Over and again, she rode him, letting her breasts bounce and her hips slide until she found the perfect place. His cock slid along the center of her being, finding the spot that sent her soaring. Kitten couldn't stay quiet. She gasped and moaned and fought to keep the sensation, riding the wave until she couldn't anymore and she fell forward.

Cole was immediately in motion. He flipped her over, taking control once again.

"You liked that, didn't you?" Cole asked as he spread her legs even wider and slammed his cock back inside. "You liked making me crazy. You liked being in control. Enjoy the brief times I give you because you belong to me. You're my sub and I'll prove I can master you."

He'd already proven that time and time again, but she wasn't about to argue with him. He drove deep inside her body, making her call out his name. He was the one on his knees, spreading her wide and fucking long and hard. He thrust inside, only to pull out and start again.

She lay back, giving over to her Master. She'd had her moment. She would satisfy herself with watching him in his.

"No, you don't." Mason was at her side, his hand sliding in between her and Cole. "You don't get to relax. I want to watch you come again."

The pad of his finger found her clit and though she'd been so sure she couldn't, the pleasure began to build again.

"Make it fast," Cole commanded. "I'm not going to last long."

Mason winked up at their Master as his thumb started making hard circles on her clit. "We have all day. I think you'll keep us in bed for most of it."

Cole picked up the pace. His cock slammed in and dragged out, sliding over her sweet spot with flawless accuracy. "Now that I have you both, I might not leave this bed ever again."

Kitten reached up, gripping Cole's muscular backside as she came again, even stronger this time. It was a fire flashing through her system, burning away all the pain that had come before and leaving her with nothing but the sweetest pleasure.

Cole's whole body tightened and he held himself hard against her as he came. She could feel the strong jets of semen entering her body, filling her up and making her warm. She would keep her Master inside her, a piece of him with her all day.

Kitten let her head fall back, hitting the pillow. Cole fell on top of her, weighing her down deliciously.

"You're right." Mason was staring down at her with stormy gray eyes. "That was beautiful." He dipped his head and kissed her swiftly.

Cole's head turned to the side, his eyes finding Mason's. "Hey, I performed for you, too."

Mason's face softened. "Yes, you did, Master, and as Kitten might say, you were very, very good at it."

He leaned over and Kitten watched as they kissed, their lips meeting briefly, but she could feel the heat between them. They needed each other. They completed each other. Separately they struggled, as though their very souls had mingled and felt the loss. Together they were strong.

Mason lay back down as Cole proved he really did have the

sexual energy of a rutting bull. He moved off Kitten and onto Mason, nestling their bodies close. Cole fused their mouths together. Her Masters tangled, being rough with each other.

And Cole's cell chirped. It was the sound of bells. Cole had programmed different sounds for different people who regularly called him.

"Ignore it," Cole ordered. "They'll go away. We don't need visitors."

The bells were from the security guard at the gate. The house was separated by a long drive and the gate in was guarded. Anyone who came to the house had to be allowed in.

Mason's hands slid down Cole's back to cup the muscular cheeks of his ass. Her Master was very good at working out. It was obvious in the gorgeous lines of his body. Kitten sighed, her system replete with satisfaction, and now she got to watch her Masters make love.

The world seemed perfect.

If she could only forget about that contract between them.

Bells went off again.

Cole's head came up and a fierce frown lit his face.

Another three sets of bells, each one more irritating than the rest.

"Fuck," Mason cursed as Cole rolled off the bed.

"No, we're not fucking and that's the problem." Cole grabbed a robe. "I'll get rid of whoever it is." He stopped and sighed suddenly. "Damn it. I can't. I'm not thinking straight. It's probably the Dawson brothers. And it might be your new bodyguard."

Mason's jaw dropped as he swung his legs over the side of the bed and sat up. "You've got to be kidding me. I don't need a bodyguard."

Cole tied the belt around his waist. "Do I look like I'm kidding you?"

Kitten studied him. Nope. There was nothing in Master Cole's demeanor that led her to think he was joking. "No, you do not, Master. I believe he's serious, Mason."

Mason stood up and Kitten took in his lovely masculine backside. It was a shame to get out of bed and it was even worse to have to put on clothes. “Again, I don’t need a bodyguard.”

Cole turned and strode out of the bedroom, and Mason followed, trying to give a hundred different reasons he didn’t need a bodyguard.

Kitten stretched and found her own robe. There was no way Mason managed to talk the Master out of a bodyguard for him. He’d almost been murdered twice. He’d also tried to sneak away without telling anyone. Master Cole wouldn’t take any chances. She wiggled her toes in the thick carpet. Alive. She felt ridiculously alive.

Kitten walked out of the bedroom. Her bedroom. The one she shared with her Masters. She’d always had her own room. From the time she’d been a baby. Even those first few months in college, she hadn’t had a roommate. Her parents hadn’t wanted her to leave their home so she’d driven an hour to and from the school. She’d come home to the same room she’d been shoved in after she was born.

When she had a baby, she was going to keep him or her in her room for the first year or so. She wanted to breastfeed. Could she do that with nipple rings?

Kitten stopped. Holy crap. She wanted a baby. She wanted a couple of babies. She wanted a family. She wanted to be a mom and she wanted to have a place in the world. They were right. She was scared. Life was scary because it could go any way it wished. There wasn’t a guarantee that things would work out. In fact nothing in Kitten’s past had given her a single reason to believe that it would with the singular exception of faith. Faith that she would be okay. Faith that she would somehow be given the tools she needed.

She’d been given the kind people she’d needed to survive a lonely childhood. Several of the churches her father had forced her into had been filled with true love, and the people had offered it to her. She remembered one pastor who had taken her into his office and told her how she deserved love. He and his wife had been worried about her. They’d told her there was no such thing as normal and she should look for love anywhere and everywhere because love was love. In her darkest hours, she’d been given Nat and then Finn, who had taken her to Julian who had brought her to her Masters.

Maybe it was time to stop worrying. Maybe it was time to begin to believe the things she'd been told.

That she had worth. That she deserved love and affection.

She stepped out, perfectly ready to speak up for herself because she knew that if Ben and Chase had come, then Nat was here, too, and Nat was her safe place.

"If you didn't want me to show up, maybe you should have answered your phone." A gorgeous blonde woman was standing in the doorway, a black Chanel bag in her hand. She was roughly five foot six, and she got right in Cole's space. She was vaguely familiar.

Cole was frowning at her. "Gemma, what the hell are you doing here? Shit. Is that Nate?"

Kitten looked out and sure enough, the sheriff of Bliss was opening a car door and stepping out. Nathan Wright was roughly six foot two and built on big lines, but the man who got out next was massive. Zane Hollister. He was Nate's partner, which made Kitten wonder…

"Hey!" Callie Hollister-Wright bounced out of the SUV they'd been driving. "I hope you don't mind. Our hotel turned out to be horrible. I couldn't keep the twins there."

Cole's jaw dropped open as the sheriff reached back and pulled a car seat out.

Babies. She loved babies. She hurried out to help.

As she passed Cole, Gemma patted him on the arm. "You should answer your damn phone."

If he had, he would have known that chaos was on its way. Kitten was happy he didn't because she loved a little chaos.

* * * *

When the hell had he lost control? Half an hour later, Cole stepped into the living room—the formerly quiet and peaceful living room. It was a place to have a quiet meeting or where he could envision Kitten doing what his mother had done in it, having tea or coffee with her friends, enjoying the peace of the day.

Now his antique, probably-cost-a-fortune coffee table was being used as a jungle gym.

And so was his submissive. Kitten was lying flat on her back on the floor, giggling as one of the Hollister-Wright twins climbed on top of her, pulling himself up, his chubby little legs shaking. There was a grin on the kid's face as he drooled down at Kitten. She reached up and touched his face, a look of wonder in her eyes.

His heart seized. She was going to want kids.

"Uhm, this one smells to high heaven." Mason was grinning as he held the other twin. "Do you want me to change him?"

Callie was on her feet in an instant. "Oh, no. Thank you so much, but I'll handle it. You've done so much already. I can't thank you enough for the gorgeously clean room. I'm not going to ask you to change a diaper."

Mason shrugged as he handed over the kid. "Hey, I have a law degree. I'm an expert in shit." He frowned. "I'm sorry. I shouldn't cuss around the kids."

Callie was laughing as she grabbed her diaper bag. "No worries. Nate mostly speaks in four-letter words, and Zane isn't far behind. It will be a miracle if their first word isn't a doozy." She smiled up at him. "It is so good to see you, Mason."

"I'm sorry I missed your baby shower," Mason replied with a wistful look on his face.

When he'd cut Mason out of his life, he'd cut him off from Bliss and their friends there. He hadn't even thought about that. He hadn't thought at all.

"Well, I'm glad someone got his head out of his backside long enough to know how stupid he's been." Callie sent Cole a prim look before turning. "Hey, Kitten, can you handle Zander while I change this one?"

Kitten winked up. "I can. They're getting so big."

Callie grinned. "Yes, they are. By the time Cole brings you to Bliss this winter, they'll be giving the Farley brothers a run for their money on the troublemaking front. I'll be back in a bit." She stopped in front of Cole. "Thank you for letting us stay. Nate and Gemma have a presentation at the national conference. They got our reservations wrong and we ended up at some smoke-filled motel. I tried to let the boys play on the floor, but the carpet was filthy. So I do thank you for giving us a place to stay."

Cole frowned. "I didn't know I had a choice."

"Cole!" Mason and Kitten both said his name at the same time.

It was good to know he had two consciences. "What I meant to say was, we're happy to have you here."

"We are," Mason said with a stare that could have peeled paint off a wall. "Very happy. I'll make sure Callie remembers where their room is."

"I'm thrilled," Kitten replied as she cuddled Zander close. The baby embraced her and giggled loudly.

Mason gave Kitten a wink as he followed Callie out into the hall.

Yes, Kitten liked babies and it seemed Mason did as well. They'd never talked about kids. He and Mason hadn't talked about having a family—the traditional type with kiddos and diaper changes and parent-teacher meetings. How would that work? Which two would be the parents? Or would they be brave and walk in all three of them?

Did he have to give up having a family because he cared for two people? Callie seemed really happy, but then she lived in Bliss.

He could live in Bliss. If he could save Bliss.

Callie walked out, smiling and greeting Gemma as she walked in.

Blonde and pretty and kind of mean, Gemma stepped into his living room and softened the minute she caught sight of the baby. "Hey, kiddo. You doing better now that we left the whore house?" She grimaced. "Sorry. I didn't mention the plethora of hookers at our motel to Callie. There was a reason the floor was so damn dirty. I hope the boys don't get some weird venereal disease."

Cade Sinclair walked in after her, his eyes on his fiancée. "They're fine, babe. Callie already bathed them. We're the ones in trouble since we…"

Gemma turned on fiancé number one. "Cade, tact. Roberts doesn't need to know everything."

So they'd screwed the minute the motel doors had closed. He didn't blame them. He would have done the same. If they'd allowed him to, he would have spent the rest of the day fucking the hell out of his subs. He wouldn't have allowed them out of bed until none of them could move.

"Gemma, you want to explain what you're doing here?" She'd been calling him. There was no question in his brain that this had to do with what she wanted from him. "I thought you were calling me because you wanted some sort of a donation."

Gemma turned to him, her face scrunching up. "I don't do the donation thing anymore. Nate made me do it once and I was awful at it. We actually came up at a negative number because Doc sued us for harassment."

Cade grinned as he sat down next to Kitten and put a hand on Zander's back. "She's actually pretty terrible at soliciting."

Jesse McCann was suddenly at the entryway. "She is and that's funny since she's a lawyer." He winked his fiancée's way. "The Brits call them solicitors. Like lawyers are hookers. I like it."

Gemma sent him a look that could freeze water in a glance. "Thanks, babe. I love having years of my life compared to spending a couple of hours on my back. How about I finally get around to talking to the man I've been trying to get on the phone for four weeks?"

Cole sank back into one of his mother's favorite chairs. There were two wingbacks and a pristinely cared for Victorian sofa. Cade and Jesse stood behind Gemma, lending her their support. "I really thought you were hitting me up for a donation. If you're not, I sincerely apologize."

"Yeah," she said as she took a seat across from him. "Start apologizing. Like a lot."

Cole simply sat and waited.

"You're no fun." Gemma crossed her legs.

Cade kissed the top of her head. "Hey, baby, while you're dealing with all the technical stuff, I'm going to go check out the pool. I could use a little relaxation after that long drive and spending all night making sure the twins didn't touch the ground. We took turns walking with them. If that's okay with our host."

Cole nodded. It had been a long time since he'd had friends out to the house. Since they were here, they might as well enjoy themselves. "There's beer in the fridge and towels in the cabana. Kitten, would you please show our guests the amenities?"

Kitten rolled over and managed to get to her feet without ever setting the baby down. She cuddled him close. "Of course. Please come with me. I think Zander needs a change, too, so I'll go and join Callie after I show Cade and the Master to the pool."

Cade's eyes widened. "I'm just Cade?"

Jesse gave his partner a slow smile. "The sub knows what she's talking about."

"I can spot a Master from a mile away." She was grinning as she left the room, followed by Jesse and Cade.

Blessed quiet. He watched as Kitten bounced the baby on her hip. She was so animated and happy. He hadn't thought about kids. He certainly hadn't thought about Kitten wanting kids. She'd seemed so far from that.

She was different than he'd imagined. Stronger. More centered. She deserved to have what she wanted out of life, and he hadn't missed the way Mason had lit up when he'd looked at those kids.

His subs might want babies down the line, children who would bind them together for all of time, kids who would have his or Mason's DNA and Kitten's. There was no contract between a parent and a child. There was just the lifelong commitment to love and protect. He couldn't ease himself away from a child.

And he didn't want to. He was suddenly incredibly aware that his contract with Kitten had an end date. Six months. She could walk away after six months. His verbal agreement with Mason was even shorter.

"I thought you and Mason had split up." Gemma's uncharacteristically somber voice brought him out of his thoughts.

He hated being put on the spot, but he was so curious about what she wanted with him. "We've recently gotten back together. Why are you here, Gemma?"

Gemma looked behind him and nodded. "Nice of you to join us, Nate."

Nate Wright strode in wearing a Western shirt, jeans, and boots. He had close-cropped brown hair and a face that could have been cut from granite. He'd been a DEA agent and now served as the chief protector of Bliss. He was quick to write a ticket and he'd held the line against everything from biker gangs to the Russian mob. He took his town seriously.

Nate was going to hate him if he lost that piece of land and it became a massive mall. Something precious would have been lost and it would be on Cole.

He had to make it work. He had to find a way to save his damn company and get back ownership of that land.

"Cole." Nate nodded his way as he passed a file folder to Gemma. "Here's the info. Where's the suspect?"

Gemma rolled her eyes. "He's not a suspect. He never was. We wanted to talk to him, but had a hard time locating him. We actually came here to see if you knew where he was. Lucky for us, he was right here."

Cole sat up straighter. Suspect? "Do you mean Mason? What the hell are you talking about? Look, I'm sorry I dodged your calls, but I would really like to know why you're here."

"Besides the fact that Callie can't handle a little dirt?" Gemma asked.

Nate held up a hand. "When you have two kids, you won't be distracted by sex. You walked in that nasty motel room and started doing it. Zane, Callie, and I had to deal with the boys and that meant actually looking at the room and not naked body parts. By the way, Cole, have I mentioned that I appreciate the fact that the Elk Creek Lodge has zero bedbugs."

"Why are you here?" They were making him nervous. Did they already know about the corporate takeover?

Nate sank onto the couch. "Gemma gets bored. When she gets bored, she starts putting her nose into everyone's business."

"Gemma is good at her job and she manages to get everything done in a quarter of the time everyone else needs," Gemma corrected.

Nate shrugged. "She does. She's got a type A personality and way too much time on her hands. She actually made a database of aliens. She's got it down to what kind of probes they use and the best place to shove the beet in order to take them out."

"Hey, Mel takes me seriously when I tell him there's nothing to worry about. I've cut down on alien involved 911 calls by twenty-five percent," Gemma argued.

"And you've brought complaints against the department up by

forty." Nate sighed. "She can be aggressive. She's also obsessed with cold cases, and that's why we're here. I needed to give her something to do so I opened our cold case files and let her have a look. Since Bliss was formed back in the sixties, we've had a handful of cases no one solved ranging from the time Hiram's outhouse was torched in '72 to the great toilet papering incident of last year. Seriously, Max couldn't open the door. Someone shellacked that sucker shut."

"It was Hal. He got sick of Max's complaints." Gemma crossed one leg over the other as she contemplated Cole. "And the burning of Hiram's shitter was a complete accident. Stella was trying to sneak a smoke."

"You didn't have to confront her Agatha Christie style in her own diner," Nate complained. "She paced and pointed and everything. She had Stella crying and offering to go to jail at the end of it."

Gemma smiled and sighed as though she'd found the event satisfying. "I got her to confess, didn't I? She even thanked me afterward because she said it haunted her because that outhouse had been in Hiram's family for two generations. I say she was a hero because Hiram was forced to get indoor plumbing after that. And I'm a freaking rock star because I've taken those forty cold cases and solved all but three of them. I don't think we'll ever truly understand the great toilet explosion of aught three."

They were starting to annoy him. "This is all terribly interesting, but how does it affect me?"

"Gemma doesn't like the reports on Emily Yarborough's accident," Nate explained.

"Technically the incident wasn't a crime. It was an accident. I happened to find the files while I was looking up another case. They were a little sloppy, but you'll have to forgive him. He was dealing with a lot at the time." Gemma picked up the folder.

Nate's jaw formed a grim line. "I was down a man. When I should have been dealing with the accident and reports, I had to handle the fallout from the Russian mob hitting town."

He knew what had happened. It was the same incident that sent Logan to the hospital and eventually brought him to The Club. From what Cole understood, it had been chaos, but he'd been too caught up in his own misery.

"Why is Emily's accident a cold case? A cold case implies wrongdoing." He didn't like the sound of that. The only other person involved was Mason. Did he need a lawyer?

"It wasn't actually a cold case, but the file on Mason alerted me to Ms. Yarborough's accident. You see there was a file on Mason, but Nate never made it formal. So there are a few things about that evening that disturb me and I would like to talk to Mason. He's the only one who's still alive. I have some questions about the party Ms. Yarborough attended. Jesse told me I should talk to you first because you're his Master. Jesse takes that shit seriously."

"Gemma," Nate barked at his assistant.

"Stuff. He takes the BDSM stuff seriously," she corrected.

"He's going to spank you," Nate warned.

A chill went up Cole's spine. "What kind of questions? What do you think happened?"

"Were you aware that three days after the accident a man named George Nelson was busted in Creede for selling the drug gamma-hydroxybutyric acid?" Gemma asked.

Nate rolled his blue eyes. "She's showing off. She practiced the pronunciation in the car. It's GHB."

Everything about this conversation put him on edge. "The date rape drug? What does a drug bust in Creede have to do with anything? Mason and Emily hadn't left the lodge except for that party in the weeks prior to her accident. They certainly weren't involved in drugs."

"That's not true," Gemma said, a fire lighting her eyes. She seemed excited about whatever was in that file. "Not the drug part. I have no way of knowing that, but Mason did leave the lodge. Credit card records show Mason took the Benz in for service the day of the accident. But he didn't go to Long-Haired Roger's shop."

"I went into Creede because Emily wanted a particular wine, and at the time there wasn't a liquor store I could buy it from. She was very insistent. She claimed she wouldn't drink anything but an Argentine Malbec. She'd gone through all the bottles we had at the lodge. Creede was the closest place to stock it." Mason was standing in the doorway, a somber look on his face. "Cole was in the middle of negotiations so I didn't want to bother him with it. And I didn't expect to have the car serviced. I had the oil changed when I went into town. Something was weird with Emily's car because I could have sworn I'd had that oil changed a couple of weeks before, but the light came on that day indicating the oil was low."

Mason took care of the cars. When they'd been together, one of the things Mason did was maintenance on the vehicles. He'd kept a careful record of each cars' service. If he thought he'd changed the oil, then he likely had.

Mason was right about one thing. He'd been knee-deep in negotiations. "Are you trying to say there was some kind of mechanical failure with Emily's car?"

Gemma sat back, considering him. "I don't know. Here's the thing. They didn't check because her blood alcohol level was so high. It was twice the legal limit, but I reviewed the photographs of the scene and there were no skid marks, no place where she even tried to brake. The car was taken to a junkyard and crushed and recycled so we can't know."

"I was overworked at the time," Nate said. "I should have done a more thorough investigation, but I left it to some outside help. When things go crazy, officers from other counties pitch in. We're a small county. We have to use our resources the best we can. There was no question Emily was drunk and her blood work proved it. I assumed they didn't find brake marks because she didn't brake. She likely passed out cold."

"It wouldn't be the first time it happened on that pass." Elk Creek Pass was dangerous and not everyone respected the mountain. There had been several fatality accidents because someone decided they could handle the pass after they'd had a few. "It's a miracle Mason made it down himself. He could have died, too."

"I wasn't drunk," Mason said quietly, his jaw a tense line. "Emily might have had too much to drink, but I hadn't. I will admit that I lost track of her. I got waylaid by a problem with some contracts. At the time I was the lead counsel for Cole's firm. I needed a quiet place to talk and by the time I got off the phone, an hour and a half had gone by. I found her and she was trashed."

"How did she get in the car if you were sober and she wasn't?" He was tired of this fight. He wanted to move on.

Mason wouldn't look at him, preferring to address Gemma and the sheriff. "You have to understand, Emily was mean when she wasn't drunk. She was pretty much evil when she'd had a couple. I tried to pick her up and take her out of there and she threatened to call the police. She said she would call the police and tell them that Cole and I beat her. She had the bruises to prove it."

Cole went cold at the thought. "Shit. The night before we'd hosted a play party and she had some paddle marks on her ass. She never minded them. She said she liked to look at them."

Mason laughed but it was a bitter sound. "Yeah, well, she also didn't mind them because she could use them. I backed away. I was going to call you, but she stole my cell. I got frustrated and I decided to wait until she passed out. I got a cup of coffee and the next thing I remember was waking up in the sheriff's department in the morning. I was in a cell and Nate told me you had left me there."

"You don't remember talking to me that night?" It was etched in Cole's brain forever.

Mason shook his head and his eyes came up, meeting Cole's with a sure stare. "I drank coffee, Cole. Coffee. No alcohol. I spent the night dealing with your contract problems and your sub. I needed the caffeine."

Gemma's eyes lit up. "I need to know who gave you that coffee, Mason. Because that's the person who tried to kill you."

Chapter Sixteen

Mason stared out at the city. He could hear the sounds of laughter from the other rooms, but he stared straight ahead. All around him the buildings of Dallas shot up from the ground, a concrete garden.

It was hours after Gemma had explained the situation to him and he was still trying to wrap his head around it. His toxicology reports had told the story. He'd been drugged. It was why he couldn't remember the accident or coming down the mountain after Emily. Everyone had blamed him and now they had to face the truth. He'd been innocent.

He knew he'd been innocent, so why was finally having the proof messing with his head?

Cole should have believed in him. Cole should have trusted him.

Why had she dragged all this shit into the open again just as he'd been starting to forget? When he'd been in bed with Kitten and Cole this morning, he'd been able to forget all the pain between them, and now his need for revenge was an aching burn in his gut again. He wanted to be back there, wanted that glorious moment where nothing had mattered except the feel of Cole's hard body against his and the way Kitten had stared at them like they were a work of art. For a moment he'd been safe and happy and he hadn't given a damn about what had happened before.

Cole had tried to talk to him but Julian had called with important news and Mason wasn't ready to listen to Cole yet. He might never be.

"You know you're going to get sniped, right?"

Mason rolled his eyes. He didn't need to turn to figure out his taciturn babysitter had shown up. "I think that should be my choice. I don't want you here, Chase. If somebody shoots me here, then I'm kind of cool with it."

Someone had been trying to kill him for a long time it seemed, and Cole had done nothing about it. Cole had blamed him.

"And if I'm not cool with it?"

Shit. Chase wasn't alone. Mason had wanted to avoid the hell out of this particular reunion. Julian Lodge owned the building he was currently in. Julian Lodge was the biggest, baddest Dom in their particular world, and he'd basically told the man to suck his cock.

He forced himself to turn and sure enough, there was the devil himself in a three-piece suit since the dinner party hadn't become a play party yet. "I can always leave. I wouldn't want to bring your party down."

"Chase, would you mind giving us a moment," Julian said.

"Yes, I would. The sniping and all." Chase Dawson didn't move. "I kind of get paid to make sure no one gets killed in this case."

"Don't you think your talents would be put to better use researching the situation?" Julian asked with a pointed stare.

"Nat got a flat tire on her way home. Ben's out picking her up. Wolf is escorting Dani and Chloe to a Mommy and Me class on kicking her legs or something. Trust me, if one of us is going to be brutally murdered in the line of duty, it should be Ben, but I'm all you've got so you two should talk because I'm not going anywhere."

Julian sighed and shook his head. "I should have fired them all long ago. Chase and Ben. Leo and Wolf. No one listens to me anymore. Of course, you rather started that trend. Didn't you, Mason?"

Was Julian about to give him the boot? How would Cole handle that? This place was practically Kitten's home. She'd spent years here. She loved Julian Lodge like a father. Would she look at him differently?

"I was never your submissive, Julian."

"No, but I rather thought we were friends." Julian stared at him, his dark eyes seeming to see right through him.

"You were Cole's friend." They had all been Cole's friends. Mason was Cole's plaything. That was all he'd ever really been. The poor kid Cole had taken in and tossed out like the trash when he proved he wasn't good enough to run with the alpha dogs.

"No. I was your friend. Do you know what I was trying to do that day I called you?" Julian asked.

"I'm not stupid. I knew what was going on. I couldn't afford the membership and I doubt Cole would have wanted me here. If it makes you feel safer, I never intended to walk through these doors again."

Julian shook his head and looked out over the cityscape, reminding Mason of a king surveying his kingdom. "I was going to offer you a place to stay. I was going to suggest you move in to The Club for a while. I was worried about you."

His heart threatened to sink because of all the things Julian could have said, that was the last he expected. "You were going to give me a place to stay?"

"As I said, I was worried about you. Many of us were. Jackson attempted to call you as well."

Jack Barnes. Mason had ignored him, too. "I was in a bad place."

"We knew. That was why we called. Mason, what Cole did was wrong. You understand that, right?"

Was Julian trying to steer him away from Cole? "I wasn't drunk."

Julian leaned against the balcony. "It wouldn't matter if you had been. If you had been drunk, you should have been properly punished and sent into counseling. He had a responsibility to care for you and he failed. He allowed his fear and grief to overwhelm his duty to you. I believe he understands that now. As it is, I've heard the new evidence. I've already sent it on to Chase, and he needs to sit down with you."

"I have some questions about the party," Chase admitted. "I'd like a guest list, but I understand the person who owned the house moved and didn't keep one. Unlike the rest of the civilized world, apparently she didn't evite everyone. She called at the last minute."

"Trish wasn't big on organization." She'd been friends with Cole's family, and he'd heard she moved shortly after the accident. "There were also a bunch of people who showed up who weren't invited. The house was packed that night. They spilled out into the yard, and it wasn't exactly a warm night. Cole had been hosting a group of his executives. Several of them went out with us that night. I can at least give you those names. Most of them still work for Cole."

"I would appreciate that." Chase's eyes narrowed. "You still keep up with Cole's business?"

That felt like more than a friendly question. "Not really, why?"

"Chase." Julian managed to make the name sound like a warning.

"Boss, this is why he's here, isn't it?" Chase asked, his big shoulders shrugging up and down.

There was definitely something he was missing. "I thought I was here because Cole's being overly protective."

Julian put a hand up and that seemed to get Chase to back down. "Again, you're here because we're worried about you. I think you're about to make a big mistake. I'm going to ask you not to."

"What kind of mistake?" He was genuinely curious. Julian wasn't behaving in any manner he'd expected. Unless Julian was setting him up for a mighty fall, he might have to believe the Dom was being honest. He might have to reevaluate. Those years he'd spent at The Club had been some of the best of his life and then he'd labeled it all as false memory after Cole had left him. He'd put everything in a file labeled lies, and maybe he'd been hasty. Tara and Darin had seemed to have actually been hurt by his distance. What if Julian and Jack had felt the same?

"Are you planning to bring Cole down, Mason?"

Well, Julian had never been naïve. Mason shrugged with a negligence he didn't feel. He might still get kicked to the curb tonight. "Would you blame me?"

"No." Julian shook his head. "I wouldn't. I understand the need for revenge. I understand the need to balance the score. I also figured out long ago that there shouldn't be a score kept between lovers. I made that mistake many times. I was unkind. I put my place as a Dom first and didn't even think about the fact that I should care for my submissives on an emotional level. Cole made this mistake with you. Don't further complicate things. This is no longer only between you and Cole."

Ah, now things were becoming clearer. It made sense that Julian would care about Kitten. She was related to him through Finn. "This is about Kitten."

"Poor little sub. You keep trying to find a way to make yourself meaningless. This is about three people I care about. I see what you're doing. If you go through with it, you're going to destroy more lives than just Cole's. Kitten is in love with you." He smiled for the first time and the sight was almost enough to make Mason sigh. Julian always looked like a dark god, but he was truly gorgeous when he smiled. "She's more open and happy than I've ever seen her. She's coming into her own and you're a big part of that. You have a place in this family. Can't you see that? You're the glue that binds them. You. They don't work without you. They were struggling without you."

And he had no doubt they would find their way when he walked out. He wasn't good for Kitten. He could see that now. She needed more than he could give her. Did he really expect that she would leave all that wealth to go live with him in some hovel? He would have to work long hours so she would be alone. She would come to resent him, and he couldn't handle that.

And she won't resent you for walking away? Even without finding a way to hurt Cole, she'll hate you for leaving her. You promised her. You promised with your body. You promised to stay with her by taking her into your arms.

He couldn't stay. He couldn't leave.

He was stuck and he had no idea how to get out.

"You understand that this plan of yours hurts more than you, correct?" Julian was saying.

He wished Cole had let him stay behind. He needed to be alone.

He needed to think and he couldn't do it here. "Sure. I hurt Kitten. I hurt Cole."

"You hurt more than merely them, Mason, and you know it."

Mason sighed. "Fine. I hurt The Club."

Julian's eyes narrowed. "I was talking about that town in Colorado. Have you given any consideration to what this will do to every family who lives there?"

Mason shook his head, forcing himself to focus. "What are you talking about? How does my leaving Cole hurt Bliss?"

Any sympathy leeched from Julian's face and Mason found himself staring at the biggest, baddest Dom in his world. "Are you going to play this game out to the end?"

He didn't even try to fight it. He let his eyes find the floor because Julian was serious when he started to look like the lord of the underworld. "I'm not sure what you're talking about, Sir."

No matter what happened between him and Cole, he'd been wrong about the rest, and if there was any way to repair the relationships, he had to try. He didn't have to lose everything this time.

You don't have to lose anything at all. All you need to lose is the tiniest bit of your pride, and it hasn't exactly been helpful.

"Did you think we wouldn't find out?" Julian asked, his voice as cold as ice.

"Find out what?" He was fairly certain he wasn't involved in the same conversation he'd thought he had been. Julian seemed to know something he didn't. His revenge plans had always been vague and unformed. He'd planned to ruin Cole and walk off with Kitten, but at every turn he'd chosen to bring them closer together rather than drive a wedge. He'd failed at the revenge thing the same way he'd failed at everything else.

Except bringing them all together and keeping them together. Julian was right. He'd been damn good at that. He could be the rock of that household if he let himself. Kitten got lost in her own world and Cole buried himself in work. Mason could be the one who drew them back to their family if he managed to let go of the past.

"Chase is not the only one I've brought into this investigation.

Ben and Chase run my personal security, but McKay-Taggart works for my business."

Where was this going? "Yes, I remember. Big blonde guy. Heavy on the sarcasm. His partner is easier to deal with."

"They have a forensic accountant working for them now." Julian managed to make every word seem like an accusation. "Phoebe Murdoch found your scam very quickly. We know about the money you have hidden. I'll be honest, I thought you would be smart enough to hide it better. Did you get it in exchange for information on the corporate structure?"

Information on the corporate structure? "Are you talking about Cole's company? I don't understand. You're going to need to be clearer. Why would you hire an accountant? I don't have any money. Are you accusing me of something?"

It sure felt like he was.

Chase sighed, a weary sound. "I think you're going to have to go through with it, boss. He's not going down easy. He should. You had to know someone would find that trail. It wasn't even hidden very well. You have to be less sloppy when you're committing crimes." Chase stopped suddenly and regarded Mason. "You're not stupid. Did you mean for us to find it? Or is something else going on?"

Nausea rolled in his gut because here he was again. He didn't even know what they were accusing him of this time, but it sounded like it would be special. This time he was trying to hurt not only Cole and Kitten, but an entire town. "I'm sure you know everything."

It occurred to him to soften, to ask what was going on, but he couldn't do it. If history was going to repeat itself, he wouldn't cry and whine over Cole this time. He wouldn't plead. He wouldn't call Cole and beg to be allowed to come home. He didn't have a fucking home and this time he would remember that. He would walk out with his damn pride intact and everyone could fuck themselves.

If he didn't have anything else, at least he had the truth.

Chase turned and looked at Julian. "Maybe I should take a couple of hours and review the report Phoebe sent again, boss. Something's not adding up."

"Or we can bring the information we have to Cole and see what happens." Julian turned, straightening his tie and smoothing down the lapels of his jacket. "I think it's time for Cole to see what we've discovered."

Yeah, that didn't sound good. His brain whirled, trying to figure out what they could have "discovered" about him. He'd done nothing but take care of Kitten since he'd gone home with her. He'd think about planning to ruin Cole and then he'd get distracted by her or by him and he'd put it off, telling himself he'd do it another day.

He would never have done it. He would have kept putting it off until he was so tied to them he couldn't get out. He never learned.

Julian stared at him for a moment. "Come along then, Mason. Let's see if this time is any different than the last. Know that no matter what you've done or what Cole does, you're welcome here. I'm afraid you won't have any place to go after Cole learns about what you were planning to do."

He watched as Julian disappeared through the doors and his gut tightened. What the hell was going on? He got the very bad feeling that his whole world was going to fall apart again, and he was fairly certain he wouldn't survive it this time.

* * * *

"What's going on? Do you know anything?" Tara sat down beside Kitten, easing onto the sofa while she glanced around the room, her eyes moving from Dom to Dom. "Can you feel the vibes in this room? The men are all tense. They don't get that way unless someone's in serious trouble."

Kitten looked around the penthouse, and sure enough, every Dom present seemed to be speaking quietly, their eyes finding hers from time to time. The sympathy she saw in them made her a little sick. She'd thought this was supposed to be a play party, but Cole hadn't brought his kit with him. It didn't look like anyone would be playing. They were all totally serious.

At first she'd been a bit relieved to put off the inevitable, but she'd rapidly realized something worse was happening.

Normally she would find her calm. She would take a deep

breath. The Doms knew best. She didn't need to worry. She could let them handle everything. They would tell her what she needed to know when she needed to know it.

Yes, that was what she'd done for years. Decades really, since before coming here, she'd treated her father very much the same way. He knew best and she waited.

Fuck that. She needed to know now. She couldn't sit here and hope for the best. Tara knew all the good gossip. "What have you heard?"

Tara's eyes went wide. "Are you asking me what I think you're asking me?"

Sometimes her reputation for perfect behavior cost her time. "What have you heard about Mason? Or me? Is Cole planning something?"

"Miss Kitten, that would be gossiping."

She didn't have time for prevarication. "Yes, and I'll take my punishment. I want to know. I want to know now."

"I don't know anything," Tara said, leaning over and putting a hand over hers. "I know that Darin believes Mason's accident wasn't an accident, but he's been busy and he hasn't had a chance to check up on it. Everything's been given over to the Dawsons and McKay-Taggart. It's weird. Darin told me he'd heard Cole was happy again."

Then why was everyone looking at her like her world was about to fall apart? "That can't be everything. I need to know more."

"Why?" Tara asked. "I'm confused. You're always so calm. You're the one who told me that in order to be a sub, I had to be more trusting."

Why was Tara throwing her own stupid words back at her? Yes, she'd said them, and yes, she'd meant them at the time. She really had. She'd meant every word. She'd thought it was the way a true submissive acted. Now she realized the idiocy in even thinking there was such a thing as a "true" submissive. She'd clung to that word because she needed something to define her. She'd needed some set of recognizable letters that made up who she was. Submissive—willing to obey someone else. It was simple. It was easy. But life wasn't easy. Love wasn't easy. She couldn't simply be submissive.

Not if she wanted to be a woman who was worthy of her men. She had to be something more. She had to become again—become the woman Cole and Mason could love.

Unfortunately, that woman turned out to be a little impatient and a whole lot scared at the thought of not getting to be with both of them.

She loved them. Really loved them. For the first time in her life, she wanted something more than to be someone's sub, someone's slave. She wanted to be Cole's love, Mason's love. She wanted to be the heartbeat of a family.

She wanted more. She'd gone through life accepting the scraps she was given and now she knew one thing. She deserved more and she wasn't going to stand for less than what she deserved.

She glanced over and Cole was standing there talking to Jack Barnes, but his eyes went toward the balcony where Mason was.

Mason was Cole's first love. Mason had been Cole's whole life as far as she could tell.

What if Cole decided he only wanted Mason?

"You went pale. What's wrong, honey?" Tara's hand found hers.

"How long were they together?"

Tara's brow rose. "Cole and Mason? They were together for years."

She knew that. She had another question. "And what was the longest time they kept a woman?"

Tara shrugged. "Never too long. I think one was with them for a year or two."

A couple of years. They were back together. Cole and Mason were getting to solid ground. What if they wanted to spend time alone? What if they were bringing her back to Julian so they could be on their own?

"I have a contract."

Tara shook her head. "Yes. I think we all know that."

"My contract is for six months." She was only a few months in. He couldn't dump her. It wasn't fair. He had to keep her for the term of her contract. She could hold him to it. She could use it like a blunt instrument.

He'd told her he wanted her. He'd let Mason take her non-virginity. He'd let her believe she was beautiful. He'd told her he would take care of her. He'd told her with the contract, but more importantly, he'd promised her with his body. He'd made love to her.

Unless it had just been sex. Maybe she didn't know the difference. It felt so much like love to her, but maybe it hadn't been the same to him.

He hadn't touched her sexually until Mason had come home. Even then, he'd allowed Mason to take her first—like an offering to keep him around.

Had he used her to keep Mason around?

She hated this. She hated feeling like this. This was why she'd held so much of herself back. She'd learned early on how horrible it felt to be unworthy.

"Kitten, sweetie, I don't know what you're thinking, but it's kind of scaring me." Tara stood up. "I think we need to go somewhere quiet and discuss this. Julian is with Mason on the balcony, so maybe we should go into the parlor."

She turned and looked and sure enough, there was Julian on the balcony. He was standing there talking to Mason. They looked deep in conversation. Mason's back was to her, but Julian frowned fiercely. He wasn't happy about what he was hearing.

Was he hearing that Mason wanted Cole all for himself?

She was being paranoid. She had to be.

"Kitten?" Tara looked down at her.

Kitten shook her head and stood up. She wasn't going to the parlor so she could be talked down. She didn't want to be talked down by anyone except her men. She needed to know. She needed to know if they would still want her when they knew the truth. She wanted more than what was outlined in their contract, more than she could get from any contract. A contract had limits. She didn't want limits. She wanted everything.

She turned and walked straight up to Cole, her heart threatening to pound out of her chest. Tears made the world a blurry place as she approached him, and every instinct she had told her this was wrong. She should step back and sit down and hope that Cole kept her. If she stayed quiet, he might decide she was easy to deal with, and they needed a woman. He might keep her.

Screw that. She wanted Cole to keep her because he loved her. Damn it. She wanted to be loved and she wasn't about to accept anything less.

She walked straight up to Cole. "I don't like the terms of my contract, Sir."

Remain polite. She could survive this.

Cole turned icy eyes on her. "What?"

Oh, she wanted to hide, but she was done with that. "I lied in my contract. I didn't think I was lying at the time, but now I know I was wrong."

"Wrong about what?"

Jack frowned. "Perhaps we should bring Julian into this. He's her guardian."

"And I'm her Dom," Cole shot back. "That means something in this place. She signed a contract with me, not with Julian."

"And it seems like she regrets that now," Jack replied with a sigh.

That made it sound like a bad thing. Cole might think it was bad that she'd become so paranoid and possessive, but she certainly wasn't trying to leave. "I don't regret it, though I have to wonder if my Master does."

Cole took her arm in his big hand. "Master Jack, I need to speak to my submissive alone."

Jack nodded. "I'll let Julian know. I think he won't mind if you use his office. He's planning on all of us retiring there anyway."

Cole stopped. "What's going on, Jack?"

Jack held his hands up. "That's Julian's story to tell."

Cole gently clutched her elbow and started for Julian's office. "This had better be good, pet. I'm not in a particularly happy mood. If you think I should change the terms of your contract, I would sincerely like to hear why."

He was walking too fast, and she nearly ran to keep up with him. She knew she should be afraid, but she wasn't afraid of him hurting her physically. Breaking her heart? She was terrified of that.

She found herself in Julian's office, the same office she'd first come to so many years ago. She'd stood with Finn and waited silently for her fate to be pronounced. She hadn't made a case for herself. She'd let Finn do it. She'd merely stood there and hoped Julian gave her a home.

She was right back here but she was a different person, and she couldn't wait and hope anymore. She had to make things happen. She had to be more than she'd been.

"Did you bring me here to return me to Julian?" She stood up straight and looked him in the eye.

Cole's jaw dropped open. "Why would you think that? What have I done to make you believe I would do that to you?"

Years and years of being unwanted had taught her that she was expendable. "You and Mason don't keep subs for long."

He softened, his arms going to her shoulders. "Only because we hadn't found the right one. You're the right one, pet. You're the one who completes us."

He was giving her everything she wanted and she was still on the verge of tears because he might not think the same way once she told him the truth.

"I work very hard sometimes to get around the rules."

His lips turned up in a gentle smile. "I wouldn't have suspected it, but I enjoy your manipulations because there's nothing malicious about them."

"I like to gossip."

He actually chuckled at that one. "Everyone likes to gossip. We simply try to keep it to a reasonable minimum. I think you'll find we Doms sometimes place a harsher influence on certain things because we know they'll occur anyway. What is prompting this? Talk to me."

Tears threatened but she had to tell him. "I lied."

"About what?" He was being so tender with her. Once she'd told him she wasn't trying to leave, he'd done nothing but comfort her. She'd expected to be interrogated but he simply asked as though he wasn't terribly concerned about the answer.

"I said I would be all right sharing you and being shared, and I don't want that."

He stopped. "You don't want to share me with Mason?"

Kitten shook her head. "No, Master. I love Master Mason. I love you. I don't want to be shared with anyone else."

His eyes went hard. "Who the hell asked to share you? I want his fucking name. Was it a Dom here?"

Oh, he was misunderstanding her. He took a step back and she reached out to hold him because as tender as he'd been with her, he looked like he was ready to be brutal with someone else. Maybe she'd misread the situation. "No, Master. No one asked. I was talking about our contract. I stated plainly in our contract that I would enjoy you sharing me with other Dominants. I meant it at the time. I thought I would like it. I thought it would make me feel sexy."

"You thought you wouldn't feel anything at all. You wanted sex to be a meaningless pleasure. You were wrong. It means more." He was staring at her again, his hands cupping her face. "Say it again. I think I missed something important in my violent rage at the thought of another man touching you."

The three scariest words in the world. She'd said them before and been rejected even by the people who should have loved her the most. Cole was right. She'd thought having sex would buy her something with her Master. She'd thought that if she was the perfect sub, she never had to deal with those three words again. She'd been so wrong. "I love you, Master."

Cole hauled her up and his big arms wound around her, hugging her like he would never let her go. "I love you, pet. I love you more than I could have imagined, so put all your worries aside. That contract is meaningless."

"But you need it." She thought she'd needed it, too.

"Mason was right. It's a useless piece of paper in truth. The love and commitment behind it are what's worthwhile. I don't want to renegotiate every six months with you. I want a lifetime. I want to know I have a life with you."

A life. A love. More than she could have dreamed. She couldn't help it. She sobbed into his neck, letting go of so much anger and fear and worry. She hadn't even known they'd been there until she'd finally felt safe enough to feel.

"Let it out." Cole carried her to the sofa and set himself down, settling her on his lap. “Let it all go. I love you. I love you more than you can know.”

She held on to him as she cried and for the first time in her life felt no shame about letting go of her emotions. Cole was her Master, her lover, her friend, and she rather intended for him to be her husband. This was his place. He offered love and comfort and she took it because it was her right. She sobbed and shook and finally settled against him. His hands moved over her, smoothing her hair and holding her tight.

“I can’t promise nothing will hurt you again. I can only swear to you that I will be there if it does.” He kissed the top of her forehead.

It was more than enough. “And I promise to figure out what I want to do, Master. I promise to figure out who I want to be.”

He tilted her head up and gently swiped away her tears. “You can be anything you want. I’ll help you. I’ll support you in anything you want to do, and so will Mason, if we can convince him to stay with us. I don’t think he’s forgiven me. I don’t blame him, but we need to get past it if we’re going to have a chance.”

“He has to stay.” Now that she knew what she wanted, she knew she couldn’t lose it. She couldn’t lose half her heart.

“He’s right. I can’t make him stay. I can force him while he’s in danger, but as soon as we clear this up, I have to honor his decision.” His face tightened. “And I’m going through some difficult business problems. I have a fight on my hands and if I lose, it could hurt us financially quite badly. You should know that before you commit to staying with me. I will always take care of you, but we might have to move.”

“I don’t care about the house.” But Cole did. Cole had grown up there. “We can move if we need to.”

“We might have to downsize.”

So it could get bad. She might need to find a job and carry her weight, but suddenly that didn’t sound so bad. “We only need one decent-sized bedroom. We can find an apartment. I have some money saved up. I also heard that Leo doesn’t like his new secretary.”

His eyes widened. “No. You’re not working. You’re going back to school, but I truly appreciate the offer.” He sighed. “I will do everything I can to keep the company. I owe it to some people I care about."

"Then I'll help you."

He stared at her for a long moment, some unnamed emotion flowing from him. "And I would never have shared you with anyone but Mason. I thought I could in the beginning but I became possessive very quickly. I love you, too, Kitten. I love you today and I promise I'll love you forever. I'm going to make this right for all of us."

She nodded. She wished he would tell her what was going on, but she was willing to be patient on this subject. Trust. Maybe she hadn't understood the word before, but trust and love seemed to go hand in hand.

She sighed and a sense of peace she'd never known before settled on her. It was all in her grasp. All she had to do was have a little faith.

The door opened and Julian walked in. "Cole, I hoped I wouldn't have to do this."

Mason stepped in behind him, his face pale, and Kitten knew that whatever was about to happen would change everything.

Chapter Seventeen

Mason followed behind Julian, aware that Chase was hard on his heels, ready to nab him if he made a break for it.

It wasn't like he hadn't thought about it. Whatever Julian thought he'd done, Mason was sure he could prove it. Julian would never bring up charges against him if he didn't have proof. Whatever was about to go down, it would be bad.

He should have demanded to see whatever this crap was, but he was far more interested in how Cole would react. What Cole did was the only thing that mattered. Cole was about to be shown evidence against him and he would believe it. Cole rarely worked on instinct. He preferred cold hard facts.

This would be done in moments.

"Cole, I hoped I wouldn't have to do this," Julian was saying as Mason entered the room.

Mason's stomach tightened as he saw Cole and Kitten. Kitten had been crying, her pretty face red and her eyes puffy. She had to get off Cole's lap so they could both stand, but she kept a hand on his body. When she was safely on her feet, she slipped her small hand in his and Cole drew her close.

Did she already know? Had Cole known this trumped-up shit all along and now he was telling Kitten?

God, he wanted to be anywhere but here.

"You could tell me what 'this' is," Cole intoned. He nodded Mason's way. "Come here, love."

Mason shook his head. He couldn't stand next to the man when he kicked him out again. It looked like he didn't know, so why had Kitten been crying? "I think I'll stay close to the door."

"He thinks he might have to run when you find out the truth." Chase leaned against the doorframe, every inch of his lean body a menacing threat. Chase wouldn't let him run. Chase would be there to ensure he took whatever punishment was about to be dealt out.

He was going to be sick. He had to hold it together.

"Should I leave?" Kitten asked.

"Yes," Julian said.

"No," Cole replied at the same time. His eyes narrowed as he stared at Julian. "I understand that you care for her, but she belongs to me. I make the decisions when it comes to whether she stays or goes in a situation like this. Mason or I do."

But Mason got the feeling he wouldn't be making any decisions when it came to Kitten after the next few moments.

Julian sighed and seemed to consider Cole's words, and after a long moment he assented. "All right. I can see there seems to be a proper bond in place now. I will step back. Please understand my prying is only because I care about the people involved."

"And the prying I get the feeling you're about to do?" Cole asked, his voice tight. "Is that because you care?"

"Yes. It is. I care quite deeply about all of you, though Mason will likely blame me for outing him."

He couldn't help it. Sarcasm was his shield and his sword in times like this. "Don't worry about it, Lodge. I'm pretty sure I outed myself when dear old Dad caught me with my tongue down the boy next door's throat."

"Mason," Cole said, his voice a warning. "I wasn't the boy next door and there's no place for you to be a smartass right now."

Mason shrugged. Cole wouldn't care to discipline him after Julian pounded whatever nail he had into Mason's coffin.

God, he wished Kitten wasn't here to see it, but she should know what her Master was really like. She should know that when the chips were down, Cole wouldn't choose them. Or maybe he would. Maybe he would choose Kitten because she was a female and loving her wasn't as much trouble as loving another man.

He would do it. When Cole struck him down this time, he would take his cue from his Master. He would find some woman and settle down because living a half life was better than living in the purgatory he'd been in for years. He would ignore his impulses and never set foot in a freaking club again. He would force himself to be normal because being himself always got him in trouble. He would move far away and after a while, he would be able to forget.

"Cole, I'm very sorry to say I was right about Mason. Remember when I told you I thought your prior actions would come back to haunt you?" Julian asked, settling in behind his desk. In the afternoon light he looked something like a mob boss about to request a hit on a former employee. He had just the right look of regret coupled with a fierce will.

"I do, but you're wrong. Mason and I might not be one hundred percent fine, but I'm going to make it up to him." Cole gave him the faintest hint of a smile, but he saw the affection in his eyes.

Oh, god. That made it so much worse. He could see everything he could have had. He could have had the right to walk over there and take his place with them, but fate seemed to have found a way to cut off his balls again.

"When you asked Chase and Ben to look into the situation, they found some problems with Mason's story," Julian began.

"Big problems, buddy," Chase said with a sigh. "Did you think we wouldn't find out about the bank accounts? You couldn't seriously imagine we wouldn't be able to link them to you. For god's sake, they're in your name, Mason."

"Bank accounts?" He had one. It had roughly five hundred bucks in it. He'd used all the rest of his money. He'd had a nest egg at one point in time, but he'd run through it. Living in the city wasn't cheap. He didn't even have a savings account anymore. They'd shut it down due to poverty or some shit.

Chase rolled his eyes and took a seat across from Julian. "Yes, multiple accounts. Cole, Mason told us he was broke but according to the accountant's calculations, he's worth roughly one point five million at this point."

"What?" Mason couldn't believe what he was hearing.

Cole frowned. "Yes, I'd like to understand how that happened. Mason, why would you lie about that?"

And there it was. Cole stared at him with that pious, never-done-anything-wrong look in his eyes. Judgment. Cole was damn good at judging him, and Mason was always found wanting. He wasn't about to cry and defend himself this time. "Why would I lie? Because I'm good at it. It's a hobby of mine."

"No," Julian replied. "You're quite bad at it or you would have known that we would find those accounts and the man who deposited the money into those accounts quite quickly."

Now that he'd accepted the inevitable, it was fascinating to watch how this whole scene unfolded. It was like a bad play and he didn't even know his lines. "Oh, I'm really interested in finding out who gave me one and a half million out of the kindness of his heart."

"It wasn't kindness, was it?" Julian asked. "It was all about business. Cole, are you having trouble with leaks in your organization? Is someone working behind the scenes to wrestle the company away from you?"

The room seemed to drop about fifty degrees with Julian's question. Holy shit. This was about Cole's company. His baby. His legacy from his parents. If Cole believed Mason was trying to hurt Roberts Corp, he would stop at nothing to destroy him.

"Yes," Cole replied quietly. "I find myself in a fight I didn't even know was happening. I recently learned that my minor stockholders are being approached and convinced to sell to seemingly various buyers, but they're all shells of a bigger entity."

Shit. "Someone's trying to become the biggest stockholder so they can take your seat?"

Whoever it was, the minute they gained the majority share, they could take Cole's place as president according to the bylaws of the company. All a person needed was majority stock and then the president would call a meeting of the board and they would very likely take over the CEO position as well. Whoever it was couldn't force Cole off the board, but Roberts Corp would effectively cease to be his company.

"Dad took the company public because we needed capital. I've always meant to buy back that stock and become privately held again, but the timing wasn't right. After what happened with Emily, I threw myself back into work and I needed the money to buy the properties and the companies I wanted to take over," Cole explained.

Mason had followed it all in the business journals for a while. He'd looked for every article that even vaguely mentioned the company. Cole had gone on several raids of smaller companies, swooping down to liquidate and take apart his competitors. "Do you think someone you gutted is looking for revenge?"

Cole shook his head. "No. This is about a piece of land I own in Colorado. It's a jewel of a property."

Shit. "The mall property? The one the board wanted to use for retail space?"

He'd negotiated the deal himself. He'd bought up land from small farms and one large ranch that had gone under. It was big enough to rival the Mall of America. It could be a tourist destination. It could also ruin the land and all the land around it.

"Mason, your acting skills have gotten much better," Julian said, his fingers steepled as he regarded Mason. "Are you trying to tell Cole you didn't plan this? You were his lawyer for years. You would know where to hit him. You would know exactly what a man needed to take over that company."

He would. He would absolutely be the person to conspire with if one wanted to take over Roberts Corp. No one knew it like he had. No one else knew the ins and outs of the business, and more importantly, how to keep under Cole's radar until it was too late for him to do anything about it.

It was a neat trap. "Who did I get this money from?"

"Do you know a Robert Hays?" Julian asked. "I can see from the look on your face that you do."

Bob Hays was a board member. Mason had worked with him for years. Hays had worked with Cole's father, and he always took a hard line when it came to profit. He was one of the members who protested when Cole wanted to spend money to clean up a property or to cede land to the government for preservation. He'd once tried to convince Cole to send in hunters to kill off any possible evidence of endangered species in one particularly large lot of forest land. He was a shark, but he'd always been loyal to Cole. "Yeah, I know him."

"He sent you five payments over the last year. Did it take you that long to figure out exactly how you wanted to take your revenge? Did you come up with the plan or did Bob?" Julian asked, his eyes hawkish.

It wouldn't do him any good to respond. He had no doubt that Julian could prove everything. And yet, he couldn't help himself. "I didn't come up with anything and I don't know how that account came to have my name on it."

Cole stepped away from Kitten and walked to Julian's desk. "Can I see this account?"

Julian gestured to his laptop. "The file is right there. I'll forward it to you, but you can read the highlights now. I think you'll agree it's quite informative."

Julian ceded his chair and allowed Cole to peruse the file. The room went quiet while Cole read the damning items. Kitten found her way to Mason and suddenly she was standing beside him, wrapping her arms around him.

One last hug. It was all he would get from her. It was stupid, but he gripped her so tight and wished he had a private moment with her. He would kiss her and memorize her so when he found his perfectly bland vanilla woman who couldn't know him, he would be able to remember the one woman who could.

"It's going to be all right," Kitten whispered.

He shook his head, utterly unable to speak. God, he wanted her. He wished he'd never met her because now he would mourn two loves, and grieving over Cole had damn near killed him.

"Mason, is any of this true?" Cole asked finally.

Mason disentangled himself from Kitten and put a bit of distance between them. He didn't want Cole to associate Kitten with him any more than he already would. She deserved a good life, and he couldn't give it to her. Hell, Cole would likely lose a bundle fighting this takeover, but Mason had no doubts that he would make another fortune if he had to. It was simply who Cole was. "Are you asking me if I wanted revenge on you?"

"I already knew that, but we can start there." Cole's voice was so wretchedly calm, as though he didn't care about the outcome of Mason's answer.

"Yes. I wanted revenge on you. I wanted to break you. I wanted to make your life hell." It was nothing less than the truth.

"Mason!" Kitten gasped as she shook her head. "You can't mean that."

Cole stood. "Of course he can, pet. Mason and I talked briefly about this last night before you joined us. I told you in the beginning that this wouldn't be easy. I hurt Mason. I nearly destroyed him. I understand his need for revenge."

Kitten's eyes welled with tears. "Master, Mason wouldn't do this."

She didn't know him very well. "I intended to steal you away, Kitten. I was going to drive a wedge between you and the Master so you would leave with me when I was ready to go. I was going to make him feel his loneliness for years to come."

"You weren't very good at it." Cole chuckled. "I gave you every opportunity to drive that wedge because I was so hesitant with her. So why did you smooth things over every single time? Are you incompetent, Mason? Did you think giving me good advice about how to love her would somehow make her go with you?"

He couldn't even get revenge right. He was a pathetic waste. Every time he'd try, he would see what she needed, and it wasn't to be used as a pawn in a game. Hell, if he was honest with himself, he'd just wanted to come home after a few days. He'd wanted to forget everything but how much he loved them.

Cole came to stand right in front of him, his big body blocking out everything else. "Mason, I want you to look me in the eye and answer my question. Did you conspire with Bob Hays to take Roberts Corp away from me?"

He brought his eyes up and was ready to tell his Master to shove it up his ass. He couldn't. He just couldn't. "No, I did not, Master."

"All right." Cole put a hand on his shoulder. "I need you to help me figure out who's trying to implicate you. Whoever set up that account is likely the person who's selling me out."

Mason felt Kitten's arms go around him again, but he was dazed. What had happened?

Julian had the faintest hint of a smile on his face. "Cole, are you telling me you don't believe the evidence we discovered?"

"I'm telling you that I believe Mason." Cole turned back to him. "Are you still planning on trying to take Kitten from me, love?"

Mason shook his head. "I can't handle her myself, Master."

It was nothing less than the truth. He didn't even want to handle her all by himself. He wanted his family. He wanted Cole and Kitten and a bunch of insane children who would make his life hell and worth living. Hope welled inside him and it felt so much better than anything he'd felt before.

Cole stepped up and gripped Mason by the nape of his neck, bringing their foreheads together. "I will never choose anyone or anything over you again. Not my pride or my honor. Certainly not myself. I make this vow to you both. You deserve your revenge, Mason, but I'm asking you to forego it. I'm asking for your forgiveness because I can't live without you."

Mason let go of his anger because it had nothing on the love he felt. "I forgive you, Master. I love you so much."

Cole wrapped him in a hug and he felt Kitten at his back. He breathed deep, trying not to cry in front of Julian, but it was hard because he'd finally come home.

Cole released him and covered his mouth in a swift kiss. "And you'll have to talk to our sub. She thought we were going to pimp her out to other Doms this afternoon."

Just like that his rage was back. He whirled on Kitten. "What the hell?"

She flushed prettily. "Master, it was in our contract."

"You're getting a new fucking contract." He wasn't going to share her with anyone. He was a deep believer in monogamy between a man, his boyfriend, and their chosen female. She would have to toe the line on that dictate.

"When you think about it, I should be punished." Kitten bit her gorgeous bottom lip as she thought. "I think figging is the only way to go."

Oh, he was going to find the biggest piece of ginger he could and shove it right up her pretty little asshole. And she would love it. He couldn't help but laugh. "You're going to be the death of me, gorgeous girl."

He wouldn't leave her until death. He would stay by her side every moment he was alive.

Cole turned to Julian with a sigh. "You're a bastard. You know that, right?"

Julian shrugged. "You needed a push."

What did that mean? "So there isn't an account with my name on it?"

Chase yawned as though he was bored with the whole thing now. "Oh, it's there. I just figured out you didn't know a thing about it about five minutes in. No one with access to millions lives in that rattrap. Even the accountant thought it was sketchy. If you read her report she says plainly she thinks you're being set up."

"You're far too impulsive to have pulled off something like this," Julian said.

"No," Cole replied. "He's incredibly smart. If he wanted to, he could do this. He's one of the only people who could. The question is who actually did it? And why would they want me to think Mason was involved?"

Cole believed him. He truly believed him. Cole had chosen him this time even after he'd admitted he wanted revenge. Even in the face of all the evidence against him.

Julian was a bastard. "He knew I was innocent and he set this whole thing up."

Julian didn't even bother to look ashamed. "Like I said. You both needed a push. Cole needed to confront his poor choices, and Mason, you needed to understand that Cole has changed. I won't have Kitten in a dysfunctional household. Now you're functional."

Kitten sniffled and then Julian found himself with an armful of Kitten. "Thank you, Master Julian."

He seemed uncomfortable for a moment, but his arms went around her, too. "You're welcome, dear. You know I'll do anything for my family."

Cole smiled as he stood with Mason, giving him a wink. "Well, you might have to house this portion of your family here in The Club if I lose everything." He sobered a bit as he looked down at Mason. "You should know I've got to try anything I can. I can't lose the company. If I do, the new CEO will likely develop that land and it will ruin Bliss and my lodge. I need you to understand."

Understand that Bliss had to be saved? That Cole would risk their lavish lifestyle to save their friends and one of the most unique places Mason had ever been to? Oh, he understood. "You have to put every dime we have into this fight, Master. No matter what the outcome."

Because a Master, a true Master, sacrificed for the ones he loved and he made up for his mistakes.

Masters…

The idea came to him in a flash of pure insight. "I know how to save Bliss and the company."

Chapter Eighteen

"How could you?" Cole turned down the lane that would lead him back to the house. He glanced down at the clock and was grateful that he had at least an hour before the Bliss crew would be back. Of course, if Mason had his way, he would have several people from Bliss constantly up his ass. "Do you have any idea what they'll do to me?"

Mason's grin showed through the rearview mirror. "They'll save your ass. That's what they'll do. Hey, I managed to get all three of them to agree. Do you know how hard that is? I had to play Stefan Talbot off Seth Stark."

Kitten laughed from her place on Mason's lap. They had been making out in the back seat from the moment they'd left The Club. Mason had been all over her, but Cole couldn't blame him for that. "Mason didn't really make it happen. He just had the brilliant idea. Georgia did all the work. She knows how to deal with men."

Georgia Stark-Warner was damn smart when it came to dealing with her husband and playing him off the acknowledged King of Bliss, Stefan Talbot. Apparently he and the Stark kid had a healthy rivalry going. They liked to try to outdo each other when it came to giving back to the town. According to Kitten, Georgia Stark-Warner had played her billionaire husband off the king in order to start the beginnings of the Bliss County Public School System. It was very likely to be the wealthiest district in the country because Bliss had a crazy amount of billionaires per capita, and their wives could be damn serious when it came to them using their money for the good of the community. They firmly believed in Bliss, and that meant making it the best place they could possibly create. But they could be so hard to deal with.

"And why did you have to bring Caleb Burke into it?" He might be able to deal with Talbot and Stark, but Bliss's town doc was a pain in everyone's ass.

Mason's smile damn near blinded him. "I had to bring in a third if I wanted you to keep our majority intact. Also, from what Georgia tells me, Caleb is very good at acting as a balance to Stef and Seth. And they're fast. They've already started contacting the rest of the stockholders. By tomorrow morning, you'll be back in control of Roberts Corp, but you'll have three new board members. I've been promised that Stark and Talbot will be silent partners as long as you promise to sell that land to Nell and Henry's new nature reserve for far less than it's worth, though surprisingly more than I would have thought those two could afford. How the hell could they quickly come up with a million dollars?"

Cole had zero idea because as far as he knew, Nell spent her life protesting things like fracking and big box stores, but now he'd promised to sell her the land in exchange for a crazy buyout deal that gave him ten years to buy back his stock and get his company firmly in his hands.

It was stupid. It was insane. It was his family coming through for him because he could continue to grow the company while he paid back the men who were already working their asses off to block the takeover.

He got to save his company and Bliss thanks to his incredibly smart and quick-thinking boy. "I love you, Mason."

He also loved the way Kitten held Mason tight, both of them cuddling in his rearview mirror.

"I love you, too, Master," Mason said with only one little hiccup. He was trying so hard to keep it together.

"You better love me because I'm going to take this deal of yours out on your backside the minute we get home." Pure arousal ran through his system. Damn but he loved them. He had roughly an hour before the Bliss crew was scheduled to show up. He'd planned to be at a play party this evening, but that had dissolved in the wake of Julian's scene.

He should be pissed about that, but it had moved them forward so much more quickly. If Julian hadn't pulled his stunt, he would still be worried about Mason and Mason wouldn't understand that he was done with being a fool. If he walked into a room and saw Mason standing over a dead body, he would ask Mason what had happened and he would believe everything Mason said. He would never question Mason again.

Not him or Kitten. They were his family. They were placed above everyone else, and now they knew that thanks to Julian Lodge.

He glanced back through the rearview mirror and watched as Mason kissed her, his tongue tangling with hers as he pressed his chest to her breasts. Mason was hot and there was no way he let that get by him. He would have them both tied down and screaming long before the Bliss group ambled their way back.

They would be gone in a few days. He should be annoyed, but he was kind of looking forward to getting up in the morning and making pancakes and watching those two kids get syrup everywhere.

Damn but he wanted a future. A future with them.

He pressed the button to release the gate. The big iron gates pushed open, allowing him to drive forward. He turned a little but couldn't see inside the gatehouse. Normally one of the guards he employed would have waved as he drove by, but there was no movement this evening. It was dark in there and he couldn't see the outline of the guard. It was early evening. The lights hadn't come on yet so there was no way to see in.

He drove forward because he didn't care if his guard was taking a nap. The kid would be forced to wake up soon enough because Nate didn't have a handy remote to open the gate and then the guard would likely get an earful. Listening to a lecture from Nate Wright was punishment enough. He wanted to get home with his subs. He wanted to get them in the dungeon where he could tie them down and they would take his cock any way he desired. They would rule his heart and his head, but in the bedroom he would be their king. It was a tradeoff he greatly desired.

Still. He couldn't help but let his brain play around the problem that was still at hand. Mason might have saved the company, but he hadn't answered the fundamental question of who had set him up in the first place. And why? Why would anyone set Mason up to take the fall?

He couldn't be certain it was Bob. Bob was too smart. If Bob had wanted to hide something, it would have taken the investigators far longer to find it. Also, what did Bob gain? Sure there would be a big bonus for him, but it likely wouldn't go over the million and a half he'd spent.

Except Bob hadn't spent it. Shit. Bob—or whoever was playing Bob—had been the one to feed the other company the information it needed to take over. There were any number of proprietary documents that the other company would need in order to quietly ensure an easy takeover that would blindside him. "Bob" was engaging in corporate espionage, and taking over Mason's identity was a convenient wall to hide behind in case Cole had discovered the plot and gotten the evidence he needed to prosecute. It was a gamble because the guilty party would lose the cash, but they wouldn't lose years of their life to incarceration. No. Whoever it was had handily set up Mason to do it.

They would have taken his company and perhaps years of Mason's life. Cole likely would have believed that Mason could do it if they hadn't reconnected. He would have believed Mason truly hated him.

If it hadn't been for that car accident. Cole pulled into the round drive and stopped the car, his mind whirling. If it hadn't been for that horrible day, the next time he would have seen Mason was as some cop was hauling him away.

Or in a casket if the accident hadn't been an accident.

Cole let the keys drop to the seat beside him as the truth hit. Shit. He didn't believe in coincidence. It was too convenient. If Mason was dead he couldn't argue for himself. Cole would have had no one to prosecute. He would have been forced to fight and very likely lose. Hell, he would have gone into a deep depression and he wouldn't have given a flying fuck about his company. He would have been a dead man walking, and he wouldn't have even swatted at the vultures who came to pick at his carcass.

This had never been about Mason. It had all been about Cole. Mason had been a pawn in a nasty game.

"Mason, love, who besides you knows the company so well that they could sell me out?" He had an idea, but he wanted to see if Mason thought the same thing. There were several people who knew their departments like the back of their hands, but only two who had known the daily ins and outs of absolutely every aspect of the business.

And only one who might be vicious enough to tear him down to his core because he couldn't love her.

"Master, uhm, I'm a little busy," Mason managed. "Can we talk about business later?"

When he looked back, Mason had a hand on Kitten's thigh, slowly drawing up her skirt. They were beautiful together. So fucking gorgeous. He wanted nothing more than to climb in the back seat and order them to suck him dry before he watched them fuck and got hard again. He would spend the entire evening inside them, playing, touching, reaffirming their bonds.

Perhaps the bad stuff could wait for a while.

"Let's take this inside." There was time enough to deal with his suspicions. When he took a break, he would call Chase Dawson, though Chase had stayed for the play party and would get even more surly if Cole interrupted him. Nate and Gemma. He would discuss his suspicions with Nate and Gemma when they got back. In the morning, Chase could run down a few leads and if his suspicions were correct, he would be cleaning house come Monday morning.

He got out of the car, letting the driver's door close before he opened the back. "You two, in the playroom. No clothes are necessary. Move it."

Mason groaned against Kitten's lips. "Damn it. I think he's serious."

"I'm more than serious. That's twenty, Mason. You're not going to screw her in the back seat. We're doing this properly." He couldn't help but smile. "It's getting too dark. I can't watch you out here, and you know how I like to watch my subs perform."

Kitten grinned up at him as Mason allowed her to exit the vehicle. Her skin was flush with arousal and she was practically glowing. "We like to perform for you, Master."

She went up on her toes and placed a sweet kiss against his mouth before winking and heading for the house.

Mason was a bit more somber as he got to his feet. "We both know who it was, Cole. She's the only person who could easily get into your e-mail, so we should assume she sent the letter blackballing me. She did everything. I don't want to think about her tonight because I believe she was at the party where I got roofied. I've got this image of her in my head. I think she gave me the coffee."

Cole's gut tightened. He might do more than fire her.

Mason shook his head, his hands going to Cole's waist. "Don't, Master. I don't want to think about this tonight. Tomorrow's soon enough. I just got my family back. Can't we have a nice night?"

He let out a long breath. Chase was going to have to live with disappointment because he was about to get a phone call. But he couldn't let Mason down. "Yes. We can have a nice night. Well, until the twins get back and then we'll likely have a night with baby drool and spit up."

Mason's smile nearly lit up the night. "One day that's going to be us." He wrapped his arms around Cole.

"If we're lucky." He kissed the top of Mason's head. "Go on and prepare her. We don't have long and I want to make it count."

Mason frowned. He was no fool. Cole was sure he saw right through his command. "I thought you said we would shelve the issue."

His brat was in for a rough time. "That's forty and I'm going to make one call. Go or you might not come at all tonight, love."

Mason was up the steps in a heartbeat. Cole watched as he disappeared behind the door. With a long sigh, he turned and touched the Bluetooth device in his ear. He wore it while driving and while he was sure it made him look like a douchebag, it was right there. He could join them in a moment, but he had to take care of this first. He stared out over the grounds, incredibly aware of how close he'd come to losing everything. He could have lost the company and the house, but more than anything he could have lost them. He had to do everything in his power to ensure that didn't happen.

"Dial Chase Dawson," he commanded into his earpiece. He would switch to the cell in his pocket when he got inside. The call went to Chase's very dour greeting. Fucking voice mail, but then what had he expected? The man was likely having a good time with his wife and would be for several hours. Julian's play parties could last late into the night. "Chase, I need you to do me a favor and call me when you get this."

"End the call, Cole," a low voice said behind him.

He felt a chill go through him because he knew that voice. He touched the earpiece, disconnecting the call.

"Don't you try anything or I'll blow a hole through her head so wide you could read the paper through it," Lea Schneider said.

He held his hands up because he was fairly certain who Lea was talking about. Hands in the air, he turned and saw Kitten with a gun to her head.

"Where's Mason?" Lea asked.

Mason had gotten away. Mason had likely heard something going on and had slipped into a closet. He knew the house as well as Cole did. Mason knew all the hidey-holes. Mason might be their only shot at getting out of this.

"I tried to tell her that Mason is a traitor and we got rid of him, but she won't listen to me, Master," Kitten said, her voice surprisingly steady.

Smart. Oh, his woman was so damn smart. "Mason Scott conspired with someone to take down my company. I found the evidence this afternoon. I told him if he ever showed his face to me again, I would kill him." It was time for some serious acting. "He didn't give you up, you know. I had no idea you were working with him. I would never have expected it."

Even in the moonlight, he could see the way her eyes widened. "You believed the evidence?"

She was completely bat-shit crazy. "I'm a logical man. I can also see the evidence right in front of me. You're the one Mason was working with."

Lea shook her head. "No. That was Bob Hays. I found out a couple of months ago. Cole, I'm sorry I didn't bring the evidence to you myself, but I was so sure you wouldn't believe me."

"I believe you," Kitten said, her eyes wide.

"Shut up, bitch. You're the reason we're here. You and that asshole. You're the ones who make him forget who he is," Lea spat.

Oh, he had to play this so carefully. "Lea, Kitten hasn't done anything to hurt you. I think you should let her go. Shouldn't this be between the two of us? We've worked side by side for years. I've always trusted you. Let Kitten go and we can sit down and talk."

Lea's eyes filled with tears. "I've ruined everything. You have to believe me. I was sneaking in tonight to leave the evidence behind. I had to make sure you got it. How did you get it?"

Careful. He had to be so careful. "When I found out about the takeover plans, I knew it had to come from the inside. I hired a PI. Unfortunately, I knew it had to be Mason. Why else would he show up now? So let Kitten go and we can sit down and talk about how to fix the situation. We're still in trouble, Lea. The company needs you."

She was a raging crazy person and he'd totally ignored all the signs because he hadn't wanted to take the time to hire and train someone else. This was his fault.

Lea shook her head. "The first thing you should do is get rid of this one. Dumping Mason was good, but she's taken you off your game, too."

"Where is he?" Ms. Hamilton stalked out of the house and as if the universe wanted to complete his daily set of crazy fucking murderous bitches, she had a gun in her hand, too. At least he knew how Lea had gotten into the house. "Where is that little prick?"

"Cole says he dumped Mason," Lea said, her eyes never leaving his. "I'm afraid he won't be joining us tonight and we have some problems we hadn't planned on, Hamilton. You told me he wouldn't be back for hours."

"You promised me. You promised me that this time I would get to kill him." Ms. Hamilton looked nothing like her normal buttoned-up self. Her hair was unkempt and her skirt sported several stains. Blood. She had blood on her clothes.

God, he hoped his guard was alive.

And Mason. Where was Mason? He had to pray Mason had called the police.

"Shut the fuck up and let me think for a minute." Lea's hand was shaking. If her finger twitched and the trigger went off, Kitten would be dead.

The device in his ear buzzed, letting him know a call was coming through. Could he touch the earpiece without her seeing? If he could, the person on the other end of the line might be able to hear and they might call the police.

"I think we should all stay calm." His heart was pounding in his chest, but he managed a cool demeanor. He needed to keep her talking, needed to give Mason time to get help. "Ms. Hamilton, why are you doing this?"

Sure enough, Lea turned slightly to attempt to see what he was talking about. Cole quickly touched the device in his ear.

Ms. Hamilton frowned his way. "You should shut up, Cole. You're not half the man your father was. You know that, right? He would be shocked by your behavior."

He'd always wondered if Ms. Hamilton hadn't had a thing for his father.

"Cole, I need you to stay calm." Mason's voice came through his earpiece. "I've already called the police and they're on their way. Five minutes tops. Keep her talking."

Mason was here with him. Talking. Mason wanted her talking.

"Lea, could you please explain what's going on here? I'm confused. And don't bother to kill the sub. It would only end up putting you in jail and I would find another one. You know I rarely care about them or keep them for long. They're disposable."

"That was a mistake, Master," Mason said quickly.

"Disposable?" Ms. Hamilton turned her gun his way.

Yes, he'd made a terrible mistake and it looked like he was about to pay the price.

* * * *

Mason kept his voice down even though he knew no one except Cole could hear him. Somehow it didn't matter. It seemed like a time to whisper. "Remember how Ms. Hamilton doted on Emily? She was cold as ice to everyone else, but she had a weird connection to Emily. Tell her no one except Emily mattered."

He stopped his slow progress through the house to glance out the window. He had to make sure they were still there. He could hear them talking, but he needed to see them. God, had he made a mistake?

Kitten had walked into the house first. He'd talked to Cole and had been a few minutes behind her. When he'd walked through the door and into the hall, the first thing he'd heard was Kitten saying that the Master had tossed him out.

Mason won't be coming back and my Master will be here any moment.

He'd immediately known something was very wrong. The door had closed behind him and he'd had to move quickly to get to the parlor. He'd flattened his back to the wall as that crazy Lea had moved Kitten outside to confront Cole. He'd dialed 911, but maybe he should have followed her out.

He'd decided to make a break for Cole's office where he kept a couple of handguns locked up in his case. He'd decided to try to call Cole because he couldn't let his Master think he was alone.

Cole's voice came over the phone. "I haven't loved any submissive except Emily."

Bingo. Ms. Hamilton's shoulders relaxed and suddenly the gun wasn't pointing Cole's way anymore. "I knew. I knew you loved her. She was too beautiful to not love. She looked like her mother."

"I'm going for the gun, Cole. Is the key still in your desk?" He watched out the window, but Cole never looked up.

"I'm sure her mother was lovely, too." He coughed a little. "No. No guns."

Shit. Cole had gotten rid of the guns. Mason had asked him to. He didn't like the idea of having them in the house, but his mind might have just changed. What the fuck was he going to do?

If there was anyone else in the house, they would have to take him out because he couldn't hold back his panic another instant. He started walking down the hall toward the back. He had no idea how long the cops would take. He couldn't risk Lea going crazy and killing Kitten.

He stopped, so much of the story falling into place in his head.

"Cole, I want you to do something for me. If Lea is the one who drugged me, then she probably drugged Emily, too. I'm coming out and you act shocked to see me. But I need you to plant the idea in Ms. Hamilton's head that someone drugged Emily and it wasn't me."

He could practically hear his Master's teeth grinding. "I think this is a bad idea. For us I mean, Lea. Let's go and sit down somewhere and talk this out. The last thing we need is other people dragging themselves into our personal lives."

He understood his Master's very deliberate words, but Cole was going to have to learn to live with disappointment. This was one argument he needed to make for himself. Besides, he seemed to be the one they both really wanted. If he could get Lea to let her guard down even for a second, Kitten might be able to run.

"I want to be alone with you," Lea was saying. Her voice was tinny, but Mason could make out her words. "I wish it had turned out differently. You weren't supposed to come home."

"I'm at the back, Cole. I'm coming around the side of the house. I'll say I snuck into the pool house," he explained quietly.

"Again, I think this is a conversation best had between the two of us."

Lea might believe those words were for her, but Mason knew the truth. His Master was pissed and wanted him to hide, but Mason was done with hiding.

He was a lawyer and that meant he knew how to put on a show. He took a deep breath and wound his way to the front of the house. He stepped out and forced his eyes to go wide. "What the hell?"

Two guns were immediately pointed his way.

Mason held his hands up. "Hello. Uhm, Cole, I know you don't want me here, but I'm surprised that you hired some new guards. What's happening?"

Cole moved quickly, placing himself in front of Mason.

"What's happening is me totally losing control, and you better believe I will have your ass for this. Ms. Hamilton, I can't let you shoot him. I know you blame him for Emily's death, but it wasn't his fault."

Ms. Hamilton pointed that gun of hers straight at Cole as though she was judging whether or not the bullet would pass through him and make it to Mason.

"Did you know the investigation is being reopened, Ms. Hamilton?" Mason asked.

"What?" Ms. Hamilton sounded surprised.

"The Bliss County Sheriff's Department is looking into it and I'm not a suspect," Mason explained. She didn't need to know it was Gemma who was actually investigating. Ms. Hamilton seemed more like a woman who preferred to deal with men. "They found GHB in my system. Do you know what that is?"

"Cole, if you don't shut him up, I'm going to kill this one," Lea said.

In the distance, Mason heard the sweetest sound ever. Sirens. Pretty sirens coming this way. They would have to plow through the gates though. It still could take some time.

He needed to change one of their targets and fast.

Cole held out a hand. "That's the police, Lea. Are you going to kill all of us? How will you make it out of here?"

Mason was paying attention to Ms. Hamilton. He knew who the real weak link was. When he wanted to turn two witnesses against each other, he always identified the weak link. "GHB is a drug that made it hard for me to think or move."

Ms. Hamilton shook her head. "Did you give this to her?"

She was obviously flustered, and he needed her to listen. "No. It was given to me. It was given to me in a cup of coffee."

"Shut him up, Cole," Lea shouted this time.

Mason could see the lights pulling up to the front of the house. He couldn't have Kitten in a hostage situation. He stepped out from behind Cole. "Lea has been in love with Cole for as long as she's worked for him. That's why she hates me. That's why she gave me that coffee that night. I believe she gave Emily the keys and encouraged her to drive. She wanted Emily dead and she wanted me out of Cole's life so she could have him."

Ms. Hamilton turned. "You were at that party? You said you were with Cole."

Cole stepped in front of him again, making himself the target. "No. She wasn't with me. She went to the party."

"I had to. You were ignoring the company. People were starting to say you weren't as smart as your father, and I couldn't let that happen. Mason did that to you. He dulled your edge. And when he was gone, you became everything I knew you could be. Ruthless and predatory. Everything I love about you. We were a real team. I always knew we could be so good for each other if I could get rid of Mason. But then you had to bring her in." Tears slipped down her cheeks. "Why did you have to come home early? You would have found the evidence and I could have arranged for something to happen to her. A break-in or something. I don't know. It's all screwed now. I have to take her with me. I loved you so much, Cole."

It was everything he needed. He just had to get Kitten away from her. "She loved Cole enough to kill Emily so Emily couldn't have him. It wasn't me. It was Lea and she's used you to cover it up for years."

A strangled cry came from Ms. Hamilton and she lifted her gun. Cole jumped for Kitten just as Mason heard the gates being forced open.

Cole tackled Kitten and Lea as the gun went off. He immediately rolled to his left, protecting Kitten with his body as Ms. Hamilton fired again. Mason jumped on her, swatting the gun out of the way, but not before he saw blood bloom across Lea's chest.

And then the world became a cacophony of bullhorns and shouted orders and red and blue lights.

"Get down now, Mason!" Cole screamed.

And Mason, because he always tried to obey an order, found the grass.

He took a deep breath because all those long years of hell were finally over.

Chapter Nineteen

Cole finally closed the door behind him as the old grandfather clock chimed three in the morning. What a freaking night.

"So Cole's personal assistant was in love with him and she set everything up?" Callie asked, patting one of the baby's bottoms as she paced. The twins seemed to be night owls.

"Apparently Lea's been working with the housekeeper for a while," he explained. "From what I can tell from the messages on her phone, at first they started working to get rid of Mason. At least that's what Lea wanted Hamilton to believe."

Callie seemed far more excited than the rest of them. "I can't wait to tell Jen. She met Lea a couple of times and always told me she had crazy eyes. I should have listened to her. She's lived in a lot of cities so she's knowledgeable about crazy eyes."

"I solved another case," Gemma was saying. "I'm kind of like a superhero. I was surprised you had never figured out that Emily was Ms. Hamilton's niece."

That had surprised him, too. When she'd talked to the cops, Ms. Hamilton had confessed everything, including the fact that she'd engineered his meeting with Emily. "I knew she had a sister, but she'd never talked about her family. I didn't think they were close. I feel like an idiot."

"Hey, the next time you have a mystery, skip the super-expensive investigators and call me." Gemma smiled, obviously pleased with herself.

"Hey, I need a new deputy." Nate took the baby from Callie and patted his back. "You want the job?"

"Ewww, polyester. Get Chanel to do the uniforms and I'll think about it," Gemma shot back. "I just wish I'd known I had solved another one before our presentation. It was kind of cool, actually. We were a little like rock stars."

"That's because you work in the town with the highest per capita murder rate in the country," Zane replied. "They're surprised Nate shows up every year and he's still alive."

Kitten was sitting on the sofa with Mason. Mason had an arm around her and her head found his shoulder. They looked soft and sweet together, and Cole couldn't quite forget that Mason had ignored his every order. Oh, he might have been the one to play the women off each other, but he'd nearly gotten himself killed in the process, and there would be punishment for that.

Mason looked up and his eyes softened. "Master?"

Kitten immediately stood. "I believe our Master has had enough stimulation for the evening. I think it's time we went to bed. Callie, do you have everything you need?"

Nate sighed. "We'll probably need noise canceling headphones from the look on Cole's face."

His wife sent him a look that could freeze fire. "Nathan Wright, you hush." She turned back to Kitten. "We're great, hon. Thank you so much."

Jesse shook his head. "Nate's correct. I've seen that look before. Come on, darlin'. Let's head to bed."

"I haven't had enough stimulation," Cade said, eagerly grabbing Gemma's hand.

Kitten came to stand in front of Cole.

He frowned down at her. "I don't have a look."

He was always stoic.

"Oh, you have a look," she said with a grin. "And you have definitely been overstimulated. Come on and we'll take care of you."

Mason followed behind. "I think a different kind of stimulation is called for."

"Don't you even start in with the sarcasm, Mason Scott." He couldn't help it. He'd almost lost them both. Damn it. He hated feeling out of control and that was what he'd been. Out of control and dependent on luck and good timing to save them. "You're in enough trouble as it is."

He stomped down the hallway toward the bedroom. He couldn't punish Mason. Not tonight. He was too angry. Too scared. Too everything. He could, however, let his submissive know exactly what he was in for. "You will wake up every morning for a week and you'll take care of me."

"Of course, Master. It would be my pleasure." Mason calmly followed behind.

"You'll get nothing for yourself and when you're done, you'll get up and you'll fix breakfast until we can find a new housekeeper since my old housekeeper is currently on a seventy-two-hour psych hold before they take her to prison."

"That might be more of a punishment for anyone having to eat what I cook, but I will do it with pride, Master."

"And I'll serve as your personal assistant since your former personal assistant is…well, dead." Kitten hurried in front of him to open the door to the bedroom. She shook her head a bit ruefully. "I know I should feel worse about that, but she was unkind and also I didn't like her filing system. Or how she called me a whore. I'm not a whore, Master. Unless you want to play a game. I might be a very good one."

"Kitten, I can punish you, too." Maybe he should. After all, she'd taken Mason's side, calling him heroic for nearly getting them both killed.

"If it would make you feel better," Kitten allowed. "Should I get the flogger? Oooh, or the canes? I love the canes."

She was going to make him crazy.

"Sit down, Master, and let me help you out of those shoes." Mason gestured toward the bed.

Before he knew it, he was sitting on the bed while his subs removed his shoes and socks. They took his shirt and he was suddenly left wearing only his slacks. Mason climbed on the bed behind him and soon his strong fingers worked the knots in Cole's neck. Over and over his hands moved, easing him, but he couldn't let it pass.

"You were supposed to obey me."

Mason moved and Cole felt the warmth of his breath on his neck. "In some things, I have to make my own decisions. As Kitten couldn't leave me behind in that parking garage, I couldn't leave you two. I would do it again."

His hands were working magic and now he tongued the back of Cole's neck, making his flesh light up. "Do you think that's what I want to hear?"

"I think the truth is I would rather die with the two of you than live alone. Should I move on to your feet, Master? You could lie down and we could work on your body."

"All this submission isn't going to save you," he said, but his heart was already softening.

"It isn't supposed to save me. It's meant to save you," Mason whispered against his ear. "I'll take whatever punishment you like, so long as you don't pull away again. I'm alive. Kitten's alive. Don't distance yourself. Let us help you."

Kitten sank to her knees in front of him. "Let us take care of you. We need to spend this evening together. You and me and Master Mason."

Fear. It had run through him so hard. He hadn't even started to process it but he wasn't going to let it rule him the way it had last time. He wouldn't let it ruin his life again. Guilt had to be dealt with, too. He was a man who held everything inside, but he couldn't. If he did, it would infect him and make him toxic the way it had after he'd pushed Mason away.

"I'm so sorry, my loves. I should have seen it." It was his fault.

Kitten shook her head. "No."

"Yes, pet."

Mason eased off the bed. "Kitten, I don't think there's a place for clothes in this discussion."

Cole shook his head. His first instinct had been punishment when they had been the ones to save him. Maybe he needed to distance himself. He needed to think of them to figure out what would truly be best for his submissives. "No. Not tonight. I need to think tonight."

Kitten tossed her clothes aside with abandon. "I believe what Mason is trying to say is you've thought far too much."

As far as he could tell he hadn't thought clearly in years or they wouldn't have found themselves in that situation. "I almost got both of you killed."

"You didn't almost get us killed. That was the crazy, mean ladies," Kitten pointed out as she sank back to her knees. Her form was perfect as always and it placed her breasts on display. God, she was gorgeous.

"Who I hired." They weren't getting the point. "I started this. I hired Lea. I knew she wasn't the best assistant and I let it go so I wouldn't have to deal with the fallout of firing her. I should have done it years ago, but I got so distracted that I almost lost the company and everything we have."

"That happens all the time in the corporate world." Mason had gotten rid of his clothes, too. That was a fine man. He didn't seem to be affected at all by his near-death experience. His cock was standing at full attention.

"It doesn't happen to me."

Kitten's hands moved to his knees. "It does and it did. Things happen whether we're smart or not. They happen and we deal with them, and it's easier when we have a family. You're my family, Master. You and Mason. Can I suck your cock?"

Damn but she knew how to get his mind off things.

"I want to suck you, too, Master." Mason sank to his knees beside her, a decadent grin on his face.

They were going to pull him out of his head one way or another.

"Tell me you forgive me again." He needed to hear it. Guilt was weighing him down, but he might be able to let it go if they would say the magic words.

"There's nothing to forgive, my Master." Kitten squeezed his hand. "But everything I have is yours."

"I forgive you, Cole," Mason said, his face shining up. "Forgive me, too. We both made mistakes. I kept things from you. I broke that trust, but I'm asking for forgiveness and another chance."

What had he done to deserve this? "You have it. You have all the chances you need. You never have to ask for another one. Know that it's yours."

A good Dom knew when he was beat. A good husband knew when it was time to give over to his spouses.

He was going to marry them. He would legally marry Kitten, but he would tie Mason up in his life by doing the one thing he'd sworn he would never do. "I'm splitting the company in thirds."

Finally he'd managed to shock his boy. Mason's eyes went wide. "What?"

Kitten shook her head. "I don't need that."

"But I do. I need to share what I have with the two people who mean more to me than life. You will accept your shares and you will both take places on the board. Mason, you're now the company's lead counsel."

"Master, I don't know enough to be a board member." Kitten was frowning, obviously worried.

Mason put a hand on her shoulder. "I'll teach you. If you don't want to take business classes, I'll tutor you, but we're a family and Roberts Corp is our business. The Master is right."

At least someone agreed with him. Wasn't the Master always supposed to be right? He couldn't help but chuckle at that thought. At one point in time he'd simply wanted a woman who followed his every order and was easy to deal with. How lucky had he been to not be granted that wish?

Kitten turned her face up, and there were tears shining in her eyes. "I will learn, Master."

She would and she would be an asset. She would be a shining light. She was smart and capable and once she got her feet wet, she would be hell on wheels, and he would love to sit around the dinner table and argue business with her and Mason. They would fill his life with meaning.

He couldn't push them away when all he wanted was to be close.

"Take my slacks off." He stood up and gave them access. The expensive slacks had become a cage for his cock, and he was ready to open the door and let it out. He was ready to be with them.

Kitten was all over it. She easily handled his belt and the fly of his slacks. His pants hit the floor and Mason immediately picked them up and folded them. He didn't have to worry about anything but the pleasure they were about to bring him.

He let go of the terror of the evening. All that mattered was the fact that they were alive and together, and he would learn from his mistakes. He would make more—so many more. He would do stupid things, but they would be by his side. They would create something unique in the world. Their family. Their children. Their future. Another whole generation would grow up in this house and they would learn to love the lodge and the freedom they found in Bliss. Another generation raised with love and acceptance as his parents had raised him.

Everything he wanted was right there in his hands, and he wasn't about to let that go.

"May I kiss you and lick you and love you, Master?" Kitten asked.

"Oh, yes. You can always do that, but tonight you can do more, pet. I think it's time Mason and I shared you." It was past time to set them on the proper path. They would share everything. They would spend their lives together, sharing their love and lifting each other up. "I believe you've been plugged before."

He knew she'd been plugged many times. She loved being plugged. She might not have been allowed sex, but Julian had allowed her Doms to train her ass. He needed to thank him for that. How did a man thank his almost father-in-law for allowing the preparation of his bride for double penetration? Maybe a cookie bouquet.

Kitten practically vibrated. "I'm ready, Master. I loved being plugged and have worked my way up to an extra-large. I assure you my anus can handle your love."

Yep, that was his wife. She was practically perfect. "I know you can. So get me hard and ready to fuck. Mason, help our future wife."

"With pleasure, Master." Mason leaned forward and licked the head of his dick.

Oh, that was what he needed. They were right. He needed them. He didn't need time to think about his guilt. He needed his love to banish it from him. There wasn't a place for guilt or remorse here. They were together and there was only a place for love. "I'm still going to punish you. I'm going to make it so you can't sit for a damn week, Mason."

He was still the Master and they would play. They would play for the rest of their lives. His beautiful subs could be ninety and he would want to play with them. And he would always discipline them the way they needed. Especially when they risked their lives. They had to know they were precious.

Mason's eyes turned up even as he dragged his tongue over Cole's cock, every swipe a pure pleasure. "I understand, Master. I love you, too."

Damn it. They wouldn't give him a thing to work with. It might be time to simply accept the pleasure they offered, but he was going to set a few new rules. "Kitten, join him and while you work you can listen, too."

He nearly groaned as she licked the underside of his cock while Mason started in on his balls. They coated him with heat, stopping every now and then to kiss each other before returning to their work. He loved to watch them as their tongues mated, sliding together in perfect harmony. "We're getting married and I won't take no for an answer."

Kitten smiled up at him. "I wasn't going to say no, so it all works out perfectly."

"I was going to play it cool for a while, but I would have eventually given in." Mason leaned over and sucked the head of Cole's cock into his mouth while Kitten's small hand stroked his base. She squeezed his dick, making him hiss at the pleasure. The two of them worked in perfect timing as though they'd served a Master together all of their lives.

"A week. No more. That's all the time you have to plan it."

Mason's head came up. "Master, that is not…" Cole shot him his coldest stare. "I will get it done and it will be lovely."

He didn't care about lovely. He cared about getting them wrapped up in legal bindings, safe and secure. He wanted it on record that they were all together. "Mason, you will legally change your name. The company is Roberts Corp. We're all keeping my name. We're the Roberts family."

"I loved your parents, Cole. I would be proud to have their name as my own," Mason whispered the words across Cole's flesh.

He wanted them all to have the same name. He didn't give a damn what anyone had to say about it. It was his life and he would live it his way. "Mason, I think it's time we prep our wife. Let her take over and you get her ready."

Mason bounced up, his cock bobbing. "It would be my pleasure."

As Mason went to do his bidding, Kitten settled in, one hand stroking while she began to work his cock into that sweet mouth of hers. She licked and then sucked, his dick disappearing behind her full lips. He couldn't take his eyes off the sight. It was so fucking gorgeous. He looked down at her, thrust his hands in her hair. She was so soft and yet there was such strength inside her. She'd handled everything life had thrown at her with enormous grace.

"Were you scared, pet?" He'd hated having to act calm when she'd been in danger. He'd wanted to rage and scream and take apart the person threatening her. He had to make sure she understood what had happened out there in the yard.

"I was." She stroked him, squeezing him with a pleasurable rhythm. "But I had faith. You were there and Mason was there and you both love me. We were stronger than she was."

"You wouldn't have been stronger than a bullet." It would haunt his nightmares. He was so glad they were finally sleeping together because he would need to wake up and assure himself that she was alive.

A secretive smile lit her face. "I knew I would be all right because you kept your cool. She wanted to talk to you, wanted your attention, and you gave it to her even though I know you found it distasteful."

Distasteful was a mild word. "You know I didn't mean a thing I said out there. I tried to tell her what she wanted to hear, but it was all a lie. You're not replaceable."

"I would have believed every word you said in the beginning," she admitted. "I would have. But you told me you loved me. When I was standing there I realized that I could only believe one or the other. If I believed that you love me, then I would have to believe that you were lying to her. In the end it was easy. I knew what I wanted to believe and I made the choice."

If only everyone had her view of the world, it would be a better place. She was a treasure. He didn't deserve her, didn't deserve either one of them, but he was grateful for them. "I love you, pet. I love you so much."

"I love you, too." Mason dropped his kit to the floor and got to his knees. He brought Kitten to hers so she faced him. "You should understand some things about me, too. I would never have done it. I wouldn't have walked away. Cole was right. I'm the worst villain in the history of time. I had so many chances and I couldn't take them because deep down I knew I wanted this more than I wanted any revenge."

She leaned over and kissed him. "Silly man. You were never a villain. You were a confused man who wanted to come home." Her eyes narrowed as she thought. "Though you could play a villain. Role-playing is fun, Master. You could tie me up and torture me. Oh, that would make me so sad."

Brat. "Get back to work and let our villain torture your little asshole before I take it."

She shuddered and leaned back over to lick at his cock.

Cole sat back, utterly secure in his place in the world.

* * * *

This was the night she'd waited for all her life. She just hadn't known it. Years of her life had gone by and she'd wondered if she would find a man who would take care of her. And when she'd found them, she realized that she had to be strong enough to finally, truly be herself.

She didn't need to be taken care of. What she'd needed all along was to be loved.

She suckled the head of her Master's cock, her tongue lavishing affection on it. She loved the way he tasted and smelled, how hard he was in her mouth. She sucked at him, drawing him deeper and deeper inside her mouth. She wanted to take all of him, all the way to the base. She wanted every inch of that enormous cock in her mouth and she wasn't going to stop until she had it.

He would be her husband, her everything, but in order to be worthy, she had to be his and Mason's everything, too.

An idea began to play in her head. They were forcing her to go back to school, but a woman didn't have to make money to find her true work. Sometimes the things that happened to a person set them on a path. Sometimes those things were bad, horrible and tragic, but that didn't mean the outcome had to be bad. The outcome could be turned by love and made into something beautiful.

They'd tried to twist her, but she'd ended up here. What if she could help others find their way, too? Her journey began with pain, but that hurt had led to love and peace.

It led to her Masters.

It led to herself.

"Don't stop what you're doing to the Master, Kitten." Mason moved in behind her. "No matter what I do, you're not to stop."

Her whole body clenched in anticipation and she simply allowed herself to feel. Everything else floated away. This was the true joy of submission. She knew the rest would still be waiting for her, but for now, she would revel in the moment.

She loved the plug, loved how it filled her up and made her aware of every inch of her skin. When her former Masters had plugged her, she'd dreamed about finding her one—the one who used the plug to make way for himself.

She'd been truly blessed to find her two.

Cole, who was steadfast, and Mason, who was as bright as the sun. Her lovers. Her men. Her Masters.

"Spread your knees wide," Mason ordered.

"Take more." Cole tugged lightly on her hair.

Her Masters were demanding men. She did as they asked, sucking Cole's monster while she spread her knees and leaned forward to give Mason access to her asshole. She shivered when the lube hit her flesh. She couldn't help but groan as Mason massaged it in, his finger rimming her and opening her up. The pressure made her want to clench, to try to keep him out, but she had the discipline to know that wouldn't get her where she wanted to be.

Mason worked a single finger in a hard circle, making her feel it. So good. It would be so good. That finger was an appetizer, but Cole's cock would be the real treat.

"She likes that," Cole said. "I felt that in my cock. You should do it again."

Mason pressed against her asshole. It had been so long since she'd had anyone play with her ass, and even when they had it had been perfunctory, a simple part of her training because her Doms weren't going to have sex with her. They didn't make sexy sounds like Mason was making. They didn't love what they did to her.

"This is a pretty asshole. She is so fucking tight, Master." He pressed against her and she felt him slip just past the ring of muscles. He added a second finger, making her groan again. "So tiny and beautiful."

"I won't hurt her?" Cole asked.

She shook her head slightly but didn't stop sucking. The Master's cock was pulsing in her mouth, tiny movements that let her know he was close to losing his control.

"I think it's safe to say she'll be all right. This little asshole is begging for a cock. She wants a big cock to split her wide while another big cock plunders that sweet pussy of hers. She's a dirty girl and so, so sweet, and I wouldn't take her any other way." Mason removed his fingers but almost immediately started fucking her with a plug. A big plug. She was stretched and had to wiggle to get comfortable.

It would be so much worse when it was Cole's big dick inside her. It would take all her concentration to not wriggle and writhe while he worked his way inside. She would be so deliciously trapped.

Mason fucked her with the plug while she sucked Cole's cock. Over and over she worked him further into her mouth. She strained to take him all the way, but she was determined. She wanted him at the back of her throat, wanted him to know he could come right then and there and she would happily drink him down if he chose.

All the while Mason worked that plug in and out of her ass. He took his time, ensuring that she felt every inch burrow in and then pull back out. Her little hole was being stretched and the ache meshed perfectly with the sensations of pleasure coming from within. She could feel Mason's hand on her back, holding her still for his work. Every now and then, that hand would leave its place and she would feel a sharp smack against her ass. The spank would jangle the plug, sending crazy sparks through her body.

Cole tugged at her hair, lighting up her scalp. He groaned and forced his cock in further. She ate him up, licking and sucking and letting Cole set the pace. She relaxed, finding that beautiful place where her brain let go of all thought except submission. It was a safe place because she trusted these men. She would let them do whatever they wanted because they would never hurt her. Never.

She gave over to the rhythms they set, finding a way to be the conduit through them. Her body seemed to flow, from her mouth sucking to her ass being filled, she floated and enjoyed the sensations, knowing there was so much more to come.

Her body heated up, feeling like liquid and moving in time to the rhythmic thrusts of the plug in her ass. The world seemed to still, to become a soft place for her to rest even as her body demanded more and more.

"Not that way, pet." Cole pulled his cock from her mouth with a forceful tug. She couldn't help but stare at it. His cock was fully erect and she could see how plump and full the head was. A drop of pearly fluid pulsed from the big slit. He'd been so close. "Not until I'm deep inside that pretty ass of yours. Mason, get cleaned up. You're on the bottom tonight."

Mason pushed the plug deep and left it there. She had to groan at the way it filled her. He gave her a nice smack that got her skin tingling and left her wanting more. "You know me, Master. I'll take whatever position I can get."

"Bratty switch," Cole chided. His hand moved restlessly on his cock, stroking. "Hurry. I find myself impatient this evening."

Her Master tugged on her hair again. He knew how much she liked that. He tugged until she was close enough to kiss and then he devoured her. His mouth covered hers and his tongue dominated. He kissed her like she was his last breath before dying, and she responded with all the softness she had inside. He'd been scared, but he wasn't going to pull away like he had before. She would keep him close. She would never let him go.

A joy she'd never felt before suffused her. She was going to have their babies and build the family she'd always wanted. One with support and acceptance and so much love.

She believed.

Mason was suddenly behind her. "Come on. I want inside that sweet pussy of yours. I want you to ride me. Dance on my cock, baby."

He tossed that beautiful body of his on the bed and spread his legs wide, welcoming her to play with him. His big cock was naked and erect, and she didn't have to get a condom because Cole had been happy with the doctor's reports. One day she wouldn't take her shot anymore and there wouldn't be anything between them, but she needed time before those babies started appearing. Just a little time to be with her Masters. Kitten straddled Mason, looking down at his movie star gorgeous face. She leaned over and kissed him. "I love you, Mason."

His lips curled in the sweetest smile. "And I love my gorgeous girl. You saved me, you know."

"You saved us both." Cole knelt on the bed behind her. "You're the reason we're here."

She wasn't sure she'd saved anyone, but it felt nice to hear the words. Maybe at the end of the day the person she'd really saved was herself. She placed herself over Mason's cock and started to lower herself down.

It felt so good to have him fill her up. Mason's eyes were on the place where his cock disappeared into her pussy.

"That's a beautiful sight." Mason's hands gripped her hips, guiding her down. "Do you know how good you feel?"

Cole's hand was on the small of her back, pressing her forward. "She'll feel far better in a minute."

She felt the plug slip out of her ass, but she wasn't given more than a second to mourn its loss because something far larger and warmer was pressing in hard. Cole wasn't taking his time. He seemed to know exactly what she needed, and she didn't want gentle. She wanted raw and hard. She wanted to feel her Masters dominating every inch of her body.

Cole was ruthless. He wouldn't let her keep him out. "Take me. You'll take every inch of me. I was nervous in the beginning, but you can handle me. You're strong, pet. So much stronger than I imagined."

Pain flared and burned and shifted to something even hotter as he worked his cock into her ass. She felt like she was going to burst, but that wouldn't be a bad thing. She wriggled, taking him even further because she was a girl who liked a little burn. She would like being sore in the morning, the ache a remembrance of how well she'd been loved the night before.

Finally she felt his thighs touch her cheeks and she had him. She had both of them. Like Mason, she loved to be with them in any way she could, but she rather thought she would always love being in the middle the most. Worshipped and adored by her men. They filled her every sense and she knew she was finally home.

Mason reached up and swiped away a tear. "I'm happy, too."

He knew her so well. She wouldn't cry from pain, but she let her emotions flow and flow when it came to love. She wouldn't hold that in. She would put it out into the world and hope it all came back to her. She'd been proven right already because she was here.

"So happy, pet," Cole whispered from behind.

"Now let's make her an even happier woman." Mason sent her the most decadent smile before he thrust his hips up.

Cole groaned and dragged his cock out of her ass.

Kitten couldn't stay quiet at that. The plug didn't feel the same as warm, loving flesh. She cried out and then there was nothing that would stop them. Kitten gave over, riding the wave of pleasure they created. In and out, over and over, they brought her to the edge with their cocks and hands and heated words. They told her how beautiful she was, how much they wanted her, how long they'd waited for her.

Mason reached around her, putting his hands on Cole's hips as he thrust up, completing the circle between them. They were together and whole and safe, and Kitten let go.

The orgasm took her like a storm, bashing against her and rolling like an inevitable wave of pure sensation. She cried out again and again as the pleasure took her.

Mason stiffened under her, flooding her pussy as he pumped into her.

Cole thrust in one last time, giving her everything he had as he went deep. He collapsed on top of her, sending her sprawling on top of Mason.

As the afterglow set in she realized this was where she'd always wanted to be, between her men, warm and safe and happy.

Epilogue

One Week Later

The door to the bride's room opened and Kitten turned, happy to see the man she'd asked to see. Julian was resplendent in his tuxedo, but then he always looked perfect to her. They were all waiting in the chapel, her whole family. Dani was sitting in the pews holding Chloe with Finn at her side. The Barnes-Fleetwood family had come along. Lexi and Aidan and Lucas had driven up from the country. Leo had hugged her, wishing her well before he joined Shelley and Wolf. Georgia had flown in from New York with her husbands, Seth and Logan. Even the Bliss crowd had stayed an extra week. Callie had said she never missed a wedding.

Her bridesmaids were waiting—Tara, Marcy, Haven, and Nat. They were standing outside, waiting for the ceremony to begin, but she had one last thing to do before she became their wife.

A bride always needed one last talk with her father, after all.

"You look beautiful, dear." Julian sighed as he stared down at her.

She felt beautiful. She felt like she glowed from the inside out. In a single week, she'd managed to plan a wedding and enroll in college and find volunteer work that served her soul. "I started training with a local women's shelter."

"What are you going to do for them?"

"I'm going to be a rape crisis counselor. I'm going to be on call so I can advocate for women when they're brought into hospitals and I can follow up and help them through. Do you know why I'm doing it?"

Julian gently brushed back a stray piece of hair. "You want to give back."

"I do. I want to be there for someone else because I had so many people there for me. I shouldn't have, you know. I didn't really have many friends. My parents believed I was responsible for everything that happened to me. I should have been alone, but I wasn't. I realized something, Sir. I realized that even though I was given a hard lot in life, I was also sent everything I needed to survive it. I was given a father who didn't truly love me."

Julian sighed. "Your father had many problems, sweetheart. You can't take his bitterness in the world as a reflection on yourself."

She shook her head. "I don't because I realized that when the family we're given doesn't work, we can find a new one. I was given a father who couldn't love me, but I found one who could. Julian, I know I acted out and even told you I hated you once."

It had been right after Chase had turned her down that terrible night when she'd wanted someone to hurt her. She'd been so desperate. Julian had taken her into his office and explained her restrictions. She'd had her one and only real fit and told him she hated him and that he was just as bad as the man who had kidnapped her. He'd been calm and patient and taken a firm stand.

Julian Lodge was the reason she'd been able to go to Cole and Mason with a whole heart.

"I knew you didn't mean it." He took her hand.

"You knew I didn't hate you, but you have to know how much I love you." Tears welled in her eyes. "You gave me a place to find myself and time to figure out what I needed. You gave me a family. I love you, Julian. I will always consider you to be my father."

"Everyone seeks to make me feel old." But he tugged her into his arms, hugging her gently. "I love you, too, Kitten. Watching you bloom has been a true joy for me. And if those men of yours ever step out of line, you know who to call. You always have a home with me and Finn and Dani."

"Julian, I've been thinking." She'd talked about it with Cole and Mason, but she'd only this morning made the decision. She'd stood in front of the mirror, looking at herself in a white gown with lace and pearls and knew she was a different person than she'd been before.

It was time.

"About?"

"My name. I was Katherine before. My parents liked the formality of the name. They never used nicknames or shortened it. I was Katherine Taylor. And then I was Kitten and nothing else." Sometimes her captivity seemed so far away, and others it was like yesterday and she sought out her Masters' warm arms to keep the memories at bay. "I think I need to be Kate now. I think I need to be Kate Roberts forever. Do you think they'll like it?"

Kate. It was somewhere between Katherine and Kitten, a mix of her past and future. A woman was a mixture of all the things she'd learned, and the good and bad that had happened to her. Kate was the woman who had come through the fire and found the beauty on the other side. Kate was the one who had found love.

"I think Kate is a lovely name." Julian leaned forward and kissed her on the forehead. "They will love Kate."

The door opened and Nat poked her head in. "It's time, hon."

Kate nodded. "I'm ready."

Julian stepped to the side and held out his arm for her to take. "If I'm your father, then I claim the right to walk you down the aisle."

She threaded her arm through his. It was more than she could have hoped for. "I would love that."

The music began as Julian escorted her out. She came to the aisle and looked down. Cole and Mason were waiting for her.

"Shall we?" Julian nodded, and the quartet Mason had hired began the march.

Kate nodded, too full of emotion to speak. She walked down the aisle, toward her future.

Author's Note

I'm often asked by generous readers how they can help get the word out about a book they enjoyed. There are so many ways to help an author you like. Leave a review. If your e-reader allows you to lend a book to a friend, please share it. Go to Goodreads and connect with others. Recommend the books you love because stories are meant to be shared. Thank you so much for reading this book and for supporting all the authors you love!

Long Lost

By Lexi Blake

Masters and Mercenaries: The Forgotten Book 4

A stolen past

The only thing Tucker remembers of his past is pain. Used in a doctor's evil experiments, his memories and identity were erased, and his freedom taken. He believed his nightmare was over when he was liberated by the men and women of McKay-Taggart, until he heard the name Steven Reasor. The idea that he could have been involved in the terrible experiments that cost his "brothers" everything crushed him. A desperate attempt to force him to remember the truth almost cost him his life. Now his world is in chaos and his only path to finally uncover the truth and atone for his sins leads to Veronica Croft.

A painful present

Veronica "Roni" Croft knew Dr. Steven Reasor was bad for her, but she also saw a side of the man that no one else knew. Even as she began to believe their employer was hiding something sinister, she was drawn to him like a moth to a flame. Their affair was passionate and intense, but also fraught with danger. When he disappeared under mysterious circumstances, she took her first chance to run and never looked back. She has stayed hidden ever since, running from forces she knows are too powerful to overcome. But now the man she believed was dead, the man she mourned, has returned and needs her help.

A dangerous future

As Tucker and Roni unravel the secrets of his past, a dark force rises and threatens to destroy them. Their only chance for survival will require them to join forces with the Lost Boys' worst enemy. Only together can they finally unlock Tucker's past. But as Tucker's memories begin to come back, will it free them both or tear them apart forever?

About Lexi Blake

New York Times bestselling author Lexi Blake lives in North Texas with her husband and three kids. Since starting her publishing journey in 2010, she's sold over three million copies of her books. She began writing at a young age, concentrating on plays and journalism. It wasn't until she started writing romance that she found success. She likes to find humor in the strangest places and believes in happy endings.

Connect with Lexi online:

Facebook: www.facebook.com/authorlexiblake/
Twitter: twitter.com/authorlexiblake
Website: www.LexiBlake.net
Instagram: www.instagram.com/lexiblakeauthor

Made in the USA
Columbia, SC
19 October 2022